BUL   Bullen, Fiona.

        The deep blue sea.

$22.95

BUL   Bullen, Fiona.

        The deep blue
        sea.

$22.95

DATE	BORROWER'S NAME	

THE
DEEP BLUE SEA

Also by Fiona Bullen
To Catch the Sun

THE
DEEP BLUE SEA

Fiona Bullen

St. Martin's Press
New York

Library of Congress Cataloging-in-Publication Data

Bullen, Fiona.
    The deep blue sea / Fiona Bullen.
        p.   cm.
    ISBN 0-312-07706-8
    I. Title.
    PS3552.U427D4   1992
    813'.54—dc20   92-1199
                                                                    CIP

First published in Great Britain as *The Dream House* by Macdonald and Co. (Publishers) Ltd.

First U.S. Edition: July 1992
10 9 8 7 6 5 4 3 2 1

To my parents,
with love

THE
DEEP BLUE SEA

Chapter One

Rio de Janeiro
September 1958

It wasn't just Papa's fault, Isobel thought. It was Eleanor's too. All right, perhaps Papa had started it but Eleanor needn't have made it worse. Everyone knew Papa had to have the last say, had to prove he dominated the household. Why couldn't Eleanor have just ignored him?

'Maybe we should have said we're sorry,' Isobel said uncertainly. But Eleanor shook her head, her mouth compressed and determined as they waited in the hall, their bookbags down at their feet. The sound of a car door banging and the clatter of dishes being cleared away in the breakfast-room broke through the still of the house. Somewhere, beyond the garden walls, a motorcycle backfired and Isobel jumped. What she had meant to say was maybe Eleanor should say she was sorry. To Papa. Tell him she hadn't meant to react – over-react really – when he said 'it couldn't be long enough'.

He had been talking about John, of course, about the length of time John had been away, and it had slipped out without him meaning it. Isobel knew he hadn't meant it. Not like that. He had just meant that it would be better for all of them, especially John, the longer he stayed away. Because of the rumours – and the memories. But Eleanor

1

had jumped up from the table, spilling her orange juice, calling him hateful, her pale face mottling up with anger and her eyes large with recrimination. Eleanor always leapt to John's defence. The look of hurt and reproach on Papa's face still made Isobel wince.

If she, Isobel, had said that, Papa would have been furious and made her go to her room. He would have barked in an angry deep voice at her and told her she was a silly child. Which at sixteen, she was not. But with Eleanor, only a year younger, he was silent and brooding, his lips folding in petulantly as though he were being hard done by. And he had stood up, creasing his newspaper very carefully into the long quarter pages he liked to read it in (as though he were still in England) and then once again in half so that it slid easily into his briefcase, and left the room. He didn't say goodbye or kiss them on the cheek; he just walked out and they could hear him talking to Honório, his driver, telling him to take him to the office now and come back for the girls after. That was Papa's way of paying them back. Making sure they would be late for school. They were.

Mama hadn't said a word. She had drunk her coffee in silence, looking down at the table, fingering the salt cellar with those long fingers of hers that were always so immaculately polished. And the girls had waited, awkwardly, in the hall.

The sun glinted off the boards, off the triangle of light cutting the window panes into white flame against which they screwed up their eyes and looked away. The girls stood by the doorway, a few minutes late and unable to join their own forms, waiting for assembly to be over. It was the long session today, when the bishop came and gave them a talk, the girls sweating in the heat, bones loose and swaying in the stifling air. Even now, so very early in the morning, they could feel the warmth on their backs and they knew it would be a hot day. It had been hot for over a week now, unseasonably so for September.

Isobel, chewing her lip, worried silently over what her younger sister had said. Eleanor would get them both into trouble and it wasn't Isobel's fault. She wouldn't take the blame, not for John and definitely not for Eleanor; not for Papa's pet who didn't care whether she hurt him with the things she said, who only cared about John. Isobel frowned again. Her skirt, pleated and tartan like all the others, flared crisply around plump knees. Eleanor's hung limply from her hips, new and bought too long to compensate for the way she had spurted into growth again. Dressed alike, they were clearly related, but where Isobel was short and curvy, Eleanor was a long stick. There was only a year between them, but a lifetime of differences. Isobel shuffled her feet impatiently.

They had been waiting for John to come home for a long time now. Their cousin John. 'Johnny-boy' to Louis, his best friend. None of them had written to him regularly, except Eleanor. Only she knew when he was coming. Which was why she had said that to Papa, Isobel realized after Eleanor had whispered to her 'today', as they clambered out of the car. Half running, their books thumping and banging against them in their bags as she said it, she tried to sound amused although it wasn't funny. He was coming home today and she was going out to meet him. Just walking out of school. And Papa had said it couldn't be long enough. Perhaps Papa had been right. Isobel shook her head.

'There's no need,' she hissed from out of the side of her mouth, her eyes down attentively on her hymn book. 'He'll be home long before us anyway and you'll get us into trouble. I won't cover for you. In fact, I'll deny knowing anything about it.' A warning glance from the stiff figures ranged along the side of the hall caused Eleanor to pause in her reply. She peered at the words of the hymn, not taking them in, lost somewhere in her own world.

Isobel, looking at her sister, saw that familiar stubborn tilt to Eleanor's chin, her long pale hair pulled back in a smooth sheath behind her head, the forehead high and

3

domed, shining in the morning light. Serious and thoughtful, the forehead creased for a moment. Then, as the morning assembly swelled into a rousing chorus of hallelujahs, the reply came back quickly and firmly.

'If he's coming home, I'm going to be there to meet him. You needn't come. There's no point in both of us getting into trouble. Besides, I didn't ask you to.' She didn't look up to see if her sister had heard her or not. She opened her mouth wide and let that shudder come into her throat, almost a wobbling shiver of excitement as the last hallelujah thundered out across the hall. Her eyes closed, the blackness warm and secret around her, excluding everyone and everything from her private enjoyment. Hallelujah! Hallelujah! Hallelujah!

Only six hours to go. She kept her eyes shut and smiled to herself, hugging her prayer book to her chest. Home at last, after all those years away in England, just so that Mama and Papa could pretend The Tragedy had never happened. The Tragedy. It was always said like that in heavy tones, immeasurably sad, signalling to anyone ignorant or foolish enough not to know about it, that what had happened was serious and should be addressed in capital letters. Even though they didn't want people to know about it. It was never to be mentioned or Papa got that frozen look on his face, his newspaper snapped angrily and he protested loudly that he wanted some peace in his own house and where was a man supposed to go to get it? And Mama grew uneasy and made shushing noises, frowning from beneath her eyebrows, smiling later once she had looked back at Papa, shaking her head.

Eleanor fingered a scar on her leg, silver where it didn't tan, like a fish or a spoon in shape. The nun had done that, trying to get the shot out. But that was over, finished with now and they could all go on with their lives. John could come home. She shifted impatiently. Soon.

She let her mind drift, thinking back. Her smile became wider, possessive in its curve of lip, its slight dreaminess. She and John were not just cousins: they were more than that. They were so close, they thought each other's thoughts. Which was why she had missed him so much. Papa knew that. He knew just how much they meant to each other. She frowned at the thought.

She couldn't remember when they had first met. Not because they had known each other for always, like most families, but because she had just been a baby when John had been taken by his parents to live in the Backlands. The Vila Serrista was a coffee plantation out on one of the tributaries of the Paraná, somewhere in the Mato Grosso, she didn't know where. Not really. She had been there, of course, but no one who lived in the cities could ever understand the jungle. It was different. There was no overlap.

And Aunt Elizabeth, who was Papa's sister, she never came back the way Papa had thought she would, even though he hadn't liked her going in the first place. But she was married and if Uncle Michael said that was where they were going to live, then there was nothing much anyone could say about it, even though Papa had tried. He hadn't liked the way Uncle Michael had changed after the war, or so she had heard when listening at night to her parents whispering as they went down the hall past her bedroom. Papa had thought Uncle Michael was odd. Violently odd. Of course, Papa had been right in the long run but no one had believed it then. They had just thought Papa was jealous. And laughed a little, the way people do, saying he would get over it.

Henry, whose father was a great friend of Papa's, had told her that Papa had been devoted to Aunt Elizabeth. Totally devoted. So when she went away, he was upset. It was natural. Everyone said so.

And then, after a few years, Aunt Elizabeth started writing to Papa and saying it wasn't right for her son to be growing up a savage, and she couldn't teach him any more than she had, so she thought he should come to school in Rio and live with his cousins. And Papa had thought that a wonderful idea, guessing wrongly that he would see so

5

much more of his sister, that he could perhaps entice her away from Uncle Michael. But he hadn't. She had sent John on his own. At ten years old.

They had been in the garden in that summer of 1950, she and Isobel and Henry, who was her special friend then and a year older than her, the same age as Isobel. Mama was there too of course because it was hot, and had made them lemonade and was pouring it out on the stone table near the terrace, her bright dress flapping in the afternoon wind and her hair mussed up as she laughed. Then this boy appeared from the library windows, stepping out on to the terrace, and they all stared. He looked at them defiantly, a slight firmness to his mouth showing his unease. Papa was there too, pushing past the boy impatiently, his face tight and his jawline working as though he were chewing on something bitter. He blurted out: 'She didn't come. She sent him alone, just like that. One of the servants came with him, but I sent him back again. Just a savage. I can't believe she didn't come.'

He had gone past the children to the table, forgetting the boy he had brought with him, and poured himself a long glass of lemonade, pushing his glasses up on his forehead and pinching his nose tightly, screwing up his eyes. Mama put a hand on his arm for comfort but he walked past her, glass still in hand, without noticing, to stare out at the gardens at some point that no one else could see. Her hand dropped and then she looked back at the children brightly, smiling and winking. Still the boy stood there, not moving in case he should suddenly give into the pain in his chest that wanted to bubble out in grief.

He knew nothing about this place or these people and now that Hatchet, his father's servant, had been sent home, he felt lost, set adrift.

'Are you John, then? My cousin?' Eleanor asked finally as the silence grew longer and the insects began to plague their afternoon: crickets and flies, wasps and dragonflies flitting through the air and making Isobel dance around and shriek. John always teased her about that later, the way

6

she said 'my cousin' and not 'our cousin', laying claim already. She was only seven then to his ten years, she said, and hardly knew the difference. But that wasn't so; she had always known the difference.

He nodded his head, cleared his throat and then Mama was there, crying out in her high, clipped English tones, 'Well, of course, this is John. Who else would it be? I'm sure you must be thirsty and tired, John. Do you want some lemonade?' And she hugged John and rattled on hurriedly, making up for the lack of greeting, not looking at her husband standing on the far steps with tight shoulders and disappointed, angry eyes.

Henry shyly held out his hand, as he had been taught, and John stared at it for a moment before shaking it quickly, wondering if there weren't some sort of elaborate joke being played on him, his smile polite, his eyes shaded, quickly taking it all in. Isobel stopped jumping up and down and flinching at a large butterfly hovering near her and obeyed her mother's admonishment to kiss her cousin. They touched skin briefly, Isobel's soft wet little mouth imprinting itself on his cheek in a way that made John rub it with the back of his hand when she wasn't looking. And then Eleanor followed suit, but her lips were dry and firm and barely there before being snatched back again. Her eyes regarded him fiercely.

'Are you going to stay with us? Mama said you would but I thought Aunt Elizabeth was coming too. Isn't she coming now?' Isobel said. Mama moved sharply as though to end the discussion and Eleanor flushed. Henry looked at the ground, scuffing his toe across the flagstones.

'Mother couldn't come. She's needed on the fazenda. Besides, she sent Hatchet with me. He's gone now,' John added and Eleanor felt the loss in his words. He looked at her for a moment, the flash of sympathy read in her eyes and then he looked away.

'But, Papa wanted to see Aunt Eliza–' Isobel began again, unaware of the tension around her, the sudden tightening in the air. But Papa heard and his hand fell from his face, his mouth screwing up tightly as though he would cry.

'Be quiet, Isobel, can't you!' he said as he swept by them, returning to the house. 'Your aunt isn't coming. And that's an end to it.'

But it wasn't, Eleanor thought later. In fact, that was the beginning.

John stayed. Papa had recovered a little from his disappointment and tried to make it up to John later that afternoon, suggesting a game of cricket out on the lawn. But John didn't know how to play, staring at the bat as though he knew it was going to be his undoing. Papa had bluffly insisted he should learn. What Englishman couldn't play cricket, he demanded heartily and John had turned still eyes on him and said, 'I'm not English, sir. I'm Brazilian.' Even then he had been so proud of his heritage, the long line of Portuguese Brazilians on his father's side that went back to the original settlers. Proud of Brazil. Papa had grunted. 'Quarter English. On your mother's side. And all gentlemen play cricket. You will too, John. You'll be expected to play at school. What did you play back home, for heaven's sake?' He glanced in keenly at the boy, not liking the composure he read there.

Charles Fawcett was an odd man, defensive and suspicious where there was no need, determined at all times to dominate the scene. He seemed so confident, so full of energy that very few realized just how insecure he was. Only his sister and – perhaps – his wife. Later, when things started to go wrong, it became obvious to them all. But in those days he was at the height of his power.

The only one who wouldn't bend to his will was his younger daughter, Eleanor, whose forthrightness he permitted. And now this boy. He smiled derisively at John's answer.

'I played with the Indian boys. We played in the jungle.'

'Played? Played at what? Hide and seek?'

John stiffened but kept his tone even and Eleanor

watched with interest the way he fingered a small sharp blade that he had palmed. 'Yes, of sorts. We played at lots of things, sir. Mostly, we played at staying alive.' It was the sort of bluffing bravado most boys of this age came out with and Charles Fawcett smiled indulgently. But John's arm snaked back and flashed out in front of him, a shining glimmer leaving his hand and embedding itself some distance away in a large lizard that had been quietly creeping along the side of the terrace. Calmly, John retrieved the blade and held the lizard up before his uncle. He half smiled, shy and proud at the same time. It had been a difficult throw and he was pleased he had made it.

'It's pretty good wrapped up in banyan leaves and buried with hot coals for a few hours. No worms to worry about. My father taught me that. You should try it, sir,' he said and then the pleasure in his eyes faded, became puzzled as he watched his uncle.

Charles's mouth worked in distaste. 'Give it to me! No, not the bloody lizard. That knife. Give it to me now!' Charles held out his hand and John reluctantly pressed the blade into it. 'Now take that lizard and throw it back in the garden, somewhere where the ants won't disturb us all.' He waited while John silently obeyed him. Then they stood staring at each other for a long moment. Charles lifted his glasses and squeezed the bridge of his nose and John recognized the mannerism from earlier. He swallowed and looked down at the ground.

'This is not the jungle, John. I'll try and make allowances for your recent arrival. Perhaps you don't know how things should be done in a civilized place yet, although how your mother ... But that's neither here nor there. What I must and will have from you right now, however, is your obedience while you're in my house and that means no knives or weapons, no killing things unless you shoot it properly, like a gentleman, no silliness. Do you have any more of these?'

Charles held up the blade and Eleanor, standing back,

9

examined it curiously. She saw the boy's colour fading from his face, his lips becoming stretched tightly across his teeth. He shook his head and Eleanor knew, instantly, that he was telling the truth.

Charles Fawcett closed his hand carefully and turned away. 'I'm afraid I'll have to check your room, John. Obviously you don't know the first thing about discipline or good manners, so I can't trust you.' He glanced over at the cricket bat and stumps, missing the sudden flash of anger and shame in the boy's face. 'Stay here and practise your swing. Elly, you show him how, puss.' And then he walked heavily back into the house, leaving the children to stare uncomfortably at each other.

'You don't have any more, do you?' Eleanor said after a moment and John half turned and shook his head.

'No,' he said bitterly. 'My father taught me to always tell the truth. It was – is – a point of honour with him. Just as being able to survive without anyone else's help was a point of honour with me. Your father doesn't seem to value either very highly.'

'The jungle's very different, isn't it?' Eleanor began tentatively but let her voice drift away when she saw that John was doing his best not to cry.

Thinking back on it, Eleanor realized he was being pompous, a ten-year-old boy hurt and angry and pretending to have adult standards of conduct. She smiled. John's standards were always high. But just then all she could think was how unfairly he had been treated and how – rude – her father had been. She ducked her head and looked away, cheeks flaming.

'I'll show you how to bat, if you like,' she said and John looked down at the bat with unfriendly eyes.

'Will I have to know how to do this, to survive here?' he asked.

Eleanor thought about that and then nodded. 'Yes,' she said and immediately he picked up the bat and ball.

'All right,' he said. 'Let's play your game.'

And he did, she realized later. He started at St George's and began to play cricket and then rugby, to construe Latin verbs and locate foreign countries, to classify animals, insects and plants into different phyla and to learn why the Magna Carta came into being. He learned quickly and excelled, first in order to please and then, after a while when he began to see that nothing he could do would be good enough for his uncle, in order to irritate. He was smart enough and subtle enough to enjoy irritating his uncle without most people knowing what he was doing. Eleanor knew and tried to make him stop. But she couldn't blame him. It was Papa's fault.

Eleanor knew her papa had decided against John from that very first day, because she and Isobel had crept down the upstairs hall, long after they were supposed to be in bed for the night, and listened in the striped gloom to the rise and fall of their parents' voices murmuring in the library, her father's harsh, her mother's indecipherable in its gentle tones.

They had listened until their eyelids had begun to droop and the banisters began to prop their heads up. Then they had crept equally quietly back to bed, whispering to each other.

But there was nothing Charles Fawcett could do. He had agreed to educate his sister's boy and to bring him up as his own family and John did nothing wrong to make that task seem unbearable. He played the game and stuck to the rules. His masters at school praised him, he did well at sports and he was unfailingly polite and helpful at home. He brought home acceptable playmates, most often Louis Preston, and included both the girls and Henry in their games.

Once he had settled in, John turned out to be a sunny-tempered, well-mannered child. His eyes were bright and open, his desire to please and be liked apparent to everyone. There was nothing Charles could think of to get

11

rid of the boy without it seeming as though he were being vindictive. And so John stayed and Charles grew to hate him more and more each day.

The Fawcetts had been in Brazil since the turn of the century, the children's grandfather, John Fawcett, amassing a small fortune first as an explorer and later as an entrepreneur. He settled down with a young wife of Portuguese Brazilian background and had a son, Charles, and a daughter, Elizabeth, before dying of a sudden stroke in 1938. His wife had not survived him by many years.

Charles Fawcett had been born in Rio de Janeiro and Rio had been good to Charles, providing him with an endless market for the imports he brought from England, using that money to start up textile factories, mining concerns, an iron foundry and, finally, to call in a loan his father had made to the Lampedusca Railway in 1905 and make it virtually his own.

The railway had formerly been a minor line serving a relatively small coffee region beyond the main coffee heartland. But as the coffee march continued across the São Paulo state, Fawcett saw that the railway would become a virtual goldmine, transporting the 'green gold' – coffee – back across the plains to the ports and, eventually, to Europe and the United States. With the backing of a couple of other British shareholders, Fawcett had called in the nearly one million pound loan guaranteed at six per cent debenture bonds in 1905 by the government and, when the railway was unable to meet the call, had taken the entire operation in forfeit. Fawcett reorganized the patchwork of various gauges, the inadequate rolling stock, and the confused management and made the railway profitable inside of the first year.

Speculation on the shares began and in three years the railway was extended to 170 kilometres of line, acting as a funnel from the new coffee sites to the coast. Gradually this area became the coffee heartland and concessions were secured to extend the railway even further into areas where the reddish-purple soil, terra roxa, so valuable for growing coffee, was to be found. Charles was content, he was young and good looking, he had money, prestige, women if he wanted – and a scintillating companion in the form of his sister, Elizabeth. What could go wrong?

However, in 1939, Elizabeth suddenly decided to marry a much older man and leave Charles to his own devices, and it was then that the seeds of Charles's dislike of John were sown. Miguel, or Michael as Charles insisted upon calling him, Campos de Serra was thirty-two when he met the twenty-one-year-old Elizabeth Fawcett at a party in Rio. Descended from the original Quatrocentões, the Portuguese nobility who first colonized Brazil in 1500 and who had lived there, marrying mostly amongst themselves ever since, Michael's family epitomized the decline of an old aristocracy who hadn't the energy to find another fortune but merely hung on in the hope that things might get better.

But Michael himself was a young major in the military forces, a former member of the young 'tenente' movement, who had rebelled against a corrupt government, and he had energy and ideals enough for two men. Elizabeth saw in him a man as strong as her own brother and immediately agreed to marry him, despite Charles's objections. After all, she pointed out, she would be living in Rio and Charles would soon be marrying himself, so what was all the fuss about?

And, as though to prove the justice of her words, Charles did meet and marry an English girl, Clarissa, on one of his trips back to England and he soon had a daughter, Isobel, to match Elizabeth's son, John. Charles bought an old palácio from yet another failing Quatrocentões family and renamed it Palácio Lampedusca, after the railway that made his fortune.

In 1944 Michael was sent to fight in Italy as part of the Brazilian Expeditionary Force and, upon his return, he insisted that his family move to the plantation his parents had owned in the backlands of the Mato Grosso, on the river Paraná. Michael was a changed man, bitterly aware of the corruption that had made certain men in the big cities rich at the expense of the soldiers who had fought and died beside him. He trusted no one now, especially not the military hierarchy who were always so closely linked to the politicians who had failed him, failed his country. He became jealous of his privacy, and of that of his wife.

As Charles saw it, he had always been an unwelcome visitor where Michael was concerned, and he was now to be cut off completely from the only person he really loved – his sister. When John was still only a tiny child, Michael Campos de Serra took his family as far away from Rio de Janeiro as possible. And Elizabeth bade her brother farewell and departed for Vila Serrista, following her husband's wishes. Charles had not seen her since.

Instead, she had sent him John. But John was too intelligent, too determined, too good at everything for Charles to like him. And Eleanor, little Eleanor, the darling of her father's heart, the replacement for Elizabeth's love that his wife had never been capable of filling, was being taken away by Michael's son. Charles lay awake at night laughing dryly to himself at the irony of it all. And hating John more each day.

Naturally Eleanor hadn't realized this at first. Not until after The Tragedy, when John was sent away. But she knew it now. She and Henry had discussed it. Even Isobel admitted it was probably so, and Isobel didn't think Papa could do anything wrong even though she was always being told how stupid and silly she was. Papa didn't think much of anyone's intelligence really, Eleanor thought uncomfortably, calling them all dim-witted at some point or another but particularly harsh on Isobel and Mama. Dumb Doras he called them with his sardonic laugh. It hurt.

In the assembly hall, the fifteen-year-old Eleanor opened her eyes and sat down, cross-legged on the wooden boards, waiting for the bishop to start his sermon. He was a nice old man really, she thought, tufted hair almost meeting across his eyes and an intense, probing look, like a good-natured eagle trying to sort out whether you were worth eating or not. He opened his bible and cleared his throat.

'Today, girls, I am going to read to you the Prologue from The Gospel According to St John, and then afterwards I shall discuss the meaning of the Good Word with you. Please turn to your bibles ...' Oddly appropriate for the day her John came home, Eleanor thought to herself. The bishop hummed and hawed for a few moments while the girls rustled away, turning pages, whispers rising and falling like sighing, trying to remember exactly where the gospel came – before Luke, or after it? Then he raised his voice and the girls fell silent. Eleanor closed her eyes again, slipping back into her memories.

When she was eight, she remembered, they had started a silly game where each of them was a member of a herd of horses. John was the leader, of course, and a stallion; black, she remembered, with a white blaze on his chest and Louis, competitive as always, had insisted that he had to be a stallion too, though not necessarily the leader of the herd. He was a bay with a long white mane and tail. Arabian, he said, to be one better. Henry wasn't allowed to be a stallion since he was younger, only Isobel's age, and as he didn't want to be a gelding, whispering angrily to Eleanor that he wasn't going to be some eunuch like out of the Arabian Nights, he was elected a yearling colt. Isobel was a mare – a plump one, Louis said teasingly, which made Isobel cry and refuse to play the game, so she had to be fed apples to make her happy again. And she, Eleanor, was the filly, since she was the youngest of them all.

They had their own ponies anyway, which they rode furiously over the back hills beyond the house near the Morro de Santa Teresa, and they kept that particular game up for months, reviving it every few days. Neighing or whinnying furiously, their legs kicking up and their heads tossing in the wind, John led them away from rustlers who wanted to steal them, or they rescued other horses who joined the herd from time to time, only to drop out as those friendships waned. It was always the five of them who remained.

Then one particularly hot afternoon when the earth plumed up in dust at every hoof print, and the wind was so dry it cut the backs of their throats and pressed suffocatingly over their mouths and noses, John rode away to quell an armed uprising, which involved going alone behind the hill, and Louis decided to take over the leadership.

Eleanor objected strenuously and Louis's eyes gleamed with mischief and determination. The dry wind rustled the trees, Eleanor remembered, sounding like skeletons rattling together.

'Hobble her, Gideon!' Louis cried to Henry, who had adopted, along with everyone else, a horse-like name. Henry stood there looking indecisive while Eleanor looked around at Isobel for support.

'White Blaze, come on! We must flee and carry the news to Midnight!' she cried, her nose burned pink from the afternoon sun and freckles standing out in her face. But Isobel merely smiled and shook her mane complacently and said she preferred to go along with Goliath. She glanced sideways at Louis, conveying some message that eluded Eleanor.

Louis smirked and pounced on Eleanor himself, whipping out a rough, knotted cord that he carried in his pocket for emergencies just like this and holding it between such grimed, broken-nailed fingers that Eleanor felt suddenly light-headed and ill. Louis had the sort of build that meant he would be a very strong man one day, already stocky and muscular for a boy of his age, his chest barrelling out above short, firm legs. Eleanor was no match for him, for all that she tried to run, tried to kick out. She was suddenly frightened.

Henry dithered, his still childish face showing all his fears and worries at once, gentle brown eyes pleading, not sure

16

whether to laugh and join in, or to try and stop it. But the others paid him no heed, shrieking and shouting excitedly in the way that children do when they have become a pack, baying for someone's blood. Henry objected when Louis pulled Eleanor along behind him and Louis carelessly told him to shut up.

'Not fair, Goliath! You're not supposed to pick on fillies!' Eleanor said, kicking out with her feet but she was hauled uncomfortably firmly up to the nearest tree and her wrists bound tightly around with the cord. She cried out sharply with the pain but Louis and Isobel were chanting 'tattletale' and laughing so loudly they didn't hear.

The heat writhed across the ground between the trees and the smell of dry earth and wildflowers, herbs and something sharply astringent wafted towards them. Eleanor could remember it all, years later, with startling clarity as though the scene were imprinted in her mind, full of colour and scent, rolling forward gently in slow motion. She had seen how Henry stood there, his eyes growing larger by the moment, his hair flopping forward over one eye, crying out for them to stop.

'Leave her alone, Goliath. You're hurting her! Louis!' But Louis wasn't listening and suddenly Henry bolted away from them, up across the scrubland and towards the hill, gasping with the desperation to get there, to get John.

'Louis, don't. It hurts!' Eleanor wailed behind him and she was crying now, sobbing as he tightened the cord to the tree and began to cinch it in.

He didn't ever mean to really hurt her, he told John afterwards, when his nose had finally stopped pouring blood and he had apologized abjectly. But the damage was done in one sharp tug and Eleanor cried out as both her wrists made a distinct cracking sound and she slumped to the ground.

John reached them just as this occurred and he launched himself on the already puzzled Louis, knocking him to the ground and punching him hard in the nose.

Isobel had gone to kneel beside Eleanor, her face

suddenly white and stricken, saying, 'Elly? Elly, this isn't funny – don't tease. Please,' in a shaky voice and John left off beating Louis and got out his penknife – all his uncle would allow him – and sawed patiently through the cord, whispering viciously to himself all the while. Henry stood over them, crying in earnest now, and when John freed the cords from Eleanor's wrists and they dangled brokenly in front of her, Henry set up a loud howl and went tearing off down the hill for help.

Papa met them halfway down, John carrying Eleanor's limp form and Louis stemming his nose with a handkerchief. Henry was running beside Papa, trying to keep up with the long strides and explain what had happened at the same time but he was still crying and all his words were coming out jumbled so that all Papa heard was the name he most detested. He saw John holding Eleanor and he snatched his younger daughter from the boy's grasp and ran with her back down the hill.

'Clarissa! Call the doctor, quickly. It's Elly!'

The children followed forlornly down the hill into the house, standing hang-dog outside the door to the library while emergency calls went out and brandy was applied. Nearly half an hour went by as they sat on the upright bench just near the door, John nearest, ranging in size down to Isobel at the farthest end, kicking their legs and staring anxiously at the closed door.

At last it opened and John stood up, looking into his uncle's face, his own tight with concern. Charles Fawcett stood staring down at him, oblivious to the other little faces behind, and then, suddenly, lifted his arm and swung it down hard, so that his palm contacted with John's cheek in a stinging, furious blow. John staggered and fell sideways, tears smarting out in his eyes.

'You're a devil, John Campos, to do that to a child, let alone one who follows you around like a puppy. I'm disgusted by you! Go to your room! All of you! Henry, Louis – out, now! Go home and tell your parents you've been naughty, ill-mannered, beastly children. You, Isobel, up to your room and don't let me hear a peep out of you. I'll deal with you in a minute, young man!' And then he walked back into the library and closed the door again and John was left standing there, his face an angry blotched red. He turned away from the others before they could say anything and bolted up the stairs and then Louis looked even more crestfallen than he had before, saying it was his fault not John's several times, and muttering 'Johnny-boy' beseechingly as though John could hear him and forgive him. Isobel and Henry started crying again. Slowly they obeyed their orders and when Papa emerged once more with the doctor, the children were all gone.

John never said a word about it being Louis who had hurt Eleanor. He just took the beating that Papa dealt out later that night, a hard walking stick applied to his backside with more vigour than was just or even sensible, and remained silent throughout the whole ordeal. His face was pale and soaked in tears but he never said a word and Louis never forgot that. Of course, it couldn't last and Louis confessed to his own father and Henry to his, so that later that evening Papa was even more angry and upset at having to apologize to John. For Eleanor however – it was worth having broken wrists to have John be her hero. And he always was, from then on.

In the winters, when the rain was falling and the great house was dank and chill, they played in the attic. The old box room was full of trunks and furniture no longer used, faded umbrellas with spokes missing and parchment lamps that were ugly and stained, threadbare rugs rolled and thrown into dusty corners and racks that were splintered, books torn or discarded, and a bison head that their grandfather was supposed to have once shot but which looked too motheaten to have even been alive. This was their Aladdin's Cave and the password to get in was changed on whim, mostly Isobel's whim since she was always insisting she was the Queen of Sheba, dressing up in the old clothes they found in the boxes up there to look the part.

19

This was where they ate their secret feasts with grape juice and chocolate dates, and salaamed to the Emperor of Egypt or the Sultan of Morocco, made secret allies with the Princes of the Seven Veils of Arabia and generally had a lot of good fun. It was also where Eleanor accidentally set the roof on fire when trying to roast pheasant over an open fire for the weary travellers of Solomon's tribe and it would have meant a very painful bottom from Papa, if not worse, had John and Louis not launched themselves on the fire with an old pair of curtains and smothered it at the cost of a few singed hairs. They all swore themselves to secrecy and signed a paper to that effect, daubed in blood, but Isobel accidentally prattled it out before the night was over and the attic became out of bounds.

Eleanor had sobbed to herself alone in bed and John, somehow knowing she was upset, had come and curled up beside her, so that she stopped sniffing and instead went to sleep in the warmth of his arms. He was always there for her, and she was always his admiring follower. And Charles grew bitter with the years.

The bishop ended his discourse by confusing everyone with allusions to the approfondimento of theological thought and the aggiornamento of current criticisms and, after the Mission collection ritual which deprived them all of their pocket money on a regular basis, he smiled beguilingly at the very little girls down the front of the hall, beneath the stage, before limping back to his seat. The assembly ended and the girls returned to their form rooms for first period, Isobel unsuccessfully trying to catch Eleanor and insist she not do anything rash. But Eleanor drifted serenely past her, her thoughts elsewhere, and passed the entire next class with little more than an occasional glimpse at the present.

In fact, she passed the whole morning so, leading to speculation by the other girls that she had fallen in love, and sharp comments by the teachers at the end of each lesson as to whether she was feeling quite well enough to be at school. To which Eleanor smiled blithely, far too intent on analysing her reminiscences and adding the insights to the past that can only be acquired by the present. And with it came the realization that hindsight could be both a useful and painful tool. Finally she forced herself to remember the events that led up to The Tragedy.

July 1954

John stood rather stiffly, his hands clasped behind his back as he waited for the reply. Around him, his uncle's library seemed even larger and more imposing than normal. It was a sombre, masculine room lined with books that were, the boy had to admit, often read by his uncle. The polished boards gleamed back a hard, uncompromising reflection. He risked a quick look at Eleanor. She seemed quite at ease. He wished he could feel like that. His uncle cleared his throat and smacked the letter held in one hand with the back of the other.

'I don't understand it,' he began quizzically but changed his mind almost immediately, his tone becoming harder. 'Well, anyway, it's your choice, Elly. I'm leaving it up to you, despite the fact that I don't really approve of you going up there. Too dangerous, as far as I'm concerned, but I'm just your father. And I know my wishes are not the only ones that matter to you.' Charles Fawcett had an unsettling and, for the most part, involuntary habit of loading his words with guilt. This time it was quite deliberate. He looked down at the figure beside him, the top of her blonde head barely reaching his chest. His daughter reached a hand up to his.

'Please, Papa. John'll look after me and Aunt Elizabeth will be there to meet us – and I've never seen the jungle before. Not the Backlands. And I'm eleven now, and big for my age anyway. We'll be careful, I promise. Please.' So insistent, so tenacious. She had worried at him like a dog for days. And now this letter from his sister. They were just alike, the two of them; they never let go once they had got their teeth into something.

21

Eleanor didn't glance across to John, knowing instinctively that this would displease her father. He was often displeased with John and anything John said, giving mocking, obvious looks at anyone else who might be around, letting John see and shrivel. Out of the corner of her eye she noticed Isobel enter the room but she focused her concentration on her father instead. He was wavering, she could tell.

'Well, I suppose I could spare you for two weeks. It means I'll be missing you in your school holidays, one of the few times I get to really see you, but I'm sure you'll have a good time anyway.' He saw his daughter wilt and continued, 'I was thinking of taking you with me to São Paulo for a few days, but I expect you'd much rather be with John.' He cleared his throat when he saw Eleanor bow her head and said more heartily, 'Well, you're both to be back in time for school, of course. That goes without saying. You understand that, John, don't you?' Charles Fawcett said firmly to his nephew, his face tightening with irritation as he saw the boy return a steady, uncomfortably assessing gaze.

'Yes, sir. I'm always back in time for school. Mother knows I must leave by the twenty-seventh. But it's my birthday on the twenty-sixth and she likes me to stay for that. I'll be fourteen!' He paused, almost shyly, expecting his uncle to say something. When nothing came, the boy continued, his eyes directed at the floor, 'Don't worry, sir. We'll look after Eleanor and have her back on time.' He felt rather than saw Isobel's shake of the head, the heavy blonde hair flying out petulantly.

'I don't see why I can't go. I'm not infectious anymore.' She almost stamped her foot but thought better of it at the last moment. Eleanor looked away: that was Isobel all over. Eleanor noticed John's eyes smiling but his face remained perfectly blank.

Isobel hadn't wanted to visit her aunt and uncle at first, thinking the fazenda, or plantation, would all be spiders and steamy jungle and boring coffee bushes but now that she had caught chicken-pox, the scheme became a conspiracy to deprive her of whatever Eleanor might be enjoying. Eleanor always had all the fun. She was the younger and Papa's favourite. Isobel looked across at her sister with veiled dislike.

'Am I, Papa? Infectious? No. So I can go too now, can't I?' she prompted more firmly. Just twelve years old, there was a disturbing precocity to the way Isobel held her body and pouted out from behind that hair. Such a lot of hair, Charles Fawcett thought absently, and so little wit beneath it. Just like his wife. He shook his head, dismissing them both.

'No, Isobel. The doctor said bed-rest and then light exercise. No heavy exertion. Going upriver is about the last thing either your mother or I would dream of letting you do. If you get better quickly, I may take you to São Paulo instead. But only if you're better. You should be in bed now. Off you go, puss, before I get cross. And stay there,' he added, wishing in some ways he could order his younger daughter upstairs to bed too. He disliked this whole scheme. That letter from his sister – so unlike her. Almost maudlin. She had never been that. He wondered if she was finally realizing what she had given up for that fellow she had married. That fellow – he frowned at the thought, tasted the same metallic anger in his mouth that had never forgiven. Never forgotten.

He realized the two remaining children were still waiting for his answer and he breathed in sharply. 'Well, all right then. On your heads be it. Especially yours, John.' He fixed the boy with a hard look, tasting the anger still. That fellow's son. Both alike. Both trying to steal his most precious possessions: first his sister, now his daughter. He swallowed over the ache in his throat. 'I'll write to Elizabeth and let her know you'll both be coming. Assuming your school marks are good enough, of course, Eleanor. You wouldn't expect me to give you a treat like this without your doing the work first, would you?'

Eleanor laughed with delight, about to run to John

23

before checking herself. She cleared her throat and stood politely beside her father. 'No, Papa,' she replied demurely before reaching up to peck her father on the cheek. He couldn't help smiling back. His girl. Isobel was her mother's; they took after each other far too closely for him to have ever thought otherwise. But Eleanor – now she was special. Taller already than her sister and about twice as bright. And straight with it. No manipulative little schemes from Eleanor, the way Isobel tried to wheedle or pout her way into his favour. Eleanor fought him straight out, all the way. Just like Elizabeth had, years ago.

That clear in his mind, he patted Eleanor on the shoulder and gave John a curt nod before walking out of the room. The boy watched that straight back and its air of command recede down the hall before he breathed a sigh of relief.

'Not one of his good days. I didn't think he was going to let you come. Did you?' he asked as he flung himself down in the window-seat and stretched his head back to catch the last rays of the afternoon sun. His hair was light too, but fairer than any of the Fawcetts, almost silver where the light caught it and glanced off the planes of his face. Eleanor shrugged and squeezed herself on to the seat beside him, pulling her legs up and tucking them in neatly beneath her.

'Papa worries. He's not trying to be mean. He's just such an old mother hen, clucking over his brood. He thinks we're too noisy, too – something. He told me not to climb so high in the tree today just because you did it. And not to ride so fast at the jumps just because you've cleared them. We're too rough-and-tumble, he says. Ramshackle. I guess sometimes he thinks that's your influence and that I'm not going to be a lady when I grow up. Or that I'll end up with more than a broken wrist or two: I'll get a broken head. You know he doesn't mean to be abrupt with you, John. It's just his way.'

She tried to excuse the hurt she knew her cousin felt whenever her father looked at him and his lips tightened in anger or dislike. There was no accounting for Papa's moods where John was concerned. The more she tried to get them to like each other, the more her papa pulled away. She sighed and John leaned against her, propping his chin on her shoulder.

He sighed heavily and hesitated before blurting out the words that had been festering in him for a long time now. Words that tried not to reveal all the hurt and pain he felt at that rejection, by accusing instead. 'He's never liked me, Elly, and you know it. He's jealous. Of us. Being together so much, I mean. You were his completely until I started coming to school up here and now he doesn't see you as much. He thinks you care more for me than for him.' At least, that was what Isobel had thrown at him the last time they had quarrelled. It made sense too, now that he thought about it. 'He was just the same about Mother. Hated letting her go. She was his sister and his companion and they were everything to each other. And then my father came along. Dad told me all about it. Uncle Charles has never forgiven Dad for that.'

He pulled away and looked at Eleanor, thinking as always how odd it was to see himself in feminine form. She was smaller and slighter and quite pretty, of course. He hoped he didn't look pretty. His features were sharper, harder, his nose like an arrow in a planed face; hers were rounded still, blurred with childhood. But otherwise, she could have been his sister – almost his twin. Except for the eyes. Hers were greener with bits of hazel swirl in them. His were just blue.

Blue like the sea, Isobel had once said dreamily when lying on the grass beside him, her mouth doing that irritating pouting trick. He hated that.

Eleanor jutted her chin forward in that way she had when she was cross. 'Don't be silly, John. Of course Papa's not jealous! What rubbish. He's just worried I might get into some sort of trouble around you. That's all. Because you're much older. He says ...' she hesitated a moment, wondering whether to repeat it, '... it's unnatural for us to be together all the time when there's three years between

25

us. And dangerous. He's just worried, that's all. But he's not jealous. All right?' She looked so upset at the thought and so determined not to admit to its truth that John couldn't help but feel a twinge himself.

'Fine. Have it your way. He really loves me like a son. But I'm a wild and terrible influence on you. That better? You prefer that version?' Fawcett's official version, John thought. The version that took pleasure in humiliating John in public and then insinuated, whispered in Eleanor's ear, that there was something wrong with them being so close.

'Oh, you're so damned touchy, John! I wasn't trying to put you down. I just feel uncomfortable being between you both all the time. I seem to always have to be sorry for talking to either of you, being with either of you. Someone's always put out. It's not fair, you know.' Her tone slid from annoyance to depression.

John put out a hand on her knee. He sighed. No, he wasn't being fair on her. 'Don't swear,' he said. That would be put down to his influence again. But he couldn't control Eleanor. She had a mind, and a sharp tongue of her own – thank heavens. He was amused by that thought and his mood swung abruptly. 'Besides, he's still letting you come to Vila Serrista and that's only ten days away now! Mother will be so pleased. I know she's been wanting to meet you for a long time. The last time she saw you, you were about two years old, I think, and a pewling, ugly little thing, probably bald and fat.'

'And you, of course, came out perfect and stayed that way, I suppose?' She stuck her tongue out at him and he laughed.

'Of course!' He pulled her in against him so he could lean on her. Eleanor squirmed until she had her shoulder bone sticking into him rather than the reverse. John sighed and let it go. They sat bickering amicably for some time and then lapsed into companionable silence, Eleanor thinking about the wild darkness of the jungle, trying to imagine what it would be like, John looking forward to seeing his home. They watched the sun ridging the line of trees on the western wall of the old palácio, the perfect order of the gardens fading as the sky purpled into dusk and the dark shapes of bats flitting through the night sky.

The children didn't notice when the door opened and Honório walked in. He had worked for the Fawcetts since before Eleanor was born. Almost since before Isobel. He was only in his forties but to the children he seemed ancient, his skin dark and leathered from the sun and his short hair beginning to show grey at the sides of his forehead. He walked forward quietly, seeing the children silhouetted against the window, sitting so close to each other they almost seemed like a two-headed beast. Honório switched on the lamp.

The room jumped forward, exerting its strong colours on the eye and immediately the night receded into blackness. Eleanor blinked. 'Oh, hullo, Honório, I didn't realize it was that late. Is Mama back yet?' She spoke in Portuguese, flipping automatically between the two languages at home. Her father insisted the family speak English. After all, they were English mostly. Just a few dabs of Brazilian, as her mama liked to put it, watching Papa's face with that teasing look that he got so impatient with. Eleanor sometimes wondered if her mama weren't being a little unpleasant when she did.

'No, Senhorita Eleanor. But your papa said you should start on your homework now, and Senhor John, he needs to go see to the dogs.' Honório spoke with all the firmness of someone who had seen the children toddling around the floor and who had smacked many a backside in the past. Eleanor obeyed without question. She slid from the seat, smiled briefly at John and ran upstairs. John, however, lingered a few moments more until Eleanor was out of hearing.

'Honório, I thought I saw Senhor Fawcett's car leave about half an hour ago. He's eating out tonight, isn't he?' John asked.

Honório's face became impassive. 'Yes, Senhor John. But

27

before he left, Senhor Fawcett told me to remind you both about your duties. I let you have until dusk to play. But the dogs need feeding and it isn't good to let them wait. They only get fed once a day, not like you.'

'Okay, okay. I wasn't questioning whether the dogs need to be fed, Honório,' John said steadily enough, despite the spurt of irritation he felt. He knew exactly how often the dogs were fed since he had been feeding them for the last three years. 'I was just wondering who would be having dinner here tonight.' And hoping his uncle wouldn't be one of them.

He stood up, taller than the other man already with long limbs and a slight stoop, as though he were always bending over to hear what someone had to say. Mostly what Eleanor had to say. He wasn't really interested in anyone else's comments, Honório suspected, although he tried hard to seem so. Honório stood back sharply as the boy loomed above him. If Senhor Fawcett, whom Honório served faithfully, thought the boy was bad, then he was bad and there would be no discussion of it as such. So he had told the other servants and they would take their cue from him. Honório wasn't sure why John was meant to be bad – he seemed a nice enough boy to Honório – but he would always be careful to watch him with the Senhorita Eleanor. Those were Senhor Fawcett's instructions.

John gave Honório a crooked smile, trying not to show the hurt. His tone became teasing. 'Don't forget the other lights, will you, Honório? Who knows what devils may be lurking in those shadows,' he said before walking briskly from the room, whistling an odd, native tune that made Honório stiffen uncomfortably. He hadn't meant to make the boy feel an outcast. It was just Senhor Fawcett's instructions.

Dinner was taken in the Small Room, so-called to differentiate it from the large, formal dining-room where they always had dinner if Charles were home. Clarissa Fawcett disliked the Large Room with its hard wooden chairs and its long, polished table; she disliked the crisp white napkins and the sombre lighting, the brown leather fender around the fireplace and the severe portraits on the walls. Even more, she disliked the heavy silences when the children dared not speak and she could think of nothing to say that her husband wouldn't mock or impatiently ignore. So she refused to eat there on the nights her husband was dining out.

She brought the children into the Small Room instead, with its flowered Portuguese needlepoint carpet and yellow painted walls, its small round walnut table and bright napkins, and she would indulge them all with ice-cream and petits-four until they were sick and had to loll back in their chairs in a way that Papa never allowed. They squabbled over who should have the last chocolate, they shrieked over the unfairness of the decision, they knocked their chairs over throwing napkins and grapes. And Clarissa laughed and clapped and adjudicated fairly. It made a nice change from the severity of most of their meals and the children adored Clarissa for it.

Clarissa came from an indulgent family herself. The only child of elderly parents, she was petted and fawned over by a large household of adoring family, relatives and servants until she began to think life was meant to be that way – always happy without the remotest bubble of worry to burst that golden haze of childhood. When, at the age of nineteen, Clarissa's parents were suddenly removed from her life by the unhappy coincidence of a train and their car arriving at a level crossing at the same moment, Clarissa discovered that the world was not at all as she had thought it. There were suddenly grim-faced men with pieces of paper waving fists in her face and demanding money and there were, equally suddenly, no kind, loving relatives or servants to whom to turn.

Gradually Clarissa came to realize that her parents had entertained and supported so many people, so lavishly, and for so long, that there really was no money left. They were gone and she was poor. It was a sobering awakening.

29

Clarissa was not particularly intelligent but that didn't mean she was stupid – something Charles never quite grasped. Very quickly she realized that her only chance of regaining the sort of lifestyle she had assumed would always be hers was to marry someone rich. And, to do that, she had to be at the parties where the rich went. Clarissa wrote sorrowful letters to old schoolfriends and before the month was out, she was installed in London for the summer and spending what little money she had left on looking her very best. Her gamble paid off. While most of the young men in English society were not interested in her – she was neither an exceptional beauty nor rich – a certain, fabulously wealthy, it was said, young Anglo-Brazilian was enchanted by her. She smiled and pouted and let him believe she was a good deal better connected than she really was and before the summer was out, she was Mrs Charles Fawcett of Rio de Janeiro. And before the year was out, her husband was heartily sick of her.

Clarissa didn't care. She liked her new name; so much better than that silly Clarissa Crewe. What must her parents have been thinking of? And she liked the lifestyle in Rio. She wanted life to be easy and charming with no financial worries and only bright, sunny faces surrounding her. She could be just as determined as Charles when she wanted. She smiled at her husband, made herself look beautiful with all the new clothes and jewels he had bought her, and ignored his criticisms and rages.

Charles took refuge in his business and other, less 'simplistic' women than his wife, as he phrased it coldly when she complained. To stimulate him mentally, he had his sister to turn to, when that fellow Michael was out of the way, and she was all he had ever needed for companionship anyway. Baby Isobel did little to change that.

From her first year, Isobel was more concerned with what colour dress she would be wearing than in whether the kitten she had been given was being strangled by the pretty pink bow tied too tightly around its plump little neck. And his wife was spoiling the child dreadfully, he thought. But it was an indifferent thought and not one that concerned him greatly. Charles continued to eat out, especially after Elizabeth left Rio for Vila Serrista with her husband and son.

And then, without any real expectations on his part, he had begun to notice his younger daughter, Eleanor. And she noticed him back. And tried to please him. He was captivated. He was unaware of his other daughter's sudden desire to catch his attention and please him also; he only saw that Isobel had a nasty habit of pushing Eleanor out of the way when she thought she wasn't being watched. And so he punished Isobel and took Eleanor on his knee in the library and closed the door. And Isobel and Clarissa were shut out.

Clarissa tried hard to make up for Charles's neglect of Isobel. She showered her elder daughter with presents and sweets, hugged her to her over-scented breast, and called her pet names. Isobel ignored her mother. She wanted what Eleanor had. Papa.

But Isobel was so intent on trying to catch her father's attention and usurp Eleanor's favour, that she didn't realize for some time after her cousin's arrival that Eleanor was equally interested in John. She didn't see that John laughed at Eleanor's long, involved tales of what had happened that day, that he helped her to ride the ponies in the garden and congratulated her for being so fearless, that he picked flowers with Eleanor to give to Clarissa, and that he often seemed to forget his other cousin entirely. And she didn't particularly notice Eleanor's pleasure at that attention. Poor Isobel. She was still intent on charming Papa, when everyone else was concerned with John.

Charles noticed, however, and began to scowl at the tow-headed boy engaged so guilelessly in rowing his little daughter around the lake or teaching her how to build pyramids of cards that went on and on up to the sky. He saw the same adoring, trusting look in Eleanor's eyes when she gazed at her cousin that she used when she looked at him. It was John she ran to with a cut or graze that needed kissing and John she prayed for first at night. Charles's world began to sour.

It was only much later, when Isobel began to see how important John had become to Eleanor, that it all began to fall into place for Isobel. If Eleanor wanted John, then Isobel would take him away. The thought was as involuntary and unrelenting as her own breathing and Isobel, aware as only a precociously beautiful girl can be of her own sexuality, began to flatter John. It wasn't difficult to find words to praise him with. He was only too attractive to her, and to all the other little girls who whispered and giggled and nudged Isobel to introduce them at her birthday party. And he was very smart, she thought, the way he came home with such good report cards. Louis and Henry thought he was a lot of fun too, always coming up with new, mischievous ideas that seemed great at the time but quite often led to them all going to bed early without dinner. She could take him away from Eleanor; she knew she could.

She smiled at him, dimpling her plump little cheeks, fluttering that strangely alluring lilt to her eyelids, standing close to him when he couldn't get away, at church or dinner. She commented on the colour of his hair, his eyes, his height. She smiled even more. And John ignored her. Just like Papa. She hated Eleanor.

Then Isobel began to notice that Papa didn't like John's influence over Eleanor either. He was jealous. She saw that with the clarity of her own gnawing jealousy and she was glad. She could take Papa away now, if she just tried a little more. He would get tired of Eleanor and then she could have Papa to herself. Who cared about John anyway?

Sitting over the creamy mess that had once been a delicately arranged chocolate and lemon syllabub, Isobel glanced from beneath her eyelashes at John. He had eaten very little of the pudding. It was too rich, he said apologetically to his aunt. Clarissa smiled good-humouredly and told him to leave it.

32

'Isobel will have some more, won't you, my darling?' Clarissa said and Isobel sighed. If she kept eating all her mother's little treats, she would soon have to start worrying about her waistline. But not yet. She smiled at her reflection in the mirror opposite her. No, not yet.

'What about you, Eleanor darling? Had enough?' Clarissa was impartial in her caring for the children. She saw and understood Charles's obsessive regard for Eleanor but she never blamed her younger daughter. It wasn't Eleanor's fault if she were more intelligent or fearless than her sister and, so, more interesting to her papa. Clarissa only wished Charles were a little more impartial in his affections. She also saw his outright dislike of the boy who now sat across the table from her and she pitied John and tried to mother him. He smiled at her efforts and thought her terribly nice but still he kept his distance.

Clarissa knew that too but didn't mind. John was not the sort to like being mothered. He had been brought up far too independently by that blue-stocking Elizabeth for that. Elizabeth, who had made those first few years of marriage so very difficult, with her well-bred contempt for following the rules and her demanding conversations that left Clarissa feeling adrift and incompetent; Elizabeth, whose relationship with her brother, Charles, had made Clarissa wonder, late at night, as she pondered over the day's events. Odd, she had shivered to herself, and disturbing. She had been so glad when Elizabeth had left Rio. So very glad!

It wasn't John's fault he was so independent, not with a mother like that. Besides, it was enough that he brought her flowers and, occasionally, a small gift that he had made at school. She still had the clay mask he had made for her, although she had hidden it away in cotton wool in her drawer so as to not have to look at that dreadful face. Like a demon. He had said it symbolized the voice of Brazil, crying out to be saved, which was just like the sort of nonsense that any child of Elizabeth's might come out with, and she had laughed at the time. He would grow out of it.

33

Chapter Two

Eleanor trailed her fingertips in the swiftly running water, feeling the surge, almost like a quiver of live wood, of the dugout as it thrust into the faster-running middle channel. The canoe was greenish in colour, the single log of wood from which it had been carved so burled and reptilian-looking that it had unnerved Eleanor and taken some persuasion to get her into it. She had asked the man at the upper trading station on the Paraná, before they moved into this tributary, about it and he had told her it was of crocodile wood. It looked like a crocodile too: low, half-submerged in the water and menacing in shape, churning up a white ruff of water as it slid between the rocks. The water was green also but cool and smelled of earth and leaves and rain.

That was a relief after the putrid musty smell of the trading station. There the jungle crowded in closely, cloyingly sweet air filled with night blooming perfumes and gassy swamps, banks of moon-flowers and orchids and rotting, badly cured skins stretched out on bamboo frames. Even the man who ran the station smelt, as though the jungle were seeping out of his pores.

Eleanor had had to turn away and go to stand on the

34

stilt-legged dock, to catch her breath. There she watched the wide channel of the Paraná sweep on and around the bend, carrying the ferry that had brought them this far out into its muddy brown waters. The ferry smartly tooted its farewell.

That sound still echoed inside her, the last link with civilization. From now on it was nothing more than Indian dugouts and oppressive, unbroken jungle for as far as the eye could see. And there were still another four hours or more, John had said, before they would arrive at Vila Serrista.

The journey so far had taken longer than Eleanor would have thought possible. They had gone by train from Rio, yesterday, across the serra and highlands to Uberlándia where they had been seen off on the night ferry by Papa, Louis and Henry, the latter two desperately jealous that they were not invited to go further. Honório had accompanied them on the ferry.

Eleanor considered it very kind of Henry to have thought to have brought a map with him that showed their journey. He pointed out all sorts of interesting sights along the way and Eleanor had wished he could come too. He always took such pains to make sure she was happy. Louis and John had disappeared along the passageway of the train to play – or cause mischief, as Charles Fawcett had remarked disapprovingly – but Henry and she had stayed with Papa and played cards or silly memory games until everyone was tired and anxious for the journey to be over.

Then she and John had passed a strange evening on the ferry, eating dinner with the captain, who was an old friend of John's, he had said with a wink, and who told outrageous tales that John said not to believe or even listen to, for that matter. Tales about the jungle and what the Indians could do to you out there. Tales of being staked to anthills or flayed alive and then eaten. When Eleanor's face had begun to get that pale, pinched look that John recognized from some of his more foolhardy pursuits, they smiled and left the table to the captain and his cronies.

They went and stood on the deck, looking down into the dark water that glinted slick and oily in the moonlight, sliding past the prows almost silently, and then they returned to the cabin to play cards with two of the other passengers, an elderly couple who were returning to their own fazenda, until it was well past Eleanor's bedtime. Honório had appeared and insisted she go to bed. He had led her to her own cabin and waited while she locked herself in before returning to the servants' quarters in the hold. But Eleanor had only stayed long enough to hear Honório's footsteps retreat down the deck before she had darted next door to John's cabin. Her cabin smelt, she said and had climbed into John's bed and fallen asleep before he could protest. But that hadn't been the truth and John had known it. She just didn't want to sleep alone so far away from home. She was only eleven; he couldn't blame her.

Then they had arrived at the trading post where Honório was to pass them over to Elizabeth. Normally John made this journey on his own but Charles had insisted, if Eleanor were to be allowed to go on this journey, that she must be accompanied by someone responsible every step of the way. John knew he was not considered responsible. So they had waited for Elizabeth to arrive, Honório whiling away the time carving a piece of driftwood, and the children poking around the trading station until the canoes should arrive. But there was only one canoe and no Elizabeth. Honório had shouted and stamped his foot much like Eleanor would expect her father to do. The Indians were stoically un-interested. The senhora could not come and there was only room in the single canoe for the children. Honório would have to catch the next ferry back. Eleanor had felt sorry for Honório and tried to cheer him up. But when they left, they could see him sitting in a hunched position on the dock, his face wrinkled with misery. Eleanor had waved but he hadn't waved back.

She leant over to glance at her reflection in the water and dabbled her fingers once more.

'You'll lose your hand if you're not careful.' The voice came from behind her, seemingly casual. She looked back over her shoulder at John.

'Why? There's no propeller and I'm well away from the paddles.' She pointed to the blue-faced Indian named Hatchet kneeling in the prow of the dugout, his skin like polished copper, and back, beyond John to the stern, where another of her uncle Michael's natives was perched, his flat face painted an angry yellow and black with mystic symbols etched across it to appease the river spirits. Monkey smiled, revealing black-painted, filed teeth in a huge maw of a mouth. John made himself comfortable against the pile of rucksacks and food carefully placed in the mid-section of the long, thin canoe.

'Piranhas,' he said flatly. He wasn't surprised when she laughed. He didn't expect her to believe him but it was enough that she withdrew her fingers and sat a little more carefully in the unstable boat. He had seen what the flesh-eating fish could do, attacking anything in the water that had the slightest cut on it, especially the cattle who came down to drink in the mist of dawn, bleeding from insect bites, scratches, and vampire bat bites. There would be a sudden creamy churning of the river, a flurry of little black triangles flipping through the air, and then just the stripped bones of the animal left, propped against the bank and starkly white in the half-light. He knew many Indians who had lost a foot or a hand or a finger to the teeth in the river. He watched Eleanor carefully after that.

The sun sometimes penetrated between the overhanging foliage as they slid into a still lagoon and there would be a flash of fire in the eyes, like crumpled foil scattering light across the ground. The natives would still the canoe for a moment to savour the feel of that golden light on their closed eyelids. Then the water would sweep the boat on into deep shade and the colour of the water would change from cucumber green to almost black.

Eleanor grew tired and lay back in the canoe, almost flat, to watch the treetops sweeping above her, the dark tangle of lianas as they looped overhead, the chattering complaints of herds of bushy-tailed, spidery-armed monkeys who fled shrieking into the jungle as the dark canoe slid swiftly beneath them. Flitting, delicately pale shapes of blue violin birds snatched the air between the water and foliage above. Clusters of fruit bats hung in the gloom and flashing green parakeets flew overhead. She heard the endless clicking of the cicadas and the drum-throb of the tree frogs, and the haunting, mystical chime of the bell-bird. Pink waterlilies with sleepy brown spotted toads basking in the sun drifted by and, as the cooler air of dusk approached, the itchy-hot summer mist gathered in the higher leaves and spattered down on them as bush rain. John strapped a jacket over Eleanor's head and bare limbs so that the poisonous saps of the trees would not burn her skin like acid. And still the river wound on.

It was almost completely dark when they slid into the clearing amidst a flock of white storks picking their way elegantly through the clear shoals. The canoe glided on to the sandbar. The last of the sun flamed the lagoon like a bowl of polished amber and, as John took her hand to steady her, Eleanor stepped ashore beneath dripping black moss that hung from the low branches and stared across at the tall woman who stood outlined against the setting sun.

'There's Mother,' John said with satisfaction. His father was nowhere to be seen but his mother, dressed as always for the day in a white blouse, jodpurs and boots, was standing on the rise above the lagoon and waving. He waved back and Eleanor gave a small, tentative wave too. She didn't know her aunt Elizabeth and her wave reflected that. John left Eleanor's side, springing up the bank to envelop his mother in a tight hug that lifted her off her feet and made her burst out laughing.

'John, darling. No need to smother me! Oh, it's good to see you! You've grown so much. Nearly a foot, I'm sure. And you're so skinny. Aren't you eating enough, darling? I'm so sorry I couldn't come down to the trading station but it was too difficult and Charles really was worrying excessively. And, quite frankly, there would be nothing I could do to protect Eleanor from danger that Monkey and Hatchet couldn't do far better. There wasn't any problem about it, was there?' Her babble of excited questions floated down to where Eleanor still lingered and, for a moment, Eleanor missed her own mother intensely. She saw John shake his head, dismissing Honório and his worries. And then the Indians, Monkey and Hatchet, were pushing past her with the luggage and she had to move forward to greet her aunt or risk being knocked into the river.

'Aunt Elizabeth?' Eleanor held out her hand and Elizabeth, looking around, saw a delicately built miniature of her son with long, pale hair plaited back from a widow's peak, an olive-skinned, oval face with serious-looking green eyes and a wide, determined mouth. The girl was standing stiffly and formally and holding out her hand as though they were greeting one another for the first time in a Rio de Janeiro drawing-room. Equally gravely, Elizabeth offered her own hand and they shook politely before drawing apart.

'Hullo, Eleanor. I'm so glad you could come and stay with us for the holidays. Aren't you and John alike? I wonder if Charles has noticed that?' She paused and thought, with a pang, how much Eleanor was like herself at the same age. And that explained a great deal. Charles had found a replacement for her after all. She knew Charles (who better?) and his possessive nature – overpowering, all-consuming, determined not to share. She had had to fight to be free of him, free of the role he had decided should be hers for life. And now, by chance, he had found another for that role. She looked at Eleanor uneasily.

Elizabeth understood finally why John said his uncle hated him. She had put that down to childish rebellion at the time. Now she was not sure. Perhaps it was time to think of other arrangements for John. Perhaps she should go back with him ...?

She heard Eleanor say something and she played it back in her mind to catch the words. Just a greeting.

Elizabeth smiled. 'How is your mama? And Isobel? Is she any better now?' Eleanor was relieved that her aunt was being sensible and not trying to gush all over her like her own mother had done over John. That would have been embarrassing.

'Yes, she's much better now but Papa wouldn't let her come. She's supposed to have lots of bed-rest.'

'Which is why she was being allowed to ride the ponies around the hillside the day before yesterday, I suppose?' John added with what his mother thought was rather sharp humour. He was changing lately, she thought. Ageing not just physically, or mentally, but spiritually as well. She wasn't sure she liked it. Perhaps that was Charles's influence? Charles ...

'Oh, Isobel wouldn't have liked it up here anyway,' Eleanor said hastily. 'She's rather nervous around insects and snakes and things. It might have made her ill again if she were constantly jumping into the air when a beetle landed on her.'

'Like you, you mean?' John teased and Eleanor flushed. It was only the once, she thought, and the spider that had dropped on her from one of the overhanging branches was larger than her hand. She couldn't help it if she had been scared. It could have been poisonous. Her face grew pink cheeked and her eyes glistened resentfully.

But John had seen her discomfort and was putting an arm around her shoulders and shaking her. 'I was only kidding, silly.' He looked up at his mother and smiled. 'It was a night spider, you know those big black ones with the red spots? It must have been weaving its net for tonight and missed its footing because it landed, plop, in Eleanor's lap. Scream! You've never heard anything like it and probably neither has the jungle because it went very quiet after that.' He grinned and added, 'No, she was very good about it actually and didn't even overturn the canoe which I'm not too sure I wouldn't have done if one of those hairy monsters had dropped in my lap!'

'Oh, my dear, how unpleasant for you. What happened

to the spider? Did you throw it overboard?' Elizabeth gathered both children to her and started leading them towards the house they could see in the distance.

'John grabbed it with his bare hands, and threw it into the water. Ugh! I don't know how he could touch it but he was so quick I didn't have time to do more than scream. I expect I would have turned us over if I hadn't been in total shock,' Eleanor admitted, now that her own courage had been established.

John shrugged. 'It wasn't poisonous. Just ugly. C'mon, let's go in,' he said, slapping at a mosquito as it droned past his ear. His mother smiled to herself.

'Where's Dad? Didn't he hear the conch shell?' John had heard their arrival announced by the blowing of the conch shell they kept to warn of visitors a good ten minutes before they had drawn into the clearing. A long blast followed by one short blast for friends, two for unknown, three for enemies. There were still the occasional raids by the local Indians who killed the tame Indians working the fazenda, for the fun of it. Like pulling wings off a fly. John shuddered at the memories those three blows on the conch had imprinted on his mind.

But their own arrival had been heralded by just one short blast and so his mother had come down to meet them. But his father, now where was he?

John felt his mother's hesitation and was even more puzzled when she answered casually, 'Oh, just working I expect. He knew I'd come and meet you.' That didn't make sense. It had been a ritual, both of them standing there to meet him when he returned from school. Why would his mother act as though it were nothing for his father to be absent? Was there something she didn't want to say in front of Eleanor? He gave his mother a worried glance but she didn't acknowledge it, talking briskly instead of what fun it would be to go and have a picnic at the waterfalls the next day and whether Eleanor didn't find the heat too oppressive?

They continued to walk up the path to the house but

John lingered, looking around the fazenda for his father. He could see the rows of coffee bushes hedged by steep reddish-purple hills around which a dripping black jungle clung, its feathered outline of ferns and lianas standing out starkly in the twilight. In the middle of the clearing was a cluster of buildings, the largest of which had light spilling from its windows out on to the gardens around it. On the west side of the clearing whispered and gurgled the tributary they had just followed from the main Paraná River; on all three other sides were jungle. This was the Backlands – O Sertão, a wild uncivilized land far from all but pockets of human habitation, an unknown wilderness. John breathed in deeply, glad to be home.

There were no workers left in the fields, just a few flitting figures carrying in the last of the coffee harvest for the day and depositing it in the barns. Tomorrow they would spread out the cherry-like fruit on the beaten earth patios to dry and then separate it from its blackened shell in a slow moving, water-powered wooden mortar called a monjolo. The coffee harvest was from May to September and this year's crop was nearly over. John could hear his mother explaining the process to Eleanor as he walked a few paces behind them. Still he could not see his father.

He quickened his pace and caught up with his mother and Eleanor. Now that they were close to the bungalow, Eleanor saw that it was not white, as she had assumed, seeing it glow lightly in the dark, but a pale yellow hung around with verandahs on the ground floor, like skirts. The massive front door was carved from a single slab of wood and stood open to greet them, the lamps within casting a welcoming glow on to the polished verandah floors.

Eleanor saw each window had equally heavy shutters, drawn back now against the walls, and at shoulder height in each shutter was a round hole. She wondered what that was for and turned to ask John but at that moment her uncle Michael stepped across the doorway and she fell silent. Both John and his mother were also silent, the first from shock, the second from embarrassment. The man standing before them was drunk.

Brownish sweat stains down the front of his shirt and heavy, unshaven jowls, folding into crevasses, suggested he had been that way for some time. His eyes were bleared and yellowed, shot through with a spiderwork of red and he smelt strongly of the local brew, chicha, a mixture of fermented sugarcane and yuca. He stood carefully upright, holding on to the doorframe, smiling foolishly.

'Hullo there. Thought you'd be here soon, John. Heard the conch. Just coming down to meet you, John.' Michael nodded, trying desperately to pretend nothing was wrong, repeating his son's name like a talisman.

John lowered his head. 'Hullo, sir.'

'Good to see you, boy. Good to have you home. I've got lots to show you, John – lots of improvements. You won't recognize the place. You'll want to stay here more then, maybe, not go off to school all the time. Maybe we should talk about that, huh? Huh, John?' He laughed, slurring his words and swung from side to side. When John didn't respond, he hesitated and looked irritated. The foolish bonhomie curdled, became unpleasant. He glanced around for something to vent his anger on.

'Well, and who's this? Huh?' Michael peered out at Eleanor. His voice rose. 'Who the hell is this? I didn't invite anyone here! Who is this?' He stabbed a finger through the air, its paleness phosporescent in the dark. His face contorted and he took an unsteady pace forward.

Eleanor shrank against John and he put an arm around her and made quiet, soothing noises to her.

Elizabeth found her voice at last, cracking with awkward emotion. 'This is your niece, Eleanor Fawcett, Michael. You remember? John goes and lives with Eleanor and her family when he's away at school and Eleanor's come to visit us for a couple of weeks. This is John's cousin – Eleanor,' she repeated so that he could follow her meaning clearly. He furrowed his brow and swallowed, licking at his lips with a large, swollen tongue. Elizabeth hurried on, 'Now, I really think you're not well, darling. You should be in bed.'

43

She tried to take his arm but he swung it angrily from her grasp.

'Don't tell me where I should be, you stupid bitch. Don't tell me what to do. You hear me? And you tell your damned brother, Mr High and Mighty Charles Fawcett, to take his brat home and keep her there. You tell —' But Michael made the mistake, at that point, of letting go of the door lintel and he felt the world begin to dip and spin sickeningly around him. His voice faltered.

'Dad? Dad!' John thrust himself forward in time to catch the tall figure as it crumpled heavily to the ground, bringing John down with him so that they both lay sprawled across the wooden verandah, the boy trapped beneath the man's dead weight. Elizabeth clicked her fingers a couple of times and two house-servants, one heavy-set with an expressionless face painted red and black, dressed in a bark apron with yellow feathers dangling from an ear lobe, the other taller and wearing old trousers with a shiny red-painted chest of anchiote and his dark hair in a bob, stepped out from the house and picked Michael up between them. They carried him inside without looking to Elizabeth for instructions. They had clearly done this before.

There was complete silence after they had left, John climbing stiffly to his feet again and standing to one side of the verandah posts, his face turned away, and Elizabeth unmoving, looking more drained than Eleanor thought she had ever seen anyone look.

'John, sweetheart, I'm so sorry. I thought I could get him cleaned up before you came back. He's normally so careful not to let you see him when he's like this. But it had to come out at some time, I suppose.' Her voice sounded flat, at odds with the concern of her words. She took a deep breath and tried harder. 'Eleanor, dear. I do hope you weren't too frightened. Uncle Michael is just a bit — sick at the moment and can't remember things and gets mixed up about people and who they are. He didn't mean to yell at you like that. He'll be fine tomorrow, I promise you. And he won't remember any of this. I hope you won't either.'

Her hands beseeched the dark air for a moment, then fell back to her side and Elizabeth slipped in through the door and went in search of her husband.

Eleanor hesitated, unsure what to do. John didn't look around and eventually she walked over to him and put a hand on his arm. 'John, John, are you all right?' She could see the light shimmering on snail tracks of tears when he turned and looked at her, his eyes huge and swimming wetly between dark fringes of lashes.

'Yes, I'm fine,' he said bitterly and Eleanor put her arms around his waist and held her cheek against his chest. She couldn't reach any higher but John closed his own arms around her and they stood like that for a long time.

'Some greeting you just got, huh? I'm sorry, Elly. Dad isn't normally like that. At least, I don't think he is. He's never been like that when I've been here before ... I'm very sorry he shouted at you.' Eleanor could tell from the tremor in his voice that John was more than sorry. He was humiliated. Everything he had ever thought he knew was now changed. His father, even his mother, were people he didn't know. In a few moments his whole world had slipped out of focus, permanently, and he wasn't sure yet how to cope with that.

She hugged him harder. 'Don't be. It isn't your fault. Everything will be better tomorrow and, anyway, I'm here,' she whispered and felt his arms tighten.

'I know,' he said, 'I'm depending on that.'

That night, John had shown Eleanor where her bedroom was and left her to wash while he went in search of his parents. Eleanor wasn't sure what had happened but John had seemed calmer when he appeared to call her for dinner. Eleanor herself had used the time to remove all her travel-soiled clothes and sit contentedly in a tin tub, washing away the day's strains. A pitcher of lukewarm water was brought to her room by an Indian woman who had appeared silently and seemingly without opening the door, smiling shyly, ducking her head so many times that

Eleanor had begun to feel a little sick and had to ask her to stop. At which the woman smiled even more broadly and pointed to herself, whispering 'Ro-sa' before scuttling quickly out of the room again.

The room itself had dark polished floorboards and a wooden bed hung about with billowing white mosquito nets and soft white sheets that made Eleanor long to climb between them and forget dinner completely. She resisted the idea and was dressed in a light cotton frock with her hair clean and plaited down her back again and her feet sensibly in sandals by the time John knocked on her door.

'It's me. You ready yet?' he called. She opened the door and pulled him quickly into her room. John had washed and changed as well and was wearing a white shirt and cotton ducks, his wet hair combed back neatly from his forehead and his skin tightly polished from scrubbing.

'Did you talk to your parents? Did you ask them what's going on?' Eleanor demanded.

John looked uneasy. 'You don't ask questions like that of my father. Besides, he's still sick. Mother –' he paused and then continued with difficulty '– Mother says dad's been like this, on and off, for most of the year. Something to do with his hero, President Vargas, and the military wanting to get him out of power. You know how Dad feels about the army after all that mess in the war; all that corruption and incompetence. He says it got good men killed, good friends of his. He never really trusted the military after that. Anyway, now he listens to all the reports on the wireless and sends messengers down to all the trading posts and other fazendas for news. It's been worrying him and he's been sick a lot, Mother says, but ... but he'll get better again.' He saw she understood without him having to elaborate.

Eleanor had a good grasp of politics and listened enough to her father to know what was going on between President Vargas and the military hardliners. There were rumours of another coup, but everyone was keeping a low profile for fear of jumping the wrong way.

'I don't see how any of it will affect the Vila Serrista or your father,' she argued and John sighed.

'It won't unless he lets it,' he said and broke off abruptly, the conversation with his mother still running through his mind. His father had been such an idealist, his mother had said, and was so soured and bitter now that even she was getting nervous. He would blank out sometimes: couldn't remember where he'd been, what he'd been doing – for hours! She had tried to get him to go down to Rio and see a specialist but he wouldn't hear of it. He would get in a rage and go off hunting – or drinking – and she would just let it drop.

John looked at Eleanor, remembering his mother's parting words: 'Until the next time. It's the chicha, I think. It can make you mad if you drink too much of it.' But he couldn't tell Eleanor that. It was too awful. He shrugged instead.

Eleanor looked troubled. 'Should I tell Papa? Ask him to write to your dad?' She began tentatively only to see John's face stiffen.

He shook his head fiercely. 'No! Your father has nothing to do with mine. Don't you say a word. You hear me?' He had taken her arm and was holding it so tightly that Eleanor was taken aback.

She shook her head. 'All right! Let me go, John, you're hurting!' He released her and stood back sheepishly. 'I won't say anything but what's Aunt Liz supposed to do all alone if . . .' she faltered, unwilling to end the sentence. '. . . if your father gets really sick?'

John turned away. 'She'll be all right. She's pretty tough. Now let's drop it, okay? I don't want to talk about it anymore.'

'Fine. I don't care.' Eleanor massaged the pinkish bruise on her arm. 'Not if you don't,' she added and then walked out of the room. She waited in the hall, silently, for John to lead the way.

He shrugged awkwardly and then, turning away from her, led her down more passageways and into the dining-room where only Elizabeth waited at the head of the table. She had changed also into a flowered dress that hung loosely around her body as though she had recently lost weight.

Eleanor looked slowly around. The walls were panelled in a red hardwood with a white burl grain, and a hissing gasoline-pressured lamp swung gently over the long refectory table in the night breeze. The table was laid with a white linen cloth and willow-patterned Wedgwood plates, silver and cut-glass crystal, and a large bowl of rose-tipped cream flowers that Eleanor could not identify. They perfumed the air with a strangely sweet, cool fragrance.

'There you both are. I was about to send someone to look for you. Eleanor, why don't you sit here, on my right and John, you sit on my left. There's no point in having to shout to each other down the table, is there? Pedro?' She looked over to the servant with the yellow feathers in his ear who was clearly the 'butler'. 'I think we'll start with the soup now. Ask Rosa to put some aside for O Patrão. He may be hungry later.' And that was how the pattern was set, from that night on.

There was no mention of Michael or his 'illness' or his occasional absences from the table. When he was present he was mostly rather silent with tightly compressed lips, surveying the table with irritability, and the few remarks that escaped those lips directed solely at his wife or a servant. Sometimes he was in a genial, almost manic mood, laughing uproariously at his own jokes, slapping the table with his large, broad hand, insisting everyone enjoy the evening as much as he. When he was absent, it was a relief.

That first night, the soup was turtle, followed by delicately flavoured fish, a dish of roast partridge, vegetables and salads of bananas, sliced papayas, grapes, zapotes, oranges, salted cashews, and roasted breadfruit nuts. On the nights that Michael was present, there were generally a couple more meat dishes, a pinkish-rare roast of tapir or perhaps a saddle of roast venison in wine sauce. But when he was absent, they kept it simple, Elizabeth explained and

Eleanor blinked. Simple? She was amazed by the abundance and excellence of the food. It could have been a dinner party her own mother would serve for dignitaries in Rio, except for the exotic nature of some of the ingredients. So much for her ideas of eating out over a camp fire and sleeping in a hammock!

After the meal, they followed Elizabeth into the drawing-room and sat in cool, slip-covered chairs, talking quietly about their life in Rio or the possibilities of the jungle if it were ever opened up to settlers, the gentle strains of Brahms or Liszt floating out through the open doors on to the verandah and carried by the night breeze into the canopy of trees. Monstrous brown moths with yellow cats' eye wings, black flying beetles, silvery flying ants, stick insects, and a three-inch praying mantis fluttered, pinged and swooped around the lamp on the table, frizzling as they made contact with the hot flame and dropping in dead piles around it.

From time to time Elizabeth would click her fingers and an Indian servant would step forward to press the pressure gauge on the lamp and sweep up the charnel house of insects from the table. Eleanor watched the process with a sickened fascination, her own eyes dancing with red spots when she glanced back into the room. And Elizabeth would continue her conversation without a pause to acknowledge the dying insects, discussing instead what latest plays were being presented in Rio or which latest author the children should read. They smiled and nodded and blinked away their sleepy eyes.

Eleanor slept soundly the first night. She was exhausted by the two-day journey, the wonder of the jungle, the fright from the spider, and the unexpectedly distressing greeting her uncle had shown her. No sooner had her head touched the pillow than she was deeply asleep; so deeply that she didn't hear the coughing roar of the jaguar that prowled the outer boundaries of the homesteads, nor the wild barking that became a yelp and a whimper as one of the dogs was killed and dragged away.

But John heard it. He lay awake for hours afterwards, knowing there was no point in going out to search for the dog but unable to simply forget and fall asleep. Nor could he forget his father. He lay on his back, staring up at the frame from which his mosquito net was suspended, feeling the night breeze stirring the nets but never penetrating through the tight mesh, and his thoughts chased around and around in the dark recesses of his mind. He sweated in the humid air, his head pillowed on his arms, his whole body aching with tiredness, but still he could not sleep.

The rain started about two that morning, sending flumes of wet spray in through the open doorway to the verandah and soaking the wooden boards. John slid from between the nets and went to close the doors. Overhead, thunder cracked and roared and, as he stood staring out at the dark, the entire clearing and jungle beyond was lit up in a blinding flash of white light, the trees silhouetted in fantastic black shapes and their canopies alive with a mass of lightning dancing against the treetops like yellow and green orchids. The smell of damp smoke and ozone filled his nostrils.

The spray lashed his face but still he stood there, gazing out at the wildness of the storm, feeling the wet running down his bare chest, soaking his cotton shorts. He felt strangely wild himself, elated and expectant and uncontrolled and he stepped out on to the verandah, the wood wet under his feet.

Somewhere, out in the dark, he could hear an insistent, strangely querulous, childlike chanting, blowing stronger now and then weaker with the wind, haunting and unsettling in its beat, threading deeper and harder into his ears, his mind, beckoning. He took a step towards the verandah stairs.

'John.' The voice was quiet and low but he heard it above the storm.

He turned, knowing already who it was. 'I thought you were asleep,' he said.

'The tigre woke me. Which dog was it?' His father was sober now, his eyes revealing the man inside whom John knew, not the shouting, incoherent stranger.

John shrugged. 'I don't know. Daisy maybe. It sounded like her bark. Has this jaguar been around before?'

'Yes. Got my prize bull about two weeks ago. Snapped its neck cleanly. I'll go hunt it down tomorrow. You want to come?' His father knew John would want to. He merely dangled it like a bait, wanting to see the boy's eyes light up with excitement, his mouth curve into a wide grin. He was disappointed.

'Yes, sir.' The reply was subdued. 'If you want me along.' There was a long silence between them. The rain was gusting harder now, soaking them both. John shivered. 'What's that sound? I've never heard it before,' he said.

Michael Campos de Serra looked out at the night and listened. 'You're never normally awake at this hour. It's the Indians. They're worshipping Pawa, the Golden Man, son of God. Idol-worshipping a Christian God. They never quite got Catholicism sorted out, got it all mixed up with their spirit world.' He half laughed. 'You stay away from there. Don't go near the chapel, their "Dream House", all right? It's not for you or any of us there. It's for them.' Then he tapped his son on the arm. 'Bed. It's late and getting cold out here. I'll see you at breakfast and we'll figure out the hunt.' He turned away and walked back down the verandah, not into his own bedroom but past it and, as his figure went to turn the corner of the house, John saw a dark shape step out from the shadows and twine itself against his father. He heard a laugh, low and repressed, and then they were gone. John stood listening to the chanting a few moments longer. Then he returned to bed, falling into a deep sleep immediately.

When John woke it was already light and he could hear voices out on the verandah by his room. He stepped out, squinting at the sun, to see his mother and Eleanor with baskets in their hands. They both smiled at the tousled, sleepy-eyed boy, his shorts hanging loosely around his hips.

51

'You slept late. Aunt Elizabeth and I've been up for hours.' Eleanor pointed to the pink and gold hibiscus that smothered the verandah. 'We're going to fill the house with these. D'you want some?' But as she went to cut the flowers, the blossoms rose in a cloud and broke into coral-pink butterflies that hovered like gilded petals and then swept away in the wind. Eleanor drew in her breath in delight, running after them to try and catch one in her hands.

'Nice child, isn't she? Like having a sister for you to grow up with,' Elizabeth said, watching Eleanor leaping across the lawn. She looked speculatively at her son.

John nodded. 'Very nice. And not such a child either. Not sometimes.' He stopped then, as though puzzled by what he had just said and ran it through again in his mind. Not such a child. What did he mean by that? Was Eleanor right then and subconsciously he knew it? His father did need help and if he didn't get it, he might . . .

His mother interrupted his thoughts. 'Your father's waiting to take you hunting. You'd better hurry up or he'll go without you. And John – you be very careful, all right? No getting in the way of that jaguar. I don't care if it's killed every animal we own. I don't want it killing you.' She softened her words by kissing him on the forehead and he smiled at her with those blue eyes that sometimes seemed so totally detached that Elizabeth had trouble in returning his gaze.

'Don't worry, Mother. I can take care of myself – and Dad,' he replied, answering her unspoken question. 'Mother? About Dad . . .' He hesitated, not sure how to ask about what he had seen last night. How did you ask if your father was sleeping with the native women? He cleared his throat and then shook his head. 'Nothing.' He turned back into his room.

Elizabeth began to cut the hibiscus blossoms, placing them carefully in her basket. He was right. He could take care of them both in the jungle. Probably better than anyone she knew apart from the Indians themselves. After all, they had taught him. How to survive, how to find food, have a quick dip first, all right? Monkey and Hatchet will watch out for us, don't worry.' Elizabeth sat down and immediately pulled off her boots and socks, wiggling the pale toes that appeared in delight. Eleanor sat down beside her and pulled off her clothes to the bathing suit she had worn underneath.

Her body was still tanned from sunning herself around the pool at home or spending the weekends on Copacabana or Ipanema beaches and she sat with her legs outstretched, flopping her feet in the water. Elizabeth was much slower and Eleanor was surprised to see how pale her aunt's body was. And then Eleanor started and stared. Against that paleness blossomed various different shades of colour: the virulent reds and purples, blacks and greens of bruises that were either fresh, or healing. There were several of them.

'How did you do that, Aunt Liz? Did you fall down?' Eleanor asked, without thinking, only to see her aunt's face become flushed and embarrassed.

'Uh, yes. I slipped down a slope and got rather battered around a few coffee plant roots. Don't worry, it looks worse than it feels and it's going now anyway.' She smiled and stepped gingerly over the shale and gravel into the deeper water of the lagoon. Ripples of light corruscated across the water in her wake. Eleanor gave a troubled sigh and followed her aunt into the shallows.

John lay silent on the ground, hoping the pium flies that were hovering in a dense cloud around him and drawing blood on every inch of his skin, would soon leave. He had rubbed his body earlier with an ointment that the Indians used to keep insects away but it had sweated off in the last two hours and he dared not move to reapply it. He gritted his teeth instead and stared out through narrowed eyes at the goat they had tethered further down the path. It bleated plaintively.

A column of umbrella ants, big red ivory-headed sauba ants, carrying the remains of a centipede over their heads

how to cure himself with their strange plant medicines, how to find the secret war trails that criss-crossed this seemingly impenetrable jungle and how to avoid the snares that were put along those trails for the unwary – and most of all, how to kill. They had taught him like one of their own sons and he had learned it well. She shook herself, trying to clear the foreboding from her mind. He would be all right. They both would.

Eleanor came running back, her hands carefully cupped around something, her face bright with success. 'I've got one, Aunt Elizabeth. I've got one!' Slowly she opened her hands and a single, pink butterfly rose into the air. It fluttered above their heads before disappearing towards the garden. Eleanor looked after it wistfully. 'I just wanted to show you it – I couldn't keep it. It would've died if I'd put it in a box to keep it safe. But I wish I could've,' she said.

Elizabeth stroked the girl's hair; she knew how Eleanor felt. But she was thinking, not of a butterfly, but of her son. 'I was wondering whether you'd like to take a look at the waterfall today. I haven't had an excuse for going up there in ages and if the men are going to be hunting, it'll be pretty dull for you around here,' Elizabeth said.

Eleanor blinked with pleased surprise. She had assumed the picnic would be off now that the hunt had become more important. 'Oh, could we? I mean, it won't be dangerous for us to go out there when they haven't caught the jaguar yet?'

'No, not up there. The jaguar stays down in the basin mostly, trying to get easy pickings from the fazenda. Besides, Michael's men tracked it early this morning and they say it's over to the south, beyond the clearing. It took one of the dogs last night so it won't be looking to hunt again until this evening, probably.' She smiled to dispel any nervousness the girl might feel. 'The jungle's pretty wild, Eleanor, and if you worry about everything, you end up not going out the door. And I like my freedom,' she added firmly.

Eleanor nodded but didn't voice her thoughts.

panied Elizabeth in the jungle, or John up-river. They were the best, Elizabeth had explained carefully, when Eleanor had asked about it. Best at what? But Elizabeth had just smiled vaguely and said, 'Oh, everything,' which left Eleanor wondering just what was out there in those impenetrable thickets.

She could hear a roaring sound now, deeper and throatier than earlier. On the last hundred yards, before they broke clear of the jungle, the sound became a vibration, throbbing through the ground, pulsing in the air and Eleanor could smell the water and the spray before she stepped out on to the rocky promontory and blinked in the sunshine.

The falls stretched up, to her right, as high as a two-storey house, and as wide as three men touching with outstretched arms. Down it cascaded a torrent of white and green water, churning and rolling against rocks, flying up in spray over the tops of the papaya grove at the foot of the falls, and swirling around into a gentler lagoon whose sun-dappled water lapped against flat black volcanic rocks. Around it the jungle bloomed in colour and perfume: pink oleander, scented cinnamon groves, white and purple orchids and fluted plumes of orange with sharp, razor-like leaves. Yellow and green parakeets flashed through the air and the birds in the dense black-green foliage sang ecstatic songs that ended, maddeningly, on an impossibly endless note. Dragonflies dipped and hovered, cicadas shrilled and monkeys clambered higher into the trees to stare at the intruders.

'It's beautiful!' Eleanor shouted above the roar and Elizabeth smiled to herself. Beautiful. Yes, but so much more than that. Violent and treacherous and staggeringly gorgeous – there really were no words, no superlatives adequate for this place, she thought. She had never named it, knowing that a name could only diminish the power it exerted over her. She saw some of that awe in the child's eyes and was pleased.

'We'll set out the blanket and food here on the rocks and

started out across the clearing and John wondered whether they would continue straight and so miss him or whether he would have to climb a tree. But they seemed unaware of, or indifferent to, his presence and continued on their journey, bearing the centipede back to fertilize their fungus plantations. John had heard they would take a man piecemeal if he were wounded and couldn't get away. He watched them with interest.

Further down the path, his father was positioned behind a rubber tree. They were both downwind of the goat and, hopefully, the jaguar that the natives were tracking. So far they had found nothing. John wiped a trickle of sweat from his forehead and blinked quickly to clear his eyes. He felt keyed up and nervous, despite the monotony of the long wait and the frustration of the flies. This jaguar, or tigre as the Indians called it, was a cunning animal: he couldn't afford to relax even for a moment or he might find he had become the bait rather than the goat.

Eleanor floated on her back, spread out like a starfish, and hung her head back in the water. Her hair swished gently in the clear shallows and the pounding of the waterfall dulled in her ears. The water was blood temperature and she found it difficult to tell whether her hand was in the water or out. She experimented by lifting all her limbs, one by one, but she simply sank under the water without feeling it. It was an odd sensation. She lifted her head again to call out to her aunt.

'I'm getting hungry, aren't you? It's quite late. Shall I start unpacking the food?'

Elizabeth waved her in. 'Go ahead. I'm just going to walk over to the falls.' She waded out of the lagoon on the far side and clambered on to the flats, the black rocks burning the soles of her feet. She winced and walked on.

Eleanor watched her aunt for a few moments before pulling herself out of the water and wringing out her hair. She slipped on her sandals against the heated rock and squatted down over the picnic basket Hatchet had carried there for them. There was no sign of the Indians but Elizabeth had assured her they would have their own food, if they didn't catch any fish for lunch.

In the distance Eleanor thought she heard a hallooing but it was only for a second and then the sound was drowned in the roar of the falls. She stood up and stared around her but the sound was gone. Perhaps it was a bird? Or some natives calling to each other. She hoped not. She wasn't sure she wanted to meet the Indians who still hunted these jungles. Not after the ferry boat captain's tales.

Eleanor laid out the food carefully on plates, unwrapping the tea towels her aunt had tied over the sandwiches and pouring out a glass of lemonade. She took a long gulp and wiped her lips on the back of her hand. Her hair hung limply down her back and she stood firmly on the rocks, feet slightly apart, with all the sure balance of a child. Elizabeth, looking back at her, thought she looked like a water sprite in her green bathing suit. She waved. Far out in the middle of the river, Eleanor could see her aunt, standing on rocks in the spray of the falling water, with her arms upstretched as though to catch it. She looked palely beautiful in the billowing cloud, Eleanor thought as she waved back.

And then it came again. The hallooing. Much nearer and louder. Eleanor started in alarm and the birds in the trees nearest her flew up with a raucous beating of wings. The monkeys swung away, clattering through the canopy and a sudden hush fell over the jungle. Eleanor looked around her. There was no sign of Hatchet or Monkey. Elizabeth, oblivious, stood out under the roar of the falls, unable to hear even a cannon fire on the opposite shore. And Eleanor began to be afraid.

John saw the jaguar some time before his father. But there was no way he could signal him. Instead he froze into position, sighting along his rifle and slowly easing off the safety catch. He held his breath tightly, focusing on the beast as it slid through the shadows, intent on its prey. It was a magnificent animal, full of power and grace, the muscles bunching silkily beneath the dappled coat, the snout wide and flat from the heavy skull. It watched everything from a blaze of golden eyes and John felt a deep regret that this beautiful creature would soon be dead. For a moment his finger hesitated on the trigger.

And then his father fired. Too low, too late, the animal already swinging away in a roar of rage and alarm as it spotted the dark shadows move and the rifle snick against a branch. The bullet caught the animal in its flank but it kept moving, disappearing instantly into the green before John could finish the job with a clean shot to its head.

John jumped up and joined his father as he bent down to check the blood on the path. There was no doubt. The tigre was wounded and bleeding heavily. It would be mean now. How could his father have missed like that? John looked at Michael Campos de Serra and for the first time saw doubt there and, perhaps, just a flicker of fear. But then his father started after the jaguar and John followed him into the forest, following the trail of blood and broken undergrowth. As they ran, John heard his father curse.

Ahead they could hear the sudden alarmed cries of an Indian tracker and as they burst into another clearing they saw the man rolling on the earth, his shoulder half ripped away. Another Indian appeared from the western edge of the clearing. He pointed silently into the jungle again and they ran on, beginning to fear as they saw the direction the jaguar was taking.

Eleanor felt as though a thousand eyes were peering at her from out of the gloom. She backed slowly away from the trees and edged into the water, her eyes never leaving the glossy wall of green that hid the watchers from her. She knew there was a myth of a forest ghost, the Curcipuri, who drove men mad in the jungle but she had always thought it an old wives' tale. Now she was not so sure. She waved to her aunt again but Elizabeth had her back to her now and didn't see. Eleanor knew she could not swim the channel of raging water that separated her aunt from herself and even if she could, what could Elizabeth do? There was something out there and the jungle had grown silent in fear. She turned back to face the trees.

Chapter Three

'It's circling around, coming up from the east so it can get the benefit of the wind,' Michael said, his breath ragged from running. John nodded. He had realized what the jaguar was doing some time ago. And that meant it would come up near the falls, near Eleanor and his mother ... He stopped and cupped his hands together and called again. Perhaps Monkey or Hatchet would hear it, or his mother. She would know it was a warning. He ran faster, ducking under overhanging branches, leading his father through the secret trails he had run as a small boy in play. He stepped off the trail abruptly, guiding his father around a hidden pit in which several sharpened stakes waited for the unwary, before resuming the path. His father groaned in protest and lagged further behind. And John had to slow rather than let his father follow the trail alone. That would be fatal.

Eleanor waded out deeper into the water, feeling it tug against her light body, trying to lift her off her feet and out into the racing millstream ahead. She crouched down and waited.

There was still no sign of Monkey or Hatchet and she thought furiously of what she would like to say to them.

Loping off to catch their lunch instead of protecting Elizabeth and herself. Unless, of course, whatever was out there had ... No, they were too experienced for that. They would have heard it long ago. Even she could hear it, twigs snapping, leaves rustling, the odd, coughing sort of grunt. Like a pig, perhaps, or a boar? Monkey and Hatchet would have done something if they were anywhere around, she knew that. Elizabeth said they were the best. But whatever was out there might be better ... And it was coming her way.

And then it was there, no more than thirty feet away, staring at her with those huge pools of yellow, like beams of light, its body blending into the colours around it, its mouth open red, snarling, hissing, full of anger and fear and hate. She screamed.

John heard the scream and left his father, running furiously over the trail, knowing he must be too late but willing himself on in an agonizing, breathless dash, his muscles aching, his chest pounding for air, the adrenalin spurting through him in a sudden rush of fear. That was Eleanor's scream. He didn't think of his own danger, or of his father left alone on the almost indistinguishable trail full of snares and pitfalls; he only thought of the little girl he had promised to look after who was now screaming in terror and dread.

The jaguar opened its jaws still further and bellowed an angry, hateful roar to see its path blocked. It hesitated, swinging its heavy head from side to side to clear the pain, slashing its tail in fury and fear. A noise behind it, crashing through the jungle made it bellow again. Then it leapt forward into the water, pulling strongly out towards the channel, towards the terrified, screaming child in its way.

Elizabeth had seen the danger now and was scrambling over the rocks towards Eleanor, yelling for her to get out of the way. But Eleanor was frozen with fear and could only crouch desperately in the shallows and watch the huge beast leaping towards her. She saw it close now, almost upon her and threw her hands up in terror.

Suddenly a shot cracked the air and the beast halted in mid-leap, sinking tiredly back into the water and slowly, half-submerged, drifted out towards the roaring waters of the channel. Eleanor screamed again and again until her throat was hoarse and her voice only came out as a whimper. Silence fell as she continued to crouch in the water, her arms lifted to ward off the ripping, tearing blow that would now never come, staring at the body of the jaguar as it was swept faster, and deeper now, out into the river. She felt light-headed and sick, her vision beginning to spark around the edges, her mouth bitter with fear. Then John was there, lifting her into his arms and holding her tightly, and she clung to him and sobbed.

Monkey and Hatchet were shamefaced that night as they came to see Eleanor. She sat up in bed, her hair pulled back behind her ears and her face still pale and shocked from her near escape. They stood with bowed heads and downcast eyes and muttered their apologies in an odd mixture of Portuguese and Indian dialect. Eleanor nodded. It was all right now, she said. No harm had come to her. John had looked after her. The Indians hung their heads even lower. Then they left.

Elizabeth poked her head around the door next and, on seeing Eleanor was awake and sitting up, she entered with a tray of food. 'Hullo there, feeling better? You've had quite a sleep. It's nearly nine o'clock. Did Monkey and Hatchet come and see you?' She saw Eleanor's nod of assent, her mouth still pinched in that pale face. 'Well, they were very sorry, my dear. They had gone off hunting, which they weren't supposed to do and Uncle Michael's been very angry with them. But they didn't mean to do anything wrong. They just forgot.' Like children, Elizabeth thought, and Michael had punished them like, like – she flinched away from the thought. He had taken out his anger at his own failure on the two Indians, no matter how much John and she had protested. Now he was drunk again. And probably off with Rosa. Oh, it was getting to be too much.

'Aunt Liz?' Eleanor looked subdued and uncomfortable. 'I thought I heard something earlier, an odd sound like maybe someone shooting and then I heard shouting, you and John – you screamed ... Did that happen? Was something wrong?' She saw her aunt's face stiffen, her thoughts immediately hidden behind a bright smile. Like Mama's smile when Papa has been angry. False.

'No-oo, dear, you've been dreaming. No shooting. I promise you. Now settle back a bit and I'll plump your pillows up, shall I?' There was an uncomfortable silence while they both avoided each other's eyes. I was right, Eleanor thought. It wasn't a dream. It was the men crying out and Uncle Michael's voice screaming at them – awful, awful words and terrible cries. Ohh! What had he done to them? And John and Aunt Liz? What had happened?

'Is John around? Could I see him?' she asked and Elizabeth thought again how close they had come to losing the girl. Just another two or three feet, a split second, nothing more, and she would have been ripped to pieces. Elizabeth shivered at the thought.

'Yes, he's waiting until after you eat to come and see you. I brought you some semolina and hot chocolate. I thought that would make you sleep soundly. Shall I feed it to you?' She sat down on the bed beside her niece and laid the tray across the girl's knees.

'Oh no, I can do that. Thank you, Aunt Elizabeth. But you mustn't worry any more. I'm fine. It didn't come anywhere near me, really. John got there first.' There was satisfaction in the way she added that last comment, Elizabeth thought. John got there first. He would always be there first for this child, she thought. Somehow that made her uneasy.

'All right. You start eating then and I'll go call John. That was quite a shot of his, wasn't it?' Elizabeth forced a smile and looked down at her niece. Green eyes studied her back.

'Yes, yes it was – but I knew he'd get to me in time. John promised Papa he'd look after me.' The girl was unaware exactly of what she had said but Elizabeth knew. John had taken this girl on and made her his own – like the baby monkey he had once found and trained and taken everywhere with him. And when that monkey ran away eventually to join its own kind, John had been distraught and swore he would never have a pet again. Never trust anyone again. There was just that hint at the same sort of relationship here, mutually dependent, mutually exclusive of any others. John depended upon Eleanor's love. And Eleanor thought it was natural for him to always be there for her. Again, Elizabeth felt a flicker of uneasiness.

'And he always keeps his promises, does he?'

'Oh yes, always.'

'Well, that's nice to hear. John's a good boy. Almost like your brother, being first cousins, isn't he?' She kept her voice casual. 'I'll say goodnight, Eleanor. It's been a long day. If you need anything, just sing out.' Elizabeth kissed her niece's cheek and left the room.

Within a few minutes John appeared, flopping himself on to the foot of Eleanor's bed without a thought to the hot chocolate and immediately apologetic about the brown stain that spread across the sheets. Eleanor shrugged and ignored it.

'Hullo. You okay?' he asked. He didn't look at her but hung his head down so that it flopped over the other side of the bed, only his stomach supported by the mattress. He seemed deliberately aloof and unconcerned.

Eleanor kicked him gently. 'Yes and thanks – but I've now got wet, sticky sheets and I don't want this stuff.' She let the spoon drop back into the semolina in disgust. 'Can you put it over there?' She pointed to the chest in the corner and, with a sigh, John got up and deposited the tray out of harm's way.

'Anything else, oh lady and mistress? Shall I plump up your pillows or stroke your fevered brow?' he asked in mock concern and Eleanor giggled.

'That doesn't translate well, does it? Lord and master – lady and mistress. Sounds quite different. Anyway, no, I don't need anything else. Aunt Liz already did the pillows. Come and tell me what happened. Aunt Elizabeth said Uncle Michael was angry with Monkey and Hatchet. Did he beat them? Is that what I heard?' She saw the grin slip from John's face and her own became uncertain. 'He didn't hurt them, did he? It wasn't their fault entirely. The jaguar wasn't supposed to be anywhere near us.'

John sighed. 'I know but it didn't have to be a jaguar. It could've been a wild boar or Indians or a snake or, thousands of other things. They had no business going off like that. Dad let them know it shouldn't ever happen again but – you know him, he had to overdo it.' He fell silent, embarrassed and feeling an odd sense of disloyalty in talking about his father. An ache deep in his throat.

'Go on,' Eleanor urged. 'What happened? I know something did! I heard ... I heard something like shooting? And screaming. Please, John, please,' she begged and he flushed.

'I –' he paused, swallowing over the ache, the words coming out in a rush now, 'I had to come across them, of course, at the worst possible moment. Dad had them out behind the back barns and he had his whip, you know the one he uses on the bullocks. Well, he let rip, screaming at them that they were useless, faithless creatures who didn't deserve to live and I think Monkey was pretty scared but Hatchet just looked down his nose, you know the way he does. Then Dad,' he hesitated, 'Dad became quite crazy, and he let go with the whip, round Hatchet's shoulders, and he was raising it again, meaning to go for Monkey so I stepped between them and grabbed at Dad's arm.'

He swallowed and looked away, not liking the look in Eleanor's eyes. She slipped a hand into his, as he continued painfully, 'Dad just pushed me off, he's so damned strong and then he used it on me. Just once because then Mother screamed and Dad seemed to come to his senses and he just stared at all of us for a moment before walking off. I can't believe he did that.' John shook his head.

'Are you hurt? Where did he hit you?' Eleanor sat up but

66

John continued to stare moodily down at the floorboards, tracing the crack with his finger.

'No, it just got me across my jacket. But he's nearly off the deep end, Mother thinks. She's ... worried,' he added lamely.

'I should think so!' Eleanor said indignantly and John lifted his head, looking at her.

'You don't understand – it's not his fault ...'

'It is! Who else's could it be?'

'No, you see, Dad's gone a bit funny again. Oh Elly, he's started drinking. That's why he's sick.' Finally he added, after Eleanor had begun to wonder at his silence, 'He gets into these rages and then he blames everything on other people, even things he's done wrong himself. He blamed me for not backing him up when he first wounded the jaguar. But I couldn't have got a shot in, in time, after it saw him. I could've before –' He hesitated, wondering again whether it really was his fault and not his father's. His voice became low and uncertain. 'But it was so beautiful and I just couldn't shoot it.'

He looked at her. 'All it wanted was to eat and be left alone. And then Dad shot and only wounded it, and it was gone before I could sight on it again.' He looked sick. 'It must have been in agony all that way – miles and miles – we chased it. Half its side was blown away but it kept going. And then I had to kill it – after all that effort it made to get away.' For a moment he looked at Eleanor and she saw his eyes were filled with tears. Then he was gone from her room, his footfalls retreating at a run.

He came back later, after Eleanor had fallen asleep and he sat on the bed beside her and brushed a strand of hair from her face, tucking it neatly behind her ear. She slept soundly, her breathing deep and even, her mouth slightly parted as though in surprise. John leaned down and stroked the fair eyelashes that quivered in sleep, his own gleaming palely in the moonlight flooding through the open doors. Eleanor stirred and rolled on to her back, blinking slowly.

67

'John? You all right?'

'Yes, go back to sleep. I didn't mean to wake you.'

'Where did you go?'

'For a walk. I didn't want to be with anyone.'

'Are you still sad you killed the jaguar?' Eleanor heard him sigh sharply at that.

'Yes – and no. I'm not sorry I stopped it before it got to you. I just wish we'd never hunted it in the first place.'

'But wouldn't it have killed more animals? And maybe one of the Indians or their children?' That was what John hated about Eleanor. She was always so logical. Cut and dried. He didn't reply and she stretched a hand up to touch his face. 'You cross with me? It wasn't my fault. I didn't try and get in its way.'

'I know. But I wanted it to get away. If only it had gone a little to the left, I'd've let it go. But it went straight for you.' He lay down beside her, pulling her in against him. 'And I couldn't let it hurt you,' he said but his voice was bleak.

'You hurt me sometimes,' she pointed out with childish obstinancy. There was a long silence.

John considered. 'That's different,' he said at last. 'I don't really mean to and anyway, I know you'll always forgive me. Won't you?'

And he wasn't surprised when Eleanor gave a gusty sigh and rolled her face against his side. 'Oh, I suppose so,' she said.

He smiled, closed his eyes and fell asleep.

He had gone when she woke but she could hear the sound of voices laughing and shouting outside her windows, high childish voices and occasional deeper ones, babbling excitedly in a language she couldn't grasp. Occasionally she heard a word or two that made sense to her, and she threw back the sheet and wandered across the boards to peer carefully through the window. A face, dark with timid eyes under a shock of black hair, regarded her equally carefully back, the body held to one side so that the head merely bobbed around the window frame, back and forth with the flow and ebb of courage. Eleanor stepped back abruptly.

There was a shriek of laughter and the face disappeared completely, the sound of footsteps drumming hollowly on the verandah boards and then the crowd out on the lawn looked towards her bedroom, a sea of dark faces milling and jostling, curious eyes, wide open mouths. She saw John out there too but he didn't look up, talking instead to two boys of his own age, dressed in loincloths and feathers, their skin painted a slick green and red. There was another, a white boy somewhat older, who stood slightly aloof, his gaze amused and condescending at the same time. She walked away from the window, back into the room, looking for her clothes.

They were talking about the tigre when she finally stepped out of the french windows and went to stand at the edge of the verandah, looking down at them. She could hear the word mentioned over and over as it flowed around the crowd, heads nodding enthusiastically, the entire mass lighting up with delight when the carcass was brought in, hanging from a pole between two bearers. The stranger, the white boy, walked over to it and lifted up the head, examining it carefully before letting it drop back with a laugh.

'Nice one, John, you massacred the coat thoroughly. Try for the head next time.' He spoke in Portuguese, excluding the mass of Indians, barely including John for all the remark was directed at him. Eleanor saw John flush slightly.

'I'll make sure I get your help next time, Ricki. I'm sure you would have been far more efficient.' There was more than a tinge of sarcasm to the words but the boy smiled broadly, revealing a row of strong, perfectly white teeth. He bowed.

'My thanks for your praise.' He clicked his fingers and the jaguar was taken towards the far barns, the two Indians loping along effortlessly with the load swinging between them. John watched it without saying a word. His shoulders were stiff though and his right hand clenched, as if taking the shot again. Or perhaps taking it back, wishing it

69

away. Then he shook himself and turned and smiled at the other boy, thanking him for bringing the carcass in.

'No trouble. Made my day, really. Haven't been over here in far too long. I hear you have a cousin visiting.' The stranger looked up at the verandah, taking in Eleanor for the first time. John followed his gaze.

'Elly! Come down and meet the local community, and especially my very arrogant neighbour, Ricardo Carvalho,' John called. And as she came down the steps, the sea of dark, smiling faces parted and John came forward to take her arm, proudly possessive. 'Elly, this is Ricardo, but don't mind him, he can't help being a pompous ass, and Ricki, this is my cousin, Eleanor Fawcett from Rio and don't bother smarming up to her, she isn't interested.' This provoked a burst of laughter from the boy who bowed once again and took Eleanor's hand in his in a formal, infinitesimal shake, before releasing it. His hair, a rich brown that gleamed like the hock of a well-groomed horse, ruffled in the wind.

'I am enchanted, Eleanor. How such a beautiful girl could possibly be connected to such an oaf of a cousin is one of the marvels of the world. You must allow me to regain favour in your eyes after such a disastrous introduction and then perhaps you will ignore the unfair comments your cousin has made about me. Let me introduce you to my people.' He was supremely confident, moving with an almost oiled grace that did little to hide the strength of his body. If anything, it was intended to show just how powerful he was – how in control of himself and everyone around him. About seventeen, tall, sturdy, and darkly tanned, he was disturbing in the way he pretended to a gallantry that Eleanor was some years short of expecting. She smiled uncertainly, wondering who he meant when he said 'his people'. His family? Were they around here too, somewhere? Perhaps with Aunt Liz, wherever she might be?

But it became immediately apparent he meant the Indians. His people. Eleanor wondered, for a moment,

70

looking at the dark colouring of Ricardo, whether he might mean that literally. But no, he meant it in the paternal fazendero way. The plantation owner to his slaves. 'My people!' he shouted, in the strange obscure language Eleanor had heard earlier, but she knew what he said. The Indians waved and hallooed, their faces splitting apart in grins. 'My people!' he repeated and John shook his head, looking down at Eleanor.

'Megalomaniac!'

'Does Ricardo have a father still, or is it his fazenda these people work?' she whispered quickly to John who was watching Ricardo with a mixture of indulgence and irritation.

'His father's been dead about three years. You can tell, huh? Ricki's really into the swing of being O Patrão. His men found the jaguar floating downstream and guessed we must have shot it. They all arrived, en masse, about an hour ago to celebrate with us. Ricki's a bit strange but he's a good enough fellow underneath it all, I guess. A small-time Mussolini maybe but he looks after "his people" well – most of the time. Funny thing is, the harsher the boss, quite often the better the Indians respond. They respect authority. Even if we don't run ours that way, you can tell his admire him.'

'So I see. What tribe are these Indians? The same as your lot?'

'Yes, Parecis, just a bit wilder. Ours have been tame a lot longer but these fellows still come and go as they please. I grew up with a lot of the warriors here.' He seemed fond of them as he looked around, waving and nodding to cries of greeting. 'They taught both Ricki and me about their war trails. I'd never have got to you yesterday if I hadn't known the path through. They can run over thirty miles in a day through the jungle along those trails. But it's their big secret, so don't mention it when we get back to Rio.' He smiled but Eleanor knew he was serious.

'All right. Are they – headhunters or anything like that?' She looked them over carefully, trying not to mind being pushed or jostled in the crowd that surged around her, Ricki yelling something to them that made them shriek in high-pitched voices, giggling like children, warrior boys looking every bit as dangerous and wild as men twice their age, and a few girls from their own village, smiling and giggling at the braves, their breasts waving in time to the curious head movement they all used.

The men had their bows and arrows slung behind them in a skin quiver, along with a blowgun and a bamboo section of darts. They had spears as well, and a skin pouch that hung across their chests that John whispered contained all the essentials of life like feathers, bracelets, anchiote, flint and steel, medicines, arrowheads and charms. Elly tried not to mind the smell of musk – warm, sweating bodies, and animal fat that clung to the air, or the dry, choking dust that was stirred up by their pounding feet.

'Oh yes, they all are round here. It's not something they do lightly though. They have to admire you as a warrior, admire your bravery, before they'll go to all that trouble. Takes a lot of skill to shrink a head just right. I know, I've seen them doing it,' John said earnestly and Eleanor swallowed, the heat and the smell beginning to invade her nasal passages and make her nauseous.

Ricki shouldered his way back through to them, shouting something above the din and John nodded.

'Dad's sent some of our boys off to catch some boar and he's supervising the killing of the fatted calf himself. We'll have a Shingirotse tonight,' he said. 'About time really, with the harvest all in. Make a nice party out of it. You'll stay, of course?' he asked politely and Ricki grinned.

'Of course. My lot'll love it. They've been a bit uppish lately, getting a bit out of hand. Had to put a couple of them in the coffin. Not best pleased, I'm afraid, so finding your tigre was just the thing. This'll take their minds off it all.' He winked. 'Come on, let's give them something to keep 'em happy. They'll get bored soon otherwise and we don't want that, do we?'

Ricki grinned again and Eleanor wondered whether he

knew just how much he unnerved her. She suspected he did.

'Crocodile hunt! Just the thing. We'll have a prize, shall we, for the biggest one caught today? What about that lousy skin? They'll like that, fix it up so the holes don't show. Be pleased as punch, I'll bet.' Ricki thumped John on the shoulder and laughed, his big face seemingly full of bonhomie but the eyes revealing just for a moment a far shrewder man intent on his own manipulations.

John drew in a deep breath, nodding, a pained smile on his face. 'Why not? The crocs have been multiplying a bit lately, Dad says. Took his best dog the other night and what with the tigre taking Daisy, he's pretty fed up. Tell them to hunt downstream though. Mother doesn't like seeing it. Get them organized and we'll be with you in a bit.' He put his arm around Eleanor's shoulder, forcing her along and out of the crowd with unnecessary speed and she wriggled away from him as soon as they were clear.

'Don't push, John! What's the matter?' She rounded on him and he continued walking, back towards the house, muttering to himself.

'Son of a bitch! Bloody Ricki! He knew they'd get out of hand, so he brought them here for a bit of fun instead. They'll be hard to control tonight, see if they're not, and he doesn't want that on his own fazenda – not with his mother and sisters there. So he brings them here. Thinks we can deal with them, and if not, well – not his place, not his problem. Bastard!' He was in a rage.

'I don't understand. What's wrong? What did he mean about a coffin?' Eleanor followed him quickly into the house, her face paling as she realized Ricki had done something unforgiveable. What, she wasn't sure, but she knew it was bad.

'Punishment coffin. We don't allow it here. Bloody beastly things. The Indians call it the "insane coffin" which gives you an idea, I guess. They're put in, head first sometimes, and left to sweat it out for a few hours, sometimes days. The garrisons use them quite often on their soldiers. Barbaric. The Parecis don't care for that sort of thing, so they'll be smarting, wanting to pay back. He brought them here to appease them. Or maybe so that the pay-back won't get out of hand. He knows Dad'll keep things in check. Too smart by half, Ricki,' he added bitterly and then said, 'I'm going to have a word with Dad. You go and find Mother. Let her know. Won't be long.' He gave her a quick abstracted smile and loped off through the house to the other side of the barns.

Aunt Elizabeth wasn't particularly surprised when Eleanor told her what had happened. She sighed heavily but continued supervising the meal that was being prepared, telling Rosa sharply to stop wasting the flour and ordering Pedro out for more spices, the key swinging from his finger by the string that normally tied it to her own belt.

'Ricardo is a strange young man. Unpleasant sometimes, charming at others. He has a drop or two of Indian blood himself, you know. I think that explains his cruelty. He doesn't feel the way we do about things. And, of course, he's very rich. His fazenda is one of the most profitable around here. His sisters are widely courted, despite how some people feel about mixed blood. Besides, you know that charming little saying "money whitens". I wouldn't worry.' She was in a brittle mood and Eleanor nodded in seeming understanding before slipping from the kitchen and back to her room, hearing her aunt speaking sharply yet again to Rosa as she retreated down the corridors.

But, by lunchtime, the party atmosphere had returned and they passed a pleasant hour around the table with all the latest news and gossip of the region being traded back and forth and Ricki doing his best to charm Aunt Elizabeth out of her irritation with him. Uncle Michael was in good form, amused and flattered that he was expected to quell the Parecis where Ricki couldn't handle them and even John had recovered at the thought of the promised crocodile hunt of the afternoon. They talked quickly and loudly, often over each other, telling tales that no one else was listening to and laughing loudly at their own jokes; Eleanor, watching, relaxed. It was all right. She understood this. This was like home.

And the afternoon did turn out to be fun, mainly because the crocodile got away after nearly taking three men with him and having crunched easily through the pieces of wood he was supposed to sink his teeth into. The idea, Eleanor was told, was that once the crocodile could not dislodge the wood, he would be unable to submerge without drowning and, therefore, he would be rendered helpless.

But it rapidly became obvious that this particular crocodile, black and ill-tempered with dark hooded eyes that made Eleanor think of Peter Pan's crocodile, had played this game before. The men threw ropes around him, they ran in and out of the shallows, yelling and shouting to each other, they jumped up and down in frustration and sometimes fear, and the crocodile splintered piece after piece of wood and dived down to the safety of his lair with many a slash of his enormous bony tail. And Eleanor, seeing no one was likely to get badly hurt, laughed herself silly.

The other Indians were more successful and they brought in two crocodile carcasses that night to loud, jubilant cheers and whistles of congratulations. The tigre skin was brought in, stretched taut between bamboo poles where it was curing and presented to the warriors in question, their appreciative grins and head rolls showing how much they valued the gift. And then they went off to adorn themselves for the evening's harvest dance and John's family moved inside again.

They washed and changed before dinner and then Ricki, Eleanor and John sat down to play Scats, a complicated card game which John invariably won. Ricki played only half-heartedly, more amused in watching Eleanor get annoyed as she lost. 'How about playing with me, Elly? Just the two of us. Fairer that way. Winner takes all.' He laughed softly and Eleanor felt uncomfortable, unsure what he was suggesting but knowing it wasn't nice.

'No, dinner's ready. Come on, John, or we'll miss the harvest dance afterwards.' She stood up and Ricki stood

75

immediately, his politeness making her feel he was mocking her all the more. John didn't say anything, just watched Ricki.

'The Shingirotse'll go on all night, Elly. No fear of missing it,' Ricki said. 'They're making the haya huasca right now. Maybe you should try some.' He was laughing, aware of John's sudden movement, but sure of himself anyway.

'No, Elly won't be trying anything that doesn't come off our own table. No Soul Vine, no chicha, no anything. You got it, Elly?' John said quietly and Ricki turned mocking eyes on him.

'My, quite the dictator, aren't we, John! What, are you to have all the fun and Elly none? She can do what she wants, can't you, my sweet? I'll look after you.' And he smiled down at her. Eleanor shifted awkwardly, irritated by John's command but uneasily aware that Ricki was playing with her. She looked down.

'Wait for us on the verandah, Elly. Please,' John said when he saw her raise a stubborn chin at his command. 'Please.' Reluctantly, she obeyed. Then he looked steadily at Ricki, almost level in height for all the difference in age and weight. He sighed. 'Elly is my cousin, Ricardo. Almost like my sister. And, I would like you to treat her as I would treat your sisters, if I were a guest in your house. With respect.' He stopped and looked embarrassed, licking his lips, hesitating. 'And, even more importantly, she's an eleven-year-old child. I know the native women are often married at that age but she isn't a native. She's only a little girl. Go look elsewhere if you're feeling randy.'

There was a long silence while the two contemplated each other, Ricki's eyes almost closed, sleepy looking. John didn't flinch.

'Of course. I meant no harm. Just a little game. My apologies if you were – disturbed,' Ricki said at last, with a smile and John took a deep breath.

Outside, Eleanor strained her ears to hear what was being said but couldn't make it out. She sighed and

76

wandered along the verandah, looking out at the fires in the distance where the Indians were beginning the evening's festivities. Already the men were decked out in their cloaks of feathers, dazzling gold and blue with ornate crowns of flowers banded with seeds. One particularly fine young warrior, dressed in a tailed puma loincloth, was swaying under a scarlet hibiscus bush, his face raised to the night sky, his mouth open, though she couldn't hear what he cried.

It was an eerie sight and she wasn't sorry when she heard her aunt calling her in for dinner. She could hear Ricki laughing again, as she neared the door, and then John saying he was glad Ricki understood, so that when she entered they were both looking friendly and amicable again. They smiled at her and lead her into dinner, Ricki rushing to pull out her chair for her, John seating his mother. Uncle Michael wasn't there and, after waiting a few minutes, they began without him.

Eleanor saw him later in the evening, after the Shingirotse had begun in earnest and night had fallen over the clearing with the suddenness of the tropics. There was light enough from the huge bonfires that were burning at intervals around the fazenda, and even some pale silver light from the moon where it hung like a huge melon low in the sky. So she wasn't nervous when she wandered away from the others to see what was happening down by the river. And that's where she saw him.

Uncle Michael was sitting, half reclined against a tree with several of the native women, who were laughing and calling to each other, passing around gourds between themselves. He was slack-jawed, casually fumbling at one of the women, his face sweaty and his eyes glazed. Eleanor knew then he had been drinking, but she stopped and watched for a moment in silence.

Then she turned and walked away, heading back in the direction of where she had left her aunt sitting on a log, smiling carefully, a shotgun down by her feet. Eleanor didn't see Ricki as he stood in the shadows, considering, a

77

gourd of creamy, clotted liquid half raised to his lips. But he saw her watching her uncle and he followed her quietly.

John was preoccupied for most of the evening, knowing the fact that his father had not turned up at dinner meant that he had started the festivities early and would, by now, be incapable of quelling any native problems. But John didn't think the Parecis looked at all sullen; they were smiling and enjoying themselves, arguing only occasionally over petty problems. He stayed well in view of the main bonfire, his shotgun beside him, talking quietly with the men, making his presence known. And his mother would keep Eleanor safe. He knew that.

Elizabeth's thoughts were bleak that night. She knew where her husband was and she knew what he was doing. He didn't bother to try and keep it a secret anymore. Not now the chicha had him. Once, long ago, he had been a disciplined man whose sense of right and wrong was clearly defined. Honour had been a word that was often on his lips. And he had loved her desperately then, and she had been so anxious to get away from Charles, to get away from his jealous demands on her time, that she had leapt at the chance of escape. Leapt at the thought of marrying a man of Michael's integrity. He had been good-looking, too, back then, slightly stern perhaps, without her brother's keen wit, but loyal and caring and so very loving . . .

He had sensed the problem with Charles, not understanding it, but determined to part them for her sake. She hadn't known whether to be grateful or sorry, torn between two strong men – but it had been the right decision then. She knew that. Those first few years of marriage had been so wonderful, so full of delight and charm, with none of the worries of her childhood preying on her, with none of the worries of her later married life even suspected. She had felt so cherished with Michael, lying at night in his strong arms, knowing she was safe.

Oh, if only he hadn't gone to war, if only he hadn't become so bitter; it was eating him up, gnawing away at his vitals so that he had become a blank automaton, unable to display affection or concern, his morals all turned upside down because all he sought was oblivion in the chicha. Don't think about it, just take another swig and all the black thoughts will fade away. Never mind that you can't feel anymore, that you don't care anymore. Just take some more chicha . . .

Ricki stepped out in front of Eleanor, a large shape looming up before she could take the path back to the main bonfire. She stepped back with a gasp of fear. He held out his cup, smiling, his big face slick with perspiration, the fire gleaming in his hair.

'Want some, Elly? Don't worry – it's nothing bad. Just a bit of native milk. John won't mind this. I was only teasing earlier about the Soul Vine.' She looked at him uncertainly, not sure how to refuse, intimidated.

'What's Soul Vine anyway?' she asked, to stall.

'Oh, something the brujas, the witchdoctors, take to give them visions. Some type of opiate, I think. But this isn't it, don't worry. Look.' He took a quick sip, holding it out again, smiling.

'What's in it? It looks horrible,' she said, reluctantly taking it from his hand. She peered at the white mixture.

'Just roots mashed up. It's quite nice. You'll like it. Come on, girl, stop being so timid, for God's sake. Take a sip!' He stepped forward, as though he would force her to drink, and she hastily tipped it up, the clotted, fibrous mass sliding easily over her tongue and down her throat. He was right. It was nice. She sighed with relief and handed it back.

'No, no, drink it all, Elly. I'll get some more in a minute. That's it. See, it wasn't so bad, was it?' He took the cup from her hand and put his arm around her shoulder, steering her down the path towards the great troughs full of this particular 'native milk'. He didn't tell her how it was made, the sugarcane and yuca root chewed up by the native women and spat into a trough where it fermented for days. She wouldn't have liked that.

John was nowhere to be seen. Probably supervising the

79

men, making sure none of them got out of hand, worrying himself silly about that coffin nonsense, Ricki thought scornfully, and he smiled down at the blonde head beside him.

'There you are, get that down you in one long swig and I'll fill us up again before we go on. Good girl! You like riding, don't you? Got your own pony? You should come on over to my place sometime. Come riding. Most of the fazendas don't keep horses. They tend to die up here. But I've got some. You should come. It's only a day by land, less by river. Come and stay a while. We don't often get white girls passing through.' He was watching her intently, seeing the sudden rock of her head, the way her eyes half closed. He held out the cup again.

'But, um, how did you get here so soon then, with the jaguar?' Eleanor asked, her wits trying to assemble themselves in the haze of swirling colours and sensations. She peered up at Ricki, seeing him smile. She smiled too.

'On a hunting trip. Thought we'd pay a visit anyway, then we saw the jaguar. Besides, heard there was a pretty little cousin come to stay. Haven't seen any white girls, 'part from my sisters, in ages. Months! And they're not blonde, like you. You're a sight for sore eyes.' He squeezed her to his side and laughed and she laughed too, drinking the cup that he held against her lips, liking the way he swung her up in his arms.

'Light as a feather, whoa, whee ...' He rocked her through the air as he walked and she laughed and the world whizzed and spun around her and then it became darker, the light of the bonfires fading. She sighed and lay her head against him. He stopped rocking her and held her against his chest, humming.

'Well, what luck! There's a nice little clearing here. Shall we sit down and have some more to drink?' And he was laying her down and propping up her head, pouring the last of the chicha down her throat, laughing as he stroked her cheek, down her throat, his fingers lingering over the collar of her dress.

'Such a pretty dress. Just like you, hm? Pretty girl, now let's undo this button, shall we? It's tight around your throat, isn't it? And this one too? Maybe we'll undo them all? It's hot out here and that dress is made for the coast, not the jungle. Such a pretty dress,' he murmured to her, soothing her with his voice, gentling her with his hands so that she lay passively, a slight smile on her face, liking the feel of his palm stroking over her skin.

He had opened her dress by now and was touching her skin, so that she made soft noises of pleasure, not really sure whether she were dreaming or not. The chicha swirled in her brain and she didn't seem to have the energy to do anything, just lie there and let pleasant things happen to her. She felt a coolness over her skin, a gentle night breeze playing over her and he was talking sweetly to her and just stroking, just smoothing so there was nothing to worry about. She smiled some more.

But then he tried to roll on top of her and suddenly she was frightened and she squirmed free, catching at her dress and pulling it close around her, saying 'don't Ricki', in a cross, querulous voice. He was trying to soothe her, holding out his hand, gripping her shoulder firmly, hurting, and she saw that strong, hairy wrist and the deeply tanned skin and she bit it as hard as she could, hearing him cry out, pull his hand away sharply.

She was running before she knew it, hearing his curses and howl of pain, and then she was almost to the edge of the clearing, her face streaked with tears, the back of her dress flapping untidily in the night air. Hastily she buttoned it up, tugging at it impatiently, her arms stretched up above her head. She couldn't hear him coming after her. For a moment, everything span sickeningly and then it righted itself and she wiped the tears from her face with the back of her hand and tried to still the sobs forcing their way out of her throat. She looked back again but there was no sign of him and so she skirted the rest of the clearing, making for the house. He wouldn't dare touch her in the house, instinctively she knew that.

She wasn't sure why she didn't go to her aunt, or to John and tell them what Ricki had tried to do. Perhaps because she knew John would try and hurt Ricki and might himself be hurt. The Indians would side with Ricki. Or perhaps because she was secretly ashamed. She had let him touch her – and had liked it, at first. Which made her nothing more than, than ... but she couldn't think what that made her, just something awful. She wasn't supposed to let anyone touch her, Mama had said. Not ever, until she married. So she was partly to blame. She couldn't face telling her aunt that, or hear Ricki saying it, with that horrible smile of his, telling what she had let him do. What would John think?

So she crept miserably into the house and into her bedroom, climbing into bed and pulling the covers over her. The room swam round and round again, so that she retched and finally had to go outside and lean over the verandah railing, to be sick. But she felt better after that and, after a drink of water, she returned to bed. The fires were still burning brightly and she knew the harvest dance would go on for a long time. She closed her eyes and drifted off to sleep.

At ten o'clock, Elizabeth started looking for Eleanor to return to the house. But she was nowhere in sight. Elizabeth stood up and looked around. Still no sign of the girl. With a slight feeling of unease, she questioned some of the Indians who gazed at her blankly, their thoughts long since departed from their minds. Angrily, she went in search of John, finding him sitting with several of the Indian boys he had played with as a child, laughing and swapping stories back and forth.

'John,' she called sharply, 'where's Eleanor?'

He looked up immediately, glancing around, his eyes clear. There were no chicha demons lurking there. 'I thought she was with you. When did you last see her?' He stood up and frowned into the leaping shadows, unable to see more than a few yards.

'I don't know. She must have slipped away. I can't think where she could've gone.'

John heard the note of panic in his mother's voice and he patted her arm, thinking hard. 'We'll check the house first. After that – where's Ricki?' But his mother didn't know that either and cursing, he set off at a run for the bungalow, his mother trailing along after him, John trying not to think the worst thoughts. But when he got there, frightened and despairing, and burst along the verandah to her room, he found a small, fair head just sticking out from the sheets, a tiny foot trailing out so that the mosquito net caught on it. Her eyes were shut, her mouth open, and she was deeply asleep. Carefully, he pushed the foot back inside the net and he turned away, laughing shakily to his mother, the relief washing over his eyes leaving them a deep blue.

'Thought for a moment ...' but he didn't finish, didn't voice the fear that had swept over him, nor the bright, consuming anger that had hovered in his chest, ready to reach out and tear away at someone. But his mother knew. And she watched him, feeling that sense of foreboding again.

Ricki and his men were gone the next morning, sliding off in the early dawn mist to their canoes and disappearing down the dark river without a word of farewell. John didn't think much of it. Ricki was like that.

The next few days passed easily, the two of them playing around the property or taking short trips into the jungle to visit some particular haunt of John's that he wanted to show Eleanor. It was late August by then and the heat was building steadily, trapping in the last breezes of the cooler season amongst the trees, turning them to stifling stagnant gasses. Slowly, as though in tune with the heat, the tension in the house began to build.

The news wasn't good. Sentiment was running against President Vargas in most of the major cities and especially amongst the military. There was talk about corruption and communism and Michael Campos de Serra sat by the wireless daily listening to the latest bulletins, before jumping up and marching out of the room in angry frustration.

Michael began lecturing them over dinner about how much Vargas had done for the country, how he had kept Brazil independent and safe from grasping imperialist countries like the United States and Britain. There were bitter looks directed at Eleanor at that point. He ranted on about how the economy had thrived under Vargas's guidance, how he had established that hallmark of Brazilian economic policy, the programme of import substitution, raising protective tariffs against foreign consumer goods and denying foreign interests access to Brazilian natural resources. How Vargas truly was the father of the Brazilian people!

When Elizabeth attempted to point out that national inflation was outstripping economic growth, or that Vargas favoured urban and industrial interests over those of the coffee growers, Michael angrily shouted her down. When Elizabeth suggested Vargas was a Fascist at heart, despite his supposed leftist leanings, Michael threw his soup bowl on the floor and stamped from the room.

But when Vargas was accused of having his bodyguard try to assassinate his leading critic, Carlos Lacerda, and killing an Air Force major instead, the house became very quiet and neither Michael nor Elizabeth said anything. It was as though even the house were listening, waiting for something to happen. John and Eleanor watched uneasily but the days passed without further outbursts and Michael stayed sober.

It was nearly halfway through the second week – two day's before John's birthday – when the trouble began. It had seemed such a calm, easy sort of day, the sun shining and the flowers, fresh from the overnight rain, scenting the air with a heady perfume that blew in through the house and beckoned to them to come outside.

Eleanor was already out in the garden, playing with the kittens that one of the barn cats had given birth to a few days before. They were still blind, wandering helplessly in tight circles and mewing weakly when Eleanor brought down some milk for them. The mother cat couldn't feed them all. She was a scrawny thing to begin with and there were too many demanding mouths for her to satisfy. So Eleanor had begged milk from the kitchen and was trying to feed it to the kittens on her finger.

One of them squirmed and fretted in her hand as she sat on the grass, trying to tempt it with the milk and John, coming out to see what Eleanor was doing, knelt beside the others and stroked them with his fingers.

'It's not going to work, Eleanor. They're not getting enough milk like that. Look at that little one – he's just about dead.' When she looked, she saw he was right. The runt of the litter was trembling on its legs, too exhausted to even feed.

Eleanor sighed. 'We need a teat, like a baby's bottle but smaller. Hasn't your mother got anything like that?' she said as she gently laid down the kitten in her hand and let it totter over to the others. The mother cat watched her efforts warily.

'I don't know. Maybe. Let's go and ask. But Dad won't like it, you know. He always says to let nature take its course. If they all weren't meant to survive, well that's mother nature making sure there aren't too many cats around,' John pointed out.

Eleanor gave him a withering look. 'If that were the case, why bother with any medicines either? If nature intended us to die of polio, why invent a vaccine? It'll just mess up the overall plan, won't it?' She was upset and it showed.

'You have to make exceptions with people because you're not supposed to let another human being die if you can do something to prevent it. But it's not the same with animals –' John faltered, not truly believing his argument.

Eleanor knew it. 'You're just repeating what your father says again. I bet you'd feed a starving dog or stop someone overworking a horse if you saw it happening. After all, you wanted to let the jaguar go, didn't you?' She knew she had him there.

85

He changed the subject. 'Has Mother got my birthday presents yet? D'you know what I'm getting?' He had reached the house and was holding the door open for Eleanor.

'Of course, but I'm not telling you,' she laughed, pausing to look back over the verandah edge at the kittens lying in the shade. And her laugh faltered. 'John? John! Look! It's huge! And it's got one of the kittens! Ugh, what is it?' She tugged at his arm and he leant over the verandah to peer into the shade.

'Oh Lord! It's one of those bird spiders. It'll eat that kitten.' He had started to run down towards the sheds but Eleanor called out again and he stopped to look. The mother cat had seen the danger too and had come to rescue her kitten but the spider wasn't about to give it up. Instead it stood up on its hind legs and attacked the mother, lunging forward as the cat backed off, edging away as the cat hissed and slashed with her claws.

Eleanor stood staring in horror. 'It'll kill her, John. Do something! Shoot it or something.' By now the spider was clearly winning, beating the cat back with its huge furry legs, its body nearly seven inches across. John looked at it in disgust. He forced himself to walk towards it, jumping backwards again as it lunged at him.

'Get me a spade, Eleanor! Quick, from the shed. It's coming at me now and I haven't got anything to keep it off.' He was almost dancing in front of the brown, mottled creature, larger even than a crab, hopping out of the way as it ran forward at him, forcing it back when it lost courage. Eleanor came running back with the spade and tossed it to him before dashing back to the safety of the verandah. She watched, half-fascinated, half-frightened, as John continued to play the spider out, calling its bluff, while the mother cat collected its kittens together.

He edged forward again and immediately the spider ran aggressively at him. It didn't stop when John held his ground but sped towards his feet. Eleanor gasped. At that moment John brought the spade down with a vicious chop.

'Ohh! Oh yuck! Revolting.' Eleanor looked at the writhing body and had to turn away to retch into the bushes.

John looked equally sickened. 'Well, it's dead all right. I guess after all that trouble, we might as well feed these kittens.' He threw the spade down and walked away, nervously shaking his head as he went. The mother cat had rounded up her offspring by now and was carefully carrying them, one by one, in her mouth off to the barn. She had clearly had enough of the garden. Eleanor agreed with her.

'Let's go see Aunt Elizabeth. Honestly, I don't know how she lives here sometimes – it's just one horror after another. Doesn't she ever want to leave?' She looked up at John but something in his expression made her pause. 'John? What is it?'

He sighed. 'Mother told me she's going to come back to Rio with us. For the time being. She can't cope with Dad anymore. She's hoping he'll come and visit her in Rio and then maybe she can get a doctor to look at him.' He looked miserable at the thought of his father being left alone.

Eleanor was wide-eyed. 'Does Uncle Michael know that?' she asked but John shook his head.

'Not yet. She's going to tell him tonight, I think. She's worried about how he'll take it.' He swallowed with difficulty.

'Doesn't Aunt Liz love your dad anymore?'

'Yes, I'm sure she does.' He sighed again and said in a strangled voice, 'It's not that easy sometimes. She's scared of him and that's starting to ruin her love for him anyway. If she doesn't leave, she won't have anything here worth anything because he'll get worse and worse and she'll start to hate him for the things he says and the way he treats her. Sometimes I almost hate him myself. But he can't help it. He's sick.'

Eleanor knew then that the bruises were no accident. She saw John's hands tense on the verandah rail. 'I don't want to leave him here alone. I told Mother I'd stay and miss school this term just so there'd be someone here with him. But she won't let me. She says he's too difficult for me to handle ...' His voice trailed off and Eleanor saw the pain in his eyes. But she didn't know what to say. She sniffed and patted his shoulder.

'Oh John – I'm sorry.' Her voice was gruff. 'But it'll get better. You wait – when Uncle Michael sees a doctor, they'll be able to figure out what's wrong. You mustn't worry so much about him. He'll be fine.' But Eleanor didn't believe that any more than John did. And he knew it.

'Elizabeth! Elizabeth! Come here! Come and listen!' The date was 24 August 1954. The children heard Michael's voice echoing through the long passageways of the bungalow and they froze into silence. They could hear Elizabeth's footsteps running towards her husband's study. The wireless was turned up, the voice of the commentator high and excited. They couldn't hear the words, just the buzz of a voice, saying something over and over. And then there was a cry, a strangled, horrible sort of cry wrenched out of John's father. It echoed down the halls to the children, dreadful in the gloom of the house, sounding as though the man's heart had been pulled out. There were more running footsteps and then a door slamming, the bolts clicking loudly into place. The children still stood against the dark wood of the hall, not moving, their breath held tightly in their chests.

'Michael! Michael! Please, open this door. Michael!' Elizabeth's voice rang out, the dull thuds of her fists beating on the door Michael had closed and locked behind himself, dying in the still air. 'Michael!'

John pushed himself away from the wall and walked towards the sound of his mother's voice. His hands were clenched tightly into fists, the nails digging into the palms of his hands. He found her outside his father's bedroom door. She was beating against the wood, tears rolling down her face as she pressed it to the door. 'Michael,' she whispered. 'Michael.'

'Mother? What is it? What's happened?'

She glanced around at that, her eyes glistening and wide, her hair falling untidily around her face. She grasped John's arm. 'Vargas is dead, John. He's shot himself. We heard it on the wireless.' She was shaking him now in her agitation. 'Your father's gone beserk. His cry! Oh God, the way he looked! He's locked himself in there and he's got a gun and I'm so afraid ... Oh John, I'm so afraid of what he'll do to himself.' She leaned her cheek against the door again and listened. 'Michael?' She rapped softly. There was no sound from within the room. 'Michael?'

John left his mother there and ran through the dining-room to the verandah and halfway around the house to where the verandah doors opened into his father's room. But the shutters were pulled to and bolted and he couldn't see anything through the hole in them – the hole Eleanor had once wondered about. John felt vulnerable with his eye to a hole that he knew was intended for the barrel of a gun. But he didn't pull away until he knew there was nothing he could do. The shutters and doors were firmly locked from the inside and nothing could break through them. They were meant to withstand a siege.

Tentatively he rapped on the shutters. 'Dad? Dad, it's me, John. Can you open up the door and talk to me? Please?' He waited but there was still no sound.

'Dad? I'm really sorry Vargas is dead. I know how much he meant to you. But it won't do any good if you kill yourself. He's gone but we need you here. Dad? Dad? Are you listening to me? Mother and I need you – you can't just let us down!' He listened some more but there was nothing to hear.

'Dad, you don't know there'll be some military crack-down. There almost certainly won't be. And even if there is, it won't make any difference to us out here. Dad, please, just come out and talk to me, talk to Mother. We're worried.' He listened again. 'At least say something so we know you're all right.' There was no reply from within the darkened room.

John waited nearly ten minutes, calling from time to time, but without success. He could feel his fear and anger building and his breaths became short and hurried. He banged on the shutter again.

'Dad, what're you going to do? Leave us to face all the trouble while you take the easy way out? Is that it? I thought you were a hero! I thought you were the brave one, the strong one in our family! And you're just going to run away from it all. You're going to run away and leave us to manage somehow, all alone. Dad, please!' He was crying now, beating and screaming at the silent doors, until his knuckles were ripped and bleeding and his voice dropped to a wretched whisper. And still the doors stayed shut. Still there was no sound.

'John, John, come away. Please, it won't do any good. Come away, darling,' his mother said from behind him and John opened his eyes to see her standing close to him, her face as blotched and ravaged as his own. But her voice was steady again and gentle, and she smiled and kissed his hair as she slipped an arm around him. 'Come away, there's nothing you can do. It'll be all right, I promise you.' She led him back around the house like an invalid as he hiccuped and retched in her arms, his footsteps unsteady.

Eleanor stood on the front porch, the brimming tears that had threatened to fall now cascading, unchecked, down her cheeks. She stared at John. 'Is he dead?' she asked in a choked whisper.

Elizabeth shook her head. 'No, no. He'll be all right. Eleanor, help me to get John to the sitting-room. I think we all need some tea and a bit of a sit down. Come on, sweetheart, stop crying. You'll make yourself sick if you carry on like that.' But John couldn't stop until they had laid him down on the sofa in the sitting-room and a glass of brandy had been forced down his throat. Then he grew calm yet despondent, and lay staring at the ceiling without thought, just watching the oil lamp swing gently to and fro in the wind.

Elizabeth left Eleanor with John and went to see about tea. She didn't try to call to her husband again.

Eleanor sat down on the sofa beside John and held one of his hands very tightly. She was shaking and cold but John didn't notice. He stared at the lamp.

Chapter Four

By ten o'clock Eleanor couldn't keep her eyes open and John had begun to look ill with fatigue. Elizabeth had given them tea and, later, tried to make them eat some dinner but John couldn't swallow anything and Elizabeth found her own throat kept closing in a convulsive choke whenever she thought about her husband. Eleanor was too frightened and bewildered to have much appetite either. Elizabeth sent the children to bed.

There was a still hush over the house and it was a long time before either of them fell asleep, huddled together as they were for comfort and security. They lay, fully dressed, in John's bed, and slept fitfully.

John woke at some point in the early morning hours and sat up with a start. He wasn't sure what had woken him but he felt uneasy. He stared out at the darkened room but nothing moved. The night was quiet. Beside him, Eleanor still slept.

He was beginning to lie back again, his breath tight within his chest, fluttering a little, when he heard it: a cry, quick and shocked, a 'No, Michael, no!' suddenly stopped by the roar of a shotgun.

John sprang from his bed and ran to the door. He

wrenched it open, ignoring Eleanor calling him back, and sprinted down the hall to his parents' room.

His stomach writhed with bile and he almost had to stop and be sick before he got there, knowing without a doubt what he would find. 'Dad,' he whispered, the pain in his chest growing tighter and deeper, 'Dad, please no!' And then he was there, outside the doorway, and he had to force himself to step forward around the partially closed door. He had to force himself to look.

There was blood on the floor and across the bed and sprayed in droplets across the walls. It flickered like fire against the white of the mosquito nets and the sheets as the gas lamp swung in the breeze, sending shadows rocking from side to side. John stared as the shadows swung across the body sprawled on the bed, light, dark, light, dark. And then, suddenly conscious, he glanced to his right. His father stood there smiling.

He glanced back at his mother's body, glad that he couldn't see her face, and then saw, moving infinitely slowly even though his mind said it was a trick, that it was at normal speed, his father raise the double barrel towards him. Oddly, John noticed his father was still smiling. But it was a foolish, manic look, a chicha look.

He threw himself backwards as part of the doorway exploded around him and splinters of wood sliced out in all directions. John felt them slicing into him but he didn't stop, running on heedless of the cry from his father. He tasted blood on his tongue where he had bitten it and something worse in his mouth. Acrid, bitter, foul beyond anything he had ever known – pure hate.

Eleanor was halfway along the passageway to him, flattened against the wall. He shouted to her to run but she looked around her in bewilderment and then he was beside her, dragging her forward with him, the two of them running breathlessly forward into the darkened gardens. Behind them, John's father laughed gently to himself, soft wheezing little giggles.

John zigzagged under the jacaranda tree, pulling

Eleanor along so fast that her feet sped from beneath her and she fell. He dragged her up again and they ran on. Another blast, casual in its aim, tore away part of the tree trunk where they had been moments before.

They slid from outbuilding to shed, from barn to hut, dashing furiously across the exposed spaces, too nervous to do more than glance over their shoulders for a few seconds, unable to focus on the dark shadows. They pressed themselves flat against dark walls while their breath jerked out in ragged gasps. Eleanor had begun a nervous gasping, her face dead white in the night.

John put his hand over her mouth. 'Quiet!' he hissed. 'He'll hear us.' Somewhere, very close to them, a foot scratched through gravel, a giggle – soft and muffled and infinitely knowing – made them freeze and then John yanked Eleanor away and round the corner of the hut as shots roared out in flashes of red. A few pellets hit them both but they kept going, close now to the jungle. Just a few feet more, just a few steps and then, suddenly they were into it and John pulled them to an abrupt stop.

They listened and then, mocking and teasing, like in a demented children's game of hide-and-seek, Michael's voice floated over the night air.

'I seeee youuu! I'm cominggg. I seeee youuu!' Then the laugh again that made them both shiver icily.

John whispered against Eleanor's ear, his voice barely heard, 'He won't find us in here if we're quiet and hide. It's too dangerous to go very deep until we can see. C'mon. I know where we can go and he'll never reach us.'

Eleanor nodded, swallowing over the terror that kept rising in her throat and threatening to slip past her clenched lips in a scream. John would save them both, she told herself. It would be all right as long as John was there.

She followed him quietly, glancing only for a second over her shoulder. In the middle of the clearing her uncle stood, looking around him, stumbling from side to side, his face unrecognizable in its wide, bright smile. 'I seeee youuu!' he cried and she turned away at once.

There was no trail that Eleanor could see but John led them surely between the snatching bushes and vines, squeezing behind trees, edging carefully by something that John didn't have to tell her was a snake, brushing through spiders' webs and against insects that clung to her skin and mouth and sent her frantic tearing at them. He led her somewhere near to the river because she could hear it sliding over the shoals, rushing by in a white blur of noise. Finally he led her up, against a rocky outcrop, and carefully beneath an overhang. It smelt damp and rotten and overpoweringly vile in there but she crouched down beside John without protest. Behind them they could hear no hint of pursuit.

They squatted there in the dark, breathing shallowly in case they could be heard, their faces blank with listening. But there was nothing beyond the normal jungle noises. Slowly they sighed and began to relax.

Eleanor felt John's arm guiding her against the rocky wall so that she partly sat, partly crouched with her back to the outcrop and her weight resting evenly on both feet. She lay her head against her arm, beside her. John didn't seem to notice.

'Has he gone?' she whispered.

John was silent a moment longer, still listening. 'Yes, I think so. He may mean to track us tomorrow. I don't know. He's drunk again and – mad, Eleanor. Totally mad. He was laughing!' He paused and Eleanor heard the anguish trying to break through but held tightly in check. 'Mother's dead.'

'Dead! She can't be! Oh God, no, she can't be ...' Eleanor began to cry and John held her face against his shirt, trying to stifle the sounds. Tears ran silently down his own cheeks. The wind rustled through the leaves around them, growing stronger as the minutes passed. It blew harder, gusting little objects along the ground beside them. Then they heard the chanting.

It was coming from over to the left, back towards the clearing, moaning higher and lower, sweetly melancholy.

Sometimes it rose in cadence and Eleanor hummed brokenly along with it, mimicking the plaintive tuneless singsong with uncanny accuracy.

John felt a shiver run along his body. 'Don't!' he said sharply.

Eleanor stopped abruptly. She wasn't sure why she had hummed it at all, except that it had seemed to seep into her mind before she knew where she was. She swallowed. 'Is that the chapel? Won't the field hands all be there? Monkey and Hatchet? They'll help us, won't they?'

'Maybe. I guess so.' John was curiously reluctant to leave their sanctuary.

Eleanor tried again. 'They have guns too. Or maybe they can sneak up on Uncle Michael and throw a net over him. So he doesn't have to get hurt.' She was startled by John's answer, by the savagery in his voice.

'I hope they kill him! He deserves to be dead. I hope he burns in hell!' He spat on to the round and Eleanor froze again, her voice stilling in her throat. He clenched his fists, digging the nails into his skin. 'I won't rest until he's dead. Oh God! Mother, Mother . . .' He began to sob then, loudly and recklessly, standing up and swinging around in the darkened space.

Eleanor caught at his arm. 'Shhh! John! Please be quiet! Please,' she hissed at him and he knocked her back against the wall. She gasped and slid into a small heap. John stood still, panting and then he dropped down beside the girl and pulled her over to him.

'I'm sorry, Elly. I'm sorry. Are you hurt?' He cradled her against him, feeling blood slippery between his fingers but unsure if it was his or hers. What did it matter anyway, he thought blackly, they would never be able to get away. They were just prolonging the inevitable. Like Mother. He started to cry again at that, the vision of her body, white and red, flashing across his closed eyes and he held Eleanor tightly to him, both crying angry tears of pain.

Finally John fell silent and thoughtful, his hands probing gently over his cousin's body for hurt. He heard her draw her breath in sharply when he touched her leg and he could feel the fabric of her trousers was wet and slippery.

'Did you get shot in your leg? Or did you hurt it when I pushed you just then?' he asked awkwardly.

Eleanor patted him on the nose, unable to see him properly and making a guess at where his face was. 'It's just a bit of shot, I think. You must have got some too,' she whispered and she felt rather than saw him nod his head.

'Yes, a bit. And some pretty big splinters too. But they'll have to wait for daylight. C'mon, let's go to the chapel.' He pulled her carefully to her feet and was relieved to see she didn't limp very much. Slowly they slid from beneath the overhang.

It took them a long time to find the chapel and Eleanor was exhausted when they finally saw the lights ahead. John knew about the place of worship. But he had never gone there before. It had been forbidden to him both by his father and by the Indians. He had never dared break that taboo until now.

The 'Dream House', the Indians called it; it stood very close to the edge of the clearing and they paused, tentatively, in the shadows of the jungle, wondering whether to risk it. Eleanor could see strange, flickering shapes in the high windowless openings of the building and hear the chanting plainly now. She breathed in slowly, terribly tired and sleepy suddenly, not wanting to face anything more.

'Come on,' John said and pulled her after him as he ran lightly over the ground and hid against the side wall. No one challenged them; there were no loud explosions splitting apart the night air, nothing to stop the throbbing insistence of the voices. They stood and caught their breath before creeping around the far end of the building. The doors stood open and they carefully peered around at the scene within.

Eleanor backed away immediately, but John held her tightly, his hand over her mouth. When she was quiet, he let her go. Slowly he edged forward again.

At the far end of the chapel, where the altar should have

been, a huge ebony idol stood, dominating the scene through the haze of smoke. Its shoulders were covered with a boa constrictor skin cape, its loins with a grass skirt. On its head was a parrot headdress with a band of cactus encasing the brow. A skull necklace hung around its neck and snake amulets were wound around its arms and ankles. Black, fanged teeth were bared in a red and black face that stared out at the two children as though it could see them and was opening its mouth to cry out at their presence.

The idol was crucified on a cross by giant pegs of black chonta from which a cascade of blood dripped into partly dried clots and, above his head, were painted the letters PAWA. That was Christ's name, John remembered his father saying. Pawa. Man of God.

The Christ figure was surrounded by offerings of raw meat and fruit on stone slabs and, in front of the altar, were several Indian girls whom John recognized from the fazenda. They were naked and greased with fat, their plump nipples rouged as they writhed and danced in a trance before the image. Their buttocks gleamed in the torch light, the sweat slicking their hair wetly against their faces. A man amongst them was slicing his arm, again and again, with a knife, catching the blood that dripped out in a bowl that he held up to the image.

Torches guttered from sconces on the sides of the walls and their flickering red light menaced the night. Beside him, John felt Eleanor trembling in the shadows.

From both sides of the chapel came the drumming and the wailing of flutes that they had heard and followed through the jungle. The men sat on the left, the women on the right, entranced as they stared up at the high priest of the Dancing Anaconda Brotherhood who jumped and wailed, throwing himself from side to side in front of the naked women, getting closer with each new movement. From time to time, he cried out but John couldn't understand what he said.

John saw the glazed eyes of the Indians, the slumped bodies, the way they dribbled, slack-mouthed in a drug-induced trance and he pulled Eleanor away.

'It's no good,' he whispered when they had reached the jungle again. 'They won't wake up for a long time and I wouldn't want them to know we were watching that. I don't know what they'd do.' He saw her shiver and put his arms around her.

'Well, what do we do then?' she asked.

He shrugged. 'I don't know. We'll just have to get out of here ourselves, somehow. Come on, it's nearly dawn and I want to get away from here.' With that, he led her back into the jungle.

They heard another shot, some time later, but by then they were nearing the falls and the sun was already throwing golden spears of light through the trees. They stopped and stared at each other but there were no further shots. They carried on in silence, each heavy with their own thoughts.

When they reached the far side of the falls, high up on the cliff before the jungle started again, John called a halt. There was an orange light over the dark rim of the basin as the light of dawn came over the canopy of trees, steaming the dew off leaves, shimmering and dazzling in its intensity. John sat down, motioning to Eleanor to do so as well. He seemed tired and listless, his normal alertness having given way to apathy. He looked down at his boots for a moment, as though summoning up the energy to speak.

'We have to make a choice from this point on, Elly. We can go south and head for Ricki's place. It's about a day, day and a half's pretty rough going but I know the way. And Ricki'll help us. Dad won't dare try and follow us there. But it takes us by the far end of the Vila Serrista –' He broke off as he saw the emphatic shake of Eleanor's head.

'Well, hold on, Elly. I know that's risky but the other option's even worse. We could go east, following the river for a while and then cut across country and we'd eventually come to a mission somewhere along the other branch of the Paraná. It's a good three days' going and I only know the way as far as the edge of the Pareci land. That's about halfway. After that,' he swallowed, wiping the sweat from his lip, 'it becomes Morcego country. They're called the Bat Tribe round here and they're pretty unfriendly to the Parecis – and probably to us. I'm not sure I can get us through without them knowing we're there.' He looked at her again, to make sure she understood but she was still shaking her head.

'I don't want to go to Ricki's,' she said stubbornly, her face closed.

John looked at her in puzzlement. 'Why not, Elly? It's much more sensible. I know it'll be hard getting past the fazenda –'

'No! I'm not going. I'll stay here. You go and come back for me,' she said and hunched over her knees defensively, her eyes turned down. John felt suddenly uneasy, the same sort of sick feeling that had swept over him the night of the Shingirotse when he had found Elly missing.

He took a deep breath and said carefully, 'Why, Elly? What happened? Did Ricki ... hurt you?' When she flinched and looked away, John paled. 'Tell me, Elly. C'mon, you can tell me, I won't say anything. I just need to know. Elly?'

It took several minutes of patient probing before Eleanor finally rounded on him, her eyes large and staring in her pale face. 'He touched me!' she hissed angrily from between her teeth. 'He made me drink that white stuff and go with him into the jungle.' She hung her head then, unable to go on, unable to explain to John that she had been partly to blame. Large tears oozed from beneath her tightly closed lashes.

'Elly? Where did he touch you? Show me.' John tried to control the quiver in his voice. Elly shook her head, grimly looking down.

'Did he hurt you? Did anything hurt?' John tried again. Elly shook her head. 'Elly, please! You must tell me!' John held her arms between his hands and shook her, so that the tears that had gathered on her cheeks flew off in a rain of salty drops.

100

'He – he undid my dress and touched me there.' She pointed hesitantly, her voice sobbing in misery. 'And I didn't stop him, John. Not until he tried to lie on me. Then I bit him and ran away.' The deep hiccups of shame penetrated John's whirling thoughts, causing him to smile briefly and tenderly.

'Don't cry, darling. Don't cry. It wasn't your fault. Ricki's a bastard. He made you drunk on chicha; you couldn't have known how to stop him. Shhh.' He held her tightly to him, soothing and comforting, trying to ease the memory from the girl's thoughts, trying to make it less. 'You did well to bite him. I hope he howled with pain!' He was smiling and trying to laugh at her fears, damping down his own tearing anger, the bitter sickness that tried to well up into his throat and mouth, tasting the sourness on his tongue.

Eleanor laughed tentatively, rubbing her face against John's shirt. 'He did! I bit him really hard on the thumb and he cried out and didn't dare come after me.' Already she was remaking the scene in her mind into a silly romp where she had come off the victor.

John squeezed her tightly to him. 'Of course he didn't. You'd have given him some more of your medicine, wouldn't you? Good girl! Now you sit up and dry your eyes while I have a think.' He stood up, pushing her away from him, and went to stand at the edge of the cliff, looking down to the rushing water, breathing deeply to still the savage anger that had taken hold of him. Silently he promised Ricki punishment. One day. Definitely, one day.

After a few moments he returned. 'C'mon, Elly. We'll head east,' he said abruptly and pulled her to her feet. She followed him without protest.

The first day was hard going but they moved quickly, taking the routes John knew, slipping along the path between tortuga trees and wild pig trails, stepping carefully around the spiky fig-leaved mato-palo lianas that twined and looped between the trees. John warned Eleanor about the snakes that, flooded out of their holes by the rain, coiled in

101

the thorny yellow acacia bushes waiting to strike. She passed the first few hours in terror, waiting for some whip-like body to dart itself around her and then, as fatigue and sorrow took over, she simply blundered after John without bothering to glance right or left, sweat drenching her clothes, her hair full of snarls and twigs.

They stopped at intervals to drink the river water, knowing they should boil it first but without the time or implements to do so. They ate berries that John gathered from a palm tree and sipped at some white 'milk' that came from a reddish tree, and later in the afternoon, John stopped to whittle away at some wood until he had a clumsy but workable bow and arrow. He stripped thin thread from the leaves of another tree and attached it to the end of the arrow and then, as the animals came down to drink at dusk, he managed to shoot a macaw as it balanced on a bush. It came down in a flutter of beating wings and shrill death cries.

He plucked it grimly, ignoring Eleanor's horrified face, and then after nearly an hour of frustrated sawing with two sticks, managed to light a small fire. It was dark by the time the bird was cooked enough to eat and Eleanor was too weary to eat much. She lay down beside John, wrapping herself in the elephant ear leaves he had picked for her to keep off the acid rain, and slept fitfully. Around them the jungle coughed and roared and screamed in the dark.

The next morning it was raining when they woke but it cleared rapidly and the heat came back in full force, steam rising from between the trees, writhing along in plumes as it hit the river edge. They ate the rest of the macaw and drank some boiled water before moving on. Already Eleanor had begun to shiver, her vision blurring from the perspiration that dripped into her eyes, her cheeks flushed brightly. John saw the signs and cursed beneath his breath.

He called a halt at midday, sitting down on a root that protruded from the ground in a huge crooked lump, like the knuckle of a bony finger. Eleanor was scratching furiously at her ankles and he lifted her feet so that he could

102

see more clearly. Large hard welts, about half an inch in diameter, spotted her ankles. He pulled her socks up and tucked her trousers down into them.

'Don't scratch them, Elly. It'll just make them worse. Roll down your sleeves and keep everything buttoned up tight.'

'What is it? Mosquitoes?' She resisted the urge to attack her ankles again and wiped her hand across her face, smearing dirt into the paleness of her face.

John shook his head. 'Tabana flies probably – big, green and brown horseflies. We'll get the bites seen to when we get to the mission.' He didn't tell her the sores would have eggs laid in them already and would be festering in a day or two. 'I need to make a couple of water bags for us. We'll be heading inland after this. We'll have to carry our own water. Go and wash if you want. It'll be the last time for a while.' He turned away, the skin from the macaw that he had carefully removed from the bird before cooking it, now proving useful as he laboriously sewed it up with a thorn needle and palm thread. He made a couple more water containers out of huge seed gourds and slung them round his shoulders.

'We'll stick to the marajá fruit for now. I'll try and kill something better for dinner, maybe an iguana, but we need to get on faster or we'll be in here forever. The rains are due soon. We need to get out before they arrive,' he said and Eleanor stood up, smiling sweetly, her cheeks blushed pink and her eyes sparkling. She laughed and put out a hand for his, humming the native tune she had heard at the chapel. John took her hand gently, knowing the fever had her firmly now.

Further on, the tree branches were covered with parasitic plants with prickles like pineapples and yard-tall red blossoms. Eleanor tried to pick one and her hand bled for some time afterwards, despite John wrapping his handkerchief tightly around it. Their shotgun wounds were nasty now – ugly, proud flesh oozing clear, straw-coloured liquid and pus when he tried to feel for the shot. He decided to

103

leave them and push on as fast as he could.

Strangely, they had seen no Indians at all by late afternoon of the second day. However, John sensed they were there. They had crossed over into Morcego country some two hours before, John becoming increasingly nervous and silent, Eleanor trailing further and further behind so that he had to keep stopping to wait for her. For a while they halted when Eleanor remembered it was John's birthday, so that she could sing 'Happy Birthday'. She was upset there were no presents for him, crying and singing and laughing alternately as the fever swung her moods. By evening, it was obvious that she could go no further and they huddled under a banyan tree, chewing miserably on a root that John had found. He had had no luck in game at all.

Eleanor was delirious by then, babbling foolishly to her father and then to Aunt Liz, asking when they were going to have the picnic by the river, and wasn't it wonderful that Papa should have arrived just in time for school? John clenched his teeth, ignoring the tears that seeped out between his eyelashes, holding her hand tightly in his. She grew restless later on, thrashing around and calling out for something that John couldn't understand, her mouth making small puckering cries like a wounded animal. Finally she fell into a deep, uneasy sleep, filled with phantoms and monsters. John lay down beside her, trying to warm the chill, shaking limbs.

Around them, in the dark, there were rustles and silent flitting movements, eyes watching. John lay still, his eyes half-shut, peering out into the shadows. He didn't dare move in case he provoked those shadows, made them more substantial as they came flying out of the trees at them. But none materialized and, at last, worn out by the day, he fell asleep beside Elly.

The third day was the worst. Eleanor was unconscious, dreaming her vivid, entrancing dreams that held her tied in deep slumber and John had to carry her in short bursts of an hour at a time. He knew they had to keep moving or there was no hope; he couldn't leave her. She would be dead to the insects, let alone the larger animals, before the day was out if he left her. So he carried her and sweated and cursed and collapsed every hour with exhaustion so that he had gone only half the distance he had wanted by the time the sun was overhead. Not that he could see the sun, but he knew it must be there, beyond the dense green canopy that rose like a sky of its own over his head. Just as he couldn't see the brief, flitting shadows that followed them through the trees but knew the Indians were there too.

They were only a day's trek from the mission, he estimated, but whether they would reach it was entirely up to the phantom shapes that glided after them so silently, so surely, menacing their every move. He felt the fear tighten his chest, his lungs becoming hard like a board, his breath gasping shallowly between his clenched teeth. But there was nothing he could do. He tottered beneath Eleanor's weight, almost losing his grip on her.

He laid her down carefully and wiped the sweat from his brow, squatting on his haunches while he took another sip of water. Then he leaned over Elly, feeling the heat thrown out by her body, trying to ease some water between her closed lips. It trickled away, down her neck and he cried with frustration, heavy, fat tears squeezing out between his wet eyelashes and sliding unheeded down his face. When, finally, he looked up, he was not alone.

There were four of them that he could see, probably more in the bushes and John, crouched beside Eleanor, his mouth suddenly dry of spit, his heart racing, knew he was going to die. Slowly, perhaps horribly. These people frightened even the bravest Parecis. The four Indians continued to stare at him, their dark eyes almost hidden in their faces except where the white showed. He knew they were Bat People by their purple painted bodies and yellow dyed hair. Morcegos. He closed his eyes briefly. There was nothing more he could do. He almost didn't care that much anymore. Only for Eleanor. Not for himself. Not really. He said a silent prayer that his mother had once taught him.

When he opened his eyes again, they were gone. For

thirty long, long minutes he didn't move. Then, when nothing more happened, he hoisted Eleanor up in his arms and carried on.

By evening Eleanor had come to and felt better. John knew it wouldn't last long. He lay beside her in the dark and wondered when the Indians would come back.

Would they come in the night? Come sliding in while they slept like dead creatures to leap upon them and tear them apart? Or would they wait until dawn, their war cries splitting apart the still morning air with a terror that would silence the jungle? Oh, God! He shook, the sweat beading over the ridge of his eyebrows to hang shimmering in the dark.

John retched and spat into the bushes, hating the taste of fear in his mouth, the dry stickiness across his tongue. There was no decision to be made: he would have to carry Eleanor through the night. They were so close to the mission now, so very close. He could almost smell the woodsmoke, see the thatched huts through the shadows. He would carry her and hope that the Indians would sleep or not dare attack until the light threaded through the deep canopy overhead. Hope that possibly, just possibly, they did not intend to attack at all but to merely shadow them until they left Morcego land. He prayed silently to his God.

The Dominican priest was out gathering firewood in the early hours of the morning, when the mist still hung in garlands between the trees and rolled over the clearing like bales of pale hay. He was a solitary man, by nature and by circumstance, and his mission was a small one. There were three nuns now and several Indian girls who were training as novices but no young men. He prayed daily there might be some converts amongst the young men but they stayed stubbornly aloof, venturing into the mission to steal food or tools but never staying. He sighed and picked up another piece of wood.

Fra Janio heard something behind him and straightened abruptly, his hand groping for the machete he carried with him always, swinging from his girdle. Then he stopped in surprise. Two children, blond, light-eyed children stood there, their bodies covered in filth and blood, their hair falling wildly over their eyes, and their faces ... He dropped the wood and held out his arms but the children did not move.

'My dears! Where have you come from? Are you hurt?' He saw the elder one, the boy, move impatiently. The little girl continued to stare out at him with desperate eyes.

'We've come from Vila Serrista. We need help,' the boy said finally, his words flat and hard. He might as easily have said the reverse, Fra Janio thought. The children still did not approach the old priest, staying carefully just out of reach and poised to run.

'Vila Serrista! But that's not on this tributary at all. And it must be three days' away by land. You can't have come through the jungle!'

'Why not? Where else could we have come from?' the boy said and Fra Janio shook his head in wonder.

'Well, come, come, children. We must get you in and the sisters will look at your cuts. When you're washed and have eaten a little, we'll talk about how you got here. Praise the Lord you are alive at all. Everyone thought you must be dead.' He tried to usher them ahead of him but the boy stopped again and stared at him.

'Who thought we were dead?'

'Why, the authorities and the girl's father.' The priest nodded at Eleanor. 'You are John Campos de Serra and Eleanor Fawcett, aren't you?' He laughed a little then. 'Of course you are! How many other white children are likely to wander out of the jungle three days after that ...' he faltered and his voice became serious, '... that tragedy. May God keep and protect their souls.'

'Is Papa here? Can I see him?' That was the little girl, speaking for the first time.

The priest smiled encouragingly, trying not to notice the haunted look in her eyes or the pinched expression of her mouth. He shook his head. 'Not at the moment, my dear.

107

But soon. We'll have him here soon.' He took her hand in his, pleased at the trusting way in which she accepted it. He looked at the boy again. 'We heard on the wireless what happened. Perhaps, when you are rested, you would like to tell me?' The boy didn't answer, just stared at the priest with what Fra Janio realized was total despair. The old man didn't press further but pushed the children towards the long, low building ahead of them, calling out as he approached, 'Sister Mary! Sister Eugénia, come and greet our visitors.'

Later, when John and Eleanor had been washed and fed, and the authorities had been contacted, Fra Janio took the time to watch the children together with interest. Extraordinary the way they almost didn't need to talk to each other, the way they knew each other's thoughts. So much silent communication going on between them. He wondered if they had always been like that or whether this tragedy had wrought a much stronger bond between them. He caught the girl's eye.

'Your father's coming here now, Eleanor. It may take until tomorrow for him to arrive, if they have to stop for dark, or else he'll be here late tonight. He said to give you his love and tell you not to worry about anything.' She smiled at the message but the boy's face – now that was odd, Fra Janio thought. He looked as though the news meant the end of the world to him. How strange.

Chapter Five

When Eleanor awoke the room was different. It wasn't the darkened alcove with the raw beams overhead and the rough cot that she slept in. It was her room at home. She sat up in surprise. Outside, a cool, rain-swept day could be seen through the window. She was wearing one of her own nightgowns, the white one with the smocking down the front, and her hair was clean and brushed. The room was exactly as she had left it, but there were fresh bowls of roses on two of the tables, and a huge bowl of fruit beside her bed. She looked around but the chair that someone had placed beside her bed was empty.

Eleanor slipped from her bed and walked over to the mirror. She felt unsteady on her feet, as though she weren't pushing hard enough against the floor, and her knees had a strange impulse to buckle under her. But she kept going and stood herself in front of the full-length mirror and examined herself.

A pale creature stared back at her, the skin sallow and tinged with yellow, the hair a dull yellow. All of her seemed yellow. She looked at her teeth, just to be sure, but they were still white. Her eyes were yellow, though, and when she lifted her nightgown to examine her right leg, the wound seemed to have gone yellow too. Then she realized that that was some ointment. She dropped her nightgown and wandered over to the window.

How had she got here without remembering anything? It would have taken days to get her out of the jungle. Had she been so sick with the fever that she hadn't noticed? Was that why she was this horrible yellow colour? She glanced out of the window and down below in the courtyard, she saw John getting into one of the cars. She knocked on the window but he didn't hear. The car backed around and then drove out of the gates. She sighed and wondered where he was going.

The door opened behind her and she heard her mother exclaiming loudly over something. Reluctantly she turned away from the window.

'Hullo, Mama.' She walked unsteadily back to the bed and was instantly seized and lifted on to the mattress. Her mother's voice had risen in an annoying, high-pitched way and Eleanor felt irritable and unhappy and curiously like crying. She pulled away from her mother.

'Eleanor! You shouldn't be out of bed, darling. You've been terribly sick. We all despaired of you – your papa and I've been half out of our minds with worry. How do you feel now?' Clarissa bent over Eleanor and felt her brow. It seemed cool. She noticed the frown on the girl's face. Such a thin, yellow, cross little face. Clarissa blinked back some tears.

'All right. A bit wobbly when I walk. How did I get here? The last thing I remember was being at the mission.' She sat back against the pillows and looked at her mother.

'They brought you out by boat. What a journey! You had a fever all the way and your papa was in such despair and I didn't know what was happening because I had to stay here. And then they brought you in here and the doctor's practically lived with us for a week. Oh, sweetheart, you don't know how glad I am you're finally awake.' Clarissa was dabbing a few more tears from her eyes and smiling. Eleanor looked away. Then, suddenly, she remembered that Aunt Liz was dead and that John had no one to cry over him. She clutched her mother's hand.

'Where was John going? I just saw him get into the car and be driven off.' Clarissa's smile faltered. She sat back in agitation and wrung her handkerchief between her hands. Eleanor could see her thinking for a way of escape.

'Now, you really are worrying and fussing yourself too much with all these questions, Eleanor. You just go back to sleep again and when the doctor comes to visit you this evening, I'll answer all your questions. Just don't worry about anything. Papa and I are here and we've taken care of everything. Go back to sleep, sweetheart.' And with that, Clarissa kissed her daughter, shushed the protests that rose ever more querulously, and left the room.

It was dark when the doctor arrived. Eleanor had fallen asleep again, despite her determination not to do so, and the curtains were drawn when she woke and the lamps lit. The room looked calm and familiar and she smiled up at the people gathered around her bed. Her father was there and he sat down beside her and hugged her to him, smelling of aftershave and cigars. Eleanor hugged him back tightly.

'That's my girl. I knew you'd be fine. You're too much of a fighter to let that fever get you,' he said and patted her back until she felt like a rug being beaten. He let her go at last and the doctor then sat down in his place. He was very nice and Eleanor remembered him from previous visits when she had been sick with measles or mumps or broken bones. Dr da Silva. He smiled at her and examined her all over, putting that cold piece of metal on her chest and making her cough so he could listen to something. Eleanor coughed obligingly.

'Good as gold. She'll need to take it easy for a while. But her chest is clear and the fever's gone. I don't know how her liver will be but she's young and healthy. I shouldn't think there'll be any problems. Bring her by for some tests in about a month, when she's fully recovered.' He smiled some more at Eleanor, packed up his black bag, and left. Clarissa accompanied him out.

'There now, what did I say? Good as gold. We'll have to get you out in the garden once the rain stops, won't we?' Charles Fawcett closed the door after his wife and sat back on the bed. His face radiated contentment. Eleanor slipped a hand into his and lay back against the pillows.

'Papa? What happened to Uncle Michael? Did someone go to the fazenda? How did they know there was something wrong?' These were questions that had been buzzing in her mind for some time. Ever since the priest had brought them in. She looked expectantly at her father, seeing the shadow drop over his face, dimming the contentment. He cleared his throat.

'Michael Campos killed himself. I suppose he must have come back to his senses, seen what he'd done and and ... Anyway, the natives on the fazenda sent for help. No one could find you or John, not even the native trackers after you went over into Morcego country, and I was frantic with worry. We didn't know what had happened. And then Fra Janio found you. We got there the next day but you had a bad fever and probably wouldn't remember that. We brought you home and you've been in that bed ever since.' He smiled, signalling that the terse explanation was all she was ever likely to get.

Eleanor pressed on. 'Where's John, Papa? Mama wouldn't tell me anything and I really want to see him. He saved my life, you know. I'd never have got away if John hadn't been there.' She saw her father look away abruptly.

'You should never have been allowed to go up there in the first place. It was bad enough I let Elizabeth go there, but she was a grown woman and married and there was nothing I could do to prevent it – although, God knows, I tried. But she's dead now and that's Campos de Serra's doing. There's bad blood there. I've always said so. You wouldn't have gone up there if I'd had my way but I had Elizabeth on at me and John making up all sorts of lies about how safe the place was –'

'John didn't lie! He never said it was safe. He just said he would keep me safe. And he did!' Eleanor jerked away from her father. 'Where is he? Where's John?' She saw her father's eyes become moist. He wasn't even listening to her.

'My poor little sister. What sort of beast shoots a defenceless woman down like that? Poor Elizabeth, poor, poor girl. There was no one to keep her safe, was there? John didn't save her.'

'It had happened by the time he got to her. She was already dead, Papa. There was nothing he could have done. But he saved me! I slowed him down and I fell over and I near got us both shot but John didn't leave me. He looked after me, and led me through the jungle, and never left me once. He even carried me for one whole day and night. Why're you saying it was his fault when you know it wasn't!' She was crying now and shouting at him.

Charles looked at his daughter in distress. 'I'm not, darling. I'm not saying it was John's fault. He just should never have taken you up there in the first place. I'm just a bit upset. Elizabeth and I were very close and now I've lost her.'

'But where's John, Papa? You keep ignoring me when I ask you that. I saw him getting into the car this afternoon. Where was he going?' Eleanor was frightened now, her voice little more than a whisper. Her father looked at her and she could see he was loath to tell her the truth. 'Please, Papa.'

'John's gone away. To school in England. We thought it best. He's been desperately unhappy since I found you both out there in the jungle and brought you back. You wouldn't know anything about that because you were in a fever the whole time. When we got back here, he seemed even worse, moping around, unable to forget. We, your mama and I, decided it would be best for him to get totally away, somewhere where no one knows what's happened, somewhere where he won't be reminded of it every day. You remind him of it, Eleanor. He could barely look at you sometimes. And I know you wouldn't want him to be

113

unhappy any more. He'll settle into a new school, a new life and he'll put all this behind him. It's the best way, I promise you.'

'He can't have! I didn't say goodbye even. John wouldn't go without saying goodbye to me.' Eleanor looked around her, hoping to see John step out of the shadows. Her voice rose. 'He can't be gone!'

'Shh, darling. Don't excite yourself. John came and said goodbye to you but you just don't remember. He wanted to wait until you were well but the new school term is just starting and we thought it best he left as soon as possible. I'm sorry, Eleanor, but you'll soon forget, you'll see.'

'No! No, I won't! How could you think I'd forget John? He's the most important person in the world to me. Papa, how could you do it? We're all he's got left and you've sent him off to strangers. He'll hate it. I can't believe he ever agreed to this. Did he? Did he!' she shrieked. Slowly she slumped back and groaned. 'Oh, Papa, why?'

Charles Fawcett's face grew tight and angry in a way Eleanor had never seen directed at her. She stared bleakly ahead of her, tears running down her face.

'Eleanor, enough! Don't tell me what's right or wrong, and never, never raise your voice to me. Do you understand?' He didn't wait to see if she nodded. 'I did what I thought best and as far as I'm concerned the further away that boy is from you the better.' He stopped abruptly and stood up. 'Go to sleep. You're still feverish. I'll talk to you tomorrow.' He pulled open the door and left. Eleanor could hear him muttering to himself as he walked down the hall about 'bad blood will out'. She curled into a tight ball, the pillow clutched to her chest, and hit it again and again.

Henry came to see her the next day. He entered shyly, his quick smile at once pleased and tentative. Did she want to talk? Could he sit with her for a while? He had brought her a book to read and some cards to play with. But that only reminded Eleanor of the ferry journey into the Backlands and she turned away sharply.

114

'I brought you some writing paper too. I thought we could write to John ...' His hair was a gentle, silky brown and flopped forward over his eyes, perhaps by design. Eleanor looked up at him and wondered whether he was really sorry John was gone. Isobel wasn't. She had said as much that morning. And Papa was glad too. He didn't say so, but she knew he was.

'Do you think John'll be happier in England at school than here?' she asked without warning and Henry glanced up from under that hair, his eyes guarded.

'Perhaps not more than here – he'll miss you and all of us. But I think he'll like it once he's used to it. And he won't have to put up with people pointing and whispering about his father going mad like that. John doesn't like people taking liberties – at the best of times – and he wouldn't be able to do anything to stop it. He's better off away from it all, for a while anyway.' Henry fingered a rose beside the bed, absently admiring its form and elegance. He didn't look at Eleanor.

'You think Papa was right then? Right to send John away?' Eleanor sat with her knees pulled up tight under her chin in the bed and wrapped her arms around her legs.

'Yes, I think so.' Henry hesitated. 'But John will want to hear from us so he knows he's not forgotten. That's why I brought the paper. I've only got one pen so we'll have to swap it back and forth.' He ignored the undercurrents in the conversation and pulled out a pad from inside the bag he had brought with him.

He settled himself comfortably on a corner of the bed, a smaller and more delicately built boy than John with none of his striking good looks. But Henry had his own charm: a self-deprecating smile, a genuine warmth in his brown eyes, a quirky humour that saw the joke in himself more often than not. Eleanor, studying him, thought not for the first time that Henry was good-looking in a subtle, pleasant way. He faded beside John but, on his own, he was a nice companion. And he was fair.

That last quality was important. She knew he would never

agree with her father unless he thought it was for the best. Maybe she was wrong in what she'd been thinking – maybe Papa was trying to do the best for John, not just get rid of him. And Henry was certainly right about one thing. There was nothing that would upset and anger John more than other people talking about him, pointing fingers. No, that would be terrible. John would shut himself away inside himself where perhaps even she could never reach him. He could be like that, she knew, from fights they had had in the past. While he might seem to forget, he never forgave anything.

'All right. We'll write to him every day. Then he'll know we miss him. And he'll be home soon for Christmas. That's only four months away now.' She rocked forward on to her knees and picked up the pen. 'What shall we say?'

'How about starting it "Dear John"?'

'No, no, "Dearest John". That sounds nicer, more caring,' Eleanor insisted.

'I'm not going to write a letter to another fellow and start it with "dearest"! What d'you think I am?'

'Oh, all right! We'll write two letters. You can call John what you like then. And I'll call him "dearest". D'you think the school reads their post first?'

'Don't see why they should. It's not a prison, you know.' Henry sounded reasonable enough, but a trace of pink on his cheeks warned he was becoming annoyed.

'Well, how do we know? I've always heard English boarding schools described as worse than prisons. And this one's run by Benedictine monks! They may make them wear hair shirts and pray in draughty cold churches for hours every day and read all their letters so no girl, even a cousin, can write to them. D'you think he'll be allowed to write back?'

'Yes, if he wants to I'm sure he'll be allowed to. They couldn't have all the boys not writing home, now could they? Parents'd get pretty fed up with that. Look, you take this pen. And you write whatever you like. Call him dearest if you really must. I'll get another pen from next door.' He got off the bed, noting that she had already begun and was not interested in what he was doing. It was always John with her. He always came first. Henry breathed in deeply. 'Eleanor, Elly?' He waited for her to look up. 'Did John ever mention anything about a history of, well, disturbances, in his family? On his father's side?'

Eleanor glanced at Henry coldly. 'No, he didn't. His father just went mad. People do sometimes. But John isn't mad and won't ever be. So don't even think it.'

'All right. But your father said something about "bad blood will out". I just wondered if he knew something . . .'

'No, he doesn't! Papa's just upset about Aunt Elizabeth. That's all.' Her mouth became stubborn and Henry stood there, chewing the inside of his cheek, thinking how careful he must be not to upset Eleanor. It was only eight days now since she had been brought out of the jungle, half-dead with fever. He must remember that and make allowances.

'All right,' he smiled. 'I wasn't trying to suggest anything about John. He's my friend too. I'll go and get that pen.' But as he closed the door behind him, he wondered if he really was sorry John was gone. He liked John, of course. But Eleanor had been his friend before John came along. Maybe now she would be again. He gave a troubled, almost guilty smile.

Downstairs, Charles Fawcett smiled the same smile as he replaced the telephone. John was safely in England. Safely away from Eleanor. He knew he should be grateful, knew John had done what few people, even grown men, could have done in getting Eleanor and himself out of the jungle alive. But it just made it worse, really, having to be grateful to someone who was trying to steal his daughter away, trying to poison her mind against her own father.

God, how he hated John! Not just because he took Eleanor away but, strangely enough, because he had returned her, alive. He couldn't bear that. He couldn't bear the fact that John had saved Eleanor, that they had gone through something like that together. That was something major, cataclysmic in Eleanor's life that he, her father, would never be able to share, never even be able to glimpse into. John had shut him out. For that he hated John.

This was his punishment. Exile. To be sent away from Eleanor so there would be years in which she grew up, grew into an adult, that John would never share in. Charles smiled tightly to himself: an eye for an eye, a limb for a limb.

The school wasn't bad, John would get used to it; in time even begin to enjoy it, as the other boys did. It was the separation that Charles intended to hurt. Charles knew his nephew. The boy would understand only too well that this was meant to teach him how unimportant he was to all of them. They could go on, live their normal everyday lives and not miss John. That would be the lesson he would learn from his uncle.

Charles picked up a cigar and lit it thoughtfully, wondering whether he ought to let the boy home for Christmas. After all, he was the boy's guardian now, in charge of his funds left to him in his father's will until he was twenty-one. It was his decision that counted around here, not Eleanor's tantrums. Christmas? No, that was only four months away. Not time enough to teach the lesson. Let him suffer a little longer; he could spend the holidays with his cousin Max in England. It was safer that way. After all, that boy was bad through and through. Just like his father. Charles blew out the cigar smoke contemplatively.

Bad blood will out. No, better John stay there a while longer. Better he never come back.

Chapter Six

Rio de Janeiro
March 1955

'Papa? Papa! Are you listening to me?' Isobel reached over
to tweak the paper from her father's face. 'You are coming
to my recital, aren't you? I told my teacher you were. You
haven't forgotten, have you?' Her eyes showed her
perpetual uncertainty where her father was concerned,
worry that he had forgotten, nervousness about reminding
him, bluffing bravado that insisted on finding out the worst.
Charles Fawcett read it all in her eyes and was irritated as
usual.

'Goodness, Isobel, you're getting plump, aren't you? You
better start missing out some of those puddings and sweets
or you'll lose your looks completely and you're only thirteen now.' He glanced at his watch. 'Good Lord, is that the
time? I must go. When is this recital, anyway?' He glanced
up at Clarissa as he folded up the morning paper. 'You
might have mentioned this to me earlier, Clarissa. I can't
constantly rearrange my schedule around children's silly
shows.'

'I did, Charles and so did Isobel. You even put it in your
diary this time. Seven-thirty this evening at the school. We'll
see you there, shall we?' Clarissa's tone remained even and
she smiled at Isobel, a secret wink that made the wilting

119

child perk up and smile tremulously back. Eleanor ignored the discussion and helped herself to more toast.

'Well, I expect I can fit it in this time. But really, no more of these this term, all right? I can't run a business and constantly take time off like this. What about you, Eleanor? Any of yours I should know about?' His tone softened and he leaned over his younger daughter.

She shook her head. 'No, Papa. Nothing.'

He waited a moment, expecting something more but the way Eleanor folded her lips in tightly, as though to seal her mouth, was final. He grunted and stood up. 'I'll see you all there then. Goodbye.' He didn't wait for the habitual kisses all round. There was no point when Eleanor barely brushed his cheek now. She was cool and distant as she continued eating her toast. Totally uninterested. He slammed the door on the way out.

'Oh dear,' was all Clarissa said before returning to her cup of hot chocolate. Isobel sat, crushed, unable to finish her breakfast. Plump? Did she look awful in the new dress Mama had had made for her for the recital? Was it too tight? Was she going to look like a stuffed pink pig up there on the stage in front of all the other parents and children? Her confidence evaporated in the still morning air and she felt tears oozing hotly into her eyes, brimming over her lashes to spill wetly down her cheeks.

Eleanor looked up at her. 'Don't cry, Isobel. Papa's just being a bear this morning. He didn't mean it about you being plump. He was just being –' she floundered, lost for a suitable explanation.

Her Mama supplied it. 'Waspish. Just plain unkind, Isobel. Because we were interrupting his schedule and he didn't really want to come. You're not plump at all, my love. You're beautiful. Isn't she, Eleanor?'

Eleanor nodded, quite in agreement with her mother. 'Very,' she said emphatically. 'Louis certainly thinks so the way he hangs around you every second he gets,' she added with a giggle and Isobel brightened and wiped her face with the back of her hand.

120

'But why does Papa always have to take it out on me? If it had been your recital, Eleanor, he wouldn't have minded at all,' she complained and Eleanor shrugged.

'You know, Papa. Business, business, business. Anyway, I haven't got any recitals or anything for him to go to so you don't really know how he'd react.' Eleanor wiped her fingers with her napkin.

'Why aren't you carrying on with the piano, Eleanor? I thought you enjoyed it,' Clarissa asked and was not all that surprised when she saw Eleanor's face become still and pinched.

'I don't know. I'm just tired of it, I suppose. I must run or I'll be late for school. Come on, Isobel.' She was gone before her mother could question her further. But Clarissa knew anyway. This was one of Eleanor's ways of paying her father back for not letting John come home. She had been so good, really talented at the piano and her father had been so proud of her. So now she wouldn't play. Not at all.

Upstairs, Eleanor gathered her books for school. She felt tired. Nothing had happened to change the atmosphere between her father and herself since Christmas. That had been the beginning of her disillusionment. She squashed her pencil case into her satchel and pulled the thong through to fasten it.

Well, she didn't care. Papa could yell and bluster and make up stories as much as he wanted but he wasn't going to change her mind about John. Papa didn't deserve to have people be nice to him if he couldn't be nice back. She would be polite but nothing more. She would continue to write to John even if she couldn't see him. No matter what.

She swung past Isobel in the corridor and ran down the stairs to the courtyard below. Honório would drive them to school and they caught the bus home in the evenings. She climbed into the back of the waiting car and was struck, yet again, by the memory of the scene she had witnessed from her bedroom window of John getting into the car and being driven away. For good. It reminded her, every day, to stand firm. Papa could go to hell!

After school Eleanor slipped away from her friends, laughing and chatting, waving farewell. She turned in the direction of her own bus-stop, anxious to be home, to see if there was a letter waiting for her. It was best to get them before Papa came home and noticed, so she never delayed anymore, never lingered with the other girls. It was one of the prices she had to pay to keep in contact with John but was worth it when there was actually a letter waiting for her. Today there should be one, she thought with a skip in her stride. There must be one today. And there was. The pale blue letter lay diagonally across the silver tray in the hallway, waiting for her. She gave a cry of delight.

She hid the letter in her blazer pocket and ran nimbly upstairs, going into her bedroom and closing the door behind her. She sat on the balcony overlooking the grove of oleander trees, staring out at the pale blue of the sea as it rolled and rose in the distance beyond Copacabana. She sat for a few minutes, putting off the moment when she would take out the letter and open it, savouring the anticipation. Then she slid her hand into her pocket.

DEAR ELEANOR,

Do you believe in ghosts? [Eleanor blinked in the late after-noon sun and could think of nothing less likely.] I think we have one here and so does my friend Nick. It makes knocking noises at night, right above our heads in the ceiling, and rustling, crawling noises as though it were some lost soul trying to find a way out or, worse still, some devil with sharp claws trying to tear its way through to us. Several of us have heard it, ripping away at the plaster. We have told Matron who thinks we are imagining things and will do nothing. If you never get another letter from me, you will know that whatever it is has got me!

Sometimes I wonder whether Mother or even Dad are ghosts now? Do you think they are? It's meant to happen when unhappy souls can't find peace. Sometimes I think that could apply to living people too but I don't know what they could be called then — except maybe zombies. Maybe there's a macumba woman who sprinkles chicken blood on me in my sleep? Do you ever get spooked by it all? I wake up in a sweat some nights, terrified my father has killed you and that the light is swinging over your body, not Mother's. I had to go and be sick the other night. But it's just a dream — a nightmare — and then I go back to sleep. Do you have nightmares? Is it still as alive in your memory as it is in mine? I hope not. Anyway, enough of all that.

You won't believe it but I won the Upper Fourth cross-country race last Friday. We had to leave the school around by the side gate, near the gymnasium, cut out to the road and down the hill to the sign for Wykham village, back up an enormously high, long hill where we all thought we would die before reaching the top, to the furthest corner of the school grounds and cut back through the woods. It must have been well over four miles by my reckoning and I beat the next person home — Charlie — by thirty-two seconds! Most people were very surprised because I haven't really bothered to try before but Father Dominic, my housemaster, who seems to lurk in every doorway or behind every tree where he might possibly catch you doing something, just remarked that it was 'about time'. Sometimes he thinks he's just so smart!

I was very glad to get your last letter with all the news about Louis and Isobel. Louis must be crazy! I hope you're not getting all soppy like that with Henry. Are you?

Nick says to say hullo. I expect it is difficult for you to know who I am talking about so I am going to send you a photograph of everyone in the Upper Fourth in our House that is being taken soon. Nick is the short, ugly one. (Just joking.) Can you send any to me? I never had a chance to get anything like that together before I had to leave. I would love one of you and of Mother if you can find one somewhere.

I expect I had better finish this and post it while the going is good. I hope everyone is well except, of course, for Uncle Charles and please don't say I shouldn't think that because I can't help it. If there is any justice in this world, there is a macumba woman sticking pins in a doll of him. Take care of yourself.

LOVE JOHN.

123

He always ended it like that. She wished he wouldn't. It seemed too much like tempting fate, or just wishful thinking, and she shivered at the thought anything might happen to Papa because of it. A shadow scudded along the balcony, plunging her briefly into shade before flipping away in the wind.

She was glad John had friends now, especially this Nick boy whom he seemed to mention a lot. He had settled in well, despite the bitter letters she had received about not coming home for Christmas. She could still remember his words, telling her that he had thought he could hold on because it was just until Christmas and then he could convince her father not to send him back. But then, suddenly the news had come that he would be spending Christmas, Easter, the summer, next Christmas ... and on and on for four long years with some unknown cousin. John had said he couldn't bear to think about it. Somehow it had seemed possible when it was a question of taking it in small slices of time, a week, a month ... But now it was four full years. He wouldn't see his home for four years. He wouldn't see Eleanor for four years!

That was when she had gone cold towards her father. How could she not, when she knew what John was suffering? He might be settling in now, but he still counted those years away as years in exile. And her father was responsible for that.

With a sigh she stood up and folded the letter, putting it carefully in her drawer. Henry would want to read the letter. He didn't write often to John anyway. Just once in a while. She wondered what he would make of the first paragraph and the ghost that ripped into the ceiling plaster. How horrible! Would John be all right? How Henry would laugh at the thought that he was getting soppy over her, the way Louis was over Isobel. They would kill themselves laughing over that. She wished she could speak to Henry immediately and not have to wait until the next day. He would know what to suggest about the ghost. She was sure he would. But she was expected to turn up at Isobel's recital and by the time it was finished, it would be too late to see Henry. The ghost would have to wait. She tried not to think about the other ghosts John had mentioned. They haunted her dreams too.

Her father was one of the last to turn up at the recital. They already had seats and had saved one for him, her mother standing up and waving her hand again and again while her father seemed to look in all the wrong directions as though on purpose. The recital was beginning when he finally saw them and squeezed between the chairs to reach them.

'For Heaven's sake, Clarissa, why didn't you take seats on an aisle so I wouldn't have to climb over all these people? And now look, my knees are up under my chin!' he grumbled. Clarissa smiled and ignored him and Eleanor didn't smile and ignored him. He wiggled on the hard wooden chairs and felt that strange sharp pain in his chest again. He kept his arm tightly pressed across his chest and breathed shallowly. Damn Isobel and her bloody recital. He'd be home and sitting quietly in his library with a good whisky by now if it weren't for her. He scowled up at the stage at his daughter.

The recital began and he let his mind wander, thinking over the day's business, the way the political climate was developing, whether it would be a good idea for him to get in with the new crowd. This new president, Juscelino Kubitschek, seemed like a good stabilizing influence on the country. He was a moderate, one of Vargas's camp, a PSD-PTB candidate. People were talking about the economy taking off in the next few years and inflation wasn't too bad, only ten per cent. There was talk about opening up the interior. Of course, there was always talk about that but this fellow might just be the one to do it. Some mining concessions up there might be a good idea. He knew the new vice-president – João Goulart. It might be worth while having him to dinner some time soon. He'd make a note to mention it to Clarissa.

125

Charles reached into his pocket for his diary and felt the most piercing, agonizing pain slice through his chest, sending daggers of hot metal slicing into his heart. He gasped and clutched at his chest, falling forward against his wife. Clarissa caught his arm but his weight pulled him forward on to the floor. Beside them a woman screamed.

Eleanor wasn't sure what was happening. She saw her father slide on to the floor and her mother leaning over him, trying to pull him back on to the chair, and then there was chaos: people shouting, a woman screaming, her mother's back still bent over her father, her father's face obscured behind other people. Papa? Papa? Someone pulled her to one side roughly and then the crowd had surged forward and someone, a doctor, was yelling for an ambulance and she just stood by the wall of the music room and felt her own heart go racing, pitapatapitapata until she wanted to be sick.

They carried him out on a stretcher and her mother went with him, not even turning to see where Eleanor or Isobel were. The doors opened and closed, engulfing the stretcher and the doctor and her parents, and Eleanor just stood by the wall and stared. Isobel came rushing up then, her face blotched and wet and her pretty hair scattering down her back in a way that made her look just a teeny weeny bit plump, Eleanor thought and then was shocked at herself. This wasn't the time for such thoughts. Papa was sick, maybe dying. She took Isobel's hand. Maybe this was happening because John kept wishing it in his letters. 'I hope everyone is well except, of course, Uncle Charles ...'

And she had been horrible to Papa at breakfast and not spoken to him, well barely at all, since Christmas, not since John ... Oh God, let him be all right. I'll be nice again to him and I'll only write to John sometimes and I won't let John write horrible things about Papa and please God, please! Don't let him die.

Isobel was hiccupping beside her and clutching her hand in a tight, sweaty hold and Eleanor felt quite frozen inside with fear as she stood there and wished bitterly she could undo what was done. She'd be better if she were given another chance. She'd always be kind to Papa and even to Isobel and she'd never try and hurt people and she'd do anything!

Eleanor jumped when someone touched her arm and then she saw that it was Honório and he had come to take them home and she leant against him and sobbed, aching inside to change things, to let Papa know she loved him, to never have been so cold.

Honório led the girls out to the car and drove them back to the palácio, the night air warming as summer approached and blowing like silk across their skin through the open windows of the car. The girls had fallen silent in the back, each staring out at the darkened buildings, the street lights flashing by, the city dropping back like strings of jewels threading the dark. They drove past dusky gardens behind high walls as they climbed into the hills.

Charles Fawcett lived. For a night and a day there was no word from the hospital and then, late in the day, Clarissa rang to say everything was all right and that Papa would be fine. Eleanor felt the bile rush into her mouth, salty and bitter around her tongue. He would be all right. Her prayers had been listened to and God had accepted what she had offered. She leaned against the wall in her father's library, feeling the bookcase against her back, solid and uncomfortable. Like Papa. And then she laughed at that thought, her laughter high and cracked with relief.

Isobel was oddly silent when Eleanor finally went upstairs to tell her the good news. She said, 'Oh,' in a blank tone and turned away to fold the clothes she had taken out of her drawer. Eleanor noticed they were some of her mother's. After all the tears and misery of the last few hours, Eleanor was puzzled by Isobel's response.

'Aren't you glad? He's going to be fine. The doctors said so,' she repeated in case Isobel had somehow mis-understood. But Isobel had understood only too well the first time. After her initial distress, her mind had quickly seen the advantages of only a doting mother on the scene and she had begun to fantasize about the party she wanted later in the year and the car she could have when she was just a little older and about how she wouldn't have to bring home good report cards anymore and really, if Papa were to be taken from them, which of course she hoped he wasn't, well, she for one could learn to cope. And now, suddenly, all those fantasies were nothing more than that. Will-o'-the-wisps blown away by an autocratic hand. She looked down at the bed.

'Um, yes. Good. When will Mama be home?' she asked.

Eleanor, standing behind her, couldn't see her face. 'Soon,' she said. 'In time for dinner. Well, I'll call Henry and let him and his family know. Will you call Louis?' Eleanor was uneasy and knew suddenly that she didn't want to understand Isobel's behaviour. A shadow of its meaning glanced across her mind and was angrily shrugged away.

'Yes, all right. You go ahead. I'll be down soon.' And Isobel smoothed out the silk shirt she had been trying on and replaced it on the hanger. A pity, but now she couldn't wear it.

They brought him home a week later, gaunt and aged, his face lined with deep furrows that had never been there before. He was only a young man, nearing forty, but the last few months had taken their toll. He looked ten years older. Clarissa hovered and soothed and mothered. Isobel smiled and sat on his bed and talked and talked. And Eleanor stood pale and awkward, out of reach, and wished she knew what to say.

Not now, not here, his eyes were busy saying to her and she relaxed a little and ducked her head. Isobel was still prattling on about something, school was it? No, some friend, some party. Clarissa shooed Isobel away, gently pushed both girls out of the door and Isobel pouted and Eleanor left, guiltily relieved, to run down and finish her letter to John. She would tell him she wouldn't keep writing if he ever said anything unkind about Papa again, she would tell him he mustn't even think it, because look, just look what happens when you do. She had promised to be kind to Papa and not write so much to John and so this would be the only letter she would send him this month and he would have to understand because she had made a vow with God.

Eleanor signed the letter and slipped it in an envelope, starting when she looked up and her mother stood there by the door. She pushed the letter into her pocket. Clarissa pretended not to see.

'Papa wants to see you but you better go quietly so Isobel doesn't get upset. She wanted to talk to him but she tires him out too much and I can't allow that yet. You'll be good and quiet with Papa, won't you, Eleanor? Don't upset him at all. He mustn't get excited or upset, the doctors say. Not ever.' Clarissa looked intently at her daughter. Yes, she was quick. She knew what was being said. A life sentence had been passed on them all. It was a terrible thought, Clarissa knew, but why did it have to be like this? He would be all-powerful now.

'I'll go up now. Mama? Papa didn't have a heart attack because of me being so mean to him, did he? I mean about John. It wasn't because of that, was it?'

'No, darling, of course not! He's just been overworking and then with Elizabeth's death and everything, he's been angry for some time. That's what does it, the doctors say. Too much frustration and anger all bottled up inside. It wasn't anything to do with you or John. You mustn't blame yourself for this.' Clarissa kissed Eleanor on the forehead and pushed her toward the stairs. 'Run along now and make your peace.'

Eleanor's steps were slow. But inevitably she arrived and knocked on the door.

'Papa? Can I come in? Mama said you wanted to see me.' The covers were tented as though he were trying to set up camp within the confines of the high canopied bed. Eleanor saw his face muscles crease up, forcing a smile.

129

'Come in, poppet. Come and sit here beside me. No, close the door. I want to have a chat with you in private.'

She shut the door carefully and tiptoed over to his bedside, peering over at the figure in the bed, sitting herself uncomfortably on the edge of the chair. She felt unhappily aware that they were going to talk about things she didn't want to talk about and that there was nothing she could do about it because she had promised Mama not to upset Papa and she had promised God to be kind. It was going to be difficult.

'Are you still angry with me, sweetheart?' He had used to call her 'sweeting' when she was little and had been ferociously angry about being sent to bed early or being smacked for some childish prank. 'Are you still angry with me, sweeting?' But now he was more circumspect. She agreed with that.

'Sometimes, Papa. I still can't understand why you're being so hard on John but I don't want to argue anymore. Mama says you must be calm or else you'll have another heart attack.' She hadn't meant it to come out like that, the veiled accusation of playing unfair. He wasn't listening anyway. Not to her words.

'I know you think I'm being unkind to John but sometimes you have to be a little unkind for someone's own good. John is much happier, believe it or not, far away from here. He's not going to ever forget if he's here. This way he'll grow into a different type of person, somewhere where that dreadful tragedy doesn't tower over his daily life and warp him into somebody you won't like at all. He's made to think about other things at school and there no one knows about it, there's no gossip or cruel taunting the way there would be if he went to school here. I know you don't agree with me but I am doing what I truly believe is best for him. After four years if he wants to come back here, he'll be old enough to have put it behind him. He'll be a different person who can't be hurt by it anymore. Can't you see that, darling?'

His tone was so sincere, so desperate for her to believe

him that Eleanor couldn't help but nod her head. She didn't tell him that the other boys at John's school already knew and they hadn't been horrible to him. That would have upset and angered him, as though she were suggesting he was lying, and she had promised to be good. She sighed heavily when he stretched out a hand but she took it in her own. His was warm against her cold skin.

'I know you think it's for the best, Papa. But I don't see why we can't see him in the summers? What good does that do?' She tried to sound reasonable, not angry, not upset. Dispassionate.

He sighed. 'Because he won't forget in that time. Each time he came home, you'd peel back open the wound; every summer, there it would be, staring him in the face. Brazil is where it happened. Can't you see that, Eleanor? John must sever all ties until he is older and he's built up a thick, protective skin over it all. Then he can come home.'

'After four years? When he's finished school? You promise?' She knew when to give up other causes and concentrate on just one. He'd give that to her now, thinking she'd forget by the time the promise ever came due. She squeezed his hand. 'You promise, Papa?'

'Yes, sweetheart. Of course I do.'

'Say it, Papa. Say you promise to let John come home after four years,' she pressed.

'All right, Eleanor! I promise. There! Are you satisfied now?' He had become angry, his face mottling up with colour, and she was instantly reminded of her own duties, her own promises.

'Yes, Papa. I'm sorry. I didn't mean to upset you. Thank you so much. I know he'll feel better if he knows that.' The moment she said it, she knew it was a mistake.

He pounced. 'So you are still writing, despite whatever I've said?'

'Yes, Papa. I can't not. You said I could even though you didn't think it was a good idea. John depends on my letters and I know he wants to hear how everyone is, to pass on his love. He sends his love to you, too.' She prayed God wouldn't strike her down for such lies.

But her father relaxed. 'Yes, all right. Write if you must. And you'll be my good girl again? You won't frown and turn away and not answer me the way you've been doing? You'll be my little Eleanor again?' It was almost a plea and Eleanor felt uncomfortable hearing her father ask for something he had always had unstintingly. She nodded, suddenly ashamed of her own behaviour. She loved him and he had nearly died and maybe some of that was her fault. She squeezed his hand again and leaned over to kiss his cheek.

'I'm sorry, Papa,' she whispered and he pulled her tightly to him.

'I'm sorry too, Eleanor. We'll just have to pretend it never happened. All right?'

'Yes, Papa. It never happened.'

Chapter Seven

Rio de Janeiro
September 1958

From many miles out the 'Sleeping Giant' could be seen dominating the skyline, like an old man asleep on his back who might waken and stride through the waters and pluck the ship from the sea like a toy. A mythical power surrounded his slumbers and John stood on the deck, staring across at the green giant as though he believed he saw the old man's nose twitch. A narrow passageway between a great rock, on the left, and the Sugar Loaf on the right swept the ship in, gathering it up into the calm green waters of the harbour and bringing it gently to rest cradled in the enclosing arms of the mountains that soared above.

On all decks of the ship, the other passengers thronged and exclaimed, pushed and laughed, pointed and photographed. Only John stood quietly withdrawn, watching a backdrop of great, jagged peaks that he knew like friends. There was Gavea, and there, there were the Dois Irmãos, the Two Brothers, and, above them all, there was Corcovado, the Hunchback, dominating all the others with Christ, the Redeemer, arms outstretched on the peak, welcoming him home after four long years of enforced exile. He smiled.

'Isn't it fabulous? I had no idea,' a girl, standing to his

left, said in tones of awe. John glanced at her. She waited for his opinion.

'Yes. There's nowhere quite like it,' he said at last and she smiled, brilliantly, pearly teeth making an ordinary face seem something quite different. John glanced at her again. 'Have you been here before?' he asked, knowing she hadn't, eager in some strange way to show it all off to her, to proudly say, see, this is my home.

She shook her head. 'Never. My parents promised me years ago that we would come one day. And now that we're here, I can't quite believe it. We're going to stay at the Copacabana Palace Hotel, even! What about you? Have you been here before?' She was standing beside an elderly couple, he noticed now, but they were engrossed in the flotilla of yachts and fishing smacks that thronged the harbour.

He turned back to her. 'Yes, but not for four years. Shall I point out the sights?' And when she nodded, he introduced her to the peaks and the Sleeping Giant, to the shining beaches of Copacabana and the white buildings that rose from the shoreline beyond, to the old fort that was the naval base and then, as they turned the corner, and the harbour proper was revealed, to the old business quarter of Rio where the passenger liners dock right at the foot of the Avenida Rio Branco, the main thoroughfare of the city.

They gazed down at the Praça Mauá, the square decked out in its formal flower beds and trees, the blacks sitting around the docks in a garish misassortment of clothes, some civilian, some military, the jostle of taxis and urchins and fruit sellers and harassed officials. The girl breathed it in deeply. 'It's quite unlike anything I ever thought, better than I ever dreamed it could be. I've never seen anything so beautiful in my life.' John smiled, glad for her, glad that she appreciated it all. He searched the crowd of people lined up along the docks, hoping against hope that perhaps Eleanor might be there. But it was a Thursday, a school day. She would be sitting, miles from there, in a classroom staring out the windows and wondering if that last passenger liner she had seen far out in the bay might not have been his. She

134

wouldn't be in the crowds below. Nor would Aunt Clarissa. Because no one, apart from Eleanor, knew he was due back today. The money had been wired for the passage home but he had never written with a date. Except to Eleanor.

The girl beside him paused, speculatively, gauging the look in his eyes. She had watched him for most of the voyage, smiled in his direction, dropped her books beside him, asked him directions as though lost. And he had never noticed her. It was as though he walked in a haze, looking out, beyond what everyone else saw, at a totally different horizon. She wanted to know him desperately – wanted . . . what? She wanted him, really, she had to admit to herself. She wasn't sure quite why. It was almost a compulsion.

'I'm sorry!' A laugh, an outstretched hand. 'I never introduced myself, did I? Lydia Forrester. We might as well be friends since we've done all the sights together already.' Another laugh, trailing off a little as she saw he had retreated into that different perspective that didn't really see her but only past her. 'And you are?' she prompted.

'Oh, um John.' No, no sign of a blonde head bobbing about in that sea of humanity. 'John Campos de Serra.' He refocused back on the girl, Lydia, and tried to be more personable, tried to stave off the boredom that already threatened to make him bite off his words, fade away from her, disappear. She was so very nice and so very eager, he thought. And so very ordinary. She would want all the ordinary things in life: security, marriage, social position; he knew that without even having to ask. But he didn't need or want anything like that; he just wanted Eleanor.

'Goodness! I thought you were English like the rest of us. You sound English, you know. What sort of last name is that?' He thought she was being coy and he just wasn't interested. He didn't want her spoiling his homecoming with her insincerity. He gave a pale imitation of a smile. 'Brazilian. What else? Excuse me.' And then he had turned and walked away, a few feet, just enough to separate them. Lydia, cheeks flaming, turned back to her parents and John thought guiltily that he had been unkind when all he had meant to be was reserved. He cursed himself beneath his breath.

It took some time for the luggage to be brought off the ship and for them to pass through immigration and customs. John noticed quite a few of the passengers were lining up at the coffee bars for their first coffee tastings, perching on stools and cautiously sipping from three or four different demitasses. He waved away the street urchins who attempted to lead him over to taste some coffee, who offered to get him a taxi, cheap, cheap, who tried to fix him up in some hotel on the other side of the city. John shook them loose and tossed them a few coins, telling them in Portuguese to be off before he grew angry. They flashed white teeth and scuttled around for the coins he had thrown.

Poor bloody kids. It was the first time he had even noticed them. As a privileged child who had grown up in Brazil, the poverty was something never noticed, just there because it had always been there. Now he watched a five-year-old boy trying to drag heavy suitcases, fighting with other boys barely older than himself, for the right to do so. Just a few centavos but it meant the difference between eating today or not. Many of these kids provided the sole income for families of four of more, the mother staying home with a new baby every year, the children sent out to forage. There was seldom a father. Just a series of men. Home was a cardboard box perched uncertainly on the hills surrounding Rio, sliding and crumpling into soggy mush when the rains came and the hills turned slick red with mud. Favelas. Shanty towns.

But he knew better than to give the little boy money. It was one thing to toss it into the air and let them scramble for the coins. That way no one got very much. But give a large sum to just one boy and that was signing the kid's death warrant. John picked up his own suitcase and slid it on to the customs counter.

No one wanted to look at it. He was too obviously the son of a wealthy house. The official scratched a sign in chalk on the top of the suitcase and waved John on. Outside, the sun was intense, gleaming brightly off the white stone buildings, the mosaic pavements in black and white. John walked slowly, ignoring the cries from the taxis, Lincolns and Packards and Chevrolets and, more and more, small Volkswagens with the passenger door cut off and the front seat missing. A variation of the motorized trishaw. John waved them all away.

He saw Lydia and her family getting into a taxi, the girl glancing around, searching for him. He stepped behind a fruit vendor's stall and bought a glass of papaya and orange juice, sitting sipping it in the sun until they were safely away. Then he resumed his walk. His suitcase wasn't heavy. He had few clothes once his uniform had been sold. And even less personal possessions. It swung easily from his arm as he hurried across the road, dodging amongst the traffic. He reached the bus-stop just as the crosstown bus pulled in.

Behind him he heard a car shriek to a halt, excited, raised voices cursing but he didn't turn around. He was searching in his pockets for some change. And then he felt a touch on his arm and he shrugged it away, telling them crossly to leave him be. The hand tugged insistently and he gave an exclamation of annoyance and rounded on the child who clung so hard to him. A tall child, nearly full-grown, with a wide serious forehead and pale greenish eyes that peered up at him from beneath the low brim of her hat. Her hair was pulled back tightly behind her ears, falling in a long sheath of honeyed silk down her back. At fifteen, she was half-woman, half-child and the sight of her caused him to feel an unbelievable tenderness for all that vulnerability he saw in her eyes. She still clung to his arm, breathless from her run.

'Eleanor? My God, Eleanor!' He dropped his suitcase then and wrapped his arms around her waist, lifting her up to his eye level and she laughed, her boater falling back off her head, her arms going around him too.

'Oh John! I nearly missed you. I had to run all the way and then the bus was late and I'll get in so much trouble when they find out I'm missing at school. But I had to

137

come. Oh, welcome home, John!' She kissed him on both cheeks, hugging him tightly.

Circling the other side of the Praça Mauá, their taxi edging ferociously into traffic, only to be blocked again and again, Lydia had plenty of time to watch John as he stood at the bus-stop. She saw the girl, a few years younger than herself perhaps but taller already, goodness, far too tall for a girl and so skinny and leggy with it. And that unbecoming uniform! What on earth was going on? Lydia straightened and stared, seeing John turn and seize the girl, lifting her up, the hat flying off. Now they were hugging and kissing! Lydia's lips compressed sharply. So that's why he hadn't seen her when she tried to talk to him. He was too busy looking for this girl. She glared out of the window and the taxi swept around the corner in a blaze of claxons and John and the girl were lost to view. She slumped back against the hot vinyl seats sullenly.

'John, let me down, you're crushing me!' Eleanor laughed and he reluctantly slid her back to the ground, not taking his arms from her waist. She smiled and he smiled and suddenly they both felt intensely awkward and shy and as though they barely knew each other. They broke apart.

'Does anyone know you're here?' John asked. Eleanor felt on top of her head, looked around, and pounced on her hat as it was blown into the gutter. John retrieved his suitcase.

'Of course not! Papa would never have let me come all the way down here on my own. I told you, I slipped away from school. I'll get massacred tomorrow for it – all round. Come on, we better get this bus if we can. We can go down to Copacabana and have a drink or something. Have you got any money?'

'Yes, enough for today. I'll need to get some more from Uncle Charles pretty soon. How is your dear papa?'

'Fine, fine.' They pressed forward on to the bus, refusing to let several people push in front of them. Once they were seated comfortably near the back and John's suitcase was stowed overhead, they looked at each other again.

'Actually,' Eleanor admitted, 'Papa isn't totally fine. He's been a bit tense and worried just recently and you know he's not supposed to get upset, what with his heart and now they say his blood pressure's pretty high as well so you won't argue with him, will you, John? You will promise to keep him calm, won't you?' There was anxiety in her voice and John sighed sharply.

'What you really mean is, his blood pressure went up when he had to wire me the money to come home. And it's going to stay up for as long as I'm around. Isn't that it?' John looked out of the window at the city flashing by, the shipping agencies, the brokers and export offices. He felt Eleanor slip a hand into his.

'Don't, John. Please. You know we all want you here but you have to be careful with Papa. Or you'll cause him to have another heart attack and he might die the next time. Please don't get angry.' With other people Eleanor was brisk and amused and a little impatient. But it was never like that with John. They already knew each other's thoughts; the words were just an added confidentiality, a strengthening of the bond. She felt the hand holding hers, warm and firm and dry. She leaned her head against his shoulder and was pleased when he put his arm around her.

'All right, Elly. I'll try and be nice. I just want to come home and fit in. If you'll help me. All right?'

'Yes, all right. Oh, let's not talk about Papa. Let's talk about you. Did you get your exams all right? Are you sad to be leaving England? I want to go there someday and see it, so you'll have to come with me and show me everything – your school and your friends and your dear, eccentric cousin Max. Everything, but him most of all.' She smiled up at him, seeing him the same and not the same. At eighteen he was older, heavier built, more man now than boy but still her John.

'What would I have done without him? I don't think your father had any idea how kind and intelligent and thoroughly unconventional Cousin Max is, or he'd have definitely sent me to someone else. I promise I'll take you to meet him one day, but that's our secret.' He smiled and squeezed her hand. 'And I think the exams went well – in fact my results should have arrived by now. Are there any letters waiting for me?'

When she shrugged, he continued, 'But I'm not really sorry to leave England. I enjoyed my time there but I always wanted to be here. It was only ever a second choice, a sort of surrogate home in exile. Nick made it all so much better, of course. And Father Dominic. I'll miss them both a lot but ... once the exams were over and done with,' he shook his head, 'I don't know, I just wanted to get back here as fast as possible. Nothing else seemed important. Cousin Max was great; he came and got me after the last exam and let me spend some time with him until I could get the berth home. Anyway, that part of my life is all over now. I don't even want to think about it. I'm home now.'

They had passed Cinelándia and the opera house and the Edifício Monroe and turned into Avenida Beira Mar. John sighed with contentment, staring out over the low stone walls that overlooked the Bay of Botafogo, where the water shimmered in the afternoon sun.

'Didn't you fall in love with anyone? Wasn't there someone you took to the Upper Sixth Dance?' Eleanor sat up straight, her eyes curious.

John shook his head abruptly. 'No, why should there be? Wykham isn't the most accessible place in the world. A lot of the fellows didn't have partners. Anyway, I wasn't much in the mood so I left early.' That wasn't strictly true. He hadn't even turned up at all, preferring to go walking in the woods where the moonlight streamed down between the trees and lit the moss like spangled silver. There was no one but Eleanor he had wanted to be with.

'Oh, that's a shame. I thought you might have met some English Rose and brought her home with you the way Papa did Mama. But I'm glad you didn't.' For a moment, sitting close beside her cousin, Eleanor was aware of something new and strange and exciting about him. He smelt different, not just of soap and water but of shaving cream and aftershave and – something. His jacket felt oddly rough and grown-up against her cheek and there was an altogether new sensation to sitting beside him. She opened her mouth slightly, staring.

'Are you?' John smiled, his face very close to hers. 'Good.' They searched in each other's eyes, but for what neither was sure. It was so odd to see himself staring back in slightly different form, the same thoughts in the eyes, the same rhythm even in their breathing. Like they weren't separate people even, just complementary halves. Odd. John leaned his cheek against hers, her skin soft and smooth. He felt it tremble slightly.

The bus swept into a tunnel under a mountain, the lights dimming to low orange, sending shadows and thick gloom through the bus. Even the sound was muffled and their ears seemed thick and clogged. John pressed his mouth against hers, barely touching. He smelled warm and fresh and disturbingly male to Eleanor. She didn't move, drugged by the strangeness of it all, the feel of his skin on hers.

And then they were out, the sunlight flashing back on to their faces, the wide curve of the road throwing them apart. They stared and then looked away.

'Where do you want to get off? Somewhere along the Avenida Atlântica?' Eleanor asked, becoming interested in their surroundings, taking efficient charge. She pushed her hat back on to her head again. John peered out as Copacabana spread out beside them.

'Yes, let's get off at the next stop. We can go have some lunch at a café somewhere and sit on the beach for a while. I haven't sat on the sand for four years.' He had broken free of that languor, knowing it was more powerful than either of them had ever sensed, not wanting to confront it. Not yet. He pulled his suitcase down and signalled to the driver to stop.

They went out the rear door and stood on the pavement as the bus changed gear and drew out in a belch of purple smog. Then they crossed the road and walked along the pavement edging the beach, staring out at the lazy, curling

141

waves, the warm, soft air caressing their skin. John loosened his tie and slipped his jacket off, throwing it over his shoulder. He watched the bronzed bodies toning up at the exercise bars, the skimpily bikini-clad girls who rushed in groups between the sea and their towels, calling shrilly and unceasingly to attract male admiration. He laughed at the boys surfing the waves with their small boards strapped to their arms and the dogs that surfed along with them, jumping and leaping into the air. It seemed so carefree and golden after the years of school.

It was all so familiar and so different that he wasn't sure how he felt. Like seeing an image slightly out of focus so that you can't quite grasp it. He shook his head.

'How're Henry and Louis? Still running after Isobel, I suppose?' He glanced at Eleanor, saw the momentary indignation, the pursed mouth. His eyes lingered and then carried on.

'Louis is. Always was and always will be. I expect he'll ask her to marry him in a few years, poor dear.'

'And will she?'

'I expect so, if nothing better comes along. You know Isobel.' A slight laugh that was both irritated and amused.

John nodded. 'And Henry?' He wasn't sure he wanted to probe this area, like tentatively touching a tooth to see if it hurt yet.

Eleanor looked sideways at him. 'Henry never liked Isobel, not in that way.' She was too casual. He gave her a discerning, questing look and she flushed. 'Well, yes, I think he does like me a bit. But he's never done anything. He knows I'd never forgive him if he did. We're just friends.' That stress, that guilty explanation unnerved her. Why was she explaining? 'Anyway, they're both well. Louis is going to study economics at the University of São Paulo if his marks are good enough. And Henry – well, he's still got a couple of years yet but I think he's going to study law. What about you?' What about him, John wondered. Was it going to be anthropology, after all? Urban studies? Or was he going for archaeology and the great unknown? He wasn't sure.

'Still up in the air. I'll decide in the next week or so, I suppose. Come on, let's get something to eat. That one over there looks all right.'

'With the striped awning?' It wasn't just a confirmatory question. It involved surprise and awe and a tinge of uneasiness. John glanced at Eleanor and wondered why it should unnerve her.

'Yes, anything wrong with it?'

'Oh, no-o, just that they're all so smartly dressed and I'm in my school uniform and they'll start asking questions, see if they don't. Why aren't I in school? Who're you? You know what it's like. This is Brazil, not England. Girls have to be – circumspect.' She looked flustered and John remembered then how prudish the Brazilians could be about their schoolgirls. Never mind the scanty bikinis on the beach, Eleanor's uniform came well down below her knees. She did look out of place and was attracting some frowns of concern from people passing by. Wondering why she wasn't chaperoned by someone older. Someone female.

'Come on then, let's just get an ice-cream. In fact, why don't you get them? Here, take my change. I just need to get something. I won't be a minute.' And then he had slipped into the traffic and across the road and Eleanor couldn't see him anymore. She shrugged and joined the queue for ice-creams.

By the time she had paid the man and stood back from the kiosk, two ice-creams melting in her hands, John was back. He smiled and took his own ice-cream and they wandered down the beach some more, seeing it stretch for miles into the distance.

'Where'd you go?' Eleanor asked, licking neatly around the cone so that the ice-cream was moulded into a bulbous mountain. John pulled a package out of his pocket. He tossed it to Eleanor. 'I thought we might spend a couple of hours more here before we have to face the music. And what do we need to be comfortable and, more importantly, inconspicuous on a beach? Hmm?' he teased.

She fished into the bag. 'Bathing suits!' she said

triumphantly, pulling them out. Except that hers wasn't exactly a full suit. It was more like a few tiny triangles. She looked at it dubiously. 'A bikini?'

'Why not? You'll look great in it. Besides, you can't call yourself a Carioca if you haven't worn an itsy-bitsy teeny-weeny bikini on Copacabana. Now can you?' He raised his eyebrows in mock sternness.

Eleanor laughed. 'Well, no, I suppose not. But Papa would have a fit.'

'Another good reason to wear it. Aagh, no, sorry I forgot. No jabs at Papa. Come on, Eleanor. You'll look sensational in it and ten times better than all those overblown sorts down there, posturing around. Be a good sport because it took the last of my money bar our bus fare home and I can't get you another.' He put down the suitcase, beginning to half frown and she nodded.

'Okay, okay. You've sold me. Where do we change?'

'The shop assistant said you could use their changing rooms.'

She smiled, taking a deep breath, 'Well, see you in a minute then. Oh! What about towels?' She paused, turning back to look at him.

He raised his hands, palm upwards and laughed. 'We'll have to improvise. Don't be so prosaic, Eleanor. This is my first day back and I want to lie on the golden sand and swim in the blue, blue sea and enjoy myself! See this?' He leaned into her and held up his ice-cream cone, minus the ice-cream. 'This,' he said in a purposely pretentious tone, 'is a symbol, a cornucopia, the horn of plenty. I'm back where I belong and all the riches of life belong to me now. Including you. And if I say wear a bikini, then wear one. And let's not worry about towels, all right?' He was half laughing, half serious, his long, planed face full of charm and devilment.

Eleanor shook her head. 'Ohh, so help me, John, you're going to get me in trouble the way you always used to and the really annoying thing is I'd rather be in trouble with you than out of trouble with anyone else!'

144

'Like Henry, for instance?' His eyes gleamed.

'Like anyone.' Eleanor said firmly. She turned and walked towards the shop not noticing the admiring looks of a group of professional beach bums grouped on the sand.

When she emerged, some minutes later, John was already changed and lounging against the low stone balustrade in his swimming trunks. His skin was pale against the tans around him, the reverse of when he had first arrived in England. It amused him.

'I feel silly, John. Look, I'm all brown except for my middle and that's like milk!' she complained, standing close beside him. She didn't just feel silly. She felt embarrassingly conspicuous, the tiny triangles of material doing things to her body that she had never seen before. It almost looked like she had curves, she thought in alarm. John looked her up and down assessingly.

'Full cream milk. And the only way to do something about it, is to wear a bikini and fry that middle. Anyway, judging by that lot over there, I'd say the bikini's a success. Come on, let's swim.' John jumped down over the wall, not waiting for Eleanor. She clucked impatiently and took a flying leap, landing in a surprisingly graceful heap on the sand. John looked back and laughed as she scrambled up and ran after him.

'Good old Eleanor. Never take the easy way out, will you?' He tweaked her top a little more firmly into place. 'Remember your modesty,' he added and then grabbed her hand and ran her screaming and whooping into the waves.

Chapter Eight

They didn't get home until dusk and by then the household was in an uproar. Eleanor's teachers had rung – had Eleanor come home, was she sick, where was she? Clarissa had panicked and rung Charles and Charles had rung the police and by the time John and Eleanor walked in, there was near hysteria in the house.

Honório opened the door for them, his dark eyes expressionless, standing back silently so that they could see the group gathered in the hall. Eleanor stepped forward, uncertainly, her face stricken. John followed behind. The group stood there, staring at them, their loud arguments and recriminations stilled, the police officers, members of the Guarda Civil, regarding them with surprise, disapproval. One, two seconds ticked by.

Eleanor swallowed. 'Oh dear, I'm so sorry I'm late. I'm sorry if I worried you all but John's come home,' she said. No one heard it in the sudden release of that stillness, the babble of voices shouting, questioning, reprimanding, the group moving again when, a few moments before, they had been a frozen tableaux.

Her father strode forward and took Eleanor's wrist angrily in his hand, yanking her away from John. 'Where have you been? How could you just walk out of school like that? Wasn't there anyone watching you, making sure you didn't? What sort of school am I paying for? I'm going to have a word with that headmistress, and as for you, miss, where've you been? How did you meet John? What's this all about, walking out of school, not telling anyone and going off to meet John when none of us knew he was due back and letting us all sit here and worry you'd been kidnapped or worse! You're a selfish, ungrateful child! I'd never have thought it of you!'

He jerked her arm to punctuate every accusation, pulling her awkwardly over to the police. 'See, you've disturbed the peace, brought these officers all the way out here. Wasted their time. We've rung all the hospitals and all your friends, the shelters and anything else we could think of. God knows what we're going to tell them all. You'll have no reputation left if you don't watch it, you stupid, stupid girl. And all that time, you've been off having a good time. Doing what? Doing what?' His voice rose even higher.

Eleanor was crying now, her cries of 'please, Papa, please,' going unheard. She twisted away from her father, but he crushed his fingers more tightly around her wrist, pulling her back to face him. The Guarda officers were uncomfortable, tipping their caps, murmuring a few words, leaving the family to discipline its own. They gave John unpleasant looks on the way out.

Clarissa was holding John's arm, restraining him as he tried to go to Eleanor, hushing him so her husband would have time to cool his rage, reminding John of his uncle's weak heart. Isobel was leaning by the door, a slightly amused look of alarm on her face. She looked John up and down from beneath her eyelashes.

Henry was there too and he was pulling Charles away from Eleanor now, calming him down, pushing Eleanor behind him. He was only of medium height and Charles Fawcett towered over him, lunging angrily at Eleanor, trying to knock Henry out of the way but Henry was steady and firm, his voice reasonable, and finally Charles stopped

147

and stood still, glaring between Eleanor and John.

John hadn't said a word through all this, his first reaction to go to Eleanor's aid thwarted by Clarissa clutching at his arm, holding him back; then his own good sense telling him his uncle would calm down soon and that his intervention would only aggravate the situation further. He realized belatedly that Charles had every right to be angry. Keeping Eleanor out that long, after she had walked out of school, had been irresponsible and selfish. He whispered his apology to Clarissa.

Silence descended again and, in that moment of stillness, Charles Fawcett and John Campos de Serra looked into each other's eyes and John saw the implacable hate there. He paled, his face becoming taut with strain. They stared at each other for a long, slow moment until Henry placed himself between their line of vision.

John's lips were bloodless, his eyes a deep troubled blue. He cleared his throat, his voice strained, 'I'm sorry, Uncle Charles, it was thoughtless of me to keep Elly out –'

'Don't talk to me, don't you say a word!' Charles broke across John's attempted apology, his words whipping out like a broken steel hawser. John breathed in deeply and said nothing.

'Mr Fawcett, please. Come and sit down. You know what the doctors said and Eleanor's safe now. There's nothing wrong that we can't talk through quietly. Please, sir, come and sit down,' Henry tried again but Charles refused to listen to reason.

'The hell there isn't! Come into the library, Eleanor and you, you come too.' He glared at John. 'Let go of me, Henry, for God's sake, I don't need you fussing over me like I'm some invalid or something. If I want to tell my daughter what I think of her, I shall and you have nothing to do with it. So, go home.' But he said that in a quieter, less aggressive tone and Henry sighed and stood back, looking across at John with pursed lips.

Eleanor walked through into the library. She felt sick with anger and fear and guilt, her face streaked with tears.

148

Her wrist hung limply by her side, throbbing painfully.

John pushed Clarissa away gently. 'It's okay, don't worry. I'll tell him I'm sorry. I won't aggravate things, I promise,' he said placatingly. He nodded to Henry as the latter left, thanking him. Henry nodded coolly back.

Standing by the door to the library, one hand outstretched to indicate that John should go first, Charles Fawcett felt all the old foreboding come flooding back to him. He looked at John with intense bitterness.

'In. Now. Clarissa, shut up. I'll talk with you later. And you, Isobel, wipe that smirk off your face and get yourself upstairs. You have homework, don't you?' He didn't wait for an answer, but followed John into the library and shut the door firmly.

Standing there, beside Eleanor, waiting for his uncle to speak, John felt like the young boy who had once asked permission for Eleanor to visit his home. He felt diminished, sick with anxiety, a deep anger throbbing in the pit of his stomach that longed to hit out. And he felt powerless. As always.

Charles told them to sit and they felt their way into the chairs behind them, not taking their eyes from his face. He continued to stand and John silently mocked him, knowing his uncle didn't want John to stand, at equal height, and confront him. Yet another way to be put down, reduced. John's face remained impassive but inside he became increasingly cynical; nothing had changed. Certainly not how his uncle felt about him.

'Your hair, Eleanor. It's wet. What've you been doing?' Charles walked over to his daughter and stood above her, almost snatching at her hair. She looked up at him for a moment before directing her eyes at the floor.

'We went swimming,' John said harshly.

Charles swung round on him. 'I didn't ask you. I asked Eleanor. Kindly have the decency to remain quiet after all this trouble you've caused. Now, Eleanor, I want the truth.' Charles's words were icy. John bit his lip but was silent.

'It's true, Papa. I went to meet John off the boat and then

149

we caught a bus down to Copacabana and we went swimming and sat and talked and then came home. That's all. I'm sorry you were so worr—' She broke off as her father cut across her words.

'How did you know he was coming home today? Who told you that when we didn't even know?'

'I, I wrote to John and asked him and he wrote back to me with the date. If you had written to him and asked, then we could all have gone down to meet him and none of this fuss would have happened. I'm sorry I walked out of school, Papa, and I'm sorry about all the worry I put you through, but I had to meet John. That isn't such a sin, Papa! You made me go round your back because you're always so unreasonable.' Eleanor felt her courage returning, her anger at being treated so harshly flaring in her breast. She barely heard her father shouting at her, telling her she was deceitful, conniving, unfit to call herself his daughter. And as for John . . .

'It wasn't John's fault!' Eleanor shouted back. 'He didn't know I was going to skip out on school and come down and meet him. I just did it. And if anyone else in this family had cared at all about John, they'd have found out when he was coming back and been there to meet him too! You cause the problems, Papa, by making it some sort of sin to see my own cousin. Your sister's son! He should be your son now and you act as though he were a beggar boy from the favelas! No, you'd be kinder to a beggar boy. You're unfair and unkind and – beastly!' she cried and Charles felt something inside him break, a lever snap, a spring go flat. His life force went out of him. He sat down heavily on his desk.

'Enough, Eleanor. Quiet,' John said, leaning over to touch her arm and still her accusations. He watched his uncle warily, seeing the bleached colour of the skin, the unhealthy dullness in the eyes. He felt pity for his uncle for the first time in a long time.

'I'm sorry, sir. It was my fault. But all we did was go for a swim. It was thoughtless of us not to realize you would be worrying ...' John broke off, realizing Charles was not even listening.

Eleanor had faltered, her own anger dying out, becoming sour in her mouth. She felt John touch her on the arm and everything came back into focus, the ticking of the long case-clock, the evening cicadas shrilling through the open window, her father sitting silently, heavily, on the desk, his face flaccid. She stood up and went to stand beside her father.

'Papa, I'm so sorry. I know I shouldn't have left school and I really, really wish I'd called to let you know I was all right. But I didn't dare. I never wanted to upset or alarm any of you, I just wanted to see John. After four years, I thought it was only fair.' She saw her father raise a hand and wipe his face with it, scrubbing at his eyes, pushing back his forehead.

He almost laughed. 'Fair? What would you know about fair?' He looked at her dully, then across at his nephew. 'So, you came back. Why was I so sure you would? Like a great heavy weight poised on a clifftop, ready to roll down again and crush us all.' He spoke in a quiet tone, a husky, whispering voice, talking almost as though to himself. 'Oh John, why did you ever have to be born? You're my nemesis, just like your father all over again. But you won't hurt Eleanor. I won't let you kill her too.' He coughed and leaned over, holding his chest as though in pain.

'Papa? Papa! What is it? Are you in pain? Does it hurt in your chest?' Eleanor leaned down beside her father, her face and voice showing her alarm. 'Get Mama, John. Hurry!'

But Charles pushed her away from him and stood up, swaying a little. 'Why worry about me, Eleanor? You have your John. I'm the unkind, unfair beast, remember? The one who never thinks about your happiness. Let me alone!' He stood away from the desk and walked out of the room, letting the door swing shut behind him.

Henry walked down the hill to his parents' house in a dark

151

mood. He thrust his hands into his pockets, walking slowly in the velvety blackness, his feet sure on the road. His mind churned round and round. So, John was back. And, already, there was trouble. Eleanor wasn't going to turn to him anymore, she wouldn't be spending long hours reading or listening to music with him, or happily playing charades with the family. No, she would be with her cousin, the two of them a set unto themselves, complete, without need of anyone else. They would laugh and whisper together, looking blank when anyone asked to join in, dismissing them with, 'Oh, we were just remembering something. Nothing, really. It wouldn't be funny to anyone else.' And everyone else would be shut out, just like it used to be. Just them. Together.

He kicked at a stone, hearing it clatter off into the dark. What was John thinking about encouraging Eleanor to go all the way down to the docks on her own? Anything could have happened to her down there and then, then keeping her out until dark, knowing everyone would be worried! But that was John. No thought for anyone except himself. Even Eleanor had to fit in with John's plans or there was trouble. That was easy enough for John, persuading a child of fifteen to do whatever he said. She trusted John, completely. Henry kicked another stone.

It would be all right if John could just share a little more, Henry thought. After all, he and Eleanor's father got on perfectly well. There was no confrontation when he took Eleanor out for the afternoon. And why? Because he remembered to return Eleanor before too long, to share her with her family, not try and snatch her away completely. Damn John. Why did he have to ever come back?

Eleanor was aghast. How could she have raved on at her father like that? When she knew he was sick and worried and it was her fault anyway? She should never have left school to see John. It had just been pure selfishness on her part, and childishness too. Not able to wait a few extra hours and see John with the rest of the family. And now she had ruined everything, made Papa hate John all over again. How could she have done it?

'Oh John! I'm so sorry. I've spoiled everything now, haven't I? And made Papa sick again. Do you think he's all right? Should I go after him?' She turned to him, her face twisted with anguish. John shook his head, feeling his anger at Charles return. That man always had Eleanor on a rack. You don't measure up to my expectations, I'm disappointed in you, you're not fit to call yourself my daughter. The most normal, thoughtless actions of a child were turned into a major crime in this household. He wrapped his arms around Eleanor and held her against him.

He sighed, 'Try not to be too upset, Elly. He'll calm down in time. I know it was our fault but he was just looking for an excuse to hate me all over again.' He half smiled, seeing the bleached look in her face and tried to explain, 'Don't you see, you'll never really please your father unless you give up any desire to be a person yourself and let him run your life for you? He wants to choose your friends, where you spend your time, how you think, what you think about. In a few years he'll want to choose your boyfriends and your university courses. Then he'll want to choose your husband. Can't you see that?' He felt her twist away in his arms and he held her tighter still. 'And every time you try and stand up for yourself, stand up for your own wishes, he'll tell you you're a disappointment to him and then he'll clutch his heart and moan and you'll just cave in. See if you don't.'

He sounded so reasonable and Eleanor knew, deep down, that a lot of what he said was true. She felt tired now, and empty. Her wrist throbbed. She leaned against John and closed her eyes.

'I don't know what I'm supposed to do, John. I can't be two people, one for each of you. Please, can't you be just a little more giving? And I'll try and make Papa give some too.' She felt his hand stroke the side of her face, turning her chin so that she had to look up at him. He had that expression on his face that most meant John to her; it was how she saw him when she tried to picture him in her mind. His lips were folded in, his chin jutting out so that the planes of his face were accentuated, his eyes guarded and sharing both at the same time.

He nodded. 'Okay, I'll try. I always try, Eleanor. Truly.' He released her and walked away, pausing to look out the window. 'Do you think I'm welcome here now? After what he just said? His nemesis! That's a good one. What's to stop your father just throwing me out?'

'Papa wouldn't do that. He couldn't. He's your legal guardian until you're twenty-one. He has to look after you – and your money – until then.'

'Whether he likes it or not. You know, sometimes I almost feel sorry for him. Almost.' He gave a half-laugh.

'Don't, John.'

John turned savagely away so that Eleanor wouldn't see his face, wouldn't read the thoughts that raged inside him. 'Don't John.' God, he was so tired of hearing it! All she ever seemed to do was feel sorry for her father. Well, Uncle Charles was the one doing all of this, making their lives a misery. Four years he had spent in exile! For what? Nothing had changed; he had seen that in his uncle's face. And now it's all his fault again? Because he had the temerity to return to his home! His mother must have been as mad as his father to make Uncle Charles his guardian. Put a narrow-minded bigot like that into a position of power over him, knowing Charles hated him, had always hated him from the moment he first came there? Jesus, didn't Eleanor realize he would walk away from it all if he could?

He turned back to her and said angrily, 'You have to realize, Elly, that I don't have any choice here. I'm stuck with your father. He's got the power over me and he's using it. I have no money and no way of earning any unless I give up all plans for university and I don't see why he should rob me of that. It's my parents' money. He has no right to it, and no right to sit in judgement over me.' He stopped, looking up to see Clarissa standing in the doorway, her hand still resting on the knob. He closed his mouth with a sharp snap.

'I wish your parents had chosen someone else too, John. But they didn't,' Clarissa said into the ringing silence. 'And that's just the way it is. For another three years you will have to do as my husband says. It isn't fair perhaps, but then,' she smiled ruefully, 'as you well know, life isn't fair. We all just have to muddle along as best we can and deal with it as it comes. You can rant against the unfairness of it all until you're blue in the face – or until your uncle is blue, which seems more likely. But it won't change anything. So get a hold of yourself, John, and you too, Eleanor, and remember whose house you are living in. Until you can pay for yourselves, you will do as he says. And I will make sure of that. Understood?' She waited until she saw them both nod, John's a mere sketch of head movement. She breathed in.

Perhaps John and Eleanor were right. Charles was unfair and unreasonable. But it was because he loved Eleanor, worried about her. And most of all he worried about John hurting her; he identified John, in some strange way, with his father, Michael Campos. He didn't want to lose her the way he lost his sister. It was illogical, foolish even, but what could you say against such an irrational fear? Charles was scared silly. She could see it in his eyes.

'Good,' Clarissa said firmly. 'Now then, your father is unwell, Eleanor, and I don't want him being upset again. I won't say anything more about this evening. I think enough has been said already. John, you may stay in your old room until university starts and I would appreciate it if you could find things to occupy yourself out of the house as much as possible when your uncle is home. Either that, or remember to agree with whatever your uncle says.' She gave him a quick smile.

'Your school report and exam results have arrived already. I meant to tell you earlier but there was no chance. Charles said you did very well and that you will have no problem entering university. In São Paulo, I hope?' she

155

added more kindly, her voice becoming softer and more recognizable.

John nodded. 'Yes, I think it'd be better. I hear Louis is going down too?' He forced himself to sound natural.

Clarissa smiled, acknowledging the effort. 'Yes, that's right. So you can both go together. That'll be nice for you. Eleanor dear, you look quite sick yourself. Why don't you go upstairs and wash your face? Maria kept some dinner for you in the Little Room. I'd like to talk with John for a while, if you don't mind?'

Eleanor wiped her hands on her uniform, feeling them sticky with perspiration. She wanted to be sick. The way her father had rounded on her, throwing out so much anger. And then John. It wasn't like a normal fight, squabbling over something silly like who was going to have the shell they had found on the beach. This was something different altogether. A dark side to him she had never seen before.

She nodded. 'All right, Mama. I do feel a bit – odd. I'll see you both later.' She walked past her mother, hearing the door click into place behind her.

Isobel was waiting for her upstairs, darting out of her bedroom to follow Eleanor, shutting the bathroom door carefully after them. Eleanor could see the enjoyment on Isobel's face. A drama, a scene in the house and Eleanor was the villain of the piece. What a change!

'What is it, Isobel?' she asked in a flat voice. She ran some water in the basin, seeing Isobel in the mirror sitting herself down on the side of the bath. The water gurgled and coughed from the taps, as antiquated as the palácio itself.

'Where did you go? You and John? Everyone's been frantic, but I couldn't say anything.' She looked defensive. 'I told you I wouldn't!' She relaxed when Eleanor shrugged and looked away. 'Did you meet him off the ship? Was it fun?' Isobel was as excited as Eleanor had ever seen her, and as friendly, despite what she had said that morning about not approving. As long as Isobel wasn't in trouble, this was something she admired.

'Yes, I told you I would,' Eleanor admitted. But had she

156

known ... no, she would never have done it. She plunged her hands into the warm water, rolling the soap over and over between her hands. 'I skipped out just before lunch, so it would take them longer to figure out I was missing. And I just caught a bus. Well, two buses. It was quite easy.' And it had been, she thought with surprise. So very easy.

'And then what? You met John and went where?'

'Well, I caught him at the Praça Mauá just as he was getting on a bus so I felt like I spent hours just travelling up and down on buses. We went down to Copacabana and John,' she smiled painfully at the memory, 'John went and bought us bathing suits so we could go swimming. And that's all we did, swim and sit on the beach and talk.'

'No! Let's see. What's yours like?' Isobel, as usual, was more concerned in the design of the clothing rather than anything else.

Eleanor laughed, knowing Isobel wouldn't know why. 'Here. You can have it if you want. It's not really me.' She pulled the bikini out of her pocket, tossing it over to Isobel.

'A bikini! You went out on Copacabana in a bikini!' There was strong admiration in Isobel's voice now and Eleanor began to wonder if her own values weren't all topsy-turvy. Both John and Isobel thought what had happened this afternoon was perfectly fine, if a little thoughtless. Maybe it was. Maybe it was nothing more than the age-old problem of youth versus parents and nothing to do with her father and John at all. The thought was a vast relief.

'Can I really have it? Oh, it's gorgeous! I must try it on.' Isobel began pulling off her clothes and Eleanor, really amused at last, sat and watched.

Down in the library, Clarissa invited John to help himself to a drink from the tray in the corner and to fix one for herself. She watched him unaware.

'Quite a homecoming, wasn't it?' she said after a few moments, liking the way he had grown up, wishing Charles did too. John brought the drinks over to her, sitting down opposite. He slouched in the chair, his long legs stretched out in front of him, one crossed over the other. He looked at her and raised his drink.

'Quite.' He was silent a moment. 'I hope you know how very sorry I am.' He paused again. 'To you, Aunt Clarissa. Thank you.' He took a long swig of the drink, gin and tonic, vodka? Clarissa wasn't sure what. He drank it as though he were used to it.

She shrugged. 'For what?'

'Oh, for everything. Writing to me and letting me know I wasn't forgotten, encouraging Eleanor to keep on writing, not letting me go tonight, when I might have done something stupid – more stupid, shall I say? Which I really wanted to do when Uncle Charles hauled Eleanor off like that. Lots of things.' He smiled and she was struck anew at how beautiful and charming – how compelling – he could be. It was a potent force, hitting her full in the face. No wonder poor Eleanor had no defence against him. If she, herself, were only a few years younger ... She blinked the thought away guiltily.

'Eleanor's still very much a child, John. You're grown-up now and you're a man. Two things that make it impossible for you to do what you did today with Eleanor again. If you can't see that, then you're not as intelligent as I always thought you were.' She took a sip of her drink, eyeing him over the rim of the glass.

John glanced at her and then looked away. He looked tired. 'I'm her cousin, Aunt Clarissa. Her first cousin. That makes me her primo-irmão.' It was a Brazilian term he used, denoting a special relationship that existed between cousins. He was Eleanor's cousin-brother. She was his cousin-sister, his prima-irma.

Clarissa understood instantly what he was saying. 'And you think I'm accusing you of something indecent? No, John, I'm not. I'm talking appearances, reputation. Take Eleanor to the beach during the afternoon, fine, no problem. Take Isobel too, as long as it isn't a school day. But don't take them out of school like you did Eleanor today and please have them back before it gets dark and people, unkind people, begin to wag their tongues.'

She took a deeper pull at her drink, wishing this was easier. 'I hope also, when Eleanor is older, you'll remember what you said to me today. You are almost brother and sister. By the Church's teachings – the Catholic Church and this is, after all, a Catholic country – you are disbarred from marriage. The blood is too close. I hope you and Eleanor understand that and can deal with it later on.' Because I'm not sure you can, she added silently to herself. She watched John's eyes. No, he wasn't sure either.

'I won't ever hurt Eleanor,' he said after a few moments. He was considering her words, fencing, trying to find a way to ease her mind without committing himself either way. In England first cousins could marry. Not Catholics except in unusual cases, of course, but in the Church of England. It wasn't all that usual, but it was quite acceptable. And anyway, he didn't need marriage to make how he felt about Eleanor acceptable. Why should he worry about other people's conventions? He remembered someone saying that to him once before, now who was it? It flickered in his memory and then slipped away as his aunt began to speak again.

'Good. I was hoping I could count on you, John. You're young men now, you and Louis. You should be going out together in the evenings, having fun, dancing and flirting with girls of your own age. Not with a child. And no matter how grown-up Eleanor can look and how intelligent she sounds, she is still a fifteen-year-old child.'

Her tone changed, became encouraging, light-hearted. 'Why don't you call Louis tonight? Let him know you're back, go out and have a drink with him. I'll give you some money, shall I?' And before John could protest, Clarissa was pushing a folded roll of money into his hand, pulling the telephone over to him. She steamrollered him along and John gave way before her, his eyes glinting amusement and admiration. Aunt Clarissa was quite something. He had just never realized before.

He arranged to meet Louis in the bar at the Copacabana

Palace Hotel, one of the best and oldest hotels in that particularly élite strip of town. This was going to be a celebration. And his aunt had given him enough to celebrate in style. He showered and changed into a dark jacket and tie with lighter trousers, pocketing the keys to his aunt's car with a pleased and surprised smile. He kissed his aunt on the cheek and told her to say goodnight to Eleanor and Isobel. And then he took off into the night with a roar to the engine that could be heard all the way upstairs in Charles Fawcett's bedroom. Charles could be heard shouting for some time.

Eleanor rinsed off her face and brushed her hair back more neatly, feeling the salt in it still. She would have to wash it before school tomorrow. But oh, it had been such a glorious afternoon. So light-hearted and happy, both of them lying on the sand near the water's edge so they weren't coated in the fine white sand further up, feeling the waves licking at their legs, the sun intense on their skin. Lying in the sun always made her feel languorous and content, like a sleepy cat. And John had been at his best. He hadn't once quarrelled with her or made her feel like a baby. He had just entertained her with his comments about other people on the beach or Cousin Max and Winchester. He even talked a little about school and about Nick.

And she had told him everything, all the scandals of the last four years and the political changes, the funny things that had happened to her, the way Isobel annoyed her and yet could still be good company. They had laid themselves open to each other, keeping very little back. Just the odd hesitation, the quickened pace of a conversation sometimes hinted at an unexplored area. They both had wondered at that. Then they had come home and it had all been destroyed, flattened by Papa. She shook her head, staring at herself in the mirror. She wasn't the deceitful one. Papa was. Making out he wanted John to come back and that the separation had been for John's good. All lies! She flung her hair back angrily.

Eleanor called to Isobel that she was going down for some dinner but Isobel was absorbed in pulling things out of her cupboard to see what went best with the bikini. Eleanor waited for a moment but when no reply came she ran downstairs.

Maria was waiting for her in the Little Room, waiting patiently for Eleanor to sit down so that she could be served. There was curiosity in the woman's eyes, dark and beadily watching everything that Eleanor did. Watching and taking note, to discuss later with the other servants. Eleanor sat up straighter. 'Leave it there, Maria. I'll serve myself, thank you. It's late and I know you'll be wanting to clean up the kitchen.' She dismissed the woman who turned away disappointed. There was little to learn there.

Eleanor had no appetite despite the long day. How could anyone eat after all that shouting and crying? She spooned her food around the plate and wondered how long Mama would be with John. What were they discussing? She felt herself grow hot at the thought, blanking out the internal monologue that told her exactly what they were discussing. She bit into a roll instead.

Outside, in the forecourt, one of the cars roared into life, its engine being revved in a way that no one in the house ever did, tyres squealing out of the sharp bend where the gate led on to the roadway and dying out as the car disappeared into the night. Eleanor sat still in surprise. Upstairs, she could hear her father yelling something and then, slowly, as though she were in no hurry to get to him, Eleanor heard her mother's footsteps going up the stairs. Who had that been?

And then, of course, she realized it had been John and she ran out into the hallway and called softly up to her mother.

'Mama? Where's John gone? He hasn't gone away again, has he?' Her hands clutched the banister, slippery with fear.

But her mother leaned down and smiled, shaking her head, putting a finger to her mouth. 'To meet Louis,' she mouthed and then waved her hand, palm down, to tell

161

Eleanor to be quiet, to wait. Clarissa disappeared from the railing and Eleanor sighed and wandered back into the Little Room. She seated herself absently, one leg drawn up under the other and scooped a finger through the cream bowl. Why hadn't John come to tell her where he was going? Why was he going out so late, anyway? Then she realized, with a start, that John and Louis were grown-up now, just like her parents, and they could go out late if they wanted. While she had to sit in and do her homework and go to bed. The thought annoyed her intensely.

'Well, I'll just have to grow up faster, that's all,' she said firmly to the salt cellar and stood up, pushing her chair away from the table. It was no good. She couldn't eat any of her dinner, particularly not when John was out there in the night somewhere having a good time with Louis and probably, if Louis had anything to do with it, a couple of girls. Horrible, stupid, painted girls who tittered over their drinks and flashed their eyelashes and had big ... She stopped her train of thought abruptly and threw down her napkin.

'Who cares?' she added crossly and then ran upstairs to her bedroom, pulled off her clothes and climbed, still salty, into bed. When her mother came to see her, she was already asleep. Clarissa turned off the light and gently closed the door.

Chapter Nine

John liked his aunt's car. It was an Austin Healey, the top folded down flat behind his seat so the wind riffled through his hair as he drove down the steeply winding roads. It was quite different from what he had imagined her driving. But then, she was quite different too. Maybe now that he was older, he was only just realizing how young she still was, only somewhere in her mid-thirties, he guessed. And fun with it. He remembered the way she had used to spoil them all when they were little, and he had never thought that behind that softness and indulgence was someone desperate to just enjoy life, to kick up her heels in defiance of her husband. How on earth had someone like Clarissa ever married a mouldy old fellow like Charles?

And how had Charles come to buy such a great car for his wife? It was not what he would have expected at all.

The thought came to him, unbidden and instantly dismissed, that perhaps he was underrating his aunt and uncle, especially his uncle. But then the lights of Copacabana reached out to him and he forgot everything else except the joy of being young and temporarily rich and in possession of a wonderful sports car. He hit the Avenida Atlântica, feeling the wind from the sea snap and pull at his shirt, blowing through his hair as he cruised down the waterfront, eyeing the girls who turned to smile at him. God, it was good to be back!

He parked neatly in front of the Copacabana Palace, fitting himself in behind a much larger Packard with no room to spare. He gunned the motor ostentatiously before killing the engine. All around him the rhythm of the night pulsed in the air, strains of music from a dozen bars, chattering voices, loud whistles from a porter trying to signal a taxi for some waiting guests. John pocketed his keys and walked along the street, his confident stride denying the flutter of his mind. He wondered for the first time whether it had been such a good idea meeting Louis here. What did he know about big hotels and ritzy bars? He'd never been in one in his life.

But then he was through the doors, across the imposing marble-floored lobby and angling into the bar Louis had chosen. Louis was there already, sitting in the half-gloom at a corner table, his dark good looks appropriate and at home in the setting. John waved briefly and made his way through the tight knot of people standing by the door, dodging between tables, shaking his head at a woman who smiled and patted a spare seat beside her. He reached Louis, who was standing now, and the two of them shook hands and hit each other eagerly on the back at the same time, old friends reunited.

'Johnny! Hey, it's wonderful to see you. You're looking great. About another foot taller but still great.' Louis was no more than five foot ten in height, a more solid body beneath the well-tailored clothes, a broad chest filling his jacket smoothly. He looked older too, by several years. When he snapped his fingers, a waiter appeared immediately.

'What'll you have? Hey, this is a celebration. What about some champagne? Yeah, let's have some champagne!' There was almost an American drawl to his accent now, his actions assured and casual. He sat back and smiled at John broadly, noting the similarities, the differences to the John he had known.

'It's good to see you, Louis. You come into a lot of money suddenly, by any chance? Or are you always such a playboy?' John grinned, sitting down opposite Louis, his legs cramped under the low table. He looked around at the discreet table settings, the darkened lights, the tiny dance floor over in the other direction where he saw a single couple trying, unsuccessfully, to tango. Good-looking people, well dressed, the girl having a terrible time. He looked back at Louis.

'I came into an inheritance,' Louis joked and they both knew what he meant. His parents were very rich and very doting. Louis didn't have to wait to inherit. 'So, let's have it. What happened tonight when you finally got home?' He grinned when he saw John's expression and he didn't stop grinning all the way through the tale, only stopping to smack his thigh and laugh all the harder when John told him how Eleanor had yelled right back at her father. By the time the tale was told, John was beginning to think it as funny as Louis, and the first glass of champagne that they both tossed down, was beginning to reinforce the hilarity.

They sat for over an hour drinking steadily, swapping tales about the last four years, and settling back into their old friendship, in a slightly altered fashion. John was no longer the leader, nor exactly a follower either. They both recognized each other as equals now and their conversation subtly shifted to give each other equal footing. It was interesting, John thought, through his haze of champagne bubbles and then he forgot about it as he glanced back and caught sight of the girl from the boat.

She was standing tentatively near the door, flanked by her parents, looking averagely pretty and averagely desirable but, to John in his state, like a Venus stepping from the sea. He stood up abruptly.

'What's up, Johnny-boy? You spotted someone?' Louis called casually. He was eyeing a dark and neat little dancer, smiling when she tossed her head and pouted at him from over her partner's shoulder. He smiled and she gave him a pert smile back.

165

'Uh, yes, back in a second. Order another bottle, will you?' John muttered and took a few steps, feeling the champagne hitting him in the knees and the room sliding just for a moment. It resettled itself and by then he found himself standing beside the girl, bending over her, taking her hand.

Lydia was taken aback. She hadn't seen John approach and, after his abrupt departure earlier in the day, she wouldn't have expected him to come over to her anyway, even if she had seen him. But he was clearly drunk. Her parents were eyeing him with disfavour, trying to draw her to one side, away from the fair-haired stranger they now saw accosting her daughter.

Lydia patted her mother's arm. 'It's all right, Mummy. This is John, from the ship. You remember – he pointed out all the sights to me this morning. He and I are friends, aren't we, John?' She knew she could ask John anything and he would agree with her. It was there in the blankness of his gaze, the smile fixed on his face. She went on, 'John Campos de Serra – my parents, the Forresters. See, Mummy, now I've met a friend, you don't have to stay with me. I'll come up in an hour or so, all right?'

Her parents were tired and they hadn't wanted to come into the nightclub at all except that Lydia had begged for just one drink and they had, after all, come all this way to please her in the first place. Such an exotic place, Rio, and so full of good-looking young people having such a wonderful time. It did seem a terrible shame for Lydia to be stuck with old fogeys when she already knew a nice young man from the ship, her mother thought uneasily. And they were so tired and did so want to go to bed. Maybe they could leave Lydia – just for an hour – with this young man?

Lydia saw the thought process going on in her mother's face. Her father didn't care. All he wanted was his bed and Lydia had always been her mother's concern. He stepped towards the door and Lydia stepped back towards John and, before her mother knew what was happening, there was already a gap between the two groups that other people had surged into and then Lydia's hand was raised in farewell. She disappeared into the throng of people with that tall, fair-haired chap and her mother sighed and gave in.

John led Lydia back to his table, wondering even as he did, what had possessed him to go up to her in the first place. She had lost that star-like glow to her the minute he had looked down into her face and seen the determination behind that shy, ingénue look. Lydia's eyes looked back at him, seeing the hesitation, ignoring it. He cursed himself, feeling a sour taste curl at his tongue. What had he done? He was drunk, yes, but not normally this thick-headed with it. And he hadn't liked her parents either, dull, bourgeois sorts. He grinned to himself at that. Bourgeois. My, aren't we being discerning tonight? But Lydia had mistaken his grin for one of encouragement and she was sitting down very close to him now, her knee against his thigh. John let it sit there, warm and rounded. He glanced over at Louis.

'Lydia – Lydia, what?' He frowned. 'Oh yes, Forrester. This is my oldest friend, Louis Preston. You'll like him. He's totally English. No Brazilian names at all.' John poured another glass of champagne down his throat and then leaned in to Lydia, close, so that he was almost touching her.

'You want some champagne?' he asked, his eyes just slightly unfocused. Lydia hesitated, smiled, nodded, yes, yes she did. She saw Louis pour her out a glass and peer at her with a hungry look, his eyes darting between her and someone out there on the dance floor. Lydia craned to see who it was. John had pulled back now and was making no effort at conversation so Lydia took a deep breath and tried harder still.

'Do you come here often?' she asked. John mumbled something that she couldn't hear but Louis smiled, giving her his full attention. The girl on the dance floor had disappeared and he concentrated now on the bird in hand. Not bad really, he thought. A little heavy and dowdily dressed but the skin was nice and clear and the face seemed pleasant. Pretty, sandy coloured hair. He watched when she leaned back in her chair, the fabric of her dress pressing tightly over her breasts. No, not bad at all.

'I come here all the time, here or one of about two dozen other places. But then, I like to go out and have a good time.' Louis edged his hand nearer hers on the table. He glanced at John. 'But John here has only just come home – after four years away at school in England – so we're making up for all his lost time. Tonight's a celebration.' He kicked John under the table, wondering if the fellow wanted this girl or not. He wasn't making much effort if he did.

John raised his head and looked casually at Louis. What, for God's sake? He saw Louis flicker his eyes over to Lydia and back again. A finger crooked towards Louis's chest. Yes, can I? John darted a look at Lydia, seeing her smile at him, her knee pressing more firmly now, her foot playing with his. He smiled uneasily and looked away. Shrugged.

'Which school were you at, John? Eton?' Lydia was probing now, trying to get a grip on the conversation and turn it the way she wanted. She saw John shake his head.

'Wykham,' he said and she opened her eyes wide.

'Oh, you're Catholic then?' John read the disappointment, the slight reserve. Lydia didn't want to get mixed up with someone who wasn't good husband material. And her parents would never take to a Catholic. They were as Low Church as you could get. She sighed, easing her knee away a little.

'Nearly everyone in Brazil is Catholic, Lydia,' Louis said smoothly. 'Except, of course, for me. I am Protestant, like my parents. And you are too, aren't you?' Louis, seeing his main chance, put himself forward. He grinned at John and dropped a sly wink.

'Oh, my, yes. Didn't you go to school in England, Louis? I'd have thought you would have, being English.' Lydia, probing again, in a different direction.

'No, no. My family like it out here. This is where I belong. Where John belongs too, if his uncle would only see that,' Louis added and saw, out of the corner of his eye,

John getting up, going to the bar. 'It was rather tragic,' he lowered his voice confidentially, bring his face closer to Lydia's. 'Oh, here, have some more champagne. We have masses to drink still. John's parents were both – killed – in rather terrible circumstances. Out in the Mato Grosso, a very wild area of the Backlands, and John's uncle was made his guardian but,' Louis sighed impressively, 'they hate each other and John was sent away to England to school. He only just returned.'

'With me – on the ship. We travelled out together,' Lydia said excitedly. She had known there was a reason for John's reserve, his look of distraction, sadness. Of course, this explained it all.

'Out here we have an expression for the emotion John is feeling, a weariness of the soul – we call it "saudade". Melancholy, sad, the weight of the world upon his shoulders. Touched by tragedy. It means many things. I can't explain it in English.' Louis had become purposely foreign in his speech, exotic, different. Lydia gazed at him raptly.

Louis looked up and saw John standing at the bar talking with some other fellow. He looked occupied, content to let things move as they would at the table he had left behind. Louis had sensed John's detachment where Lydia was concerned, almost dislike or contempt. It was odd. She wasn't too bad. Louis smiled and pressed his foot against Lydia's. 'And,' he added, delivering the *coup de grâce*, 'John is in love with his cousin. It's very sad really, because there's no hope there. They can't marry.' He drank a sip of his champagne, filled Lydia's glass some more.

'Is she tall and blonde? About sixteen or so?' Lydia asked, trying not to feel the disappointment coursing through her. What did John matter to her anyway? But she couldn't quite shrug off the smart, the jealousy.

'Yes, that's right. You've seen Eleanor? Oh, yes, that's right. She went to meet John today so you probably saw her there when the boat docked. Quite a beauty, isn't she? Fifteen. And the apple of her daddy's eye. John's uncle.'

'And John's in love with a fifteen-year-old?' There was

shock and disapproval – and yes, still jealousy there. It made it all the worse really. She drank her glass down and felt quite light-headed.

'Oh, he doesn't really know he is. But there's never been anyone else for him.' Louis stopped playing the game for a moment, eyeing his friend with affection and worry as he leaned against the bar. "There's going to be one hell of a problem in a few years. John's waiting for Eleanor to grow up; her father's trying to keep her a child. There's going to be a reckoning and I don't know who's going to end up paying.' He looked at Lydia, seeing her disapproving expression with a tinge of impatience. 'I expect it will be Eleanor.'

When they both looked at the bar again, John was gone.

John drove home at a wild and reckless pace, the wind ripping at him as though it would blow right through him, blow the smoke fumes and the alcohol right out of his body, purge him of the night. The car responded well to his throwing it around the bends and curves that led up to the palácio, gripping the road no matter how much he thought it would slide out from under him, slide out towards the twinkling lights in the blackness below him. He drove with a concentrated ferocity, trying not to think.

Lydia was forgotten, as she had been moments after he left the table. Louis could have her, he was welcome to her. He wanted nothing to do with the Lydias of this world. He slowed down as he approached the final bend, seeing the palácio walls begin and following them around, the car barely moving now, its engine throbbing low and quiet. The gateway came up and he slid the car through the opening, rolling gently to a stop. One of the servants, Fernando, was sleeping on the doorstep, his body curled into its low cot as though to bar entry to the house. John stepped over him quietly and closed the massive front doors behind him.

The lights were off in the house except for a lamp in the hallway, near the stairs. Maria had forgotten that, or

170

perhaps it had been left especially for him. He clicked it off as he passed it, the hallway falling into sudden darkness, only a few panes of moonlight silvering the floor. There was no need for light. John knew where he was going. He climbed the stairs swiftly and padded down the long passageways, his feet silent on the tiled floor.

Eleanor woke with a start, feeling something shake the bed, someone breathing in the dark beside her. She lay perfectly still, her heart hammering in her chest, her throat twisted at an angle, listening. The person was lying down now beside her, sighing and in that sigh she recognized her intruder and she turned to him with relief.

'John? It's very late. Have you only just got home?' She put out her hand, touching bare skin. She hesitated and withdrew her hand.

'Yes. Can I sleep here? You don't mind, do you?' His speech was blurred, mumbled. He lay his head beside hers, his breath on his cheek. She could feel him pressing against her, the warmth of his body coming through her nightdress. She smelled cigarette smoke and alcohol mixed with his aftershave and she reached out and touched his side, flinching back when she realized he wasn't wearing anything at all. He is drunk, she thought in surprise.

'Yes, you can stay here,' she whispered, pleased and touched that he had come to her – and excited in a strange, breathless way. She tried to stare into the dark, to make out his face lying on the pillow beside hers, but it was too dark. An arm suddenly encircled her and pulled her tightly against him, the hand spread out to press into the small of her back, pressing her against him. She didn't try to struggle or push him away. There had never been any such thought in her mind. Instead, she lay relaxed against him, savouring the feel of his body, the warmth of it burning through the cotton.

When he pressed his lips against the side of her neck, opening his mouth to taste the soft salty skin of her throat, his breath heated where it lay trapped, she gasped softly, feeling a tremor run through her. He pushed her back

171

against the pillow, searching with his mouth for the long sweep of her throat down to her breasts, unbuttoning, pushing away the fabric that blocked his passage. Eleanor felt his fingers travel lightly over her nipples, tightening them in a shiver as he pushed her nightdress away, down, trapping her arms as his mouth roamed lower.

She knew she should push him away, call out, but something torpid and heavy lay across her mind, the very night air she breathed seemed filled with the languor of drugged dreams. These were her dreams. And in them, John was always there.

She lay still and relaxed, letting him taste the skin in the hollow of her throat and lower, to her breasts and she opened her mouth in a silent exclamation at the exquisite pleasure that touch provoked; his tongue was warm as he sucked quickly and then pulled away, her wet nipples chilling in the cooler night air, standing fiercely erect. There was a scent to the night air, salt and smoke, alcohol and the warm, male skin of him.

He roamed with his hands, flat and hard against her ribs, down over her stomach, grasping her sides between thumb and fingers with strong, sure movements so that a deep shudder went through her, shaking her. And then he lay his cheek against her breasts, holding her tightly and she encircled him with her own arms. He murmured something and she only knew what some minutes later. Her name.

She called to him softly, 'John, John?' but there was no response. When, after a long time, he didn't move, she realized he had fallen asleep against her, his head pressing heavily against her breasts. His breathing was loud in the stillness of the dark.

She lay like that for hours, stroking his hair, his cheeks, holding him tightly to her, wishing he could always be there beside her. For the first time since she was a child, she felt totally safe, totally loved. And then, before dawn, she reluctantly eased herself from beneath him and refastened her nightdress, curling into his side to sleep. When she woke, John had left.

172

Chapter Ten

Friday morning meant school. Eleanor climbed, heavy with tiredness, out of bed and stumbled into the bathroom. Isobel was already in there, washed and dressed and brushing her teeth. She stared at Eleanor, seeing the lids over her eyes half-lowered.

'You'll be late. I'm not going to be late just because you didn't wake up on time. Mama will have to run you down, because I'm leaving in fifteen minutes and Honório hates waiting. Why're you so tired? You went to bed before me,' she pointed out and Eleanor felt a moment's fright. Had she heard anything? Their bedrooms were right next to each other. But no, the walls were thick and anyway, there was no hint of suspicion in Isobel's eyes. Just impatience.

Eleanor sighed. There were dark rings under her eyes and she looked unhappy. Isobel assumed she was worrying about the trouble that awaited her at school. She wasn't surprised when Eleanor said slowly, 'I don't feel very well. Maybe I'm coming down with something?' Isobel yawned and lifted her hair from around her neck, tying it up neatly into a long plait. 'Well, don't think you can get out of school again today. Papa will never allow it. I'd hurry up if I were you or you'll be in even more trouble.' Isobel put her toothbrush back in the mug and wiped her face on the towel. 'Where did John go last night?'

Isobel didn't see Eleanor's flush, or the way she had to look down, as though searching for her own toothbrush. She just saw a careless shrug. 'Out somewhere with Louis, I think. You better ask Mama. And go away now and let me get ready. I can't get ready if you keep asking me questions.' Eleanor covered her embarrassment with irritation and Isobel gave her a squinty frown and left, her footsteps heavy as she receded down the passage. Eleanor leaned over the basin and splashed cold water on her face.

Oh, now what was she supposed to do? She couldn't face John at breakfast – or ever again. Why hadn't she stopped him? Why let him kiss her, touch her like that? They had no business ever touching each other, especially not after the terrible scene last night. It was so very stupid of her that she almost couldn't believe it had happened. Perhaps she had dreamed it all? Perhaps he had never been in her bed, never ... But she couldn't think of it without feeling guilt and revulsion – and a deep pang of longing – and she had to lean over the basin, staring at her pale face in the mirror. They were first cousins!

She felt genuinely sick at the thought and it didn't take much more to convince herself that she really was sick, her brow breaking out in fine perspiration, the colour fading from her cheeks. Her wrist hurt too from where Papa had squeezed it so tightly. In fact, it looked terrible. Swollen and black. She held it up and stared at it. Why hadn't she noticed it until now?

'Eleanor? Are you coming down? You won't have time for breakfast if you don't hurry.' That was Mama calling. Eleanor wondered whether Isobel would be able to resist adding her mite, telling the news that Eleanor had woken up late and said she was feeling sick so she wouldn't have to go to school. She waited and yes, sure enough, there were her mother's footsteps running up the stairs, coming down the passage towards the bathroom. Eleanor leaned over the basin, stuck two fingers down her throat, and retched.

*

By the time Isobel left for school, Eleanor was back in bed and the doctor was on the way. She had protested the need for a doctor but her mother was insistent and Eleanor didn't care enough to fight it. She lay back against the pillows and tried to smile at her mother but it was a wan effort.

'My wrist isn't broken, is it?' She knew it wasn't but it never hurt to give the impression it might be, something to explain the way she looked, the way she was behaving. It certainly hurt anyway and even simple actions were giving her pain. Simple actions like arranging her nightdress tightly around her neck. She felt a silly, choked desire to cry and had to blink back the tears so that her mother wouldn't see.

'No, of course it isn't. Just bruised or maybe sprained. You just lie still and I'll go get some aspirin. But you did bring it on yourself, you know.' Clarissa sniffed but Eleanor heard her mother muttering to herself, 'Honestly, Charles! He always has to overdo things', as she disappeared down the passageway to her own bedroom for the aspirin. Eleanor buried her face in the pillow. It still smelt faintly of John. For a moment she nearly threw the pillow out of the bed, as far away from her as possible. And then she hugged it to herself instead, staring hollow-eyed at the wall.

Papa had already left for the office. He always left early and this morning, Eleanor thought, especially early. Perhaps he didn't want to see John? Or her? She touched her throat nervously, fingering the buttons. That must never happen again – not ever. Nothing must ever happen between them. He was her primo-irmão! She sighed, from deep within her chest, as though to force more air into her lungs. To clear the suffocated feeling she had. She wondered what John would say to her when she saw him next, the embarrassment, the shock of those few hours of intimacy, lying between them forever more. The thought made her cry.

*

But Eleanor didn't see John again for some time. He had already left the palácio before anyone awoke, walking silently down to the bus-stop in the early morning light and standing with all the workers who rose early every morning to go and tend some rich person's children or house or garden. He shrugged the collar of his dark blue woollen peacoat up over his neck where the cool morning air nipped in at his ears and he nodded to the greetings that were offered.

He didn't want to stay in his Uncle's house until January, when the new year would start at university. And he didn't really want to spend every evening with Louis drinking and carousing around the bars of Copacabana or Ipanema. He would get a job instead. Somewhere outside of Rio. Just for a few months.

He didn't think, just so I don't have to lie in bed at night sweating at the thought of Eleanor only a few feet away in her room. He didn't have to. He knew that deep in his belly and had known for some time. But she was still too young and he would have to go away.

He was uneasy about what had happened last night. So much champagne, so much exhaustion from the turmoil earlier, had left him with no recollection of how he had come to be in her bed. She had been asleep, curled up beside him, and hadn't woken when he slipped from her bed, dressed and left. But now he was worried. What had he been doing in there? Had anything happened? But no, surely not, with Eleanor so peacefully asleep, her nightdress chastely around her. There was nothing to worry about there.

The bus arrived, billowing diesel fumes and John waited patiently behind an old woman with a large bundle of washing. She was coarse featured, her hands twisted into claws from years of washing and scrubbing. John lifted the washing for her and carried it up, on to the bus, depositing it with a brief nod on a seat. The old woman ignored him,

176

sitting heavily in the next seat and searching for something in her pocket. John looked at her without expression. Then he went up to the back of the bus and sat, hunched over, his feet up on the back of the seat in front of him, staring out at the morning.

What sort of job could he get? Something manual, a labourer's job? It would have to be out of Rio. His uncle would never forgive him if he disgraced them by working as a labourer in Rio. Besides, he wanted to get out, get away, where none of them could find him for a few weeks, a couple of months. Not even Eleanor. He felt again a strange uneasiness, a compulsion not to think about her too deeply, not to think about last night, that unnerved him.

He could hire out on a tramp steamer, some old freighter plying up and down the coast. Or maybe along some of the inland waterways, the Paraná even? Earn some money, see a bit of the other side of Brazil – that would always help if he decided to read anthropology – have a bit of fun that didn't involve middle-class English girls looking for husbands or chic nightclubs where every drink cost more than most of these people's weekly earnings. He looked around the bus, seeing the weathered faces, the set expressions. They knew what life was about.

He could write to his uncle, asking permission to enrol at the University of São Paulo. Louis could take care of all the rest of it. He had said so last night, before the champagne had got to both of them and before Lydia had joined them. Idly, John wondered what had happened there. But he didn't really care. He sat back in his seat and nodded off to sleep.

The old woman woke him, halfway along the Avenida Rio Branco, jabbing her knuckles into his arm with force. He blinked and sat up and stared around him. Shops and theatres, businesses and sidewalk cafés lined the sides of the road, all closed up, their fronts metal-shuttered and chained. Down the middle of the street was a row of trees with taxis lined up under them, their drivers asleep still at their wheels. Pieces of paper, food, refuse, blew along the

177

gutters, waiting for the street cleaners. For a moment John was lost and then he oriented himself, his face dropping back into the bored, heavy-lidded look it had acquired just lately. The old woman waited and he grinned reluctantly and dipped into his pocket, placing a few coins in her calloused palm. She waddled back down the bus, hissing to herself, a small grin twitching at her cheek.

John yawned. It was cold and he felt in need of a cup of coffee and a sticky roll. He hunched himself into his peacoat and stood up, swaying easily toward the doors. The bus stopped and he stepped off, glancing to left and right. Everything was still shut.

He leaned against a wall, one leg crossed over the other, his bag slung over his shoulder and lit a cigarette. He could wait.

Dr da Silva was gentle when he examined Eleanor's wrist. He could see the tear stains on her face, even though they were dry now, and there was something in the dark shadows under the girl's eyes that made him more tender than he would have been otherwise. He knew Charles Fawcett's temper. And while he couldn't blame the father for his worry, he also pitied the child.

'Well, Eleanor, I think we have a bad sprain here. Your wrists are weak anyway, you know that. I think we'll have to bandage it and keep it very still for a while. A week, maybe two. Can you do that?' He smiled encouragingly and saw the girl nod, her eyes sliding away from his. Natural really, for her to be embarrassed. She had been disobedient and her father had been angry with her. Perhaps too angry, Dr da Silva thought with a momentary frown, as he bound the wrist. But then, these English. Who knew what they would do with their children?

'Good. I knew I could count on you to be sensible. You were very patient last time I came to see you, oh, ages ago, years ago when you had that terrible fever. Let's see if you can't be just as patient this time.' She hadn't, of course, been patient at all but he always believed in praising the sick to get the best behaviour out of them. And for a fever she couldn't be blamed for being a bit difficult. He remembered suddenly the way she had struggled and cried out and fought him in that fever, calling for someone, her cousin if he remembered rightly. John somebody. The one who had got her through the jungle. And then, like a light going on in his head, he realized that the fuss last night was about the same boy, the same cousin. He glanced at her again.

'I hear your cousin John has come home. You must be very pleased.' There was no mistaking the way she jumped when he mentioned her cousin's name. Jumped and looked furtive and embarrassed and – upset. Because of the débâcle last night, with her father wringing her wrist for her like that? Dr da Silva rather thought not. He gave her an uneasy look and packed up his black bag, putting it on the bed beside her.

'There isn't anything wrong, is there, Eleanor? Anything you might like to talk to me about?' The door was partially closed, the mother somewhere else in the house. Such a pretty woman, Senhora Fawcett, the doctor thought fondly and then redirected his thoughts at Eleanor.

She was shaking her head. 'No. Everything's fine.' Except that she was crying again. She snatched a hand up to wipe the tears away.

Charles Fawcett had a busy morning. By nine o'clock he had been at the office for two hours and had decided just what should be done about Eleanor. By ten o'clock he had a list of several convent schools in his hand; by eleven, he had reduced the list to just two. One was the Colégio Santa Ifigénia, the other, the Colégio Sagrado Coração – Sacred Heart. He called for Honório and went to visit them. By twelve, he had decided on the latter school, liking the demure attire of the young ladies enrolled, their polite manners, their good exam results and, most importantly, their restricted freedom. No one could walk out of Sagrado Coração without permission, no one could see a boy

179

without a parent present, no one could spend an afternoon on a beach without anyone knowing where she was. He liked that and promptly signed his two daughters up. The nuns were pleased.

After lunch, Charles set about securing John's future. He rang the University of São Paulo and spoke to the registrar, reading John's exam results to the man over the telephone. The registrar was pleased. He said he would be grateful to receive a notarized copy of the results and would, himself, personally submit John's application. Charles hung up, satisfied, and tried hard to think of what to do with John in the meantime.

Clarissa hadn't liked to disturb John's sleep but, by midday, she did feel it was time for him to get up. She sent Adélia, the upstairs maid, along to rouse John and went, herself, to see Dr da Silva out. He was a kind man, she thought, and charming. She loved the way he flirted so punctiliously, never for a moment stepping outside the decreed boundaries of polite society. She held out her hand.

'Thank you so much, Dr da Silva for coming so promptly. I didn't think it was anything more than a sprain but it's good to be sure.' She smiled as he bowed over her hand, his lips kissing the air exactly five centimetres above her hand. Punctilious. Not for him the clumsy slobbering of a Don Juan, she thought with amusement.

He rose and twitched his tie minutely back into place. 'It was nothing, my dear senhora. Nothing at all. The child is more comfortable now but, I feel, still upset. You will perhaps be good enough to talk with her? I tried but –' he shrugged his shoulders delicately. Ah, he thought, she understands me so very well. Such a pity there is Senhor Fawcett. Such a pity there is Senhora da Silva. We should deal so very well together, the pretty Senhora Fawcett and I. Such a pity.

He took his leave, doffing his pearly grey homburg briefly as the door was shut behind him. Clarissa turned back into the hallway, pausing to rearrange a vase of orange

180

canna lilies and straightened the mirror that hung above them. She glanced at herself in the mirror, brushing a cheek with her hand.

'Senhora! He isn't there! See, here, he has left a letter for you.' Adélia came running down the stairs, her body stout in its uniform, unused to such exercise. Clarissa turned and stared at the maid, her pleasant thoughts of a moment before, stilling, becoming painful. Oh, why hadn't she thought to check on him before this?

She almost snatched the envelope from Adélia's hand, slitting it open immediately. Adélia stood patiently, wondering, at her side. Clarissa read the contents of the letter, folded it up again with sharp movements to her fingers, and put it in her pocket. She pursed her lips, thinking.

'Thank you, Adélia. Please strip the sheets from Senhor John's bed. He won't be using it again for a while.' She began to walk away.

'But, senhora, the bed has not been slept in. It is as new. You still wish me to take the sheets off?' Adélia was loath to lean over a bed that she had made only yesterday with difficulty, due to its ornate wooden frame, and due to her increasing stoutness. She pressed her hands together, hoping.

Clarissa stood perfectly still, her mind darting about furiously to find an explanation. He had left soon after he came home last night. But no, his letter was dated today and said he was leaving this morning, early. So perhaps he had just lain down on top of the bed, without disturbing the bed linen? But, no, it had turned cold in the night and he wouldn't have been comfortable without blankets. So, where had John slept last night?

She glanced at Adélia, grateful for the maid's slow wits and laziness. 'Leave it then. Just as it is. It's nearly lunch time. Why don't you go help Maria in the kitchen?' She walked past Adélia and into her husband's library, closing the door behind her.

Something was troubling Eleanor. She had sensed it herself and Dr da Silva had said as much just a few moments before. Something beyond the anger last night and the pain of the wrist today. Something perhaps to do with John? And where John had slept last night?

But when, eventually, she went upstairs to talk to Eleanor, her daughter was asleep, her hair spread out on the pillow, her nightdress demurely buttoned around her throat. She looked very young and quite innocent. Clarissa closed the door on her doubts and shook them away. Almost.

When Charles returned home that evening with the news that Isobel and Eleanor had been enrolled at the Colégio Sagrado Coração, Clarissa was surprisingly relieved and supported her husband's decision despite the tears of rage and indignation from Isobel. And perhaps even more so because of the guilty, averted look from Eleanor. Perhaps a convent school was a good idea? Perhaps.

Charles was also pleased to read John's letter. Good, that was one less worry. He could have arranged to have John sent away somewhere but it would have been difficult and uncomfortable against the boy's wishes. So now it was all taken care of and Eleanor couldn't say that it was her papa's fault as always. She would have to admit that John hadn't cared enough to stay with her. That was good.

He smiled over dinner, apologized to Eleanor for her wrist, and remained in fair spirits for the rest of the evening. Isobel sulked and complained that it was her last year at school and she hadn't done anything wrong, so why was she being separated from all her friends? Eleanor looked distraught, her thoughts unvoiced and all the more disturbing for that silence. Clarissa watched them all with a pain lodged somewhere up inside her chest, just beneath her ribs. For the first time in her life, she hoped John never came back.

The breeze blew fresh and steady from the north, whipping the sea into mountainous waves into whose troughs the old *Espírito Santo* crashed with regular monotony. Metal screamed against metal, seams groaned as though they would crack open and let the waters pour in, and the twin propeller screws shrieked as they lifted clear of the water. And then they bit again and the freighter would shake and right itself and start to climb the side of another mountain of green glass.

The dawn lit the early morning sky with an eerie light, more silver than golden, with sullen hues that picked out the water as it rolled over the bow and forecastle of the freighter, turning it translucent, like purple and pink and black cellophane across the scuppers. John watched it with a strange feeling of indomitability, sure no matter who or what else foundered, he would survive. The spray hit his face, the wind gouged at his lungs, and he laughed at the savagery of it all. At that moment, he was sure he would live forever.

His body ached from hours of manning the pumps in the bilge, four on, two off, and his head reeled with the fumes of diesel oil mixed with something more unpleasant still, fish perhaps, or rotting fruit or maybe a legacy of all the different cargoes that had been plied up and down the Atlantic coast by that old barque. His hammock beckoned down below in the crew's quarters, and he knew he should be sleeping but the dawn rising over those fantastic shapes of water, flinging its light over a terrifying landscape of moving, rolling green filled him with such awe and fear, such a joyous feeling of life that he couldn't tear himself away but stood, clinging furiously to the metalwork, staring out into the scene as though he might command it with his will. The first mate yelled at him to get below, but the words were snatched away in the roar and thump of seas landing on their bows, sluicing across hatches to roll angrily back into the green landscape. John stood and marvelled.

They had drawn out of Vitória the day before yesterday, bound for Pôrto Seguero, John just one more crewman aboard a leaky, rust-caked freighter that should have been retired years ago. He had joined the *Espírito Santo* in Rio. The ship was carrying a cargo of light machinery and some food stuffs, powdered milk, soap, medicines, and luxury items that could not be obtained in Vitória such as china, saddles and riding equipment – and a burial casket. That last item had caused some concern among the other crew members, two of them signing off the list immediately and waiting for another freighter, the rest muttering uneasily and making small offerings to the sea of chicken gizzards and flowers and chanting mournful prayers to the accompanying sound of the berimbau, a single wire string connected to a gourd that the bosun struck with a stick.

They were a hard lot and John was treated with suspicion. But it was the only freighter who would hire him. And he had to get away.

That feeling, almost a compulsion, to distance himself from Rio, from his family, seemed odd now that he was afloat and miles away from land. For four years he had done nothing but long to be back where he belonged and then, within twenty-four hours, he had run away from it all again, set out on a mysterious pilgrimage to what or where he neither knew or cared. It was enough to be away.

The ship had put in briefly at Vitória, a sleepy, untidy town with a harbour dotted with small islands and hillsides scarred by the rusted tin roofs of coffee sheds and favelas. The town itself boasted little more than one main street of purpose-built modern blocks and a few back streets, narrow and mean with poverty. Moreira, the first mate, told him the fina gente, the upper classes, lived in plush villas on the islands or well back in the hills, the poor clustering along the coastal strip with all their practicalities of life defacing the graceful curves of the beaches and the town beyond.

John made no attempt to go into the town. The rest of the crew wanted to go eat at the churrascarias, great halls where slabs of meat, roasted on swords and sliced off on to their plates, could be gorged and washed down with beer, before going into the back streets in search of further pleasures of the flesh. He shook his head at their urgings and headed instead to the market where he filled a basket with fruit and bought a rolled-up woven mat to lie on the beach with.

The harbour waters were turgid and deep green, lapping around small islands of black volcanic rock and sprouts of green vegetation, in all hues and shades. John sat on the beach and ate his fruit, shaking his head at the boys selling popsicles and the men shouting their wares of fresh fruit juice, carried in two silver coolers that hung suspended from their shoulders by a pole. Washed up on the beach were the heads of sword fish and the remains of flower leis, macumba offerings. An old black woman, turbaned and dressed in orange and pink and yellow garments, one over the other, squatted with her skirts pulled up over her knees. In the sand by her feet, a fire, over which a cast-iron griddle was set and surrounded by palm leaves, burned without smoke, the embers glowing. Occasionally she poked the food from the griddle on to the leaves. She was selling acarajé, a shrimp cake fried in palm oil. In the eddying heat from her fire, she plied a steady trade.

John watched from beneath half-closed eyes, his body becoming as burnished as those around him as the sun beat down on the bright sand and the heat nailed him to the ground. He spat out the last of the black, pepper-like, papaya seeds into the sand and lay back, feeling the scorch of the mat against his back. Low in the sky, thunder clouds hung like grey mountains above the sea, the air sullen with heat. He fell asleep.

Later, as the afternoon cooled, he swam out to some of the islands, hauling himself out on to the flat volcanic rocks to hunt for crabs and small shellfish trapped in pools of water that almost boiled with heat. He swam from one to another, fighting the strong pull of the current, alarmed only once when something large brushed against his leg in the murky waters. It was a lazy, solitary day for John, full of awkward, previously avoided thoughts. A day that did much to clear his mind. He returned to the ship reluctantly.

They had left the next morning, at first light, and hit the storm late in the day. There had been no warning that it was coming in, no hint from the weather report or the look of the sky, just an ache in Moreira's shoulder that made

185

him order the hatches battened down and the cargo tied more firmly into place only hours before it had hit. And then the night had fallen in that raging torrent of sound and motion and John had been set to the pumps.

He turned and grinned at Moreira, feeling the force of wind suck the air from his lungs, smother his nose. Water streamed down his face. Moreira shouted something again and pointed at the wheelhouse and John nodded reluctantly. He released his grip on the iron railings and slowly, lurching from side to side, made his way along the ropes tied to guide him back to shelter. And that was when, with his back to the sea, the ship suddenly tilted alarmingly, plunging down into a trough much deeper than any they had entered before, a wall of water, many times higher than the bridge towering over them. John, looking back, saw Moreira open his mouth wide, whether in terror or warning he wasn't sure, and then the wave was on them.

It tore at him, battering, suffocating, brutal in its weight and he felt himself flung up hard against the metal door and jammed in a corner of the bridge, drowning under many feet of water, the seconds becoming minutes, the minutes seeming to never end. It seemed as though his lungs and heart would burst, the pounding in his head, the pain became so overpowering, so crippling and then, as he opened his mouth to breathe the waters in, they flung themselves back from him, clawing him with them towards the sea. He held on desperately to the safety rope, wedging his feet against the metal rim that ran around the bridge and choked on ragged, gasping mouthfuls of air.

Moreira was nowhere to be seen and the second trough was sliding out beneath the old ship, tilting the bows down again into the depths. John felt the motion and looked around frantically, his bravado and joy in the sea's savagery gone, replaced by an emptiness in his stomach. He recognized it as fear.

Jesus, where had the man gone? Had he been swept overboard or was he still clinging somewhere to a last guyline, a last ledge that separated him from those black waters? John took a deep breath and released the safety rope, tottering forward against the shrieking wind to where the metal railing of the bridge edge now fell away beneath him, nearly sending him over. He clung to the railing and looked down over the forecastle, tilting frighteningly towards the pit of the trough, and then, finally, he saw the figure rolled up against one of the davits, gripping to the metal base with grim intensity. John called to him but his voice was ripped away by the wind, unheard even by himself.

The second wave was on them almost before John could throw himself back to his corner of safety and wrap the rope tightly around the palms of his hands. It struggled and howled and tore at him and then was gone, more quickly than the first wave. John prised himself free and crawled towards the bridge ladder, and the forecastle, blinded by the spray and wind, feeling his way and all the while his stomach knotted in anticipation of the next wave, the one that would rip him from his precarious position and fling him out into the nightmare seas beyond.

He was at the base of the ladder when it came and he wrapped his body around the rungs, hanging on, knowing it was smaller this time. When it passed, he had about fifteen, perhaps twenty seconds to reach Moreira. The man was still there, jammed up again the davit, his left arm lying awkwardly, his right wrapped tightly around the metal lifeline. John reached him by the simple expedient of letting himself fall down the tilting deck towards the man and then grabbing at the davit at the last possible moment. He pressed his face up against Moreira's, seeing the man's eyes screwed up tightly, the water streaming from his beard, the blood oozing from a cut.

There were other figures now, dark and slick from the rain and sea, staggering about the bridge, two making their way down the ladder. They carried a rope with them and John, glancing back at them a moment before the next wave engulfed them, saw they were gesturing to him. He held Moreira tightly and the wave sucked and eddied and smothered before rushing away again.

When the rope came, snaking into his grasp on the fourth try, John tied Moreira in a tight noose underneath his arms and got him up on his knees. A wave, taunting and fickle, knocked them down again before sluicing down the side of the ship and then John had them both up, staggering, tottering forward across the slanting deck as the safety line drew them near.

They reached the ladder just as the next huge wave crashed down on them and, for a second, John felt himself being plucked free of the line to which he clung, tearing along in the wave's wake and then a hand grabbed his jacket, pulling him back. He hung gasping and coughing against the ladder and then they were wrenching at the door of the lower deck that another crewman had opened from inside, feeling it fling itself back against the wall, falling forward into silence and dryness and John felt the deck roll up to greet him. The door slammed behind them with a heavy metallic clang.

They battled their way up the coast for another two days, overshooting Pôrto Seguero and making, instead, for Salvador where, on the third day, the storm ran itself out and they coasted into Todos os Santos bay past the lighthouse into waters of mint-green and blue that glinted in the rays of the sun. The crew were exhausted, lining the sides of the old ship, and raising a faint cheer to see São Marcelo, a circular fortress long since abandoned, rising up on its island in the centre of the bay. Many kissed the crosses they wore around their necks, or touched the good luck ribbons they wore plaited around their wrists. Others called out to Imanjá, the goddess of the sea. Some simply blinked in the sun.

John leaned against the rail and stared across the flat glare of water at the city basking in the heat. A soft, balmy breeze blew through the ship, relaxing, relieving the tension of the last few days. He looked briefly at the men around him and wondered whether any of them would sign back on the *Espírito Santo* for the return voyage. With, or without, the coffin. He decided he wouldn't be one of them.

The sea was a wonderful thing unto itself, but he preferred the land. He thought he might stay a while in Salvador, maybe travel around Bahia a little. See the land, work where he could. It seemed a better idea than going up and down the coast endlessly for the next four months or so.

They anchored out in the bay and John went ashore in the long boat, his pockets comfortably lined with money, his few belongings slung over his shoulder in a carry-all. Moreira shook his hand on the quay, his dark eyes smiled for a brief moment promising many things, perhaps even lifelong friendship, and then they walked away from each other, as separate as they had been a week before, the storm forgotten. John breathed in the smell of the land.

Salvador was a city divided by steeply terraced cliffs into two parts, the Cidade Alta and the Cidade Baixa, upper and lower cities. He wandered past the market along the waterfront and up into the narrow streets, thronging with noise and colour and people intent on selling their wares.

It was cooler between the tall walls, shadows stretching out across the old cobbled streets that rose steeply up to the quiet Cidade Alta. Colonial mansions and modern office blocks, baroque churches, the plaster peeling from their walls, and courtyards filled with fountains that splashed and tinkled wetly amongst the foliage. He wandered, lost, up and down amongst the streets and narrow lanes of the city, pausing to rest occasionally at a café or fruit bar, or stare admiringly at the dark-skinned girls who sold flowers or incense and leaves, good luck charms, to protect from the 'evil eye'. They admired him back, their looks both bold and uncertain. John continued on.

It was late afternoon before he began to tire, his belly churning to remind him that no food had been forthcoming in some time. He began to look for somewhere to stay, a cheap café at which to buy some food, a bowl of ensopado, or perhaps some caruru. He wanted something spicy and warm, something with seafood and tomatoes and garlic after the monotony of the food at sea. His mouth watered at the thought. The shadows were drawing out across the stones now and he began to look more urgently.

He noticed the number of terreiros, temples for voodoo worship, were nearly as numerous as the churches and he remembered then that this was Bahia and, like the Backlands, many believed in magic and sorcery. For a moment he recalled the scene in the chapel, the 'Dream House', out on his property the night his mother had been killed. Voodoo and Christianity flung together and churned up into a mixture that was neither one nor the other, just a blur of frightening images imprinted on his mind.

For a moment he stood, undecided, outside the thick walls of a terreiro, daring himself to enter, daring himself to put the old nightmares to rest. Sweat had broken out on his forehead and the palms of his hands. He wiped them carefully, his face still and calm. There was nothing to fear. He would prove that to himself.

A girl, selling plaited ribbons and leaves, watched him from the corner of the street. She saw the sheen on his forehead, the bright, unfocused look in his eyes. Curiously, she looked him over, wondering if he had a fever. That look in his eyes – odd, really. She shrugged and turned back to her wares.

John paced backwards and forwards in front of the doors, glancing inside in brief, fleeting looks. At last he entered, his breath tight in his chest as he wandered around the main building, his footsteps echoing sharply across the stone floor, his shadow large and disconcerting, walking before him. He smelled incense and the heavy, sweet scent of lilies but saw nothing more unusual than blood and strange drawings on the walls. Chicken blood.

He stopped and laughed with relief and shook his head, thinking how childish fears can be so unnerving until confronted as an adult. He moved nearer the altar, into the darker recesses, forcing himself on but more relaxed now, more in control.

Suddenly he started in fear, almost crying out, as he came upon the black shadowed sacristy. Staring up into the eaves, he saw they were hung about with arms and legs and hands that gleamed palely in the gloom. He threw himself back in horror, hitting a wall, tasting blood in his mouth where he had bitten his tongue. A hand swung gently in front of his face.

And then he realized with a bubble of relief, sour in the back of his throat, that they were wax castings, moulds made of body parts that had been blessed with a 'miracle' cure. He smelt the oddly sweet and fetid odour that had permeated the chapel in the jungle, like an animal den, and he turned and ran blindly through the building, out into the street. He leaned against a wall, gagging for air.

The girl saw him come out, strangely agitated, and she put down her tray of ribbons and commanded one of the children beside her to guard it. She walked uncertainly over to the young man, seeing him pant and lean against the wall, his face wet and pale with sweat. She touched his arm.

'Are you unwell? Do you need help?' Teresa asked, wondering why she bothered with him. Yes, he was good-looking but she didn't need a man in her life, there were enough on a business basis as it was. And there were many ill people in Salvador, many more who were just hungry, and she never went to their aid. She had herself to look after, and that was hard enough. But as he turned to stare at her, the girl felt her mouth become dry, her skin prickle into gooseflesh. There was terror in those eyes and they seemed to engulf her, swallow her whole into their blue. She stepped back.

'Teresa! Come, come quick!' The wail snapped the trance she seemed to have fallen into, breaking her eye contact with the stranger as she craned around to see what the child wanted. There was a scuffle going on, the tray being snatched back and forth between her own little helper and another girl. Teresa sped across the street and slapped the other girl away, raising her hand to hit again before the would-be thief could escape. She raged, kicking and swearing, and then the girl gathered her skirts up and dashed away, her wails of grief and disappointment soothing to Teresa's ears. She stood back, breathing heavily, her hands on her hips.

When she glanced around again, she saw the young man was moving away, his footsteps uneasy on the cobblestones, his hand pressed to the walls every few feet, as though to steady himself. She called after him but he didn't respond. She fitted two fingers between her lips and let out a shrill whistle.

John, still shaking from the terror of the limbs swinging in the dark, felt his way dimly along the street. Suddenly he wanted to be free of the buildings that clustered dark and close around him. He wanted to step out into a square, see daylight, see the sea, take a deep breath of salt-laden air.

He had thought the girl part of the nightmare at first, the way she clutched at him, her face shadowed and hard. But he now realized she was nothing more than a street vendor and he relaxed a little, wondering which way to go to get out of this maze of streets. He heard a sharp whistle behind him and turned back to see what it was.

She was beckoning to him, walking after him, the tray swinging from side to side as she balanced it on her hip. Her skirt was caught up on the tray, revealing a long, firm leg the colour of polished teak. She was part Indian, part black, part European, he thought. All three races melded together in exotic proportions. He hesitated and then turned back.

'Where you going, Senhor Louro? You look all lost to me. You come in off a ship?' He didn't look like the Europeans in Salvador, not with that blond hair and those blue eyes and that faint air of sophistication despite the rough clothes he wore. From further south perhaps, one of the big cities like Rio de Janeiro or São Paulo. But not Salvador. She was certain of that.

John thought her bold and impertinent, the way she addressed him so familiarly as 'Senhor Blond' and swayed her hips as she suggested he was lost, the way she laughed in her dark, shiny eyes and licked her lips. Bold, impertinent – and seductive. His mouth was still dry from his fright and he had to swallow before he could reply.

'Yes, I've been on the sea for a few days. What's the quickest way down to the waterfront again?' He looked her in the eye, coldly, disinterestedly and her eyes laughed back.

So, he was a Carioca with his Rio twang so tight and sharp, saying 'Atlântchio' rather than 'Atlântico', saying 'p'ra' rather than 'para'. A very good family Carioca. Perhaps playing at being poor, being a seaman for a while until he went back to his rich life and his rich family? She pursed full, dark lips together and swayed the tray.

'It will be dark very soon, I think. You will have difficulty finding your way. Salvador is not an easy place to find your way around. And after dark, it is not safe for strangers. If you like, I could show you?'

'Are you going down to the waterfront? I don't want to take you out of your way.' He knew he should get away, walk past this street girl and pretend she didn't exist. That was what Louis would have done, or Henry. But he was tired and still a little frightened, and he wanted company. He gave her a cool nod and she hoisted the tray even further up on her hip and called quickly to the other children, telling them to go home, to come back tomorrow. If they even had a home, John thought, seeing the ragged clothing, the pinched expressions. The girl didn't seem to notice.

He followed her down a different lane from the one which he had been about to take.

'What's your name, then?' she asked, over her shoulder.

John strode out a little faster and caught up beside her. 'John,' he said.

She gave him a quizzical smile. 'Just John?'

'For now, just John. And you?'

'Teresa. Just Teresa. For always.' Her black eyes glittered at him, mocking.

'How do you mean?'

'My mother abandoned me very young, my father I

193

never knew. I learned to survive but I have no last name. Just Teresa.' She didn't ask for his sympathy or even pity herself. She said it matter of factly. There, that's how it is. Take it or leave it. John felt ashamed.

They walked on in silence for a while, the girl leading him up and down a bewildering number of passageways, crossing over stone steps, down dark alleys. She hummed to herself, a sad, plaintive tune that didn't match the bright expression on her face, the seductive sway of her bottom as she walked ahead of him. Every now and then she glanced around, smiled at him. John followed her blindly, too tired to care where she led him.

'How long you here for, then? You mean to stay in Salvador – or Bahia?' She didn't look at him now, just kept walking on, fast and sure.

John cleared his throat. 'Uh, I don't know exactly. A while perhaps. Is it hard to find work?' He didn't like to tell her he was only passing the time until university started. It seemed so callous in the face of her struggle to survive. She sensed it anyway.

'Not for you. Not with an education and a few months to kill. How old're you, John?' She was direct with her questions and equally blunt with the answers.

John smiled in spite of his tiredness and low spirits. 'Eighteen. And you?'

'Seventeen, I think. Near enough anyway. What sort of work you want? Good hard labour or clerk in some office? I guess you could do either, couldn't you?' She sized him up, seeing the broad shoulders, the height. Yes, fed well all his life, grown up a strong young man. She felt a flicker of anticipation, touched her tongue to her lips, moistening them.

'I'd prefer labouring or maybe something up country. I don't really know yet. I just got here.' He felt uncertain about everything since that shock in the terreiro. What he was doing here, why he wanted to go out amongst the poor and pretend to be one of them. It all seemed laughable now and stupid. Immature. He ought to stick to his own sort and not condescend to these people, not try and live their lives and then walk away when it all became too unbearable and monotonous. Walk away because university called. He looked at her, hoping she wouldn't judge him too harshly, too contemptuously.

But Teresa didn't think to criticize. He was one of the fina gente and that was all there was to it. They chose to do whatever suited them, changing their minds on a whim. If he wanted to work as a labourer for a while, then why not? She just hoped he would become fond of her, in that time. Because she needed someone to be her meal ticket for a while, to help her put some money away beyond the selling of trinkets and good luck charms that brought her no luck at all. When he left and returned to the south, she wanted to have something to show for his time here. She looked at him, hoping he wouldn't judge her too harshly, too contemptuously.

They saw the uncertainty in each other's eyes and smiled, each for their own reasons.

'You got somewhere to stay yet? Somewhere to sleep?' It was growing dark now, the streets becoming menacing in appearance. John had no idea where he was, nor even in which direction the harbour lay. He shook his head.

'Then you can stay with me tonight. Not very good but just me. If you like?' She had to have her own room, a dingy, plaster-peeling room with little more than a bed and a tiny balcony, if she wanted to make money in the evenings. Tonight she would forfeit those earnings in the hope of greater rewards to come. She swung her hips more languorously, her brisk walk slowing and becoming more tantalizing. John stared, nodded again.

He felt dazed, as though he were walking through a maze of unknown, unforeseen pathways, each one leading to a different life, a different John. But she led him on inexorably and he was too tired and too confused by the feelings she provoked in him, to fight it. A strange, giddy anticipation began in the pit of his stomach.

He noticed they were in an older part of the city now, the

houses once gaily painted but now crumbling at the edges, fading into damp, dingy boarding houses, brothels. The balconies were lit with lamps, many pink in hue, and John became increasingly uneasy. He glanced at Teresa, wondering.

But she was darting into a passageway now, stopping at a darkened doorway and he saw her beckon to him, come on, quick, what are you afraid of? It was all there in the impatience, the teasing flick of that wrist. Further down the road a band of drunken seamen were being evicted from a bar, several single men loitered in doorways, a few women hung over balconies, their hair hanging down, their blouses cut low. John stared at them, looked back at Teresa. Dark eyes assessed him. Yes? Or no? It was not a place to wander alone. He sighed and shook his head at himself, at his folly.

John followed Teresa up a flight of steep stairs and then another until they were finally at the top of the house and she was fumbling with a key at the lock of a door. Several other doors opened, just a crack, like oyster shells, and then snapped back again.

Teresa shrugged, 'They want to know who is here, who might be trying to steal from them. It's a good enough system. Everyone watches everyone, no one trusts anyone. Come on in.'

He followed her into a single room, feeling the heated air of the attics, seeing the scratched doorway, the lock barely hanging in place.

She was shrugging again, deprecating. 'Not so nice, is it? But it's mine and there are two doors between me and those people out there on the streets.' She almost spat when she said 'those people'. John nodded.

There was a mattress on the floor in the corner, scuffed wooden boards, a fringed shawl hanging like a curtain to divide the room. A metal bucket underneath a cracked, once white porcelain sink and a metal tub in the corner served as the bathroom. There was a mirror above the sink, pitted and broken in the top left corner where someone had tightened the screw too much, and a glass and metal shelf on which stood a toothbrush, a jar, some bits of make-up. A balcony that looked as though it might crumble to the street below if any weight were put on it held a butane bottle and a small gas ring. A few clothes hung from hooks behind the door and a pile of palm leaves and ribbons lay, unplaited as yet, in the far corner. That was the sum of Teresa's life.

'You want to lock that door behind you? Safer that way,' she said, laying the tray down on the floor and straightening to look at him. He seemed to fill the room making it even smaller, even more cramped. He locked the door and stood awkwardly, waiting for her to tell him where to go, what to do.

She was fumbling behind the curtain now, pulling out a box from which she produced a half-bottle of cheap wine and two tumblers. A tin cigarette box contained a couple of joints, already rolled. Ready for her clients, she thought with misgiving and then shrugged the doubt away. What the hell, enjoy him one way or the other. Even if he walks out tomorrow. How often do you get someone like him here? How often? Huh? She stared up at him, at the fine, pale hair, the smooth curves of his face, the firm, long body. The way he wasn't presuming, but waiting, still dressed, for her to invite him. How often?

The answer wasn't hard to find. Never. Only the pig sailors or the scum who worked around here, cheating on their wives or their girlfriends, or too ugly to have either. She deserved better than that. So go ahead, give him some wine, give him a smoke. Give him everything. Who the hell cared?

'I'll sleep over here, shall I? I'm sorry I'm going to crowd you. I didn't realize how little space you had,' John paused awkwardly, half wondering why she was looking at him like that, the roll-up cigarette dangling from her lips, the lids of her eyes lowered so that only a glint of eye remained. He felt that giddy shiver again. 'It's very kind of you to let me stay. I – I can pay you some board, just for the night. If it's not too much,' he said stiffly, uncomfortable discussing money.

197

She grinned to herself at that. Only the fina gente had trouble talking money. 'You've never had a woman before, have you?' she said after the silence with which she had greeted John's offer had become intolerable to them both. John coloured a deep red, looking away, out the window. His shoulders hunched up tightly at the collar of his peacoat, his back became tight. He didn't say anything. Teresa sighed, smiled to herself, stretched out full on the mattress so that her lean body seemed to arch in the middle.

'Look, I like you, John. I don't know why, but I do. It doesn't matter if you've never had anyone before, because I know what to do and I am very, very good.' Her voice became low and husky, tantalizing. 'And you have to start somewhere, don't you? So, come on, have a glass of wine and a smoke with me. It'll make you feel better.' She held out a glass and he glanced around, reluctantly coming to take it from her hand. He didn't look her in the face. Teresa sighed even more gustily. 'Okay John, I don't care if you do or you don't want it – there's no pressure. It doesn't matter. Just come and have a drink with me. Tell me your life story.' She was laughing now, and he tried to smile, his cheek muscles tight against the flesh.

He sat down on the floor, cross-legged and raised his glass to her. 'Later. You tell me yours first,' he said and she sat back on the mattress, her back against the wall. She settled her legs beneath her, fished around inside her blouse for a moment, readjusting something, and took a deep drink of wine.

'All right. So, I told you the beginning already, right? How my mother just dumped me, left me sleeping on some steps she'd chosen for the night, and when I woke up she was gone? I was about four, maybe five then. Old enough to know some things, not old enough to know others.' She shrugged, and he realized she wasn't talking about her schoolwork. This girl had been to a different sort of school. He wondered, idly, what Eleanor would make of her.

She leaned forward and poured him out some more

wine, her blouse falling open as she bent from the waist, her skin the same burnished teak as her legs except for dusky pink nipples. She had long thin breasts that swung low, beckoning to him and dark, curling hair that fell loose somehow from the plait she had worn it in earlier, feathering over her skin and lying like coiling tendrils against the white of her blouse, the gloss of her bare shoulder. John looked away, slinging back the second glass of wine. It hit his empty stomach and seemed to burn some warmth into him. A bead of perspiration began between his eyebrows. He tried to listen to her words, tried to wrench his mind away from the sudden thoughts that flashed and exploded in his brain.

'Some old woman found me and gave me some food. I don't remember her name. She looked after me for a few days and then I ran away, got a few cruzeiros a day plaiting flowers and ribbons, begging, stealing from people in the street. If you look in the rubbish tips, there's lots of things that are still good, thrown out by people like you because you're bored with them. I dressed myself like that and fed myself too, when I couldn't make any money. Slept in cardboard boxes, drains, people's outhouses.

'Then, when I was about eleven or so, I started, well – you know.' She signed crudely with her hand. 'Made enough to live a lot better, get my own stall going in the market.' She took a puff of her joint, holding the smoke in her lungs. Then a sip of wine, running it around her teeth, her gums, with her tongue. John watched the pink tongue dart up and down, round and round. He felt like a mouse before a snake. Stunned, stupefied.

'I'm saving up, enough money to get out of here. But it's slow. You don't make enough to live and save both at the same time. Sometimes I think I'll never get out of here. Sometimes I just want to kill someone, take their money, and run!' Her voice became harsh, her eyes glittered. She saw John watching her steadily. 'But I don't. I'm still here. And you know, I think I deserve better.' Her voice became amused, considering, and she dipped her tongue around her lips again. 'I'm a good-looking girl, aren't I? I could be a lady if I had some money, couldn't I?' She straightened her shoulders, throwing back her hair, staring him straight in the face. 'Couldn't I?'

She wasn't beautiful, he thought. Not to him, not like Eleanor. But she was wildly sensual, exotic, provocative. All the superlatives came to mind, he thought, eyeing her body, the curves beneath the cheap cotton stuff she wore, the hair coiling dark and vibrant, with a life of its own, her long legs thrust out beneath her rucked-up skirt. She had an aura to her, a carnal, intemperate appeal that could not be denied. Not, certainly, by him.

Yet despite all the allure, the temptation, he also read uncertainty, fear, need in those eyes that stared at him now, begging for some words of praise. She needed him. It was an exhilarating feeling. He leaned over towards her, tracing a finger down the curve of her cheekbone.

'You could be anything you wanted to be, Teresa. A lady if that's what's important to you, maybe an actress, a model. A very rich man's mistress. Whatever you choose.' Their mouths were close together, the white of her teeth showing between the dark, thick lips, a slight fuzz on her upper lip oddly appealing. John stroked it with his finger.

'How? How can I be any of those?' she demanded.

His eyes stared at her, from too close, blue and large and staring. 'By wanting it enough – and by seizing every opportunity that comes your way.' He smiled vaguely at her, knowing what she was thinking, his mind thick with drugged smoke and wine. Deliciously, deliriously blotted out, his fear was lost back in the dark recesses of his memory. He felt her arms go round him, pulling him against her warm flesh, those moist, dark lips sliding on his own, inhaling him, pulling him down to her.

'Seize the opportunity,' he mumbled as he slid down beside her on the mattress, her breath hot now on his cheek. He felt her fingers loosening his shirt, his belt, skilled, quick and light, fleeting over his skin, making him shiver as she lay half on top of him, panting, running her

200

mouth over his chest, down his stomach, down further still. Thought had become blurred, feeling overriding his senses. He slid and rocked against her, arching his back, gasping. Teresa could hear him still muttering the phrase to himself, trembling now as she kissed and nuzzled him, feeling his strength drain away in shock and then return again, triumphant. She laughed deep in her throat and moved up to straddle him again, plunging herself down hard on to him. John groaned, his mouth remaining open in astonishment.

'Seize the opportunity,' she teased him and then she quickly tightened her stomach muscles so that John could do nothing more than lie there, racked with shivers. Her breasts swung down low over him. 'Seize the opportunity,' she taunted and was not surprised when he finally did.

Chapter Eleven

Rio de Janeiro
December 1958

Eleanor lay on the grass, a book, *Gabriela* by Jorge Amado, abandoned by her side. She was tired of it. It was too difficult to read in the sun, especially the strong summer sun and she now lay on her stomach poking at a snail with a twig. It ducked inside its shell and she left it alone. Poor thing.

Henry was still reading his book. She craned around to see what it was. Something about Senhor Carrar's Rifles. She sighed and flopped over on to her back. It was two months since John had disappeared. She wondered whether he intended to join them for Christmas? Only another week to buy him a present. She had all the others already. Only John's was so difficult that she had rejected everything she had seen as too young, too boring, too silly, too old. Nothing seemed quite right for him. She chewed on a piece of grass.

'You think John would like a tie?' she asked.

Henry looked up from his book. 'No,' he said mildly enough but Eleanor spat out the grass. She saw Henry didn't want to talk about John and, perversely, she pressed him to it.

'What then? What can I get him for Christmas? What would you like, if you were him?'

'I'm not him. I don't know what John would want. I would like a new pen, or perhaps some cufflinks, but John? I've no idea,' Henry said coolly and Eleanor kicked his shoe.

'Don't be difficult, Henry. Or I won't get you anything for Christmas at all. I know you could think of something if you just tried,' she threatened, and saw him dart her an indifferent look. At least, he tried to be indifferent. But he couldn't quite be. She sat up and crossed her legs. 'How about a book? Something he's interested in, like archaeology. Ancient ruins and earthworks with lots of pictures of amphora and pottery and oh, I don't know, megaliths and barrows and stuff like that. What d'you think?'

'Maybe. It'd be pretty expensive and anyway, you don't know if he's going to turn up at all. Or have you heard from him?' The jealousy hit Henry in the back of his throat, clenching tightly so that he could barely swallow. He forced it back down and tried not to mind, tried to remember that they were first cousins and could never be anything more to each other.

Eleanor leaned over and closed his book with a snap. Bertold Brecht's version of the Spanish Civil War. He had been enjoying it until now. 'No, nothing at all. Where on earth can he be? I worry about him sometimes but I know, deep down, he has to be all right. I'd know if he weren't.' She paused and considered, 'Oh well, I'll think of something. You hungry? I could do with some lunch, couldn't you? I think Maria's cooking some of her moqueca. Oh, I forgot, you don't like fish much, do you?' Eleanor thought with regret of the simmering fish and sweet peppers, onions, tomatoes, and garlic. She loved moqueca. She and John. They loved all the same things, often getting the same cravings at the same time, unknown to each other. Like identical twins. She saw Henry watching, trying to read her thoughts. John would have known them, she thought, and then was ashamed of herself.

'Well, no, not much,' Henry was saying, oblivious of her long internal monologue. He was still considering lunch.

203

'But I could have an omelette or something instead. Maria wouldn't mind that, would she? When are your parents due back anyway?' Henry asked and Eleanor smiled at him, thinking how like Henry it was to offer to eat something else just so she wouldn't have to forego one of her pleasures. Not like John. He would demand that they had what he wanted and then he would want the largest share and she would fight him for it, noisily and angrily until they both realized what they were doing, burst into laughter and shared the food equally.

That wasn't Henry's way. He was always kind, always considerate. Why then didn't she feel anything for him? Everyone else thought he was wonderful at her school. But then, she reminded herself cynically, they never saw many boys anyway.

'Late this afternoon, I think,' Eleanor replied. 'Mama hates São Paulo and only goes when she has to, when Papa forces her to. She says it's so industrial and so ugly. But it was the shareholders' meeting on Lampedusca and I think Papa wants to sell some shares so he can invest in the Brasília scheme, so he insisted she go along. Won't Louis and John be sorry to go there to university? I'd've thought they'd've stayed here, wouldn't you?'

'I'm going to stay here,' Henry said, ignoring her question. Or perhaps it had been rhetorical. He looked at her from beneath long eyelashes, his face thin and attractive now that he was sixteen, almost seventeen, and through the awkward stages of adolescence. Not that Eleanor seemed to have had any awkward stages. She never changed, he thought, just drew out a little longer every year. Henry admired the way her hair fell from a widow's peak over a high, wide forehead, her body just as lean and lovely as a young child's. Well, not quite a young child – she was, after all, just sixteen now and beginning to fill out in certain areas. His eyes lingered over her blouse, unbuttoned one lower than he thought seemly, at the brown skin disappearing down into that blouse.

'Are you? What, read law here? I thought your parents

204

wanted you to go to São Paulo, too?' Eleanor sat up again, conscious suddenly that Henry was staring rather hard at her chest. She gave him a reproving frown. Henry cleared his throat and became, as Eleanor phrased it in her mind, slightly pompous. He always became pompous when talking about his future. It was so very decided, so very mapped out, she thought with a sigh.

'No, it's all settled. I'm finishing a year early and going straight on, as long as my exams are all right. I'll have to work very hard from now on but my masters think I should do fine. I'd have to wait another year if I went to São Paulo. My father wants me to get on as fast as I can, and join him in his law firm. And then, once I'm a lawyer and established, I can enter politics.'

Henry dropped his pretence at being interested in law and gave way to his real enthusiasm. 'There are so many reforms going through now, Eleanor, and most of them are half-baked. I mean, how about this one of giving the masses land without any technical skills or credit facilities? They haven't even got any tools! What're they going to do with that land? And who's going to pay for free education with inflation galloping ahead like this? This Brasília idea's got totally out of hand, with everyone trying to climb aboard, and who's going to foot the bill? Kubitschek seems to be invoking the "Law of the Miraculous Solution", hoping like mad that the next party can sort it out because he sure as anything can't!' He coloured slightly as he realized that Eleanor's father was one of those climbing aboard for a quick profit.

Eleanor tossed her hair. 'Papa thinks he's a very good president. The economy's booming and everyone's becoming terribly proud of being Brazilian. We don't need anyone else telling us how to run our country. And, anyway, we've had the vice-president to dinner lots of times. He and Papa are very good friends and he says the economy's never looked better and Brasília's a wonderful idea because it's opening up the interior. Besides, Papa's investing quite a lot in it all, not just trying to get money out of it, which is what you're trying to suggest.' Eleanor had become haughty, annoyed with Henry's criticisms.

Henry became equally annoyed. 'Well, that's wonderful, Elly. I'm happy for you. Never mind that we can't afford to break off relations with the IMF or stop foreigners coming in and investing in property and business. Let's all be terribly nationalistic. Except don't forget that's how your family got started out here, will you? You may feel Brazilian but you're mostly English. Foreigner. Estrangeira.' He said each word slowly, forcefully and watched the way Eleanor's jaw became tight.

'That may be a problem later on, mightn't it, if things keep on the way they're going?' He paused and looked across the gardens, at the fountains throwing out water and the clipped formal hedges, the rose garden. Privilege and wealth as far as the eye could see. But for how much longer?

'And I wouldn't go getting too chummy with Goulart if I were your father. My father thinks Goulart's a self-serving politician who'll adopt any policy as long as it keeps him in power. He plays musical chairs with some skill now, but one of these days, it'll all come down on him, see if it doesn't. And on anyone who's too good a friend, too. They'll be looking for scapegoats.' He was serious now, looking her straight in the face, his soft brown hair flopping over his intelligent-looking brow.

Eleanor felt a moment's uneasiness. She shook it off. 'So you say. Who made you all-knowing? You always lecture at me about politics, Henry, as though I don't have any idea about it all. Well I do, and if I don't agree with you, that's too bad. Come on, it's lunch time and Maria hates us to be late.'

He saw her flick her hair back and stand up, signalling the discussion was at an end. Perhaps he had gone on too long, bored her? Been too prosy? He didn't have the knack Louis and John had of putting across their views firmly, impressing. But it didn't change the way he thought or the distant concern in his mind about how the future was shaping up. He wanted Eleanor and her family to be safe and happy. That was why he went on sometimes and perhaps bored her. But he saw now she was looking thoughtful as they wandered back to the house, and worried. He put his arm around her shoulders, gave her a slight squeeze.

'Don't mind me. I'm just a doom and gloom merchant. Forget what I just said.' He twisted his lips into a self-deprecating smile, his thin face full of charm and concern.

Eleanor smiled. 'You know what worries me, Henry? Sometimes I think you're the only one of us all who's really got his head screwed on right and we're just so busy thinking we're smarter and more fun that we're riding for a terrible fall.' Her words were out before she considered them, wishing she could take them back as she saw his mouth tighten slightly, wince. She hadn't meant to suggest he was dull. She hadn't meant it like that at all. Because he wasn't. But, just sometimes, she wished he would do something wild. Something totally crazy that said, oh, to hell with everyone and everything, this is what I want to do.

But he didn't. He was the perfect son, the perfect friend, the perfect student. She saw him smile now, painfully.

'I doubt it, Eleanor. The world doesn't really work like that. Only in fairy tales does it work out that the drudges are the big winners. I shouldn't worry too much if I were you.' There was irony and a touch of embarrassment in his voice. He held the door open for her and she walked in before him.

'You're not a drudge, Henry,' she said guiltily.

'No, I don't think I am really.' His brown eyes watched her. 'I guess I just care too much. Silly of me.' And she felt so sorry for him, so sorry for her own careless remark, that she drew his arm through hers and kissed his cheek.

'You could never care too much, Henry. That's what I like about you.' She was rewarded by a smile of such sweetness that she wondered yet again why Henry was not the man she hoped one day would be hers. And then she sighed at the thought of that other figure who dominated her dreams.

*

Christmas was a big event in the Fawcett calendar. Clarissa spent weeks preparing the palácio, 'spring-cleaning' it, as she liked to call it, polishing the silver and brass and decking the doors and fireplaces with pale gold, gauzy ribbon holding up long swoops of plaited greenery and wreaths. The hall blazed with white candles and bowls of roses, the sideboards groaned under plates of nuts and oranges studded with cloves, glass tiers of sugared fruits, pears, sugarplums, kumquats all tied with a pale silvery green ribbon, gold-wrapped chocolates, iced stollen and miniature croquembouches. Wonderful scents wafted through the rooms of spices and fragrant potpourri. Lamps were lit in every room, and poinsettia blazed in the hearths instead of the real fires that would have been too unbearable at that time of year.

It wasn't like an English Christmas really, there would never be any snow and the sun shone brightly outside, but the atmosphere was all important, Clarissa felt. She hoarded pine cones from each previous year, saving them up as they were so difficult to find, and gilding them with gold paint. Isobel and Eleanor helped, fighting over who should tie the orange ribbons around the paraffin lamps and who should tie the cinnamon sticks in bundles and leave them in every bedroom. Dried flowers, herbs and seed pods were hung in corners, and mistletoe hung in every doorway. Clarissa made the plum puddings herself weeks in advance, leaving them to darken in the larder.

Maria and Adélia cooked biscuits and glazed breads which Eleanor painted red and green with food colouring and proudly presented on the library table.

Isobel and Clarissa made pomanders out of nuts and spices and wrapped them up as presents for anyone who dropped by during the twelve days of Christmas, along with jars of spices, pears and slices of fruit cake, pickled quail eggs and savoury chutneys.

Charles invented new and alarmingly potent versions of eggnog and punch and insisted that everyone taste his

208

creations, resulting in a rosy glow that lasted for hours.

The Christmas presents were spread beneath the tree, flowing like a gaily coloured tapestry across the floor and brightening the otherwise sombre library. The tree itself was tied with hundreds of red ribbons and posies of white dried flowers, clear glass baubles that spun in the air and reflected the lights of the room, and intricately sewn toys of velvet and brocade. From every branch a small white candle balanced precariously. It was a beautiful sight and they gathered around it, exclaiming at its perfection, vowing there would never be another tree quite so wonderful.

Still there was no word from John.

On Christmas Eve, it was traditional for the Fawcetts to throw a party. Not more than forty people, all close friends, who stopped by for champagne and canapés, rather than the more English sherry and ginger wine and fruit cake. Some concessions had to be made to the weather, Clarissa thought. They gathered in the library and the drawing-room and the hall, the women elegant and gleaming in cocktail dresses, the men darkly suited, mingling and chatting and laughing, drinking too much and eating too much, their enjoyment obvious in the deep, throaty murmur that filled the air. Almost like purring. Eleanor helped Maria and Adélia pass around plates and Honório and Fernando served the drinks.

Isobel was radiant in a new dress that she had begged and sulked and threatened for, and Louis was appreciative as only Louis knew how to be. Henry was there, smiling politely at an older woman's tales of her latest trip to Europe, darting occasional looks across to Eleanor. She smiled mischievously and disappeared between the dark shoulders of two men, her white broderie anglaise skirt all that remained for a moment and then that too was snatched through the gap out of sight.

Charles Fawcett stood near the drinks table in the hall, talking to Henry's father, Senhor Arreas de Botelho, one of the foremost barristers in Rio. They were discussing politics, of course. Everyone in Brazil discussed politics. Charles raised his glass and drank deeply. He smiled at his old friend, about to renew his attack, when there was a commotion behind him. He saw his friend's eyes widen, his face remaining coolly well-bred, detached. A ripple of astonishment, quiet and subdued ran around the room. Charles turned around, his fist tightening in anger. His breath exhaled sharply.

John stood in the doorway, his peacoat hunched over his shoulders, a bag dangling from one hand. He was unshaven and red-eyed, his jeans torn across one knee, his shirt open at the neck. In his other hand, he held tightly to the reason for everyone's astonishment.

Teresa stood awkwardly beside John, staring at a sea of faces, wide-eyed, closed-mouthed, all looking at her. She knew instantly that what she had worn was wrong. Totally and humiliatingly wrong. From the feathered pincushion of a hat over her left ear, to the red satin dress that clung so tightly, to the four-inch stilettos on her feet that she had been so thrilled with only a few moments before. All wrong. These people were in subdued shades, even the reds somehow less red than her dress, few shiny materials, no very high heels – no hats at all! They stared at her for a moment, a blink of the eye, and then gently, involuntarily turned back to whomever they were talking to before her appearance had so surprised them. There were no unfortunate lapses of manners on their side, they seemed to say, even their astonishment had been toned down, discreet. Like themselves.

Teresa turned to run. But John had her tightly by the hand and he wouldn't let her go, holding her by his side. And then she saw a girl come up to them, a tall, very fair girl in a simple white dress and almost flat shoes, who smiled and stood in front of Teresa, mercifully hiding her from the curious sidelong glances still being darted across the room. Teresa's mouth dropped open.

She had never seen such a girl, all fair and smooth and gentle, such a young lady! The girl held out her hand, stooping over a little in the same way John had, as though her thoughts were entirely centred on the person before her. Her eyes seemed to smile, not by any particular movement, no fluttering of eyelashes, but by intensifying some inner light so that they appeared warm and welcoming. Teresa felt John release her hand and, tentatively, she reached out and shook hands with the girl.

'Hullo, I'm Eleanor. I'm so glad you could come to our Christmas party. We weren't sure whether John was going to turn up or not,' the girl said, her voice low and pretty, infinitely appealing.

Teresa closed her mouth carefully and swallowed before attempting to speak. 'I'm Teresa. Are you John's sister?' From the surprise on the girl's face, it was obvious she wasn't. Another mistake. Teresa groaned inside, knowing there was nothing here for her. Oh, why couldn't John have mentioned more about his family? Why couldn't he have instructed her in more of the social graces that obviously came so naturally to him and everyone else here? He had told her she was beautifully dressed when she had surprised him and gone out and bought herself a completely new outfit. Now she knew what that tremor to his mouth had meant. He was enjoying humiliating her!

Eleanor saw the shame and anguish in the girl's face, the way her eyes sought for an escape, and she felt terribly sorry for her. How could John have brought her here, dressed like this? Where had he picked her up? Oh, he was impossible!

'No, no, I'm John's cousin. This is my father's house – Charles Fawcett – John's uncle. Please, do come in. You must have come a long way.' She glanced at the bag in John's hand. 'Why don't you come upstairs so you can freshen up a little first? John, your bedroom's all made up and there's a suit laid out for you, if you mean to come down and join us.' Eleanor's voice became cool when she addressed her cousin. She saw him nod briefly at her before looking back across at the people gathered in the hall. So, this was to be their greeting! After what had passed between them last time. No matter, it was all for the best.

She swallowed hard over the pain in her throat and smiled at Teresa.

'Come along, Teresa. John can find his own way. We'll go upstairs together, shall we?' She led the girl through the press of expensive scents and cigars, talking to her all the way of trivial pleasantries. Anything to keep the girl's eyes on her and not on the people they passed. Eventually they were in her bedroom and she closed the door on the laughter outside.

Teresa had never seen a room like it. The rest of the house had been magnificent, yes, and she had been overwhelmed by it all but this, this one room! Oh, what she would give to have a room like this. With walls of a papered print, flowers and birds and Chinese pagodas in pale blues and greens, and with that rug on the floor, covering the polished wooden boards, that almost seemed to match the wallpaper and the curtains at the windows. A little writing desk and a chair, a big wooden bed with soft pillows and sheets, all white, and an embroidered counterpane of fine handkerchief-linen and sheer white gauzy curtains that fell around the bed. She looked at the row of dolls in the corner, sitting on a wicker chest and the large, earless teddy bear that had lost most of its fur. She felt a deep pang of loss. Teresa knew a little about nice things. She had looked in the shops in Salvador, the very expensive shops many times. But she had never seen anything like this. Not with its mixture of graciousness and homeliness, its nest of security. This was what she had been deprived of as a child.

She wandered over to the dressing table and picked up the heavy silver-backed mirror, rubbing her thumb over the handle like a talisman, examining the initials carved into it.

Eleanor watched her in silence. 'Would you like to use the bathroom and get changed, Teresa?' she asked after some moment's debate with herself. Perhaps she could bluff her way through this, play the fairy godmother to this girl, and make her emerge presentable. Soften some of the rage she had read in her father's eyes, some of the dismay in her mother's. One of Isobel's dresses would fit Teresa.

212

'Oh, um, I don't have anything else to wear. I – we didn't know you were having a party.' That was a lie. John had warned her that there might be one in progress, that there always was a party Christmas Eve. Which was why she had bought the dress and shoes and hat. She reached up suddenly and wrenched at the hat, pulling it free from her hair, and squashing it tightly in her hand.

Eleanor's hands fluttered in the air, as though to say, no, no, don't do that, don't worry, we'll sort it all out. She saw the shame in the girl's eyes and she pitied her intensely.

'I won't be a moment. Why don't you just sit down and I'll be right back? I know just the thing for you.' She slipped out of the room and reappeared, seconds later, with the dress that Isobel had worn last year and rejected this year as being too threadbare for anyone to wear. It had only been worn twice.

Eleanor held it up, a discreetly cut green silk dress with satin bindings on short filipino sleeves.

Teresa glanced at her, questioning, then shook her head. 'Oh no, I mean I couldn't!' What she meant was she wouldn't. She wasn't about to be patronized; wasn't going to be given hand-me-downs from anyone. What was some old dowdy dress like that going to do for her? Make her fade into the brickwork and let this beauty bloom all on her own? Teresa frowned, thinking the girl was probably more cunning than she seemed, was probably trying to put her down in some clever, fina gente way. Make a joke of her, the way John had made a joke of her. For a moment she felt tears prickle in her eyes and she brushed them away angrily.

'Oh, please, Teresa. It'll look lovely on you, really. And while you look so nice now, I don't think it's really right for the party, is it? So just try it on. If you don't like it, then you can take it off again. All right?' Eleanor coaxed, reading the resentment and hurt in the girl's eyes. She cursed John beneath her breath. Arrogant, selfish, hateful. She ran out of words and fumed instead.

Teresa didn't know how to refuse, so with sullen grace,

213

she took the dress and waited for Eleanor to leave the room. Eleanor, used to a sister and a convent school where none of the girls thought twice before stripping off in front of each other for sports, stood waiting for Teresa to undress. When, finally, she realized her error, Teresa had already begun to pull her dress off, angrily, with short jerks at the zipper. Eleanor apologized and stepped out of the room.

She closed the door after her and turned, almost bumping into John. He was shaven and dressed in a suit and tie and looked once more appropriate to his surroundings. So easy for him to be a chameleon, back and forth, just a game really, Eleanor thought. And that poor girl in there, trying desperately to follow him, was the one who had to pay the game's penalties. Eleanor shook with indignation.

'Merry Christmas, Eleanor,' John said, smiling. He seemed relaxed and happy. He leaned forward and kissed her cheek and she jerked away from him. He didn't notice. 'You coming down? I got you something for Christmas I think you'll like. From Bahia. It's very exotic and different up there. I had a fabulous time and I earned some money too. Not much but enough to buy some presents and have a little spare now. You should see Salvador. Amazing place. I'll take you one day, if you like.' He seemed unaware that she was angry with him, chatting easily on about where he had been, what he had seen. As though he were a different person from the John she knew who read her every thought. He didn't notice her short, clipped replies, her stiff back.

He didn't once mention Teresa and for that alone, Eleanor could not forgive him. Eventually she introduced the subject herself.

'Is that where you met Teresa? Up in Bahia?' She saw the lids droop lower over John's eyes, his face become still.

'That's right. Where is she now?'

'In my bedroom, getting changed. Good of you to finally ask. Tell me, didn't you think she would look out of place here, or was that your idea of a joke?' She saw his eyes glint

214

beneath the eyelids, his face become aloof.

'Don't be stupid, Eleanor!' He was impatient and annoyed at her accusation. 'She went out and blew all her savings on that outfit, especially for tonight. How could I tell her it wasn't appropriate? I was just hoping she wouldn't notice and to hell with what anyone else thinks. Why on earth would you think I'd find humiliating her a joke? Or has dear Papa been working on you again?' He leaned close, his head to one side, quizzing her.

'I think you're forgetting whose house you just brought your – friend – into. I feel sorry for her, and I feel sorry for my parents who, in case you didn't notice, were also humiliated in front of a lot of people who matter to them. So don't expect me to be sorry for you. Why should I? You just do whatever you want and damn anyone else, damn their feelings – damn mine! Why don't you go downstairs and show them how much you don't care, John? I better see how Teresa's getting on.' She turned and walked back to her bedroom, lifting her hand to knock on the door.

John pulled her roughly back beside him. 'Is that what you think? That I don't care about you?' He stared at her and she stubbornly refused to match his gaze. 'Eleanor, you're the reason I went away to begin with. You ought to know that.' Why, she thought, why should I know that? But he continued on in a rush. 'Because I couldn't –' he broke off, searching for the words. 'Because it's too difficult being near you for long at the moment. You're still only a child, although you don't look like one. And I can't always be responsible for my actions.

'So I took off and had some fun upcountry and met Teresa and had some fun there too. It's normal, you know, for someone of my age. And I brought her back with me because I like her and I owe her that much. She wanted to get away, get out of Salvador and I was her only chance. She helped me while I was there, and now I'm going to help her. Find her a job down here, help her get started. But that's all. When she's on her own feet, I'll edge out of her life, get on with my own. It's just an – an arrangement if

215

you like – that suits both of us at the moment and no one's going to get hurt. No one.'

He was surprised when Eleanor laughed. A derisive, scornful laugh. 'No one except Teresa if you plan to keep introducing her where she's neither expected nor, quite frankly, wanted. I'm sorry, I probably sound like a snob to you but I'm truly not trying to be. You put Teresa through hell when you brought her in here like that. Didn't you see her shrivelling up inside? She thinks you enjoyed making fun of her – I could see it in her eyes – and she's very hurt. You've brought her somewhere where she doesn't know a soul – doesn't belong – and can't survive the way she did up in Salvador, and now she thinks you're going to humiliate her in public like this. Those people down there aren't going to accept her. You know that. Why on earth did you subject her to that?'

She could see anger, both at himself and at her for pointing out his insensitivity, beginning to crowd out the light from his face, the joy he had had in coming home. He brushed his hair back out of his eyes with a jerky movement of his hand and became even more unapproachable.

'I didn't think she would notice. Okay, so tonight was a bad idea. That was – stupid, thoughtless, of me. I'm sorry. I'll keep her out of things, away from your parents. But I didn't mean to hurt her. She's been begging to meet my family ever since I first met her. I thought she'd get a kick out of it.' He sounded confused, even annoyed, as though he were the one who had been hard done by.

Eleanor shook her head at him. 'Go downstairs and make your peace with Papa. Don't get him angry, John, or that'll be it. You'll be banned from here for good. I'll try and do something to make Teresa presentable. Tell me something, is she planning on continuing – what's she thinking of doing down here, anyway?' She carefully skirted around mentioning Teresa's previous profession. Perhaps John didn't know? Perhaps she oughtn't to know about such things herself, though it was hard to think how she could avoid knowing in Rio, of all places. What did people imagine convent girls talked about anyway?

'I thought I'd try and get her started in modelling. Louis should have some connections; he runs with that sort of crowd. I don't know, we'll have to see.' John didn't want to discuss it anymore. He was tired of the subject already and would have liked to just give Teresa some money and show her the door but he couldn't. That look of need in her eyes and trust that he would help her, prevented him from saying anything, from ever hurting her. Like a rope binding her to his side. He sighed and walked down the hall, leaving Eleanor alone.

When Eleanor returned to her room, she found Teresa turning from side to side in front of the mirror, a pleased, even triumphant, expression on her face. She stopped guiltily when Eleanor closed the door behind her and looked embarrassed.

'Is this all right? I know it's a bit loose but –' She shrugged and faltered as Eleanor stood still, staring at the girl.

'But it's fabulous on you, Teresa. My sister never looked half so good in it. Oh, just wait till John sees you!' She forgot for a moment that she didn't want John to continue seeing this girl. She was entranced instead by the way Teresa looked, all the cheapness and flashiness of the girl who had walked in the door gone, a totally different girl standing now in her bare feet looking elegant and exotic and quite, quite beautiful. Eleanor felt a moment's pang that she would never look so good.

'We'll put your hair up, in a tight roll and here, how about this necklace? Gold will look good with that green colour.' She held up a plain but heavy chain that encircled the throat and a pair of matching earrings that she had been given by Papa for her birthday; Teresa's eyes gleamed. A pair of shoes from Eleanor's own cupboard, since both her and Teresa's feet were much larger than Isobel's, were pulled out and the two girls laughed and chatted excitedly over the transformation.

When Eleanor heard Teresa had no surname, she

217

thought hard for a moment. 'You must have one. Everyone will expect it and besides, if you want to go into modelling, you'll need one. Just pick a last name, right now. Go on.'

'Well, I don't know really. Maybe, Lopes? How does that sound?' Teresa said uncertainly.

Eleanor shrugged. 'Why not? You can always change it later, if you find something better. But at least for now, you have one. Teresa Lopes. Yes, that goes well.'

By now Teresa was dressed, her hair pulled back severely from her face, showing the beauty of her cheek bones and the lovely lines of her throat, the dress flattering her figure as no other had ever done before. The gold glinted against her tawny skin. She looked like one of the expensive models seen swaying elegantly down the catwalks in the better couture houses of Rio. Eleanor felt quite plain beside her.

When they descended the stairs together, more than a few pairs of eyes were focused on Teresa, but none held the same expressions of an hour before. Most didn't realize it was the same girl. Those eyes were filled with admiration or envy, depending upon the gender of the beholder. Some did recognize her and sniffed disapprovingly but not with any amusement or contempt. Teresa's appearance put her far beyond those strictures. Isobel stared in outrage at the dress, mouthing furiously to the two girls by her side. Louis's sisters. Eleanor ignored her and led Teresa over to her mother.

'Mama, this is John's friend, Teresa Lopes. She's just come down from Salvador to work in Rio. Teresa, this is my mother, Senhora Fawcett. Mother knows lots of the big fashion houses, don't you, Mama? Teresa wants to get a job as a model. You could help introduce her to somebody, couldn't you?' Eleanor felt guilty pressuring her mother in such a way. But someone had to help the girl and John obviously hadn't thought further than the next ten minutes. Her eyes pleaded with her mother not to be angry.

Clarissa obliged, holding out her hand. 'Hullo, Teresa. How nice to meet you. So you want to be a model? Uh, well, I expect I could mention you to someone. Since you're a friend of John's. Perhaps we could discuss it later?' Clarissa smiled smoothly, her calm expression showing none of the turmoil within her. None of the dismay. She glanced at her daughter. 'Why don't you take Teresa over and introduce her to some of your friends, my dear? I must just go and check on the refreshments. Excuse me.' She drifted away and Eleanor had to admire the way her mother had handled herself. Not a hint of displeasure, not a trace of condescension.

Teresa was thrilled, her speech thickening with excitement. 'Your mother is so nice. Very charming. Do you think she will introduce me to a fashion house? I would work very hard and do everything they said. Truly I would. Oh, that is my dream, to become a model and to live in Rio de Janeiro. Nothing can compare to that. You don't know how happy this makes me.'

Eleanor smiled, thinking what a nice, straightforward sort of girl she was. Naïve almost. There was a quality to her that was endearing, and Eleanor understood easily how John could have become involved.

And then, as though Teresa's mind had been completely wiped of her thoughts of a moment before, she parted her lips and gazed up at someone behind Eleanor's shoulder, with evident fascination. It seemed that something could, and did, compare to Teresa's dream. Eleanor turned and saw Louis was standing there, smiling broadly, holding out two glasses of champagne. She sighed.

'You both seem to be without drinks. Here you are, Eleanor, and this is for you, my dear. I don't think I caught your name? And such a beauty as you should have a name. I'm Louis Preston and a good friend of John's.' The implication, Eleanor thought angrily, was that good friends share and share alike. Well, not Teresa, Louis. You can think again.

'Teresa Lopes,' Teresa murmured, still in a daze of admiration at the young man before her. She smiled and took a sip of her drink, trying not to pull a face when she found it sour on her tongue. She dipped her head and gazed up at Louis in the same movement, fluttering her eyelashes. Louis put out his hand and leaned, very close, to Teresa's shoulder. They gazed into each other's eyes. Eleanor looked around desperately for John but met instead the watchful gaze of Henry, sizing up the situation and coming to her rescue. She breathed with relief as she introduced Henry to Teresa, slipped her own arm through Louis's and led him, protesting, away to where Isobel was sulking in a corner.

John was outside on the terrace beyond the library. He had made his apologies to his uncle, fortunately catching him with several people so that few words could be exchanged, and now he was purposely absenting himself from the rest of the party. God, these people bored him! He leaned back in the chair, crossed his feet on the balustrade, and tossed back a double whisky. From his uncle's decanter. It burned down his throat, warming him, lifting some of the depression from his mind.

Everything had been so different in Salvador. There he had worked hard, enjoyed the simple pleasures of a meal and bottle of wine, enjoyed Teresa. He had been accepted for himself, without any of this social posturing, this gauging of how much money a person had, what clothes they wore, what cars they drove. Teresa had needed him and made him feel good and he had enjoyed that unqualified esteem. Here, there was no such thing. His uncle was never pleased, no matter what he did, his friends were caught up in the social whirlwind as though it were the most important thing in the world, even Eleanor – she was judging him and finding him lacking because he had the temerity to mix with people who weren't from her circle.

He was sure that was what she was so angry about, making hypocritical noises about how unhappy poor Teresa was, not wanting her hurt. God, it all made him sick!

He leaned his head back and looked up at the night sky, at the different constellations, trying to make them out.

220

That one there was Ursa Major and the one just below it and to the left had to be Ursa Minor, he thought. And next to that, Cassiopeia and Andromeda and above that, Perseus. He wasn't sure about the others. Nick had been the one who was good with the stars but those were in the northern hemisphere, when they slipped out on the roof of Wykham at night to stare up at the flashing points of light. Here, in the south, there were many John couldn't recognize.

For a moment he felt at a loss, missing intensely the easy friendship he had built up with Nick. It would have been so nice to have had Nick here to talk with, to laugh away the melancholy that plagued him. Who else knew him like Nick? Who else had seen the black moods, the anger, and could still joke him out of it? Just Nick – and Eleanor. He shrugged away from that thought. She was angry with him and appalled at what he had done. Her disapproval soured all the joy of the last three months, the feeling he was doing something entirely on his own that didn't ask anything from his family and yet that was still good. Still admirable. Now, after Eleanor's few choice words, he began to think of it as a self-indulgent lapse of good sense. A callous use of another person. Perhaps she was right? He wished Nick were there to tell him what he thought. He stared up at the sky again.

'How could you, Eleanor! Just take my favourite dress and give it to some tramp that John's dragged in! You can damned well pay me for it. I'll never be able to wear it again after this! You're just so high-handed, aren't you, Miss Bountiful, helping the poor!' Isobel's whisper became vicious, 'But I notice you didn't give her your dress, did you?'

'Oh, for God's sake, Isobel, I had to do something and nothing of mine would have fit her. She's so much smaller than me. And she was so miserable, so humiliated – anyway, she's wearing my shoes and my gold jewellery, so you got off quite lightly. And she's a nice girl. You'd like her

221

if you talked to her. Louis, can't you talk to Isobel? The last thing we need is a scene with Isobel demanding Teresa take off that dress.' Eleanor appealed to the equally sulky young man beside her, wishing somebody apart from Henry could be relied upon to help out occasionally. She couldn't see John anywhere.

Louis shrugged. 'I don't care if she takes her dress off right here and now. Be quite a sight, I should think. Damn that John, he's a sly dog, now isn't he? Never breathed a word to me about it all and I had a couple of letters from him too. Where is he now, anyway? I need a word with him.'

'Not about her, you don't!' Isobel said firmly, and pushed him back against the wall. 'Come to think of it, Louis, I'd say I need a word with *you*' – she emphasized the pronoun, jabbing at his chest with her finger – 'about quite a few things. Eleanor, go and tell that – that creature – that if she gets anything down my dress, I'll personally throw her out of here. Which is what should have happened to begin with, anyway!'

Eleanor left them to it and thankfully eased her way towards the library. John might be in there and she wanted a word with him herself.

She found him out on the terrace, still staring up at the stars.

'Hullo there,' she said.

'Hullo there, yourself.' There was a long pause.

'Teresa's making a big hit in there with the men. You better watch out for Louis.' She heard him snort.

'Louis goes for anything that isn't nailed down – and sometimes for that sort too. Teresa can look after herself, believe me. Who'd you leave her with?' he added, as though not quite believing himself.

He laughed when Eleanor answered, 'Henry.'

'Oh well, she's perfectly safe then. Good old Henry wouldn't dare touch a hair on her head,' he mocked and Eleanor felt a flash of resentment.

'Just because Henry's loyal in his affections, unlike Louis

222

and obviously, unlike you, doesn't make him scared of women. Believe me, he's not!'

'Oh? Really? And just what would you have me believe? You know this through personal experience, I take it?' John's voice had become low and mocking. He turned his head sideways, to look at Eleanor.

'None of your business, I'd say. I haven't asked any details about you and Teresa, have I? I'm just saying Henry's worth a lot more than you give him credit for, you and Louis. He's two years younger than you both, for a start, and he's a lot more decent and caring than either of you. You can bet Teresa's quite happy in his care and quite safe too. Whereas Louis would very much like to move into your shoes, or perhaps I should say, your bed!' she snapped.

John stood up abruptly, the chair rocking back and falling, with a clatter, on to the stone terrace. 'What exactly are you trying to say, Eleanor? Has Henry taken your fancy, finally? Is that it? Or is it Teresa you're really cross about?' He gave a quizzical smile. 'You know I like Teresa but I don't much care what she gets up to. She's her own girl, so if she wants to get involved with Louis, that's not going to bother me. And it shouldn't really bother you either. It's entirely Teresa's choice, not any of ours. So leave her alone.

'You, on the other hand,' he took her arm and pulled her up close to him, 'do bother me and if dear Henry has been romancing you, then I'll be the first one to let him know how much you are my concern. Are you saying he has?' His voice was very quiet, totally serious.

Eleanor shook her head. 'Don't be so stupid, John. The only one's who ever done anything more than kiss my cheek is you. And you have some nerve acting like an outraged father where Henry's concerned. You're the lecher round here, not him!' She almost spat it out.

John's face became pale beneath the deep tan, his cheek bones seemed to protrude more acutely. That awful compulsion of his to get away, that dread of thinking too hard about Eleanor. No, he couldn't have. Surely not! He looked uncertain, shaken. 'I don't – what do you mean? When have I ever – done anything to you? When?'

'The night you came back from England, in case you were too drunk to remember. The night before you just disappeared for the last three months and shacked up with the nearest ... Anyway, it doesn't matter, does it?' She was appalled by what she was saying, the words spewing out of her mouth, the hurt that had been bottled up inside her over the weeks taking charge of her speech. But she was equally appalled that he had no memory of that night, had not spent long hours, days, weeks agonizing over what had happened as she had. As she still did.

'What, what happened between us? I didn't–?' His voice was broken, faltering.

Eleanor saw the dismay in his face and felt a flicker of pity. He didn't know. She put a hand on his arm and he clasped it tightly in his hand.

'No. Not that. But you were – oh God, never mind! I can't go into all this. It's humiliating enough that you don't even remember.' Her voice became husky. 'Well thanks, John, I guess I rank even lower than Teresa. At least you remember her, even if you don't particularly want her anymore.' She snatched her hand from his hold and would have walked away but John reached out and touched her face, stroked his fingers along her cheek, and she hesitated.

'Tell me,' he said, his voice hoarse. And so she did.

When she finished, he was silent for a few moments, shaking his head. Inside, he raged at himself. 'I'm so sorry, Eleanor. My God, don't you know that's why I had to get away? Because I was scared of something like that happening. My poor girl, holding all that in and thinking I'd just shrugged it off, gone off with the nearest girl who came my way.' He pulled her into his arms, cradling her against him, his face against her hair. 'You are the most important person in the world to me, Eleanor. Always remember that. No one else matters except you.' He leaned back against the balustrade, still holding her against him and he felt her give a shuddering sigh.

'Except that we can't ever be together, John. Not ever. We're first cousins.' Her voice became firm again, only a little whisper inside her saying over and over, 'Oh God, why do we have to be so close in blood? Why? Why? It's so unfair.'

'I know. But that can't stop us caring about each other most, can it? You do love me best, don't you Eleanor?' His words revealed the fear that lurked deep in his mind, always tantalizing, always debilitating. That need for her to love him more than her father, more than Henry, more than anyone. For her to need him too.

Eleanor heard it and recognized that appeal. 'I love you like everyone else in my family – except a bit more. But I can't love you any other way, John. Just as family. You know that.'

'Yes, but you still love me best. Don't you? That's good enough,' he said, silently adding 'for now'. He relaxed and Eleanor relaxed against him.

Henry and Teresa found them like that, in each other's arms, out on the terrace. They had been looking for them for some time, Teresa wanting to go, Henry wanting finally to talk to Eleanor himself. The drawing-room and library had been searched, and both Henry and Teresa had been stopped and questioned and drawn into conversation by people along the way, so that it had taken some time for them to work their way over to the terrace and the open french doors. And there they were, John and Eleanor. Pressed together in the dark, just one combined shadow.

Henry stiffened and tried to lead Teresa away, before she could see, but she resisted, peering out into the gloom until she too saw them both. She stopped and watched, waiting for something to happen, for herself to feel something beyond the enormous sense of betrayal she had first sensed when John brought her into this house. Beside her she heard Henry shift, uncomfortable and unwilling to be a spectator any further. He started to move back, into the library and, after a moment, Teresa followed him.

225

Henry was a nice young man, she thought. Attractive and beautifully mannered and – very, very nice. Much nicer than anyone she had ever met before. She looked up at him and saw the pain in his face.

'You don't want to go caring about her,' Teresa said roughly. 'She's got something going with John and has had for a long time. I knew there was something between them, the minute I saw them both together. She'll go breaking your heart, Henry. Don't you let her.' But he was smiling sadly at her now, taking out his handkerchief and she realized suddenly that it was for herself, that she was the one crying and that made it all worse somehow. She had to get out, get away.

'Eleanor can't help herself where John's concerned. Nothing has ever happened between them – you mustn't think that. But they're very close. Always have been, ever since we were very small children all playing together. And he saved her life. That makes her his, in some ways,' Henry said, trying to explain and excuse.

Teresa sighed and coughed a little. 'He never told me. He never told me anything. We lived together for nearly three months and I know nothing at all about him. How d'you figure that?'

'That's John. I can't explain him to you. Only Eleanor.' Henry shrugged and smiled, his thin cheeks creasing into a smile of charm and slight puckishness.

Teresa nodded, 'Yeah, that's John all right. Say, Henry, do you know anywhere I could stay? John isn't going to want me here and I don't know Rio yet. You know any little hotels, or something? I don't have much money,' she added, in case he should suddenly think to put her up at a hotel he would be familiar with himself. She saw him consider her request, his brown eyes steady and intelligent.

'Well, maybe. One place I can think of that Louis told me about. It shouldn't be very much for the night and I can give you some money to help out. You sure you don't want to stay here? I thought Eleanor's mother was going to try and find you a place at a couture house?'

226

'I'm sure. Besides,' she snorted, 'they were probably just saying that to shut me up, stop me pestering them in the middle of their party. Come on, I want to go.' She took his arm and pulled him towards the hall, ignoring his requests that she reconsider. She had had enough of this place and the sort of people that went with it.

'And where might you two be off to then?' Louis stepped in front of them as they were nearly to the door.

'Nowhere that need concern you, Louis,' Henry said firmly but Louis wasn't paying any attention.

He was smiling at Teresa and Henry felt her insistent pull on his arm weaken and stop altogether when Louis continued in a low and pleading voice, 'But you can't leave me like this, Teresa, with my heart snatched from my breast the moment I set eyes on you, and with no way of ever getting it back unless you let me see you again.'

It was flowery and, as far as Louis was concerned, grossly insincere but Teresa had never heard gallantry before. She opened her mouth wide with surprise and pleasure and told Louis not to worry, she wasn't going to run out on him. Why, she'd be happy for him to find her somewhere to stay and no, Henry, you needn't stay. Louis'll look after me.

Louis gave Henry a side grin, a bad luck, old fellow, try again in a few years sort of look that made Henry want to punch him hard and wipe that grin from his face.

Reluctantly, since to stay was only to annoy them both, Henry left Teresa in Louis's care and returned to the library. It was only eleven o'clock but he felt desperately tired. He wondered how long the evening would continue.

It was well after midnight when the last of the revellers were let out into the night and the large front doors bolted into place. John had discovered Teresa was missing with some guilt and had been about to go and look for her when Henry had discreetly revealed her whereabouts. John shrugged uneasily and then decided Teresa was in better hands with Louis than himself. Louis could help her more. He thanked Henry and turned away, yawning slightly and

Henry shook his head with a slight lift to his lips that was not in any way amused.

Eleanor was upset that Teresa should have fallen into Louis's clutches and Isobel was angry that Teresa should have gone off with her dress. The evening came to a less than harmonious close.

'And she took all your jewellery and shoes too, Miss Bleeding Heart. You'll never see those again, I'll lay you odds,' Isobel said bitterly.

For a moment Eleanor wanted to say, 'Yes, and she took Louis too,' but she would never have hurt Isobel like that and perhaps, after all, Isobel was right. Perhaps Teresa was just out for the good things in life.

Eleanor saw Henry to the door and thanked him for devoting so much of his evening to looking after Teresa. Around them their parents were busy calling farewells and Christmas wishes and laughing and joking loudly. Eleanor was surprised when Henry gave her an odd look and shrugged.

'Yes, well, you were so very occupied elsewhere, what else could I do? I'm just sorry I couldn't keep Louis away. But then, I'm not the sort a girl's likely to go for, am I? Merry Christmas.' He kissed her on the cheek and went out into the warm night without looking back at her. Eleanor felt as though she had neglected a dog she loved and depended on and then that dog had turned around and bitten her. She went to bed silently and lay awake long into the night, wishing she had been nicer to him.

The next two weeks were strained and difficult for everyone. John did his best not to be there much, seeing friends from his earlier schooldays and going out to films or to dinner. Charles had given John an allowance out of his trust fund and made few comments about how or where John should spend it. Charles didn't really care, as long as it took John out of the house and away from Eleanor.

Eleanor made an effort not to spend too much time with John, not to annoy her father, not to neglect Henry. She smiled at John's urging her to come out with him and shook her head. No, she said, she had arranged to see someone else that afternoon. Perhaps later? John nodded with feigned indifference and went out anyway.

Isobel was showing signs of a broken heart since Louis had barely been to see her and when he did, it was with distracted thoughts and impatience. Rumour had it that he had been seeing a great deal of Teresa and had arranged for her to be auditioned as a model for one of the lesser couture houses. Isobel sulked and cried but Louis refused to discuss it and was so transparently eager for university to start that Isobel began to suspect Teresa might well be moving down to São Paulo fairly shortly. There was nothing Isobel could do about it but she made sure she was not the only unhappy one in the house during those days of joy and peace on earth.

Clarissa, as usual, tried to keep everything calm and without friction, going out of her way to nip arguments in the bud and see that Charles was spoilt so outrageously he could barely muster the energy for an annoyed grunt. Merry Christmas, she told herself, joy to the world. But her mouth drooped a little and her eyes showed none of her former sparkle. Clarissa began to feel middle-aged.

Chapter Twelve

The three years of university passed rapidly. Louis and John set themselves up in an apartment together near the University of São Paulo but saw little of each other outside the walls of those rooms. Their interests began to diverge early on in the first year.

Louis continued his carefree, enjoyable life of parties, nightclubs and women and yet, somehow, managed to do enough work to make passing grades in his courses. He saw Teresa occasionally, on his return trips to Rio, but they were drifting apart also, she in her increasingly successful career, he in his desire to become comfortably settled after university in a good job that Isobel's father could provide. He wrote to Isobel a great deal.

John, his decision finally made in the months before university when he was up in Salvador, began to study anthropology, specifically urban poverty, and became increasingly disillusioned by the huge gap he saw between the rich and the poor in Brazil. He began sitting in on student meetings to discuss political reform, to bring down inflation, bring in state education. He gave speeches about how Brazil must fall in line with the process of democratization and socialization that the powers of Western Europe had adopted. He waved banners, wrote posters, agitated, and rebelled. The other students thought him a natural leader, his professors thought him brilliant, and the university authorities found him difficult and looked forward to his graduation.

He went on rallies, mixed with radical socialists, some covert Communists, drank heavily, smoked dope and began to avoid returning home during the holidays. He stopped writing to Eleanor.

For Isobel and Eleanor, they were also busy years. Isobel finished school and took a part-time job as a secretary for the Red Cross. She went to a great many parties, flirted with every eligible man in Rio de Janeiro and a number from outside, and made a few mothers raise questioning eyebrows at her modesty. But the offers of marriage poured in and she graciously refused them all, thus soothing a few of those mothers' anxious brows. In Louis's third and last year at university, she accepted a large diamond ring from him and began to plan her wedding trousseau. The wedding itself was to take place late in December 1961, after Louis had graduated.

Eleanor worked hard at school to keep her mind from other matters and passed her final exams with 'notable'. She decided on university in São Paulo and carefully began introducing the subject at dinner. Her father was uncooperative. Henry, also, thought university so far away was a bad idea. He told her of the student unrest down in São Paulo, the rallies, the riots, the crackdowns. He told her how ugly São Paulo was, how far away from her family, how lonely without her schoolfriends. Eleanor listened with deaf ears.

She didn't want a nice safe job like Isobel's and the chance to receive hundreds of marriage proposals, although she privately doubted whether she would receive any, not being as popular as Isobel with the young men of her circle. They found her intimidating both in mind and body, she realized, with the small frown that tended to form between her eyebrows when something worried her. It wasn't her fault she had a brain and could use it, nor was it her fault she was taller than most of the men she knew. It was their problem, not hers. Besides she just wasn't interested in any of that.

She wanted a degree in history and literature from São Paulo University. If John were there and going on for a master's, she wanted to be there too. In the meantime, to please her father she studied French at the Alliance Française and, to please herself, she began spending her free time teaching the poor women of the favelas how to read and write in some of the church schools the Colégio Sagrado Coração organized. It was charity work, she pointed out, when her father protested, perfectly acceptable. Just like Isobel's. It wasn't anything like Isobel's really and they both knew it. But Eleanor won that one.

Henry was now in law school and nearly finished. Just two more years and he would be joining his father's law firm. The thought gave him little joy. But he would also, soon, he thought, be earning a good salary. Be able to buy a place of his own, start campaigning in local politics ... get married. Soon.

He had become tall and lanky in his last year at school, his shoulders broadening, his body filling out into that of a man. An attractive, elegant man who hid a sharp mind behind a lazy, self-mocking smile and a shock of light brown hair that fell over brown eyes. He was surprised and discomfited when he suddenly became the object of a good deal of matrimonial speculation. He wasn't interested in mowing a path through the single girls of Rio. He just wanted Eleanor.

'Where you off to tonight then, John? Another fascinating discussion on the rights of the people and the wrongs of the government?' Louis was peering at himself in the mirror, adjusting his tie. He smiled with satisfaction and folded down the wings of his collar, giving the tie one last tug.

John, stretched out full length on the sofa, his nose in a book, made noncommital noises. 'Not sure yet. Something'll turn up. Pedro's coming over later, I think.' Pedro,

John's like-minded, politically active friend, was the son of one of the most prominent journalists in the country. A man known for his unbending stance on the issues of corruption and governmental inefficiency. A man the present government would dearly love to see fall under a bus – or even push. John saw Louis smother a yawn.

'What about you? Dinner party?' He knew it was, knew he had been invited himself and had even been tempted. But how could he justify his speeches about inequality and profligacy when he still attended the parties of the privileged himself?

Louis glanced at him and grinned. 'Yeh, well, Johnny-boy, you know how it is. Too many girls, too little time. I've only got four months left before I marry your fair little cousin. Let me enjoy it while I can.' He laughed when he saw John look annoyed and then indifferent. But Louis wasn't particularly bothered by John's disapproval. Johnny, he thought, was disapproving about just about everything these days. He was getting to be no fun at all.

Louis was thinking that same thought, later that evening, when he ran into John again outside a particularly well-known nightspot where certain members of the government were wont to spend their time and money. Most especially their money. John was in the grip of a policeman, looking calm and unperturbed despite the angry shouting going on all around him, directed both at himself and at the flustered-looking group standing around waiting for their cars. Louis recognized the minister in question.

John wasn't alone but part of a group of some five or six agitators who were simultaneously crying out for the policeman to release John, and for the minister in question to explain a certain military contract that seemed to have worked a rather excessive amount of money into his own pocket and provided inferior quality goods to the army. Louis saw Pedro, his dark face working angrily as he screamed denunciations, and he recognized most of the other members of John's group. All old political cronies, he thought with a sigh and wondered if it were too late to slip quietly back into the shadows.

But John had noticed him now, and was looking amused. He bowed his fair head in a mocking salute, ignoring the way the policeman tightened his grip. Louis grinned back. What the heck? He might as well go see what he could do. He strolled over.

'Hi there, ole buddy. Got a bit of trouble going here? You disturbing the peace again?' Louis's sudden appearance, casually elegant in dinner jacket and accompanied by equally well-dressed companions startled the policeman. He wrenched John's arm up a little tighter, just to be sure.

John grunted in pain and then forced himself to appear calm again. 'Not especially. Just thought we'd let a few people in on what our friends in the government have been up to again. But the minister seems a bit upset. They've sent for a squad of police, I suspect, so I wouldn't hang around.'

Louis looked uneasy for a moment. 'You really get a kick out of this, Johnny-boy? You like going to gaol?' He glanced at the policeman, saw the way John's arm was being pulled up behind him. The policeman lowered it slightly.

'No, not really. But if someone doesn't say something, who's going to ever look into all the corruption going on round here? Besides, Pedro's father'll bail us out. We haven't done anything wrong.' John seemed so very sure of himself, so quietly aloof and in command that even Louis was uneasily impressed. He could see how John was gaining such a following. He made brilliant, plausible speeches, always seemed to have some new scandal to reveal, and he certainly looked good when there was trouble. Yes, the guy had nerve, you had to give him that.

'Right, old son. Anything I can do?' He slipped his hands into his pockets, looking casual, as a police van careened down the street and spilled out several uniformed men. John smiled grimly as he watched them rush across the pavement. He looked back at Louis and grimaced. 'Yes. Don't tell my uncle.'

*

Clarissa waited patiently for Isobel to finish making her choice of material for the wedding dress, a difficult decision that involved draping herself first in raw silk, then in moiré and satin, and finally in taffeta. A long and complicated discussion was entered into with the seamstress over each of the fabrics, its crushability, its weight, the way it would cut, the way it would look in candlelight. The seamstress answered fully, as engrossed in the subject as Isobel herself.

Clarissa edged a glance at her watch. Nearly three o'clock. The fashion show started at three-thirty. Would they make it? Oh, why couldn't Isobel have waited until after the collection was shown? After all, Eleanor would be meeting them here then, and she could give Isobel the benefit of her advice as well. Clarissa sighed when Isobel threw all the bales of material down on the ground and announced that none of them were quite right and that she wanted to see more. The seamstress pursed her lips and clapped her hands and several assistants came running. Clarissa hoped Isobel only ever got married once.

By three-fifteen, the room was strewn with different fabric samples, each a lustrous shade of white, off-white, opaline, cream or ivory. Clarissa preferred the ivory taffeta herself and said so several times but Isobel's taste was not quite that of her mother's and the final choice was of a heavy cream silk that made Isobel's skin seem like milk against it. Sour milk, one of the assistants who had carried all the heavy material bales upstairs to the showing rooms, was heard to remark. Isobel gave her a narrow-eyed warning. After that, the veil of tulle was an easy decision in comparison.

By the time Clarissa was able to drag Isobel away from her wedding dress and next door to the fashion show, the first mannequins had begun their sway down the catwalk and Clarissa and Isobel had to settle for seats near the back of the room, rather than their normal, front-row places. Isobel wanted to make a fuss but Clarissa told her quietly

235

but firmly to sit down. Isobel saw the glint in her mother's eye and sat.

'I don't see why we can't go and sit in our usual seats. No one else is sitting there. And I can't see from here, Mama. That woman in front is totally blocking my view,' Isobel murmured petulantly but a glance at her mother's set profile caused her to sink back in her seat with a sigh.

Clarissa wondered whether Isobel would be more bearable once she was married and left home? When she only had to see her elder daughter perhaps once or twice a week? It was an exhilirating thought. One she had been indulging in for some time. Yet Charles was so set on offering Louis and Isobel a whole wing to themselves in the palácio. Daughters were supposed to be lost to a father, weren't they? Even if future sons-in-law were working for the family firm. Clarissa wished Charles would see reason before they gained a son who drank and played around too much, a daughter who would soon be a sour, dumpy matron, and a wing in their house that would echo to the battle lines already drawn up. She would lose the peace of her own house. If not her sanity.

'Oh look, Mama! Isn't it just too exquisite? I could wear that colour perfectly. It's really me, don't you think?' Isobel pointed out pale green silk pyjama pants that swirled elegantly around a particularly tall and lean black model and a matching silk top that haltered around the long, slender throat and exposed a daring amount of flesh. Clarissa could think of few things that would less suit a five foot three inch, buxom blonde.

'Write the number down, dear. There are quite a few more to come. We'll see them all first, don't you think?' Her attention was then caught by a particularly attractive girl modelling a black sequined cocktail dress, her bronzed skin smooth and taut where the back of the dress lowered in a deep 'V' shape down to a tiny waist. There was something familiar about the girl, Clarissa thought, waiting for her to turn back and approach them again. Something in the face that reminded her of someone. The girl turned, her head held high, her hair pulled tightly back from her face in a severe chignon. Heavy onyx and gold earrings hung beside the taut jawline, deep black eyes surveyed the audience calmly. It was Teresa.

Isobel realized at the same moment and gasped aloud. It was an angry, impatient, petulant sound. For once Clarissa didn't blame her. So, this was the street-girl that John had brought to Rio and Louis had so conveniently inherited. And moulded into his idea of what a woman should be, Pygmalion-like. Quite a change. Clarissa silently applauded both Louis's taste and Teresa's determination. She was more than a match for any woman now, particularly one who, though beautiful, liked her sweets far too much. Clarissa understood that gasp only too well.

'Mama! That's that creature! That beggar girl who stole my dress!' Isobel said loudly. Several people glanced at her, or shifted in their seats.

Clarissa cleared her throat. 'Hush, Isobel. There's no point in making a fuss. Besides, you never wanted that dress anyway. Just let it be.'

'Let it be? What about Eleanor's gold necklace! And what about Louis? This is the trollop who took him away from me for nearly a year, who utterly humiliated me. No, I will not let it be. Look at her, prancing around up there as though she were the cat's whiskers, thinking everyone's admiring her so. Well, I know what she really is, and I'm not going to let her get away with it,' Isobel hissed furiously and her mother winced inside. Oh, don't let Isobel make a scene, she prayed. Not here, not in front of all my friends.

'You'll just make a fool of yourself, Isobel,' Clarissa warned. 'Everyone will think you're just jealous and unsure that you can keep Louis. Just forget it. I promise you, you'll be sorry if you don't.'

'Not as sorry as she's going to be, depend upon it! But it's all right, Mama. I won't do anything to embarrass you right now. I was simply wondering how much Madame Chervil values our custom? My wedding trousseau alone should make us one of their bigger accounts this year, I would imagine. How much do you think Teresa's worth, compared to that? Or at any of the other better named houses? We're clients of all of them, aren't we?' Isobel's voice had dropped, become calmer, more controlled, more cutting.

Clarissa sighed. 'Leave her be, Isobel. It's all over now. Louis hasn't been seeing Teresa for nearly two years now. She can't do anything to you. Why go raking it all up again? What's the point?'

Isobel opened her pale blue eyes very wide. 'Why, revenge, Mama, of course! Just revenge.' She settled back in her seat, her pretty features showing to best advantage now that she was smiling. Isobel was made to be happy. It was a shame she so seldom was.

The show was ruined for Clarissa. She barely saw the swirl of colours and fabric adorning the girls who paraded up and down in front of her. The summer collection. Her favourite. And her favourite couture house. All ruined. Because all Clarissa could do was sit there tensely, anticipating Teresa's return each time, holding her breath tightly within her when Isobel muttered loudly at each appearance. Hoping nothing more would come of it but, of course, knowing it would. She knew Isobel.

When the show was over and everyone was filing out into the vestibule, Eleanor joined them. She had seen very little of the collection, arriving too late from her French language course to do anything more than stand at the back of the room and crane over people's heads at the fantasies flaunted before them. She was impatient with fashion shows; so little seemed to be practical or wearable, so much seemed to be self-indulgence by the designer who thought his creation so precious that good sense was lost and absurdity became the order of the day. But she had promised she would meet Isobel and Mama and help with the wedding dress decisions. God, she hoped Isobel only got married this once. What a palaver!

'Hullo there! Thought I'd missed you at first. I was busy looking for you over there, in your usual places. What on earth were you doing sitting right back there?' Eleanor greeted them with kisses on the cheek, and swept them sideways out of the exited throng. Clarissa sighed and looked at Isobel. Isobel rolled her eyes and made a sideways motion with her head towards her mother. Eleanor nodded at them both. Ah, I see. And she did.

'Eleanor, you won't believe who was in the show. As one of the models. That Teresa creature. Can you imagine? Looked quite ridiculous too, trying far too hard to look soignée and elegant. No one's likely to ever miss her beginnings, let me tell you. Once a tramp, always a tramp, is what I say.'

'Oh, you would know, would you?' Clarissa asked acidly. 'Oh do come on, for heaven's sake! Eleanor, tell Isobel to stop being such a wasp about it all. No good's going to come of badgering the girl, or getting her hounded out of the modelling business in Rio. She'll only go elsewhere – maybe to São Paulo. How would you like that, Isobel dear?' Clarissa's fine features were flushed, her eyes angry. Isobel's more rounded face was sullen and determined. Eleanor wished she hadn't agreed to meet them there at all.

'Why should I care? Louis will be back here by then and married to me. Let her go to São Paulo, by all means. Perhaps John will take her back in?' Isobel snapped.

'Oh shut up, do, Isobel!' Eleanor's temper surged and then she controlled it. 'Come on, I came all the way over here to see your wedding dress and all I've heard so far is a lot of nonsense about someone who really doesn't concern any of us. She's no threat to you, Isobel; you should know that. You're marrying one of the most eligible men in Rio, you're having a spectacular wedding with over five hundred guests, and you're going on your honeymoon to Europe! Everyone I know is wildly jealous of you. What does someone like Teresa matter? You can afford to be generous and just forget all about her. Come on, let's go see which material you chose.' Eleanor combined irritation and flattery to coax her sister out of her vindictive mood. For a while it looked as though it might work.

They headed back through the fashion house, towards their own private room where the cream silk was still waiting for Isobel's return. Clarissa trailed along after them, wishing unpleasant come-uppances for her elder daughter. But not really, she added, looking up at the ceiling. Not really.

As they were almost into the room and it looked as though the danger had been averted, Teresa came down the stairs with another model and walked right past them. Isobel's hand shot out, catching Teresa's dress in her fingers.

'Just a minute, my dear. I want a word with you about a certain green dress, a pair of shoes and a gold necklace and earrings. I'm sure you remember those items, don't you, Teresa? You stole them from our house three years ago, on Christmas Eve, after you gatecrashed our party.' Isobel's voice had always had the ability to carry clearly. Now it seemed particularly loud, particularly penetrating. Many of the guests looked up in surprise at the group by the stairs. Their expressions showed embarrassment and shock in equal measures.

Teresa's small, neat head turned to face her attacker. Her expression was contemptuous and, carefully hidden but still there, frightened.

'I don't know what you are talking about. Please let me go. You have mistaken me for someone else, madam.' Her accent had changed, become smoother, more acceptable in the circles to which she aspired. But it was still Teresa.

Eleanor tried to pull Isobel away. 'For heaven's sake, Isobel, don't! It doesn't matter anymore. And you're causing a scene. Everyone's looking!' She couldn't help her eyes meeting Teresa's, the model's eyes dark and liquid, full of fury.

Isobel ignored the warning. 'Let everyone look. I want everyone to know that this girl is a thief! She came from some slum, some whorehouse in Salvador, uninvited to our Christmas Eve party and then, when we treated her kindly and lent her some better clothes and jewellery to wear, she walked off with them all and never looked back. That's the sort of girl you're employing here, Madame Chervil.' The manageress of the fashion house had appeared, alerted by staff that an unpleasant scene was taking place between a model and a valued customer. Isobel put her hands on her hips and tapped her toe.

Madame Chervil looked aghast. She saw the determination in Isobel's chin, the tapping foot, and she saw one of her more esteemed customers walking out of her fashion house never to return. And all for what? Some model, some girl who, though very pretty and popular, counted for nothing. Everyone was watching, all her clients, having heard this girl accused of thieving. It wasn't possible for Teresa to stay. No, not at all!

Teresa read her employer's thoughts, saw the mouth opening to dismiss her and smiled bitterly. 'Don't bother, Madame Chervil. I wouldn't dream of staying here a moment longer.' She looked around the room, at the people still standing staring at them all, their ears straining to catch what was being said. She raised her voice and looked back at Isobel, smiled again.

'As for you, Senhorita Isobel, you should be more careful whom you accuse of stealing. Because I only took that dowdy old dress that you didn't want yourself in compensation for what was stolen from me that night. By her.' She pointed dramatically and everyone followed her finger, saw Eleanor standing by Isobel's side, her face drained of colour.

'Your sister. I wonder how many people here know she's having an affair with her cousin, her primo-irmão, John Campos de Serra?' Teresa paused, looking around. 'That's right. I caught them at it. Right there in her father's house, right in the middle of that dreary party that I was invited to. By John. That's why I walked off.' She was breathing heavily now, stoking up her rage, her eyes dark and dangerous.

'And when I did, your future husband, Louis Preston, insisted on accompanying me. That's why you're mad! Because he was my lover for a year and we made a fool of you. He cheated on you all the way through. As he still does. How do you like that, Senhorita Isobel, and you, Senhorita Eleanor? How is John now? Still sharing your bed?' Teresa spat on the ground, very close to Isobel's feet and walked past the horrified faces that stared up at her, mesmerized by her words. She pushed by the assistants who were trying not to laugh, past the doorman who made no effort to get the door for her, flouncing her hips as she slammed the door after her. No one stirred.

Suddenly, everyone looked back to where Isobel and Eleanor still stood together, their faces white, taut with shock and embarrassment. A hundred eyes stared at them both and then Isobel made a choked noise and dashed into the private salon, out of their view. Eleanor took a deep breath, looked around for her mother who was standing, clutching her throat a few feet away.

'It isn't true, Mama. Believe me. It isn't true,' she said softly, holding out her hand.

Clarissa nodded and walked forward, took the hand in her own. She smiled. 'No, I didn't think it was true for a moment. Teresa was just lashing out to hurt. I feel very sorry for her. It was so unnecessary of Isobel to make a scene like that. That poor girl had nothing when she came to our house, so I don't really blame her for taking the few things we loaned her.' Clarissa spoke in a clear voice, letting everyone near her know that Eleanor was innocent as charged. Then they both walked into the private room and closed the door after them.

No one outside believed them for a moment. Many had remarked before on how close the nephew and younger daughter of the house seemed to be. Now they knew why! Not surprising the girls had been suddenly put into a convent after that young man came back to town. But it obviously hadn't done any good. That younger one must be quite something and still only eighteen. Heavens, what a story! Who would have thought? She seemed like such a nice girl too, hardly the sort to be having affairs and with her primo-irmão too!

242

And all along it was the elder sister whom everyone had thought fast. One couldn't blame her entirely for showing some spleen with a little bit of baggage like that model girl going off with her future husband. Not that she was a terribly nice girl herself, that elder daughter. Vicious tongue and flirted rather too hard and fast when she was un-attached. Quite a few mothers were concerned she'd come home as the daughter-in-law. Well, this was a pretty come-uppance! What a joke! Charles Fawcett would have his haughty nose put out of joint by all this. Just wait until everyone hears!

So it went on, spreading faster than the wind, changing and distorting in the telling until it seemed that neither Eleanor or Isobel would be able to hold their heads up again in public. There were tales of a brawl, Isobel tearing the clothes off a model in public, accusing her of having an affair with her husband-to-be, the model screaming back obscenities and slapping both Fawcett girls' faces, telling terrible tales of orgies with both Louis and John, spilling the beans about Eleanor and John sharing each other's beds for years. Since they were children! It was all too shocking for words.

Eleanor, once they returned home, refused to speak to anyone and locked herself in her bedroom. Isobel furiously threw her diamond ring out of her bedroom window and then made Honório and Fernando spend hours searching the gardens for it, in the dark, by torchlight. She wrote Louis letter after letter, dismissing him from her life and then, in tears, crumpled them in her fists and threw those out the window too.

Clarissa sat drawn and pale in her sitting-room, staring blankly at nothing. Was it true? John and Eleanor? Were they lovers, as she had once feared, once suspected? Had Teresa actually caught them together? She wrung her hands, twisting the fingers into knots and still stared at the wall. Waiting for Charles to come home.

She knew he had heard by the time the front door was closed. The sound echoed through the house.

'Clarissa? Where are you?' He sounded odd. Not exactly angry, more sickened, disgusted. He had lost his honour, when the girls lost theirs, she thought. And all because Isobel wouldn't leave well alone, had to have her revenge. Some revenge!

'I'm here, Charles. In my sitting-room.' She waited until he appeared in the doorway. 'Come in and close the door, my dear. Here –' she passed him a glass of whisky, a double '– you'll probably need this. Now, before you start, Charles, I want you to listen to me. Hear our side. Then you can say whatever you want, all right?' She saw him open his mouth in surprise, his lips fleshy and wet, and suddenly quite repugnant to her. She looked away.

'All right. Go ahead,' he said and he continued to pace the carpet of the small room, five steps up, turn, five steps back, while she recounted the afternoon's events. Eventually, she stopped and looked down at her hands. The fingers were still twisted together.

'Then it's not true? You've asked Eleanor and she says it's not true?' he demanded. He didn't care about anything else. She realized that in a flash. Isobel and her reputation, Louis's didn't matter. Everyone had known that part before. But Eleanor. Eleanor and John. No, that was unthinkable!

'I didn't have to ask her, Charles. Eleanor immediately denied it. And I believe her. I think this Teresa just said whatever it was she could think of to bring the most shame down on our family. Eleanor's totally innocent. I'm sure of it,' she repeated, even more firmly. Her fingers twisted some more.

'But who's going to ever know that? The damage is done, isn't it?' Charles said harshly, but Clarissa could see some of the colour flowing back into his cheeks, some of the stoop to his shoulders falling away. It wasn't true. As long as he knew that, he could cope with the rumours. He tossed back his drink and went to fix himself another, sitting sprawled in the chair opposite his wife. He sat there, silently communing with himself for some time, the ticking of the carriage clock on the mantelpiece going on and on. Clarissa stayed still, wondering whether her husband would be able to come to terms with such a disgrace. Perhaps she would never know.

There was a knock at the door, and Clarissa looked up expectantly, surprised when she saw Henry's face appear in the doorway. He looked composed and polite, as always, but Clarissa noticed how gaunt and pale he seemed, his eyes burning darkly from behind that wisp of hair.

'I came as soon as I heard what people were saying. It's not true. You mustn't believe it. I was with Teresa all the time at the party. We just saw Eleanor and John standing together on the balcony. They were leaning against each other. Nothing more. The way they always do. Teresa got upset and left with Louis, but that's all there was to it. I promise you. I was there.' The words spilled out of his mouth tumbling over each other to get clear, to make sense of the denial he was issuing. He stopped finally, still leaning in the doorway. He panted, out of breath.

'You're sure, Henry?' Clarissa asked and he nodded firmly.

'Oh, thank God! Thank you, God, and thank you, Henry!' Charles laughed, the sound breaking free from him as though it had been prised from deep within him and had exited, not through his throat, but actually through the ribs of his chest. He got up and walked over to Henry, slapping the young man on the back, pulling him into his arms in a tight hug. 'Thank you, Henry!'

Henry was embarrassed. He smiled and edged himself out of Charles's clasp, looking around at Clarissa.

'Is Eleanor all right? I've been telling everyone I know the true story. It won't be long before her name's cleared. But she must be going through hell right now. Can I see her?' He was shy yet pleased that he had done well, but mostly anxious to see Eleanor.

Clarissa nodded. 'I'll just go check, Henry. Why don't you have a drink with Charles? I'll call you if she's up to seeing you. But I don't think she is. She was quite – upset.' Too much so, Clarissa wondered for a moment, and then

245

shook the suspicion away. It wasn't true and Henry could prove it. Couldn't he?

Eleanor was lying across her bed, when Clarissa knocked and entered, a half-finished letter beside her. She covered the letter quickly, slipping it under the pillows.

Clarissa cleared her throat. 'How are you feeling, darling?' Clarissa searched Eleanor's face for any sign of tears but it seemed calm enough, if a little pale. 'Henry's here. He came over as soon as – as he heard. But it's all right, you know. Henry was with Teresa all that evening.' She felt a flush rising across her cheekbones and fought to seem equally calm and unembarrassed. To seem to believe her daughter entirely. 'Henry knows there's no truth to Teresa's allegations and he says he's going to tell everyone he knows. He's already told quite a few people. She just saw you and John together out on the terrace, Henry says. And got jealous.' Clarissa wanted to ask why, why did Teresa get jealous at something so innocent? But she couldn't bring herself to say it. It hung, instead, between them. 'So it's all all right now, isn't it?'

Eleanor looked up at her mother, and gave a sad smile. 'I'm not and never have been John's lover. I know you're having trouble with that, worrying about it for some reason. But it's the truth. What Henry's just said proves it, doesn't it? What are you so worried about, Mother?'

'I'm not! I said I believe you and I do! Don't be silly, Eleanor, please.' Clarissa was sharper than she meant to be, her denial too emphatic. She took a deep breath. 'Henry wants to see you. You up to it?'

'Yes, of course. I –'

'Good. I'll tell him,' Clarissa cut across Eleanor's words, ending the discussion. She smiled awkwardly, her eyes pleading with Eleanor to leave it alone, not force the issue between them. Eleanor looked away. And Clarissa went in search of Henry.

Good old Henry. Loyal, always there for you, right by your side, back you up all the way Henry. Thoughtful, patient, dependable Henry. Eleanor shook her head. Maybe she should start trying to like him as more than just a trusted friend? Maybe there was more there than she had ever tried to see. But a vision of John flashed across her mind and she knew instantly that it was no good. Everyone had to be compared to John, and everyone was lacking. If only John didn't exist. Or if only he weren't her cousin. If only ... But there was no point to thoughts like that.

She drew the letter out from beneath her pillow and looked over it. At the shame and pain that was there, between the lines of unemotional prose. He would read it all but he wouldn't care, she thought. He would think it a ridiculous fuss about nothing. He disliked the whole idea of society and what other people thought about you; he didn't care what anyone thought. She wished she could be like that.

There was a knock at the door.

'Come in, Henry.' She slipped the letter back under the pillow and sat up.

'Hullo. I thought I'd just come and see how one of the notorious women of the Fawcett household was. You sure I should close the door behind me? Is it safe? You won't attack me, will you?' His thin face was alight with amusement, his eyes teasing.

Eleanor threw a pillow at him. 'Wretch! You might think it a joke, but I promise you, I'm ruined! What mouldy old mother's going to want me even talking to her son, let alone marrying them. I might as well lock myself in the convent for good, become a novice! Except, of course, even they wouldn't take me now.' She said it in a tone of mock horror, but there was too much feeling behind her words for Henry to think she was joking.

He came and sat beside her on the bed, flopping back on it when he realized just how weary he was. 'Thought you weren't interested in getting married or going to debutante parties or any of that side of things?' He was still teasing. Pushing to see how far the hurt went.

'I'm not – if I can be the one to turn them down. I just

don't want to have them all turn *me* down!' She lay back beside him, staring up at the ceiling. Thinking how true that was. Perhaps equally true for John, if he would only see it? 'I'll be struck off everyone's list in Rio. No one will dare associate with me,' she said gloomily and Henry laughed.

'Don't be silly. I know Brazil's a bit backward still, but don't you think that's taking it a bit far? Besides, I'll associate with you. Isn't that good enough?'

'Oh Henry! Of course it is!' Eleanor rolled over and kissed his cheek. 'But no one's going to believe your tale about being with Teresa all that night. They all know you're – you're my friend,' she said. There was a pause.

'And that I'm in love with you? Is that what you were going to say?' he said slowly. He didn't look at her.

A silence fell between them and then Eleanor took a deep breath. 'Are you?' She didn't really want to hear the answer.

'Yes,' he said at last. He turned his head and looked at her.

'Is that why you're trying to clear my reputation?' Eleanor asked softly. Their faces were no more than six inches apart, both lying still on the counterpane.

Henry shook his head. 'No. I'm just telling the truth. On that night, at least, Teresa saw nothing except you and John leaning against each other out on the terrace.' But what about other nights? His eyes watched her carefully, trying to read the thoughts that came so easily to John. He couldn't be sure.

Eleanor saw the flicker of doubt cross Henry's face; his expression, normally so humorous, was now purposely blank. He didn't want to judge her, she knew. And he wouldn't, no matter what.

'I don't think I've ever been in love, Henry,' she said hesitantly, wondering if how she felt about John qualified. But no, he was family. She loved him as family.

'No? Well, it doesn't matter. You'll find someone to love one day. You're not exactly ancient,' he said, his cheek quirking upwards into a gentle smile.

Eleanor, on impulse, reached over and kissed him

quickly on the lips. 'I hope it's you I fall in love with,' she said suddenly, and then realized that what she had said was true. If anyone was worth loving, it was Henry.

He blushed, unexpectedly pleased and embarrassed and had to sit up and look away, out at the night he could see through the still uncurtained windows. For a moment, as though he couldn't help it, he touched his fingers to his mouth. Then he dropped his hand and stood up, still with his back to her.

'I hope so too. I've got to go. I told my parents I'd be back in time for dinner. I'll see you tomorrow, all right?' he said, turning back to face her. She saw he had recovered, his face as whimsical and charming as ever, the eyes smiling at her from beneath that shock of hair. He moved his jaw forward, pressing his lips together, a gesture of acceptance. So, now they knew where they stood with each other. And he would wait and see.

Isobel knocked on her door later that night, long after the lights in the house had been turned out and long after Eleanor herself had gone to bed. But neither of them were asleep. Eleanor moved over on the bed for Isobel to sit down. She could see the blotched and swollen eyelids, the tremor to the mouth that threatened to lapse back into tears and she pitied Isobel.

'What is it, Isobel? You knew Teresa and Louis had had an affair, so what's upsetting you so much now?' Her voice was gentle and she touched her sister's arm.

Isobel hunched deeper on to the bed and covered her face with one hand. 'It's Louis. When he hears about all this, he'll be bound to blame me. Maybe even believe something worse. You know what he's like. His reputation, his image, are so important to him!' She was sniffling into a handkerchief again and Eleanor had trouble understanding her.

'So what? He's not being put on trial by most of Rio society. We are! Why should Louis care?' Eleanor felt irritated that Isobel should only care how Louis felt. How about how she felt? Then she heard the anguish in her sister's voice.

'But he may not want to marry me! Don't you see?' Isobel wailed suddenly and Eleanor, looking at the stricken, tear-blotched face, realized for the first time that Isobel really did love Louis.

Her face softened. 'Oh Isobel, of course he'll want to marry you! Why wouldn't he? A bit of nonsense like this won't matter to Louis. The only thing that'll make you lose Louis will be if you don't show him how much you care. You know, until now, I didn't really think you loved him? I thought he was just the best, most convenient choice that had come along,' she said and Isobel's head snapped up in amazement.

'How could you? Whatever makes you say such a cruel thing? Of course I love Louis!'

'Then you better start changing your way of showing him that. All you do is nag at him, Isobel. He's young and enjoying life and you want to chain him up and make him sit in every evening with you. You need to lose some weight and go out with him, make him see how much other men admire you. Be more fun. Don't say bitchy things to him when he does something wrong – try and coax him out of his bad old ways. You can do it if you put your mind to it, Isobel. And tell him you love him.' Eleanor stopped abruptly, realizing she was in danger of alienating her sister for good. But from the serious, thoughtful look on Isobel's face, it seemed her words had already taken hold.

'You really think that? You really think he loves me still?' It was so unlike Isobel to sound unsure, to sound so humble that Eleanor was filled with guilt. She hugged her sister to her.

'Of course I do. Just think before you open your mouth. Make an effort to woo him. He'll fall at your feet, see if he doesn't.'

Isobel was so relieved that she quite perked up again, going to stare at her ravaged face in the mirror and exclaim in horror. She borrowed Eleanor's slender make-up collection to repair what she could and prattled happily about what she would do. Eleanor, leaning back against her pillows, absently agreed with whatever she said. Eleanor had her own worries.

'You know, we should do this more often, you and I,' Isobel said suddenly, halting as she lifted a tissue to her face to blot at some powder. She stared in the mirror at Eleanor's reflection. 'You know, talk like this. It's about time we had some sisterly chats. I could help you with your make-up, if you like. Lend you some clothes so that you make more of yourself. It'd be nice.' It was such an unexpected offer and so sincerely meant that Eleanor, looking up, was startled. For a moment, a silly, maudlin moment that owed more to the afternoon's trauma than to Isobel's words made her own eyes blurred as tears rushed in. She smiled.

'You're right. We should. We don't talk nearly enough together.' She paused. 'Isobel – you ... you don't believe any of that nonsense about John, do you ...?' Her voice faltered and died away as Isobel turned around to face her.

'John?' Isobel queried, then she looked down at her hands. 'No, I know you haven't done anything with him.' She smiled sadly. 'Not yet, anyway.'

She turned back to the mirror and Eleanor stared at her, her own mind suddenly chilled.

Chapter Thirteen

'Cut the cake! Cut the cake!' The crowd took up the cry, laughing and surging forward around Isobel and Louis, pushing them towards the towering edifice of plaited white marzipan and flowers that had taken three men to carry from the palácio out into the gardens. Eleanor, standing beside them both, laughed and pushed along with everyone else, her face eager and happy and carefree. Just like a child, John thought as he watched her. Except, at nineteen, she wasn't anymore.

There was a circlet of flowers in her hair, the ribbons streaming out in the wind, and her bridesmaid dress was of the sheerest, lightest yellow, clinging to her figure like a nymph. A long, pale golden beam of light, bouncing between the leaves of the trees, blazed across her for a moment before moving on, and then back again, dazzling her. She closed her eyes against it, flinging up an arm.

When she opened them, she saw John standing in front of her. She smiled and took his arm, leading him over to the others. 'Don't they look wonderful! I never thought Isobel would manage to lose all that weight in time, and I thought the seamstress would have a heart attack trying to take the dress in every few days, but look now! Isn't she absolutely gorgeous? She was quite right insisting on the cream silk even though both Mama and I thought she was wrong at the time. But then, Isobel generally knows what she's about, doesn't she?' She babbled gaily, trying too hard not to be aloof, not to let what other people thought spoil what they had between them. But she couldn't quite stop herself glancing from left to right, checking.

'Don't worry. For a few minutes at least everyone's got their eyes on the cake. We're second fiddle to that,' John remarked caustically. He felt Eleanor flinch beside him. 'And I must say, Isobel is well worth looking at today. You're quite right, she's got all her looks back again. No wonder Louis is mooning like a besotted calf. Oh, speaking of which,' he nodded over to the left, to where Henry was standing beside one of Louis's little sisters, lifting her up where she could see the cake, 'has Henry proposed yet?'

'Don't be silly. Of course he hasn't! What on earth made you say something like that?' Eleanor said, protestingly. He shrugged, giving her a cynical smile. She wished John didn't have to be so abrasive all the time, lately. Was that what his student life was doing to him? She wished he could just relax and enjoy the day like everyone else.

Around them the gardens blazed in the full heat of summer, a large tent of pale green and white providing shelter from the sun, and the fountain spraying out arcs of glinting water. It made a cool place to sit and trail fingers in the water. Bowers of flowers were arranged around the elaborate buffet and the cake itself had been set up on a table of its own, strewn with rose petals and camellias. As many of the five hundred guests as had accepted and actually appeared today were clustered around the table as possible; Eleanor knew there was no chance of fighting a way through them to see Isobel cut the cake. She leaned against a pillar instead and surveyed the people around her.

'You really are serious about going to university in Paris? I can't talk you out of it?' John asked beside her. He looked straight ahead at the well-dressed, polished crowd who cavorted and pushed and cried out in laughter in what was,

253

for them, a very unseemly manner. Old, familiar scenes he remembered from his childhood that were now almost offensive to him. He felt as though he belonged and was separate, both at the same time. It was unsettling. His lip curled.

'Yes, of course I am. Papa's never going to let me go down to São Paulo. That's pretty obvious, what with all the riots and student arrests going on.' She glanced at him but he was still looking ahead. 'And I just need to get away for a while. I don't want to stay here and go through university and live at home all that time. I want a little freedom.'

'You're not running away, are you? Because of that stupid rumour about us? Running out?'

'No. That was over three months ago now. People forget pretty quickly and besides, Henry backed us up and told them that Teresa was making it up,' she said firmly. She saw his cheek twitch. 'I hear you've been seeing quite a lot of Teresa again.'

'So? Considering you and your family got her thrown out of her job and pretty much loused up Rio for her altogether, why shouldn't I try and help her out a bit? I feel I owe her that,' he said coldly.

'Oh John! Why can't you ever just say you like Teresa and enjoy being with her? Why does it always have to be a duty? You owe her! I'd hate someone saying they had to spend time with me because they felt they owed it to me to be kind,' Eleanor said abruptly and stared at him. He gave her one of his particularly stonewall expressions. She sniffed. 'Well, I'll see you later. I'm going to help Mama pass out the cake.' She walked away from him, her back very straight.

Isobel and Louis were feeding each other bite-size pieces of cake and the crowd were cheering and clapping now. John edged away and joined Henry at the table he had finally chosen as a vantage sight for Georgina, Louis's youngest sister. He sat down beside Henry and held out his hand.

'Henry. You seem to have your hands full playing Mister

254

Nursemaid. Hullo, Georgy – can you see up there?'

'Only their heads. Now they're kissing! Ugh, Louis's got cake all over his mouth and Isobel's still kissing him! Forget it, I don't want to see anymore.' She jumped down from the table before Henry could stop her and ran off to find her mother.

John laughed. 'Sounds pretty revolting to me too. How're things, Henry? You getting into politics yet?' he asked casually and Henry grinned back.

'Oh, only on the sidelines. I'll have to wait until I've finished my law studies before I plunge in. But you seem to be pretty active. I hear you're fairly vocal down in São Paulo,' Henry said, leaning back in his chair. He took a sip of champagne and offered John some.

'Thanks. Yes, well, you know how it is. You never intend to get involved and then everyone else seems to be making such a pig's ear of it, that you can't stand it anymore and find yourself just leaping in with both feet, figuring you can't do any worse. Besides, someone's got to make this damned government do something for the poor.' John drank his glass very quickly and poured himself another.

Henry watched him. 'And you're it, huh? All on your own, the knight in shining armour? You think we can just suddenly become a modern democratic state, with a full social welfare system in place, just like that?' Henry snapped his fingers. He saw John look at him and smile. Not a pleasant smile.

'Why not? What's holding us back except for a lot of corrupt officials who'd rather all that tax revenue went on their pet projects so they can siphon some of it off for themselves? You know there's a certain customs official in São Paulo, just a minor guy who's got the docks so sewn up with bribery that he can actually afford a penthouse down here on Copacabana Beach? And no one does anything!' John said angrily. He brushed his fingers through his hair, pushing it back from his forehead.

'But they will, in time.' Henry leaned forward. 'Don't you know the most dangerous time for a newly emerging

255

country is just when that freedom is in sight? Everyone starts grabbing for it, and then the government comes back with repressive moves, and the whole thing blows up in everyone's face. Look at Hungary, for God's sake!' He pointed out quickly as he saw John's face become irritated, 'We've got to get a broader base before we start implementing change, John. I mean, all the successful countries you look at who've made the transition to a fully modern democratic state had elements that we don't yet possess. A high rate of literacy, an industrial revolution, a sufficient supply of domestic capital, and a technological trad—'

'Oh Henry! Wake up, can't you? You can spout all your political science at me forever, and we'll continue to wait until doomsday before anything's done, while the government makes soothing promises that they have no intention of keeping and people like Goulart continue to make themselves rich. Anyway, a western capitalistic society may well not work but then again, maybe that isn't the way to go to begin with. We need some dramatic changes. About the only way we're ever going to get the population educated and have full employment is to start handing out some of the wealth – like this.' John waved his arm around at the fine clothes and jewellery, the silver and china, the gardens, the palácio in the distance. 'Make everyone equal, redistribute the wealth –'

'Turn Communist, you mean? That's new for you. When did you start believing Russia's way is best?' Henry asked in a quiet voice. 'You really think Communism is the answer?' To himself he thought – that's a problem, that's dangerous. John could end up on a government list that wouldn't do anyone any good, particularly not Eleanor. But Henry didn't voice those thoughts aloud. 'You won't find any grass-roots support for that. The masses aren't politicized enough for it and they've basically too much of a happy-go-lucky nature to want it either. They just want a house and some food and if the government tell them that's what they'll get as long as they're patient, then they'll wait. They can see reform's coming . . .'

'When? When is it coming? In the next century? I'm no more Communist than you are but it might be the stick we need to try and force a change. For Christ's sake, can't you see Goulart isn't going to be able to handle things any better than any of the others? He's been vice-president twice and he's never yet come out with a firm policy. And now that he's president, he just blows with the wind. And this wonderful change you foresee won't come at all if the military get back into power,' John said heatedly. He threw back another glass of champagne, the perspiration beginning to gather on his brow in the still heat of the tent.

Henry took another sip from his glass. 'No. Which is why we mustn't scare the military with talk of a Communist overthrow. Must we? I don't like Goulart any more than you do, but we must work within the framework that already exists. Not just scrap it all and try and start again. That won't work,' Henry replied mildly. They locked eyes, each as sure of their views as the other.

Then Henry smiled. 'It's too nice a day for all this. Come on, let's go get some cake.' He stood up and waited for John but John shook his head.

'You go. I'm too hot. I'll just sit here and try and cool down.' He gave a rueful grimace, both of them laughing for a moment as they had as boys. Then Henry smiled again and nodded, seeing Eleanor instead holding up a plate for him and laughing. He sketched a wave and moved over to join the crowd gathered around the buffet tables.

John left them all to it and retreated into the house, going up to his room. He closed the door after him, depressed beyond anything he had known before.

He had been waiting for Eleanor to come and join him in São Paulo for three long years. Once she was away from her family, he knew he could convince her that the rules of the society she was born into didn't function outside of that small circle anymore. She could be or do anything she wanted. Eleanor had a kind heart. Why else would she be volunteering her time to teach the poor? And she had a loving heart. She loved him. He knew she did. Yet she was going to Paris instead.

He felt as though all his careful planning, all his thoughts of the last few years had been for nothing. He had been outsmarted even before he had started. By whom? He didn't think Eleanor would have thought of going away to Europe herself. She wanted to get away, yes, but not that far. So, the idea had to have come from her father – or from Henry. Something made him think it was the latter. Far too subtle for Charles Fawcett. His method was heavy-handed, autocratic rule. You will not go to university in São Paulo and that is that. But Henry was much less obvious. Equally against the idea of São Paulo, he would make Eleanor see how much better Paris was than anywhere in Brazil. He would make her want to go away, far away. Out of John's reach. Clever Henry.

John lay on his bed and put his arms over his head. It was all settled now. Nothing would make Eleanor change her mind. Not even how much he loved her. He closed his eyes tightly, trying not to think about her leaving, not to think about how bleak the future seemed.

'Where's John gone?' Eleanor asked Henry, after he had slowly weaved his way through the crowd to her side.

Henry looked back at the table where they had both been sitting and shrugged. 'No idea. Gone off to get some air, I should think. He's tossing the champagne back and it's pretty warm. How about abandoning your post and coming out by the fountain for a while. I feel like I'm about to die of heat exhaustion.' He pulled at his cravat, easing his starched shirt collars away from his throat. They were wilting in the humidity.

Eleanor wiped back a strand of hair and breathed deeply. 'Twenty more people to go and then I'll pass it over to Maria. She's dying to get out of the kitchen and see what's going on anyway. You want to go call her for me? I'll see you by the fountain in about five minutes.' Henry nodded and eased out of the crush again, taking his own plate with him.

Eleanor smiled and continued to cut cake and serve it, her thoughts barely on what she was doing, grappling instead with what John had said. Was he hurt that she was going away? Running out, he had said. On whom, him? But he had barely written to her in the last three years, barely come home to see them, and now he was seeing Teresa again. What difference should it make to him whether she went away to Paris to study or not?

Besides, he was twenty-one now and coming into his inheritance. He could start looking seriously for someone to love, someone to spend the rest of his life with. Why would he want her in São Paulo? She would just cramp his style, make other girls jealous of their special relationship, make more rumours. No, he was better off without her around.

'Eleanor dear, just a tiny slice for me. I don't want to go ruining my figure entirely!' One of Isobel's closest friends from school, Guillermina, or Mina for short, drew Eleanor's thoughts back from her reverie. She smiled and obligingly cut a much smaller slice.

'Though why you worry, I simply can't imagine, Mina. You could be a model you're so skinny,' Eleanor said frankly.

'Oh, you are such a dear but goodness me no! I'd never be a model – you know what sorts they are, don't you? I mean, who better? I hope you're not too upset about that girl moving in with John. I mean, not that there's any truth – but still, unpleasant for you, I expect.' Mina floundered her way through her explanation, her thin, dark face entirely without malice. Surprised, she saw Eleanor pale, her hands falter over the knife.

'No, Mina. There is no truth to any of that. You should know that as well as anyone else,' Eleanor said after a moment's pause. She passed the plate of cake over. 'And I know all about Teresa, and I think that's just fine. I always liked her, despite the – the things she said about me.'

Mina moved on, her cheeks flushed. The next person in line, however, was equally interested in how Eleanor was coping with the news, and she was far less easily embarrassed than Mina. One of Clarissa's acquaintances, Senhora Borges. She probed and pushed and remarked, her dark eyes avid for news, until Eleanor's hands shook with distress and anger.

'And she's such a very good-looking girl too, that Teresa, although not quite in my style. I don't like them so florid, but all the men seem to, don't they just! Your John must have quite a few jealous friends wishing they knew what it was that made her like him so much. But then, I expect you could tell them that, being so close as you are to him.' Senhora Borges smiled and ran her tongue quickly over lips. Her plump face quivered with intense pleasure as she realized she had made the girl opposite her begin to shake. She saw Eleanor glance up at her, fury in her eyes.

'Please! I would think you would realize just how unpleasant I find such a rumour and how unjust! I'm sorry, but I really don't want to talk about it any more.' She looked over to her side and saw Maria standing there, sturdily surveying the woman who had made such offensive remarks about her little girl. Maria sniffed and took the knife from Eleanor's hands, pushing her silently towards the gardens. Eleanor fled with relief.

'Now, senhora, how can I help you? I expect you would like a very big slice, yes? You look like you have such a large appetite and appreciate food,' Maria said loudly, cutting a double slice of cake and offering it to Senhora Borges with a withering smile. The woman compressed her lips angrily but moved on without another comment.

The rest of the guests eyed each other, and whispered with interest over Eleanor's reaction. Quite upset, wasn't she? Rather too upset, perhaps? No smoke without fire, is there? They glanced over at Charles Fawcett who could be seen in the distance talking and laughing with President Goulart, his voice self-satisfied as it carried faintly over to them. And they raised eyebrows, smiled to each other.

Eleanor found Henry picking a rose from the trellis near the fountain. She stopped to watch him, unaware that he was being observed, and she smiled when he pricked a finger on a thorn and cursed fluently.

'Heavens, Henry, I never thought you knew those sorts of words. And you had me believing you were such a gentleman!' she mocked and he turned swiftly, his face a mixture of mortification and amusement.

'Oh well, now you know my darkest secrets. You think I'm bad, you should listen to the clerks of the courts. Now they know some altogether different uses for the language! Here, this was for you anyway.' He passed her the rose, pale yellow like her dress and gilded along the top of the petals with pure gold. She took it and sniffed it cautiously. Almost no perfume. What a shame.

Henry paused and looked at her again, more closely. 'Come on over here in the shade and sit down. I brought some champagne – it's chilling in the fountain – and some food from the buffet because, quite frankly, I would prefer to save my cake until later, if you'll excuse the pun. You don't have any, I see.' He knew something was wrong, despite the light tone she had adopted. Her face was pale, her eyes sparkling as though she were close to tears. What had happened? Had John been having a go at her again?

Eleanor let herself be led over to a stone seat under an overhanging vine, the blast of the sun withdrawn abruptly as they entered the shade. She sat with a sigh of relief.

'Your wreath's crooked,' Henry said, smiling. He adjusted it carefully in her hair, pulling the ribbons out to trail down her back, lifting her hair away from her face. He stroked her cheek with the back of his fingers, gently. 'Better now?'

'Yes, much!' she said with a shaky laugh. How did he always know how to comfort her? And what did any of them matter as long as she had people like Henry who cared about her? She gave him a grateful smile. 'Now, how about some champagne? I've barely had a glass since this all began and I don't think I've sat down since the church. It's my turn to enjoy it all now.'

'Good! That's the spirit. We'll have a whole bottle to

261

ourselves and take all afternoon to enjoy it.' He slipped the foil from the top of the bottle, released the wire and eased the cork out expertly. Eleanor held a glass up. 'And you know what I've been thinking, sitting here like this?'

'What?' Eleanor demanded. They both had glasses now and Henry set the bottle back in the cool water of the fountain.

'I've been thinking that I might just come out and visit you in Paris at the end of next year. I finish law school then, and I think I deserve a trip abroad for a month or so. How does that sound to you?'

'Oh Henry! That'd be wonderful! I can't think of anything I'd like more.' Eleanor's eyes lit up, her mouth split apart in a wide smile. Thrilled. They brought their glasses together, toasting Isobel and Louis, Paris, and Henry's visit, breathing in the heady perfumes of the garden and the odd, slightly metallic, wetness of the fountain. Enjoying themselves. Except, just for a moment, Eleanor thought how much better it would be if it were John who were coming to see her instead. She blanked out the thought, angry at herself for ever allowing it.

A band started playing later in the evening, and Isobel and her father opened the dancing with a graceful waltz. Then Louis danced with Isobel, Charles with Clarissa and, gradually, more and more people moved on to the dance floor and the waiters began clearing the tables for the dinner buffet and lighting the candles. Eleanor had left Henry to some of his friends and gone off to the house to make sure Isobel's change of clothing was all laid out and her bags carried out to the car. She knew some of Louis's friends had probably tied old shoes and balloons to the back of the car already but she hoped they had not written obscene comments on the windows. Isobel wouldn't find that very funny. On the way upstairs she asked Honório to check.

It had been a long, hot afternoon, the moisture in the air plumping up the flowers into bloom and wetting the grass so that it shimmered a vivid green in the heat. As the light had faded from the day, a heavy dew had come down. Her dress clung damply to her now and her hair had become limp and heavy against her neck. She shivered in the cooler night air.

She felt quite light-headed from the champagne and she hummed a tune to herself as she twitched a couple of creases from Isobel's leaving dress, smoothed her hand over the delicately laced lingerie. She caught sight of her reflection in the mirror and paused, pushing her hair back into place, trying to make herself look more presentable. Then she giggled and wandered out of the bedroom and down to John's.

He was asleep on his bed, his long frame sprawled out carelessly, the morning coat and cravat thrown on to the ground along with most of the rest of his wedding attire. He now wore nothing more than a pair of old shorts. Eleanor remembered him as a boy, stepping out on to the verandah of the Vila Serrista one morning, wearing just that, a pair of shorts hanging loosely around his hips. She wished they could go back to a time when John had been happy and carefree, when his words weren't bitter or angry, when he could just look at her and smile and know her thoughts.

She closed the door behind her and stepped closer, leaning over him, unable to resist stroking the silver blond hair back from his brow, running her fingers over the contours of his face. He was thin, she thought with a pang. Too thin. Perhaps Teresa wasn't feeding him properly or he was too busy, too active with his rallies and riots to remember to eat. Now, sleeping, his face had lost all its cynicism, all its anger and become untroubled and sweetly smiling, the way he had looked as a boy. She kissed the tip of his nose but he didn't stir.

She trailed her hand down his shoulder and arm, liking the feel of the taut sinews, the lack of fat anywhere on his body. Not like Louis. He was already beginning to look meaty, his smooth playboy looks blurring a little, his waistline paunching out. Too much drink and too much food, Eleanor thought with distaste. She was glad she wasn't marrying Louis. She glanced back at John and realized, with a shock, that he was awake and watching her.

'Oh! You might have said you were awake!' she said accusingly, her face flushing bright in the shadows of the room.

John smiled lazily. 'I was enjoying myself. Don't stop. That feels good.'

'What does, this?' She stroked along his arm again. 'Or this?' She tugged hard at the hair in his armpit, her eyes glinting mischief.

John cried out at the sharp pain and pulled her over him, manhandling her on to the bed so that he held her pinned beneath him. 'Not funny, Eleanor,' he said, annoyed. She giggled again, feeling wildly amused by his reaction and the headiness of the champagne mixed with the afternoon's heat. So, he would think twice before pretending to be asleep again, she thought.

John held her pinned down, panting slightly from having jerked her off her feet and on to the bed. He leaned over her. 'What made you do that? I thought you were being nice for a change, gentle the way you used to be.' His tone held irritation and perhaps, just a touch of dismay.

'When was I ever gentle, John? We used to fight about everything! Have scraps on the floor, you pulling my hair, me biting your hand. But it never meant anything. And I wasn't really trying to hurt you, you know, just then. I just wanted to shock you.' Her smile faltered, sensing the oddness of his mood but unable to follow it.

'Well, consider me shocked. I was having a nice dream before you came in. And then you were so −' he paused, unable to find the words. '− So gentle. So enticing. I thought, maybe ...' He trailed off, looking disappointed, letting go of her.

Eleanor continued to lie there, looking up at him, a frown between her eyebrows. 'Maybe what, John?' she asked. When he didn't answer, she wondered whether he had been remembering how good it had been between them when they were young and belonged only to each other. She reached up and touched his arm, stroking it again.

'Maybe you really did still care,' he said finally.

She opened her eyes wide. 'But, why would you think I didn't care about you anymore? You know what you mean to me, don't you? I thought we had that all clear.' A sound of protest broke from his lips and he turned away, pushing himself off the bed. He stood up and went to stare out of his window at the marquee below in the gardens and the candles that flickered in the night breeze.

Eleanor got off the bed and went to stand behind him, putting her arms around him and leaning her face against his bare back.

'What is it, John? What's gone wrong lately?' she asked in a soft voice, almost a whisper.

John reached down to touch her hands, holding them tightly in his own. 'I don't know, Eleanor. It scares me the way we're going in two different directions. We're not meeting anywhere anymore. There's no middle ground.' He turned suddenly, before she had time to pull back, and he pulled her in against his chest in a fierce embrace. 'I'm scared,' he repeated.

He leaned down to bury his face in her hair and she held him tightly back.

'Don't be. I'm here and I always will be. Don't be scared,' she whispered and then she felt him lift her quickly and carry her back to the bed, laying her on it with his own body beside hers.

'Tell me what's going on, Eleanor? What's in your mind right now? What're you thinking?' he said urgently and Eleanor felt a moment's dismay.

'Don't you know, John? Can't you tell anymore?' she asked softly and he shook his head, the loss heavy in his eyes.

'No, no, I can't! I don't understand. What's happened to change things between us? Why can't we read each other's thoughts anymore, why can't we be together without fighting, trying to hurt each other anymore? I don't understand it and I don't like it!' His voice rose, choked.

Eleanor reached over and pressed her hand across his mouth, shushing his words, trying to soothe some of the fear and hurt in him. 'It'll be all right. Just as long as we both know we still care and want to be together. I'm – I'm sorry I'm not coming down to São Paulo. I hoped that would sort things out between us.' Eleanor felt him twitch away from her. 'But Papa won't hear of it and I won't have any money of my own for several more years. I'm not free to make my own choices like you, John. I have to make compromises. And that's what Paris is. A compromise. Going away from home, but not into an area of political strife. And you're part of that strife. So that makes it even more unacceptable for me to go down there. I tried hard, John, all this last year but I couldn't budge Papa and then, when all this nastiness came up, about you and me, well, I just wanted to get as far away from everything as possible. Even you.' She sighed heavily. 'I'm sorry.'

His breath came out in a rush, a long, warm exhalation against her cheek. So that was it.

'Don't be. I guess it's as much my fault as yours. Maybe if I were more like Louis, or Henry – more conservative and ready to fit into whatever mould your father wanted to press me, then I guess he'd act differently where you're concerned. But I can't be like that, Eleanor. You do see that, don't you? I can't just be – perfect.'

'No,' she said slowly. 'I know you can't. It's just – fate, I guess. Bad luck maybe even. That we're always going in opposite directions and Papa won't let us change. He keeps us apart because he thinks we'll hurt each other, I think. Or him. Something like that. His nemesis, remember?' She pressed her cheek against his shoulder, holding her arms around him. Outside the sky had become a deep purple and the throb of music carried up to them through the night air. The room became very dark and she felt that strangeness between them dissolve, become something different entirely.

When he kissed her, she wasn't surprised. Maybe she had been wanting him to do that for a long time. Ever since that night he had climbed into her bed, drunk and unhappy with the way he had been greeted by the family on his return to Rio. Even before that, when she had looked at him on the bus, startled by his maleness, the heaviness in the air.

She pressed herself against him, opening her lips to him, wanting him to hold her more tightly still, tasting him and finding that taste both familiar and strange. She had stopped worrying about his relationship to her, stopped worrying what other people might think. In that moment when he kissed her deeply and groaned with all the frustration and pain of the last few years, all she could think was how much she wanted him. And how right it was.

'Don't say no, Eleanor. Please, my love, don't say no,' she heard him murmur and his hands were holding her waist tightly, lifting her up towards him. She held his face between her own hands and kissed him back, hard and with a rising passion that unnerved her and exhilarated her and swept her on.

He pulled the wreath from her hair, tossing it out into the darkness of the room, neither one aware of hearing it land. Her dress was pulled down, ripping over her shoulder where it became caught and John was too impatient. Eleanor cried out in protest but he was beyond listening to her, intent only on having her body next to his. He pulled harder and the dress tore clear of her shoulders and was thrust down over her hips, falling away. Eleanor began to be afraid by the force with which he pushed her back against the bed, the way he didn't hear her muffled cries for him to be calm, to be gentle.

She clung to him, feeling his body, his skin cool and firm against hers, and involuntarily, she twisted herself beneath him so that they lay more comfortably together. She wrapped her arms around him and he pushed against her, kissing her face, her neck, lower down to her breasts. Eleanor arched her back, still reaching for him and he shook with some deep distress.

'Don't ever leave me, Eleanor. Not ever,' he whispered and then she was filled with such pain and pleasure, the one barely separate from the other, that it was some time before either of them was aware of the room again or the bed on which they lay.

Only when the noises of Isobel and her bridesmaids, laughing and crying out to each other as they trooped down the passageways intruded, did either of them realize how much time had passed. They froze together, entwined around each other, as they heard Isobel remark petulantly on Eleanor's absence. And then Eleanor felt John's hand sweep down her back, cradling her against him, protecting her and she made a choked sound — aghast at what they had both done. There could be no going back now.

The voices swept on down the passageway, out of hearing and still they lay against each other without speaking, without moving. Gradually Eleanor became aware of where she ended and John began, where before there had been no sense of separate identity or separate bodies. She shuddered and leaned her face against his throat, her tears falling hotly on to his skin.

'Oh God, John, what have we done?' she whispered and he twisted, so that his face was looking into hers and he could wipe the tears from her face with his fingers. He kissed her mouth and she still felt an almost uncontrollable urge to wrap herself around him, yet again to commit the same folly all over again.

'Don't cry, sweetheart. We made love, nothing more. It's not so terrible. Because we love each other. Shh,' he soothed her and she let him hold her, welcomed his kisses and words of heresy. 'It doesn't matter, Eleanor. Not to a great many people in the world. A lot of those people marry their cousins. It's only here in Brazil or amongst Catholics that it's made out to be a sin. And you're not even Catholic, so how could it be wrong? It's not, my love. Nothing like that between us could ever be wrong. You know that, don't you? You can feel the truth of what I'm saying? We couldn't have helped ourselves – it was always supposed to be like this between us.' He lay on top of her, feeling her gentle curves, the swell of her bottom where his hands cupped around her, her warm skin beneath him.

'You'll always be mine,' he whispered and then she knew he was right because she became a part of him again and all her doubts, all her thoughts were swept aside in a rush of emotion so intense that she simply closed her eyes and let herself be carried away by the need to hold him against her, to move in time to the thrust of him inside her, to love him as he loved her.

Eleanor awoke, some hours later, knowing by the intensity of the silence that it was the middle of the night. She lay, face pressed down on the bed, smothered by the pillow, John half on top of her. A painful ache between her legs reminded her of the madness that had engulfed them both and she would have risen from the bed and crept, silently, along the passage to her own room but John held her pinned down and she could not bring herself to separate that warm flesh from her own. She moved slightly, coming up on to her elbows, arching her back at the pain.

John woke and pressed his lips to her shoulder, slid his hands around to clasp her breasts, running his fingers over nipples that became hard and tight, until he felt her arch her back further and gasp out silently in the dark.

They fitted together as though they had been made for this, she thought dazedly, as though every curve in her body matched a concave surface to his. He pressed himself forward and they slid together in a long exhalation and he whispered he loved her, over and over into her ear. When they could bear the intensity no longer, they both let themselves go, and he moved tightly against her and held her like that long after they had both spent themselves.

Finally, John went to sleep with his mouth on her breast and a feeling of security enveloping him as surely as her arms. For the first time in a long time, he didn't dream of fire and snow.

269

Chapter Fourteen

Eleanor left two days later for Paris.

No one had noticed her set face the morning immediately following the wedding. Too many others were showing the after-effects of the champagne and the heat to even be surprised by her pale face or the way she sat very still in the library window-seat and wrapped her arms around herself.

Isobel had managed to pour Louis into the car and leave for her honeymoon but few people had been sober enough to wish them farewell or throw rice and rose petals after them. Eleanor's absence had not been remarked upon. It was assumed she had succumbed to the champagne and taken herself off to bed. Which, she reminded herself painfully, she had.

No one suspected. That was odd in itself, she thought. After all the rumours, she would have thought more people would have been paying attention to her absence – and John's. But then, they had all been drunk too.

She had been avoiding John ever since. Avoiding his eyes, his words, his very presence. Ignoring his attempts to catch her alone, barely speaking to him at meal times, locking her door against him at night. It was her fault, not his. She had gone to him and she had never protested, never pushed him away from her, so the fault was hers. She knew it was wrong, whereas John didn't feel anything except the will to possess her. A will that was so strong, she had been swept along before it, unable to hear the voice within her that cried, no, this is not allowed, we must stop. But now that voice was awake in her again and only too clear. They were primo-irmãos and too close in blood, no matter what John said. She must get away.

It had all been planned long before, anyway. She had always intended to leave two days after the wedding. There was no unseemly haste, no reason for eyebrows to be raised at her hurried departure. Only John seemed surprised and unable to accept that the preparations were continuing, unchecked. That she really was still leaving. He watched her, distraught at her aloofness, and he brooded alone in his room and then, leaving a letter for Eleanor, he left again in the night for São Paulo. Eleanor was miserable and desperately relieved and then guilty even at that.

The pain and confusion in his face that sought some answer, some flicker of recognition from her, followed her in her thoughts and ground into her with accusations of heartlessness long after everyone had fallen asleep at night. She loved him but why, why did she always feel out of control when he was around, as though she were being pulled along faster than her feet could carry her? Why did his will always supersede her own?

She was driven, the next morning, out to the airport by her parents and Henry, and checked in, her hands shaking, her face streaked with tears as she suddenly realized she was leaving them for at least a year and that she loved them all very much. They hugged and kissed and cried farewells, Henry holding her tightly for a moment before smiling and letting her go. When she was past the barriers, walking out to the waiting plane on the tarmac, she felt a completely new sensation that she had never known before overtake her – she felt free!

*

271

John sat in front of the television and watched a children's programme on TV Globo with the sound turned down. Flickering images of balloons and party hats were reflected in the orbs of his eyes, staring without blinking at the screen. He didn't see them. He was lost in thought. A totally different image filled his mind's eye. He poured another glass of wine from the bottle, rolled another joint and sat back in the clouds of smoke, his eyes blank and unfocused.

Teresa watched him uneasily from where she stood cooking the evening meal. It was hot in the kitchen, the windows wide open to catch a breeze but the still night air of January throbbed with heat. If it weren't for the fact that he hadn't eaten a proper meal since he came back from Rio de Janeiro, she wouldn't be in the kitchen now. She disliked cooking and cleaning, disliked anything that didn't involve her looking her best and wearing beautiful clothes, anything that might make people think she was perhaps his maid. But John had lost even more weight, looking gaunt and ill, and she couldn't ignore the situation any further. If sweating over a hot stove was the way to get him to eat, then she would cook. Today and tomorrow – and the next day.

She liked this apartment with its separate kitchen and bathroom and its two whole bedrooms! She liked the way it was furnished so very casually with polished boards and rugs and lots of white walls, the space never cluttered by unnecessary furniture or bric-à-brac. And she liked the man who lived here, his calmness, his intelligence, his caring. More than that, she thought ruefully: she loved him.

But he didn't love her. He had always been honest about that. He liked her, he enjoyed her company in the evenings when he was tired from his days at the Escola de Sociológia e Política, when his graduate studies kept him awake long into the night. He liked to make love to her. But he didn't love her. That was reserved entirely for that cousin of his. Eleanor. Teresa chopped the mint on the board with small, precise movements. Chopping Eleanor up, very finely.

272

'Are you going to work tomorrow?' Teresa looked up and saw John standing there in the doorway, smiling at her. A painfully forced smile, but still a smile. She had begun to think he would never show that emotion again.

'Not if you'd rather do something else,' she said immediately. 'It's just a cattle call, one more audition and hundreds of girls to fill it. I can always miss it.' She saw the flash of concern cross his face, knowing that she had said the wrong thing, worrying him that she was becoming too involved. But then it was gone, and he was shaking his head.

'No, no. I just wondered what you were doing, that's all. There's a student meeting late in the afternoon that I've got to attend, so I may not be back until late. We're going to denounce Goulart and the way he's running the country. Should be fun,' he added ironically and Teresa felt a shudder go through her. She wished he weren't so involved in all those political rallies. Sooner or later there would be a backlash – and he might be caught up in it. Oh, God, why couldn't he be a lawyer or a doctor or something stable?

'Well, if you're sure. I guess I probably should go to this audition. There's talk of a film – an American film being made down here and they need extras. Who knows, I might get lucky.' She laughed as though the chance of her ever being lucky was absurd. 'Come and eat. I made soup.'

She pressed him to sit, enticing him with just another bowl, just another piece of bread, just another slice of cheese until John felt as though he might burst. He hadn't eaten so much in a long time. In fact, he couldn't remember when. It made him feel heavy and stupefied, the gnawing pain stilling for a moment, becoming bearable. He reached over and took her hand, kissing the palm.

'I don't know why you stay with me, Teresa. And look after me, and feed me, and care about me. Why?' His brow was furrowed as though he truly were puzzled by her behaviour.

Teresa shrugged. 'Why not? We suit each other. Neither one of us is a sentimental fool.' She forced her voice to sound indifferent, as hard as she once had had to be. 'We're both getting what we want out of this. And when it doesn't suit either of us any more, we'll part. Just like before.' So don't think I'm in love with you and that you can do whatever you want with my heart, because I'll never give you that satisfaction. That's my secret. Teresa smiled and John didn't notice the muscles that wobbled in the effort to keep that smile in place, or the look of anguish in her eyes when he nodded and turned away.

'Fine,' he said. That's what he wanted to hear. 'We're happy enough, aren't we? Who needs love?' He went into the bedroom and lay on the bed in the dark. Teresa heard him exhale heavily. She continued to sit at the table, thinking bitter thoughts.

Finally, she got up and cleared away the table, stacking the dishes in the sink and tidying his papers in the sitting-room where they were spread around the floor. Notes for his thesis. Teresa looked at them, hesitated, and then sat down in a chair to read them over. It would be painfully slow, her reading skills still not very advanced, but in these notes she might find out, perhaps, what made him do what he did, what made him the person he was. She began to read.

'... the better study of man and of human society in its present form ...' The notes went on in the same way for several pages, discussing communal and associational relationships and tribalism. Teresa could make no sense of it. Then, further down, she saw a quote that had been marked with an asterisk.

'There is a marked lack of "esprit de corps" in Brazil. Sergio Buarque de Holanda discusses a "peculiar characteristic" of the peoples of the Iberian peninsula as "... the index of value of a man is inferred ... by the extent to which he does not need to be dependent on others, to which he does not need anybody."' Teresa studied the words, sure that here was a clue that would give her an insight into the man she so desperately loved. But the sense of the words eluded her. In frustration, she read on.

'I believe the same to be true here in Brazil. In Brazilian

274

culture, a great man is a man who does not need anybody
...' The last four words had been heavily underscored.

For a moment Teresa felt cold, staring at the notes.
Maybe that was it then; maybe it wasn't that he loved
Eleanor and not her, Teresa. Maybe it was that he just
didn't need anybody at all. She shivered before reaching
over and putting out the lights. Well, that was just too bad.
John would just have to learn to need her, the way she did
him. Because she meant to have his child.

Eleanor had never been so cold in her life. The wind blew
her scarf across her face, muffling her mouth and nose as
she headed across the street and slipped between the cars
parked, almost bumper to bumper, in the snow. She cursed
and pushed on, pulling her basket of shopping further up
on to her hip, searching with frozen fingers for her keys.
The Rue D'Amélie was only a short distance up on her left
but it seemed as though she had trudged across a waste-
land, a frozen tundra before she arrived at the door to her
apartment. She fitted the keys into the lock and gratefully
leaned against the door.

'*Eleanor, c'est tu là? Attends, j'arrive!*' a small, dark-
haired girl cried, seeing the door handle wiggle. She
jumped to her feet and quickly unbolted the door, pulling it
open to let in the taller, fairer girl who leaned, as though
one of the last survivors of Hannibal's trek through the
Alps, against the entrance. 'Come on in, you imbecile!' the
girl said in French and Eleanor thrust the basket against
her flatmate's stomach and pulled the door shut after her.

'So help me, Sophie. I am never going out there again.
Not until spring,' Eleanor said and her companion nodded
understandingly, taking the basket and depositing it in the
kitchen.

'Yes, yes, I know. But tomorrow there will be classes and
then what will you do, hmm? You will brave the blizzards
yet again and tell me how warm it is in Brazil right now,
just as I will tell you how warm it is in the south. And we
will shiver together and trudge home in the snow and

complain like mad.' Sophie laughed and Eleanor closed her eyes.

'Are we that predictable? Oh well, just as long as you know it's coming, I might as well tell you how everyone I know will be lying around the pool, or playing tennis and the sun will be blazing down and the flowers will be blooming and, oh God, I hate Paris!' She ended in a loud shout that did nothing to faze the French girl who simply took a bite of the baguette Eleanor had brought in and smiled.

'So do I. I'll come back with you to Brazil, when you decide to leave. I could do with some sun. And some gorgeous men who don't look like they spend all their time sitting in cafés drinking coffee and smoking and talking politics.' Sophie lit her own cigarette and used the match to light the gas top. She put the kettle on, for coffee.

'Oh, but that's just what all the men I know do! What makes politics such a riveting topic for discussion? I can think of a hundred things I'd rather discuss,' Eleanor complained. She shed her coat, throwing it across the sofa that took up nearly all of the tiny sitting-room and going to stand in front of the fireplace. At least they had an open fire.

'Like what?' Sophie asked. She tossed the packet of cigarettes to Eleanor, who took one and tried, unsuccessfully, to smoke it.

'Oh, how about literature or travel, restaurants, theatre, music . . .' she began and Sophie took up the litany.

'Magazines, fashion, film, sex,' she said loudly.

'Well, yes, that too I daresay,' Eleanor admitted. 'But as long as they keep their pawing hands to themselves. I'm getting tired of slapping them down.'

'Don't Brazilian men ever make passes? I thought all that hot Latin blood would make walking the streets of Rio a painful experience for your behind.' Sophie looked disappointed and Eleanor giggled.

'Not my behind, anyway. Here, you might as well have this.' She passed the cigarette over to her friend and coughed away the last acrid taste from her throat. 'I'm

276

never going to be able to do it with any panache, so I might as well not try at all. I'll just drink lots of coffee and look broodingly remote.' Eleanor struck an attitude, as though she were sitting at a café table and Sophie shook her head.

'You're remote enough. You don't need to look any more Garbo-esque. Try and look more come-hitherish, can't you?' But Eleanor couldn't and wouldn't and they sat over their coffee and discussed their day instead, laughing over their professors and the other students, moaning about the cold and the meagreness of the size of their apartment.

Eleanor had met Sophie Gastambide at the small hotel on the Left Bank near Les Invalides where her father had arranged for her to stay until she found herself somewhere suitable to live. Sophie's father had done the same, since Sophie lived in the south of France, just near Perpignan. Her father was an artist, she explained over breakfast their first morning, and needed the light. When they got to know each other better Sophie admitted her father also needed the money and it was cheaper to live down there than in Paris.

They took a flat together after their first week of classes, Eleanor supplementing Sophie's share of the rent from her own overly generous allowance and Sophie introducing Eleanor to the subtleties of the French language and café society. They had shared for two months now, very happily, and Eleanor thought she could not have been more fortunate in having Sophie as a friend.

'And I might tell you, that Maurice de Baudet is very taken with you. You fulfil his image of the Aryan blonde his mother has been dinning into him for years. And you're rich. You could help him renew the family treasures, like that old mausoleum of a place on the Ile de la Cité. He likes you a lot,' Sophie said, puffing away on her cigarette and trying to look as worldly wise as was possible for a small, dark-haired girl with a gamine face and large mischievous grey eyes. She looked at Eleanor, wistfully, thinking how much she would give to be tall and blonde. How she would love to be remote and have endless men languishing miserably after her.

Eleanor, from her extreme height of five foot ten inches – ten and a half if she were honest – could think of nothing nicer than being tiny and delicate and sexily dark the way Sophie was, and she would neither believe nor listen to Sophie's ridiculous stories of how much French men wanted Aryan blondes as wives. Good heavens! They were all so small themselves, what would they do with a hulking great girl like herself?

'I'm not interested,' she said and Sophie shrugged.

'Oh well, if you don't want to be a marquise, why should I worry? Here, have an éclair and ruin that wonderful figure of yours. Please!'

Eleanor took the pâtisserie, placed it neatly on a plate and picked at it with a fork. Sophie shook her head. Nothing was going to change that girl.

'But I don't want to stay here when I finish my course, Sophie. My life is back in Brazil. Why would I care about being a marquise?' Eleanor stretched out the syllables until it became almost ridiculous in sound and Sophie threw her hands up in that quick manner of hers, begging for no more.

'How anyone could hate Paris, the most romantic of all cities, the most beautiful, elegant, refined – ugh! You are too much! A peasant! I shall marry Maurice instead, despite the fact that I am short, dark and poor. Perhaps his mother won't notice? After all, once I have a man in my bed, he is my slave forever more!' Sophie often made claims of equal magnitude but Eleanor had never noticed her do more than flirt outrageously with the other male students at university or in the cafés after classes. Sophie was a born flirt, but nothing more. Which made it all the more necessary that Eleanor keep her own experience to herself. She winced at what Sophie might think, if she knew.

'You do that. And I, poor peasant that I am, shall come to your wedding with my wonderful tan and my many lusty Brazilian men who pinch bottoms, and you will run down the aisle away from pasty-faced Maurice and beg me, yes, beg me on your knees to take you away from Paris and let you see the sun again, just one more time before you die! There, you see what happens to title-hunters!' Eleanor said in a gravely mocking voice and Sophie went into hoots of laughter and sank back against the pillows of the sofa.

'Alas, I am born to be a ragamuffin like my father, always in search of the sun and something new to divert me. Rest easy, Maurice is safe from my clutches.' She wiped the crème pâtissière from her fingers. All gone, she thought sadly and Eleanor resignedly offered her half of her éclair. Sophie brightened and popped it into her tiny mouth, still finding room somehow to talk around it. 'You get any more letters from your dear friend Henry – who is not a boyfriend and should never be thought of as such – but who still writes to you once a week at least and tells you how much he misses you and can't wait to come and see you. You know the one I mean?'

'Yes, I know the one you mean. I just got a letter today but I haven't read it yet. It's over there in my bag, if you're so keen to hear the news from home,' Eleanor said and settled herself more comfortably, one foot underneath her, in front of the fire. 'And anyway, I don't hate Paris. I honestly think it is beautiful and elegant and oh, whatever else you called it. Truly I do,' she added as she saw Sophie pull a cynical face. 'I'm just so cold! My God, is this what John went through in England for four years?' she added, almost as an afterthought to herself. But Sophie sat back from where she had been rummaging in Eleanor's bag and raised her eyebrows.

'And who, might I ask, is John?' She saw the flush start on her friend's face and knew, instantly, that here was the reason for Eleanor's disinterest in other men. This John was the reason why Eleanor had earned the nickname of the 'Ice Princess' amongst some of the more disappointed young men in her class. How interesting!

'Oh, just my cousin,' Eleanor replied abruptly and reached out her hand to take Henry's letter. 'Would you like me to read it to you?' she asked, hoping to divert Sophie's interest.

279

The clear grey eyes smiled. Who did she think she was fooling? 'All right. But you'll have to translate it for me. My English isn't nearly up to the standard of your French. And my Portuguese is non-existent. Whichever he writes in.'

'Mostly English. His mother's English so I guess it comes just as easily to him. Okay, let's see.' Eleanor flipped open the letter, and began to read, translating clumsily as she went, compared to the elegance of Henry's prose.

'Dearest Eleanor,

'You sound as though you are having such a wonderful time that I am terribly jealous and wish I could throw my law books out the window and fly out to join you immediately instead of waiting a whole year.' Eleanor and Sophie pulled faces at each other and laughed. 'But I console myself with the thought of all the freedom I will enjoy once I become a lawyer and have a career and money of my own. Then I will take you on trips and Paris will pale beside the beauty of your own country and you will never want to go away and leave us again.' There, that was Henry at his finest, Eleanor thought. She smiled.

'Isobel and Louis are settled into the west wing of the palácio now and Isobel has, of course, ordered a team of decorators to refurbish the apartments and make them "habitable". Your poor mother was, I think, quite hurt and not without reason as everyone knows the Palácio Lampedusca is one of the most beautiful private homes in Rio and entirely without need of refurbishment. But Isobel can be extremely insensitive and Louis, well, Louis is so under Isobel's thumb that she can do no wrong and he assents to every whim she has. I cannot think what provoked your papa to allow them to live with you all but perhaps it will work out better in time.' The words of criticism were so unlikely, coming from Henry, that Eleanor opened her eyes wide. Poor Mama.

'My parents are going away on a cruise to the Greek islands this winter, which will be good for both of them. Father suffers from arthritis in the damp cold and Mother is feeling run down and in need of change. I have promised to look after everything while they are away, so there will be no problem there.

'There is news about John and I hesitated for some time over whether to write and tell you or not. Your parents have not done so yet, nor Isobel, and they left it up to me whether you should be told. But I don't feel I have the right to withhold any information from you concerning someone as dear to you as John.' Eleanor's voice faltered, her translation failing her and she read on rapidly in English so that Sophie exclaimed and protested she could not follow the sense of the words. But Eleanor paid no heed.

'John has married Teresa, just a few days ago, I think. We heard of it via friends of Louis's in São Paulo and they tell us that Teresa is going to have a child – John's child – and that it was the best solution for them all. I don't know how John feels about it nor when the child is due. Perhaps it would be best if you were to write to him about that. I do not like to intrude where I, almost certainly, will not be welcome. Forgive me if this gives you pain, but I thought you should know.

'I know nothing I can say now will hold much interest for you and so I will end this letter and write again to you in a few days when, I hope, you will have adjusted better to this news.

'My love and best wishes to you, Henry.'

Eleanor sat quite still in front of the fire, feeling it scorch the side of her face and almost welcoming the pain. John was married. To Teresa. And having a child! For a moment, a wild, uncontrollable moment, Eleanor wished desperately that that child were hers. That she and John had made a child between them that night of Isobel's wedding. But then, reality hit her and she realised nothing could have come of that. She could not marry her primo-irmão. No matter how much she loved him.

'Well,' she said shakily, 'that was quite a surprise.' She folded the letter up carefully and slipped it in the pocket of her skirt. She would read it again later, in the privacy of her own room. Along with the letter John had left for her before he returned to São Paulo. That letter had spoken of love, of waiting for her, of always knowing they would be together in the end. And yet, barely two months later he was married and having a child. She laughed at the bitter absurdity of it all.

Sophie had seen the colour fade from Eleanor's cheeks, the tremble that had begun in her voice as she read the last few lines of the letter in English. Only some of the words had been clear to Sophie, but she had understood the gist of the matter. This cousin, John, was married. And Eleanor would never show the pain, never reveal anything intimate about her life, unless Sophie could somehow understand what this man was to Eleanor. More than a cousin clearly; how much more?

'Tell me about this John, Eleanor. You never mentioned him before tonight. What has he done that has you all in a fright?'

'He's, um, married someone – a girl he's been seeing on and off for a few years. She's going to have a baby.' Eleanor strove to make her voice seem normal. She failed miserably.

'And so? What is his connection to you?' Sophie probed. She knew Eleanor had some secret, something that seemed big and dark and terrible to her that she longed to share with another person but was too restrained, too private to reveal without pressure.

'I told you, he's my cousin. My father's sister's son. My primo-irmão!' Eleanor's voice had begun to shake badly now, tears quivering in her eyes. She began to get to her feet, but Sophie reached out and took her arm.

'And you are in love with him. Does he know that?'

'Of course he does! My God, you don't understand ...' Eleanor cried and then she began to cry, heaving, terrible sobs that made her hunch forward and hold her head in her hands, her hair falling over her face. She sobbed for some time, Sophie sitting beside her, holding her in her arms and then, once the extreme emotion was spent, Eleanor told Sophie everything about John, from the first time he had

282

first walked into her life at the age of ten until the night of Isobel's wedding.

Sophie made some coffee and they sat late into the night, huddled in the flickering light of the fire against the howl of the wind beyond the steel shutters they had pulled into place over the windows.

'I may be very stupid here, or crudely insensitive,' Sophie said finally, 'but I still don't understand why you ran away from John. You love him. He says he loves you, he has always been the most important person in your life, and then he makes love to you. And you run away. Why?'

'Sophie, haven't you been listening to anything I've said? John's my first cousin! In Brazil, that's almost like being my brother. And marriage is forbidden between people so close in blood.'

'You're not Catholic and you're half-English — more, in fact. So go live somewhere else in the world and be with him. He doesn't find it a problem, does he? No, so what's yours?' For a moment Eleanor was startled. She had never heard it put so bluntly before, so very clearly, and yet she still fought the answer.

'My father and John detest each other. It would tear my family apart,' she began and Sophie snorted contemptuously at that.

'Your father wouldn't have much to say about it on a daily basis if you lived somewhere else, now would he? Families adapt. And anyway, you are going to be twenty this year. How old do you need to be to finally stand up and say, "Hey, this is my life and my decision. You're not going to live with my husband, I am!" That's what you tell your family.' Sophie waited, seeing the hesitation, the awkwardness in Eleanor's eyes and wondering what more was hidden there, even perhaps from Eleanor herself.

'He wouldn't ever leave Brazil, Sophie. He's caught up in its politics, determined to lead it to democracy. He loves me but I come second to all that. Anyway, I can't now. It's all over. It's too late! He's married and Teresa's having a baby. There's nothing that can be done now,' Eleanor pointed out wretchedly, her mind retreating from any further thought. Nothing can be done now, she repeated to herself.

'No,' Sophie sighed, 'I guess not.' She lapsed into deep thought and Eleanor sat on the floor beside her, her back against the sofa, her head lolling on to its cushions. 'You got a picture of John? And Henry too?' Sophie asked suddenly and Eleanor nodded, not moving. She was too tired to move.

'Top drawer beside my bed. Help yourself,' she said and Sophie darted up the stairs and back down again, several photographs in her hand. She knelt back beside Eleanor and passed across the photographs.

Eleanor sorted through them. 'That's Isobel and Louis and my parents. Taken in the garden last summer,' she began. 'And that's Henry, taken some time last summer too. I can't remember where. He's such a dear.' Sophie noticed how warm Eleanor's voice became when she mentioned Henry. She looked at the photograph hard, liking the look of the young man's expression, amused, self-mocking, as much as the way his features were arranged so neatly and pleasingly in a lean face, the body at ease and well proportioned. She looked up at Eleanor.

'This is the one who writes every week? And you want more?' she said in mock surprise, indignation. Eleanor smiled painfully and took the third photograph from the pile and showed it to Sophie.

'And this is John.'

There was a long pause while Sophie stared at the last photograph. It had been taken the day before the wedding, when he had first arrived from São Paulo and was getting out of his car. Eleanor had snapped it without his knowledge and hidden the camera behind her back before he noticed. A memento, she had thought at the time, to remind her of him when she was away. She saw the startled expression in Sophie's eyes.

'You see what I mean?' she said simply.

Sophie looked up and nodded. 'Yes, I guess I do. He certainly is quite special – looks a lot like you but in masculine form. The expression's different, but ... anyway, I didn't know they made them that good-looking,' Sophie joked and then glanced back at the photograph uneasily. So, now all was clear and Eleanor was right, no one else was likely to ever fill his place. She passed the photograph back. 'All yours,' she said without thinking.

There was a heavy sigh and Eleanor shook her head. 'No,' she said, 'all Teresa's.' And she slipped the photograph in amongst the rest.

Chapter Fifteen

Eleanor wrote to John, a halting, awkward letter of congratulations that sounded nothing like her. She wasn't surprised when her letter was never acknowledged nor replied to. Henry kept her informed about John's activities along with those of the rest of the family but there was little depth to the news. Simple bulletins to the effect that Isobel was expecting her first child, that John was still agitating against President Goulart's government, and that more and more of the middle and upper classes in Brazil were unhappy with the government.

But Isobel had begun writing too, and was proving a far more entertaining correspondent, despite her inattention to grammar and her laboured descriptions of her own pregnancy. She wrote that Teresa was becoming a popular figure in São Paulo's local television commercials and had been offered a part in a film. There were caustic comments about casting couches that Eleanor smiled at and ignored.

And she wrote that John himself would be leaving São Paulo once his studies were completed at the end of the year. There was no mention yet about where he would be going but there were rumours that he intended to return to the Vila Serrista. Eleanor shuddered at the thought.

Henry reported that President Goulart was trying to dredge up support from the urban masses and the trade unions with little practical success and that Goulart's policies were becoming increasingly leftist and radical. He was blaming foreign interests for a sliding economy and rocketing inflation. Henry assured Eleanor that her own family's position was secure enough and that she was not to worry, but still, Eleanor did worry both about the political situation and about John. She wondered whether, at the end of the year, she ought not to return home.

But, in the meantime, it was spring in Paris and Eleanor had fallen in love with the city. She loved the sparkling, tree-lined boulevards washed with water every evening, and the Seine with its endless, graceful bridges with the *bâteaux mouches* gliding beneath. She loved the lights reflecting on the water at night and the warm, fragrant air in the mornings that smelt of cherry blossom and bakeries and freshly brewed coffee. She loved the dappled shade of the Bois de Boulogne, where the leaves glowed transparent green with the sun overhead and the dust blew up in warm clouds and she and Sophie sat at La Cascade and ate endless *chocolat liègeois*. She loved shopping in the sixteenth arrondissement, strolling up and down the Boulevard Victor Hugo with its elegant mamas and beautifully turned out children, and she loved her apartment, despite its cramped size and the number of steps she had to climb to reach it.

On that particular Saturday morning in late June, she sat reading her latest letters and listening to Sophie clattering around in the kitchen with guilt.

'Oh, Sophie, please leave all that until later and come out here and sit in the sun,' Eleanor urged from where she sat, squeezed on to the tiny balcony of their apartment and basking in the golden warmth. Already her skin had begun to take on a faint colour and her freshly washed and still drying hair shone in the light. Sophie eventually emerged, drying her hands on a tea towel. She edged out beside Eleanor and sat down on a pillow, her pale face angled back to lean up against the window frame and soak up the sun's rays.

'Bliss! Absolute bliss!' Sophie murmured and Eleanor smiled.

'Isn't it? But are you referring to the sun or to a certain young man who seems to be receiving a lot more of your time than most of the others? Marc-Antoine something-or-other?' She saw Sophie shake her dark head and grin.

'Old news. I've found someone much better but I expect he'll bore me by the end of the week. They're such callow youths compared to all your admirers.' There was a twinge of jealousy to her tone, a slight pique. Eleanor didn't notice. 'Who're you taking to Claudette's?'

'I don't know. Perhaps the morose Maurice. I hadn't really thought.' Eleanor sighed at that. Maurice had already asked her and she felt it would be rude to refuse him and go with someone else. But he was so very proper and dull. She wished Maurice would understand that she had no feeling for him beyond casual friendship. And not be so downcast by it all.

'Oh no! Not him. You've got lots of men dying to take you. Why go with Maurice? After all, Claudette's party is going to be the last one this school year. Probably the last one before the autumn, the way everyone's going away for the summer. It's bound to be quite spectacular. You don't want Maurice dripping around after you all night long. You really are so ridiculous sometimes, Eleanor. What I wouldn't give to have just a handful of the other men who pine for you throw a mere glance at me,' Sophie protested and Eleanor shrugged and smiled.

'I told you, I hadn't really thought about it yet. Who're you going with?' She glanced across at her friend, seeing the concern and perhaps, yes, just a touch of irritation in her eyes and wishing Sophie wouldn't worry so much. She was over John completely now. And that was all for the best, really. They had never had any future, anyway. It was nothing to do with John that made her so reluctant to go out with other men. She just wasn't that interested in them.

They were boring. She prompted Sophie again. 'Well?'

'Oh, either Georges or Laurence. They both asked and I said I'd let them know. It's only a week away now and you really should have someone lined up. Besides, you've only got one exam left and I have two! So what's your excuse?' Sophie pouted and Eleanor laughed.

'You always have twice as many exams, Sophie. And twice as many boyfriends, even if you do think they're all callow youths and you much prefer my admirers. Why can't you just take things a little easier? You're such a tiny, fragile creature to be trying to gulp life down in one swallow. One of these days you're going to choke.'

'And you're too beautiful to be trying to ride life out on the sidelines,' Sophie retorted quickly. 'If that's what this fellow John's done to you, I for one say you're better off without him.' She saw the sudden stricken look on Eleanor's face, the way her eyes became filled with pain, and she cursed herself for being so clumsy. Let Eleanor sit it out for a while. What did a few months matter? She was entitled, surely?

Sophie was not the only one who felt Eleanor was sitting life out; quite a few of the young men who hovered around Eleanor without success felt there had to be a reason for her reserve, her inattention. But neither they nor Sophie had any real idea what was going on in Eleanor's head that particular summer.

Claudette's soirée was held in Neuilly, overlooking the Bois de Boulogne and Eleanor found it quite, quite beautiful and quite, quite dull. Like herself, she thought ruefully. Everyone told her how exquisite her dress was, how it complemented her colouring, how very smart Maurice looked beside her. And she smiled her thanks and smothered a yawn.

There were many faces she recognized either from university or from the parties that Maurice had insisted she accompany him to throughout the first months of the year. Not quite as comfortable as the parties in Rio, where she knew everyone from birth, but certainly not a party of strangers. She smiled and circulated on Maurice's arm, making small talk and listening to jokes, wondering how soon she could politely leave. People nudged each other and made predictions about whether Maurice would have her for his marquise before the year was out and whether she would accept. The odds were fairly even.

Sophie, however, was in her element and enjoying herself tremendously. She bubbled over with excitement and enthusiasm for the evening's pleasures, eating her way through the spectacular buffet display like a starved cat and whirling her way across the floor in the arms of a steady flow of men. She waved to Eleanor and saw Eleanor smile and wave back, looking stiff and tired beside Maurice's serious figure. Looking bored. Sophie felt a flicker of guilt and then was caught up in the flow of the music and forgot Eleanor completely.

When, later in the evening, Sophie looked for Eleanor again, she wasn't surprised to find that she was gone. A headache, Maurice explained with his usual turgid manner, gone home in a taxi, refused to allow him to leave the party. Sophie sighed to herself.

He was waiting for her on the stairs, huddled into a corner and leaning back against the wall. The stairs were dirty and old, splintered in places where the wood had been broken by heavy furniture being dragged up them. John didn't seem to notice. He just sat there, smoking, watching her come up the last flight and the hall light was so dim that it lit only his brow, leaving his eyes in shadow. The time switch clicked off as Eleanor came forward slowly.

'I wasn't sure this was your place at first,' he said. 'It seemed unlikely.'

'John? What ... what on earth are you doing here?' Eleanor stopped in front of him, wondering whether he intended to rise or would continue to sit there in the dark. 'When did you get here?'

There was a rustle in the dark and then he was standing

close beside her in the cramped corridor, his body almost touching hers. She smelt the cigarette smoke and tired, sweat-stained clothes. But it was also John's smell and she breathed it in deeply, snatching at her moment of private pleasure.

'About an hour ago. I hope you don't mind but I didn't have anywhere else to go.' There was silence between them.

'Find the light and I'll let us in.' It was an abrupt command, showing her agitation and John leaned on the switch, flooding the hall again with shadows and faint dim light.

'Better?' He surveyed her while she fumbled in her bag for the keys. 'You're home early, aren't you? It's only ten o'clock. You look like you've been out on the town.' He didn't say how good she looked, he didn't compliment her on the dress that he had never seen before, he didn't comment on how sophisticated and adult she seemed, but he thought it all to himself. Eleanor became acutely uncomfortable.

'There,' she said, as the door swung open, 'let's go in. I hate this hallway.' The flat was welcoming after the bleakness of the stairs. John sighed, almost with relief, and closed the door behind him.

'Will you stay long?' she asked, moving forward into the small sitting-room, her back to him so that he wouldn't see the expectancy on her face, nor how she reacted to his answer. She put her bag down, delaying turning around.

'Perhaps a few days,' he said vaguely and then added, 'this is nice. You've really made it comfortable. After that entrance I thought it would be some sort of dive. Did you do all this yourself?'

Eleanor turned around, glad that he had provided such an easy opening into conversation, edged away from the difficult issues. She surveyed the room with pride.

'Yes, mostly. Sophie contributed a few bits but she's not very interested in her surroundings. You know I like things to be ordered and attractive or I can't think straight. I'd never get any work done if the place were a mess.' She laughed, self-consciously. 'Sophie cooks though. She's much better than me and it works out an even split. You want some coffee?'

'Mmm, yes.' John sounded distracted, looking around the small room with its bookcases and comfortable chairs, the pot plants and rugs. It was casual and charming and an oasis of calm. Like Eleanor herself. He smiled and breathed in deeply.

'Is that Henry?' He moved forward to the mantelpiece, abruptly picking up a small silver frame and staring at the photograph it contained.

Eleanor, watching him from the kitchen, saw his shoulders tense. 'Yes. I think Sophie's fallen in love with him from afar. She reads all his letters and moons over his photo. She put it up there, so she could see it every day,' she said quickly, lightly, trying not to make it important. She thought of the photograph of John, still in her bedside table drawer, still hidden, still private.

'Oh. You like this Sophie? Is she fun to live with?' John asked and Eleanor, taking mugs down from the cupboard, smiled.

'She's wonderful. You'll meet her later. She's still at the party I was at tonight. Absolutely mad and never stops running for a moment. Wait till you see her.' She came back into the room, carrying the mugs of coffee.

'Does she know about us?' John asked baldly and Eleanor shook suddenly at the intensity with which he said it. Shook with fear and something else, something that made her stomach quiver almost as though in delight. She glanced up at him.

'There isn't any us.' She saw his mouth twitch, as though in pain.

He sighed. 'There's always been and always will be. You know that, Elly.' He turned and walked out, through the french windows.

It was a tall, fair-haired man looking out from the balcony window, out at the night sky and the rooftops surrounding their apartment, that caught Sophie's attention as she climbed out of Laurence's car. Then Eleanor joined the man, both standing close together, looking out, not down. He seemed – different, foreign, from all the men Sophie knew. And, seeing them together, Sophie realized for the first time that Eleanor was also different – also foreign. She glanced at the stranger again, taking stock.

He was a man of striking good looks with pale hair and a sharply planed face, a slight stoop to his figure as he bent over Eleanor and spoke to her. Sophie saw the tension in both figures, the look on Eleanor's face. She knew instantly who he must be. The man was clearly Eleanor's cousin – John.

They looked like brother and sister, Sophie thought in astonishment. The shared blood was apparent in more than their features; it was there in the tilt of their heads, the grace of their movements, their mannerisms. And, from the expressions on their faces, they were unaware that anyone else existed. Sohie caught her breath in dismay. Now what on earth was he doing here?

'Laurence? We must go out again. Just for a while. Another drink.' Sophie commanded and Laurence, bewildered first by her demand to come home early, and now by her demand to go out again, hastened to open the car door.

'John, what are you doing here? Tell me, please.' Without knowing it, Eleanor repeated Sophie's own question. Eleanor's face was pale, her mouth so dry that she could barely whisper. John shrugged but didn't smile. He was holding Eleanor's hand in his, tightly. Not letting her go. She stared at the pale hairs on his wrist, the way they curled against his skin. She barely heard what he was saying.

'I wanted to see you, wanted to get away from Brazil for a while. I needed to, really. What's the matter, Eleanor? Aren't you pleased to see me? Not at all? Do you still want me out of your life?' He had become deathly pale, the two standing like alabaster figures in a night sky. Eleanor watched his lips folding in, his chin jutting forward. She

293

saw the intense look in his eyes. She shook her head, turning back into the room, away from the balcony.

'Why are you here? You're married. To Teresa. And having a child. What do you want me to say to that?'

'Teresa lost the baby.' There, just like that, the room span out of focus and all Eleanor could see was a deep blue sea of colour surging out at her, engulfing her like the tide. She lost her balance and swayed to one side and John put out an arm and steadied her.

'Oh John! I'm so terribly sorry! Oh my God! What happened?' Her voice became a hoarse whisper.

John sighed. 'Teresa wanted a part in a film. It was her first big break. An American film too. She – she starved herself so the baby wouldn't show and I, well, I was too caught up in my studies and my political rallies and – myself – to notice until it was too late; she lost it. Miscarried. At four months.' He swallowed and looked away, around the room. He didn't see any of it.

'And how is she now? Was she terribly upset?' Eleanor brushed her hair back out of her eyes, wondering how she would have felt if the situation had been reversed. Wondering how John felt.

'She's all right. Working hard. I've barely seen her in the last few weeks. I think maybe she's relieved – I mean, not that the baby's dead, but that she isn't going to have to stop her career to have the baby. It's odd, I don't really know how she feels.' He shrugged, dazed at the idea. 'And I guess I'm sort of ambivalent myself. I don't love Teresa and she doesn't love me. It just happened.' It just happened. He wondered if that were really true.

'Like us, you mean?' Eleanor wasn't sure why she said that. Perhaps to provoke a reaction.

'No! We never "just happened". What's between us is totally different. You know that.' His voice though still low was clear and hard.

Eleanor shrank inside herself. 'Yes, I suppose I do. Though what good that will ever do us ... Anyway, I thought you had decided things were going to be different, you know, when you and Teresa married. I kept thinking how funny it was really, because I missed you more than ever, missed the family, missed Brazil. Wanted to come home but knew I couldn't, shouldn't. I love Paris but – I don't fit.'

John nodded. 'We're the foreigners. Strange thought, isn't it? It's not till you're away from Brazil that you really see where you belong. I learned that for the first time in England.' He smiled awkwardly. 'Come out on the balcony again. I like the night, and I like looking out at it. We'll talk.' He looked as though she had just eased some burden from him, lightened his load a little.

Eleanor wondered whether it was because she had accepted him. But what else could she do? He was part of her. 'All right,' she said.

It was a cool night with a fresh wind plucking at their clothes, ruffling through her hair. Eleanor shivered slightly and John slipped his jacket off and put it around her. He seemed indifferent to the cold himself, pulling his tie from his throat and unbuttoning his collar. John never liked to be constrained, not by clothes and not by people, Eleanor thought.

'What are you going to do?' she asked after they had sat in silence for some time. The streets edging the river were dark and the street lights shed little light. The night air smelled of damp pine-needles, exhaust fumes and grass.

'That depends on various things, I suppose,' John said and looked at her.

'On me?' Eleanor queried. She felt that tightness begin again in her chest. She pulled his jacket in more tightly around her.

'Yes, partly. On several things.'

'Such as?'

'I'm on a list,' he said abruptly and Eleanor felt her heart give an extra beat, a lurch of fear. In Brazil, to be on a list, could mean persecution, arrest, torture, perhaps death. She tried to breathe evenly.

'For your political involvement? Is it a military list or a government one?'

'I'm not sure. The word was just passed through to me to get away for a while. Teresa's not involved. She doesn't know anything about all this. I told her I was going out of town for a while but I wasn't sure where. She didn't seem to care all that much. And the film's going well. She doesn't need me there for her anymore.' John had thrust his hands into his pockets and they were clenched now, tightly, in fists. He cleared his throat. 'It's my country and they can't force me out. I'm going to stay but it may be difficult.' He looked at her obliquely. 'For everyone.'

'Then why are you here, John? What do you want from me?' Eleanor wished she could phrase her questions better, not sound so cold, but the fear that was pressing in on her mind made thought almost impossible. She shivered in the wind.

'I want – Oh God, you know what I want! I want you!' he cried out harshly and she shrank back, frightened by the longing of those words. John shook his head and his voice dropped away to nothing more than a murmur, almost lost in the wind. 'I know I shouldn't have come over here but I had to see you, at least for a few days, before I go back. I'm going to have to go into hiding for a while – maybe permanently – and I just wanted a few days of normality with you before it all begins. That's all I'm asking, Eleanor. I wouldn't want you mixed up in my affairs back home. That wouldn't be safe. And, anyway, as you've already pointed out, I am married.' He half smiled, despondent and amused at the irony of it all.

Eleanor put her arms around him, wanting to shelter, to comfort. She ached at the thought of losing him again. 'Don't go back, John. Please. Leave it alone for a year or two – until Goulart's term of office is up. When's that? 1965 or so, isn't it? That's only three years away. You could continue your studies over here, couldn't you? Get a doctorate? We could be together. Why go back, knowing they'll be looking for you? Why?' She held him tightly, feeling for a moment that if she just held on to him, he could never go away, never go back.

296

John stroked her hair and rested his chin on her head, staring out into the dark. 'They won't know I'm back. I flew out on purpose, so that would go on record, as soon as I heard about the list. They didn't have time to catch me then. And now, I'm officially abroad. If I sneak back into Brazil, no one'll know. I'll be safe, you see?' He tried to reason with her but she wouldn't listen to him, knowing what he said was not true. Once you were on a list, you were never safe until the government changed.

'And us?' she said awkwardly. He kissed her hair but didn't say anything and the moment drew out, passed away so that Eleanor knew he had already decided.

They sat quietly, each silent with their own thoughts.

Finally, Eleanor reached out for his hand. 'Come to bed,' she said.

He looked at her steadily, sadly. 'It won't change anything, Elly. I'll still leave,' he said quietly.

Eleanor nodded. 'I know that. Come to bed anyway.' And they rose together and walked inside, holding each other tightly, almost desperately.

They were almost to the stairs when the front door opened and Sophie came in. She saw them immediately, saw the way they clung to each other, the direction in which they were headed, and she coloured awkwardly.

'Oh, I'm sorry. I didn't mean to intrude. I just, I mean, it's late. Hello.' Her words became disjointed, spilling out and falling dead before the two lovers. They split apart, John looking remote, Eleanor distracted.

'Oh, Sophie, I didn't realize it was that late. This is John.' Eleanor sought to cover the awkward moment. What else could she say? It was all so obvious.

John nodded, suddenly aware of Sophie's presence and shocked by it. He had been so close to Eleanor, so caught up by her, that he felt as though someone had wrenched him back into the present without collecting all his thoughts with him. It was almost a misery to stand apart from Eleanor, to let his hand drop from her waist, fearing she would not let him return to her side. How he wanted this girl, this small dark girl who had intruded so abruptly, to go away! He forced himself to be polite.

'Hullo.' The word was so impossibly inadequate and yet he couldn't think of anything else to say. He racked his mind but it remained obstinately blank.

Sophie looked up at the tall cousin, sensing the impatience, the indifference and she closed her mouth tightly.

'Well, hullo too. Look, I didn't mean to get in your way. I'm off to bed. We need to leave early tomorrow, Eleanor, don't forget. Father's expecting us.' She moved past them quickly, letting them see she was offended.

Eleanor swallowed. 'Um, Sophie? I probably won't come with you tomorrow. I'll come later, in a few days. When John's gone.' She smiled painfully at the other girl, wishing Sophie wasn't looking so surprised, so hostile, so – jealous. The word sprang into her mind and Eleanor blocked it out abruptly. Of course Sophie wasn't jealous. She was just worried that things would go wrong, that John might hurt her. She saw Sophie shrug, her mouth small and annoyed.

'All right, if you like. You'll let me know? Nice to have met you, John – however briefly. Good night.' And she went into her room and closed the door firmly behind her.

'Oh dear. That didn't go too well, did it? D'you think she was upset?' Eleanor asked worriedly. She looked at John who smiled, his arms going back around her, his chin resting on her head.

'My little worry-guts. She'll be fine. Don't fuss.' He leaned down and kissed her gently on the lips, experimenting. He was reassured by the way she pressed back against him. 'Come to bed,' he said and she nodded, slipping her arm around him. She led him up the stairs, both leaning on each other heavily.

They made love differently this time. Slowly, lingeringly, as though they were old lovers who had shared many years of intimacy together, hushed and laughing as they slipped each other's clothing from their bodies, stroked and caressed and clung together. They seemed to know how they should fit, what part would provoke most pleasure.

Eleanor lost all fear with John, letting him do whatever seemed to please him, losing her own modesty so that she explored his body with her mouth, her tongue, examining and teasing and learning every part of him.

When, finally, John slid into her, his body lying heavy on hers so that their skin became damp and warm, Eleanor opened her mouth in a silent exclamation of pleasure. They pressed more tightly together, shivering with urgency, rolling and writing within the sheets until Eleanor gasped and cried out and then John let himself go and came deeply within her.

He held her cradled within his arms all night, refusing to succumb to the tiredness that washed over his body and tried to drag him down into heavy slumber and he smiled tenderly as she slept against his chest. More than once he wished he could stay with her, never leave her side again; but there was a stronger compulsion which overrode even his love for her. He knew he would never rest until he returned to Brazil.

John stayed for five days. And five nights. Eleanor threw her fears and her sense of what was right or wrong out of the window and welcomed John into her life as though they might never have any more time than this. As though this must last them for a lifetime. Privately, they both wondered if it weren't all the time there was for them.

They barely slept, so intent on savouring every hour, every minute of their time together that they begrudged the heavy stupor of sleep that parted their minds. And when they did sleep, it was closely entwined, her head on his chest, one or the other reaching out, even in sleep, to touch skin, to find reassurance that the other was still there.

Eleanor cooked the spicy, savoury dishes of seafood and tomatoes they both loved and they sat, basking in the sun, on her little verandah and drank wine and held each other, touching intimately, privately, enjoying the closeness that had returned again. Occasionally, they ate out at some of the more famous places like Brasserie Lipp and Café Flore, people-watching, laughing, hands linked like lovers. They walked through the parks, and along the wide boulevards, casually window-shopping but with no real desire to buy. They sat in wicker chairs at round café tables on the pavements and drank wine or café-crème and espresso and read the papers and talked and talked and talked.

Theirs became a world peopled by just two. That same exclusive, intimate world that Henry had recognized in them as children and resented being kept apart from, slipped back around them. All the old quirks, the silent communications, the shared jokes came back to them and they smiled together, each staring hard at the other's face at odd, frozen moments, as though they might imprint it on their minds, each knowing that it was already there, carved into the memories as if it were their own flesh.

And then there were the moments of passion and loving that made all the rest of it more perfect, like cement in between the bricks of a house they were building just for themselves, a house for two. Eleanor could barely even think that it must come to an end. That he must leave.

On the last day, they lay in bed together as the late afternoon sun poured through the shutters, striping the sheets in shadow and light, the heat of the day lying still and heavy in the air. John lay outstretched beside Eleanor and she turned and surveyed his face, the lines beginning around his eyes, the smooth planes of his cheekbones, the wide, firm mouth. She glanced along the length of his body, running her fingers over the ribs that were outlined beneath his skin, kissing the sensitive areas of his chest, under his arm. She breathed in the scent of him, warm and clean and male. He stirred and murmured something, his eyes still shut.

'Did you sleep at all?' she asked and his mouth curved up briefly as he murmured an assent.

After a few moments, he roused himself enough to ask, 'Did you?'

Eleanor leaned over and kissed his lips, reaching past him for the glass of water on the side table. 'No. I didn't want to waste this time,' she said. She drank some water and offered it to him. 'Here, you'll be thirsty soon from all the wine at lunch. What time is it, anyway?' It was late, she could tell from the angle of the sun. He sighed and opened his eyes. He smiled and tweaked the sheet away from her body, caressing her breasts so that they stiffened and became erect. He kissed each one lightly, a salute. Then he replaced the sheet, tucking it in tenderly around her.

'Nearly five. I'll have to leave by six if I'm to get to Le Havre in time. I join the ship there,' he added, knowing that she wanted to know now, whereas before she had always changed the subject, refused to discuss his travel arrangements. Not during their precious time. But now, it was almost over and she wanted to know.

'How will you get through immigration in Brazil? They'll pick you up there, won't they?'

'Not if I use a false name to get that far, and then jump ship while we're still in harbour. It's done all the time, believe me. They won't see me go, and they wouldn't care that much if they did. I'm just another seaman. That's all.' He drank what was left of the water and replaced the glass on the table. Then he pulled her in against him, marvelling at the smoothness of her skin, the faint lingering perfume in her hair.

Eleanor clung to him. 'How will I know if you make it all right? How will I know you weren't picked up?' She was frightened and determined not to show it, determined to be as calm as he was himself.

'You'll know. Somehow I'll get word to you. Maybe not immediately, so don't worry. But – eventually – you'll hear. Don't come back for a while to Brazil, all right? It would be too much of a temptation for me, to come and see you. And I need to stay out of the way.' He kissed her forehead and stroked her face with his hand, her neck, sliding his fingers down her back to cup her buttocks, pressing his thumbs into the little hollows in her lower back. He held her tightly against him for a moment. 'Finish university, have a good time, and don't worry about me. All right?' He felt her shift in his arms, as though to begin the separation before it became impossible for either of them to move.

'All right,' she said. He knew she would do as he asked when she leaned over and kissed him. It was as though they were saying goodbye forever.

Sophie had left for her father's home early the morning after the party and Eleanor had never even heard her go. For a few days Eleanor had felt a pang of guilt at having abandoned her friend but then, she reasoned, she would follow Sophie shortly and surely her friend would not have begrudged her those few days of happiness. No, Sophie would never do that.

So, when it eventually came time, Eleanor packed her bags briskly and silently and left them by the door, as she turned off the gas heater and made sure every window was locked. It was a relief to leave the flat, to have Sophie to turn to. John had been gone twelve hours and already she knew, for them, it was over. She picked up her bags and closed the door.

The summer passed quietly for Sophie and Eleanor, their time spent swimming or bicycling up the coast, shopping, cooking and keeping house for Sophie's father. Sophie's mother was never mentioned and Eleanor did not like to ask. John was never mentioned, and Sophie did not want to ask.

When they returned to Paris, it was the end of August, and the months flew by until Christmas and the arrival of Henry in person, rather than by letter. Eleanor was surprised at how excited she was, so full of expectation and pleasure that she flew around the apartment cleaning it and putting fresh flowers in the sitting-room. Sophie laughed and made sport of her efforts, as excited as Eleanor herself, and Eleanor caught sight of herself, duster in hand, and gave a cry of horror. She dropped the duster where it was and went off to bathe and make herself presentable.

Then the doorbell rang and Henry stood there in the

doorway, his face alight with charm and slight shyness and Eleanor threw herself into his arms and hugged him more soundly than she had ever done, almost as though she could bring herself closer to John that way. Henry was a link with John, with Brazil and she realized, just then, how she missed them all desperately. Eventually, she stood back and released him, looking him up and down. A fully grown Henry stood before her, a lawyer now and a man independent of his parents. He looked happy and relaxed.

Eleanor beckoned him in. 'Sophie, may I present Henry, whom you have heard so much about and whose letters you tease me about so much. And Henry, this is Sophie. Who needs no introduction at all.' Sophie stepped forward and clasped Henry's cool hand in hers. They smiled at each other and shook hands, looking each other over assessingly and liking what they saw. Then Henry glanced back at Eleanor and Sophie saw all the love there in his eyes, held in sternly in case it should intrude or embarrass or be unwelcome. Love just for Eleanor. Sophie felt a deep pain inside her.

'Come on in, Henry, and tell us all the news. How was your trip? Did you have any trouble finding us? I'm sorry we couldn't come out to the airport but we had our last exam today and you know how that is.' Eleanor guided Henry into the sitting-room, pushing him into a chair, her face alight with pleasure. Henry smiled and nodded or shook his head obligingly, unable to fit a word in now that Eleanor was in full flood. 'Aren't you lucky with the weather? Last year it was just atrocious and now look at it, sun shining, barely cold at all. It must be your presence, Henry. Oh, what do you want to drink? Some coffee, wine? Are you hungry? You must be tired after that long trip. Oh! It's good to see you!'

Impulsively, Eleanor leaned over and kissed Henry on the cheek and he laughed, his colour remaining steady now where only a year ago he had flushed like a beacon. He looked at her.

'And it's wonderful to see you. Home hasn't been the

same with you away. Everyone says so. We all miss you.' He spoke slowly in English, knowing Sophie could just about understand. His own French was passable but not up to conversational standards. 'And I'd love some wine if you've got any. I'm not tired at all, for some reason, but I could do with a boost. So, how were exams?' He included Sophie in his question and she thought how very different his behaviour was from Eleanor's cousin. Then, there had been no words wasted on her, no courtesies beyond a curt hello. The two men in Eleanor's life were like chalk and cheese, Sophie thought. And she knew whom she preferred.

'Oh well, the exams are over, that is about all I can say for them,' Sophie said carefully and Eleanor smiled.

'Pay no attention to Sophie. She's the smartest thing around, cleans up on all the exams, and will be finished long before I am at this rate. And look at her! Does she look like a swat?' Henry glanced over at Sophie, as requested, and saw a tiny, delicate pale-skinned creature with a tumbling mass of dark locks and huge liquid grey eyes. Eyes that were not full of their normal mischievous delight but more embarrassed and shy. He smiled.

'No, truly, Sophie, you look far too much like a hot-house flower to be such an intellectual. But I like girls to have minds, so I am doubly delighted to make your acquaintance,' he said gravely and she smiled back, at a loss for her usual smart backchat. She stood up instead.

'I'll, um, get the wine. You two sit and talk. You must have masses to catch up on.' She reverted to French but Henry understood her perfectly well. He stood as she left the room.

'Oh Henry, for heaven's sake, don't go being so formal. Sophie doesn't want you standing every time she comes in or goes out. Relax, this is Paris and the Sixties. You don't have to be on your best behaviour with us,' Eleanor teased and Henry nodded and sat down again.

'I don't know why you include yourself in that. I wasn't about to stand up for you. Sophie seems a dear. You're very lucky to have found such a good friend,' he remarked and

Eleanor wondered, just for a moment, whether Henry found Sophie attractive. She hoped so.

'Yes, she's the most wonderful girl. I'm trying to convince her to come out to Rio for a few months when we finish. She could take a course in Portuguese in her last year here and oh, it'd be so much fun to show her around and introduce her to all the people she's heard so much about. She'd love it. Don't you think?'

'Everyone else does so I'm sure Sophie would too. Certainly all my friends would love her.' Henry grinned. 'But I'm forgetting. I brought photographs with me of Isobel and Louis's baby. They were disappointed you couldn't make the christening but they understood about your studies. Here we are, little Charlie. Your father is as pleased as though it were his own son, rather than his grandson – and named after him too! Isobel gets smarter as she gets older.'

His tone was ironic and Eleanor thought again that this was new for Henry. He never normally criticized, not even obliquely. He never used to make sharp or cynical remarks. But then, he was a lawyer now, and grown up. He wasn't entirely the Henry she knew anymore. She wondered if she had changed too.

They pored over the photographs, sharing them with Sophie, for some time. And filled each other in on what had been happening in the last few weeks. John was mentioned briefly and Eleanor stilled, her hands falling into her lap so they wouldn't show her disquiet. He was officially listed by the government as an agitator who had fled the country. Henry said he suspected John was up in the Mato Grosso somewhere, but they had had no word. He looked at Eleanor speculatively, but she refused to meet his eyes, shrugging instead. Then the conversation passed on to safer ground and Sophie and Henry engaged in a lop-sided French-English discussion about the latest films, and Eleanor allowed herself to sit back over her wine and think bleak thoughts.

She missed John so very much. Sometimes, more than

she could bear. His letter, purposely vague and unsigned, had reached her in October. He was alive and well, that was all she knew. She had burned the letter.

Henry was staying in a pension quite close to them in the Rue Patrice Le Fèvre and they enjoyed his company for nearly a week, going to concerts and films, sitting inside the large glass-fronted cafés that lined the Champs Elysées, taking walks along the Tuileries and seeing the paintings at the Louvre. It was too cold to stay long in the Jardins Luxembourg, the trees bare and bleak in the wind, on the last day before he took off to tour France and Italy and so they returned to a snug evening in the flat to discuss his trip and plan where he should meet them later.

'I still think you're being positively archaic about me coming along with you. No one's going to think twice about it and if they do, well, I'll say I'm your sister,' Eleanor said, picking up on the argument that had been raging all week.

'No, Eleanor, and that's final. What would your family think if they heard? And anyone else for that matter. It's totally inappropriate for an unmarried girl to accompany a man on a trip. I won't have it.' Henry was remarkably adamant for once.

Sophie was quick to second his opinion. She glanced at her friend. 'Don't be silly, Eleanor. We'll see Henry down in Gassin for Christmas. You just can't go off with him. It's all wrong.' But her eyes watched Henry anxiously in case he should change his mind at the last moment. She knew how much Henry would have liked Eleanor to come with him. She thanked heaven that Henry was too punctilious to give in to his own desire.

So Eleanor had to comply with their strictures. Privately, she thought it was ridiculous. Nothing would happen with Henry. He was too much of a gentleman and she wasn't interested in him in that way. They would have separate rooms and just travel with each other. Besides, she had never seen Italy. Who cared what other people thought?

306

But Henry, especially, was firmly against the plan and she gave way with ill grace.

She thought about John and how he had stayed with her in her apartment, how they had never been separated for a moment, and she wondered what Henry would have said about that. She hoped Sophie would keep her promise and never mention it to Henry – or anyone else.

Sophie had invited Henry to join them for Christmas in Gassin, a town up in the hills above St Tropez where her father had recently moved to, and he had promised he would work his travel arrangements around that date. The two girls then bade him farewell and took off themselves for the warmer air of the south. And Eleanor wondered how long it would be before Henry realized Sophie was in love with him. Not long, she hoped.

Vila Serrista
December 1962

A keening sound came from the outbuildings, hushed and choked. John walked over the rough ground of the clearing with his breath held tightly in his chest, the small hairs at the back of his neck standing cool and erect in a way that upset him as much as the noise. He wasn't frightened. There was nothing to be frightened of.

In the late afternoon the smell of decay and dry, baked earth filled his nostrils so that they flared and quivered with disgust. He snorted and folded his lips together, wiping his arm across his brow. His shirt was soaked with sweat. He stopped and stared into the glare of the sun.

What was it making that noise? Only a few of the Indians had stayed. The rest had run off, into the jungle or to the next plantation where there was hope of work and food – and protection. Only Monkey and his family and a couple of others were left. And almost no animals. So what was making that noise?

The day was swollen with heat, thunderclouds bruising the sky along the edge of the clearing and rumbling out

307

warnings from time to time. Flies clung to John's skin, moving slowly, drugged with the heaviness of the air. He brushed them away and continued walking. His right hand tightened on the machete it held. His left hand opened and closed, convulsively flexing itself, wriggling the fingers as though something were trying to catch at him, to pull him down.

The shed was falling apart, its door half hanging in place, the roof collapsed at one end. There was a closed-in, rank smell to the straw and wood, as the jungle grew back and tried to claim its land again. The sound had stopped now and John peered into the darker corners of the shed. His eyes gleamed palely in his face. There was nothing there.

He went right in and poked around in the far end, where he had thought the sound was coming from. Nothing. Just like last time, and the time before that. Just a sound, a crying perhaps? He didn't know. But it was there. He heard it. And then – nothing. He breathed in again, sharply, and turned to leave. Out of the corner of his eye, he thought he caught a glimpse of motion, a hint of something out of place. He whirled back but whatever it was had gone. He shook his head and backed out of that dark shed, walking tightly and slowly, stilling his desire to turn and run. He returned to the house.

It was a mistake coming back. He knew that. But where else could he go? He had some money left, that he had withdrawn from his bank accounts before the government had frozen them, but the way inflation was going it wasn't going to last long. And where else could he lose himself from the public eye so completely? Disappear, utterly, for three years? He didn't have any choice.

He looked around the bungalow, at the way the wood was swelling from the years of neglect and rainy seasons, at the broken windows, the mould-infested furnishings. He had never entered his parents' room since he had come back. It was locked and he didn't want to open it. So he slept in his old room and cleaned the house as best he could, throwing out the rotting fabrics, the beetle-infested wood, the spore-ridden, brittle rugs, and he lived in spartan surroundings. He couldn't get the Indians to enter the house. For them it was possessed. They wouldn't come near.

And now these noises. He knew he heard them; he knew they were there. But Monkey told him none of the rest heard anything. The Indian looked at his master with a blank face and eyes that doubted, wondered whether there would be more blood in their clearing before long. John angrily sent him away.

If only he had someone else to talk to, someone who could spend the evenings with him, the nights. If only Eleanor were there. He began to understand why his father had begun to drink, why people spoke of the jungle pressing in around you, smothering and dark and sinister, of jungle madness taking hold. This was his home but he began to be afraid of it.

It was the house, he decided that evening. Too much had happened there. The walls were steeped with the sounds, the emotions of those dreadful times, his mother's screams, his father's rage. If pressed, he almost expected the walls to ooze blood. Like the blood that still covered the floor and bed, the curtains of the room he would not enter. He shuddered and closed his eyes. Saw fire and snow, fire and snow, flickering in the swinging lamp light. A strangled cry broke free from him and he held his head in his hands. No more!

No more. Tomorrow he would burn the house. To the ground.

He was up before dawn, piling the remaining furniture together in the middle of rooms, sluicing it down with kerosene, trailing the liquid out into the gardens. When he lit the kerosene trail, the flames sped over the ground like fluttering insects, seeking the lure of the wooden house, blossoming out in rosettes of pink and red and orange that danced from the windows, hung delicate and enticing from the roof, beckoning. John thought, just for a second, he saw the shutters of his parents' room part, a dark crack that seeped fear and pain and horror, and then the house went up in a dull crump of searing wind. John stood and watched it burn.

The Indians, from their own end of the clearing, also watched it burn. They glanced at each other with still, silent expressions that knew something more but would not tell.

It was Christmas Eve.

Gassin
Christmas 1962

It was colder than Eleanor expected. She had thought the winters in the south of France would be balmy, sun-soaked months in which to recover from the heat of the summer. But it was actually cold. The wind blew sharply in from the sea, the walls and stone floors now held the chill where, during the summer, they were protection against the sun. The rain fell steadily; the light was grey and obscured. For Sophie's ailing father, Philipe Gastambide, it was a time of rest.

He lay by the window, on an old chaise-longue, and Sophie and Eleanor threw on heavy woollen sweaters and thick, corduroy trousers and boots to see to all the chores. They carried in piles of wood for the fireplaces. They lit lamps and cooked rustic, satisfying soups and stews. They tended Philipe with loving concern when he coughed long into the night. And they waited for Henry to arrive.

Four days before Christmas, exactly when he said he would, Henry appeared. The house suddenly seemed warm and lively and full of the joys of the season, even Philipe Gastambide with his cough and his aches and pains, falling under Henry's charm, emerged from his study to join them in charades and silly parlour games that they remembered from when they were children. Only Eleanor could not shift the strange feeling that had taken hold of her in the last few days, an inexplicable foreboding that left her

310

shivering in bed at night, too frightened to peer closer into the dark.

She became withdrawn, even aloof, and the others sent puzzled looks to each other, whispering in corners about her behaviour. Missing her family, they wondered? Missing the heat of Brazil? Worrying about exam results? They didn't know and Eleanor didn't notice. Still the foreboding grew.

Sophie and Henry spent more time together since Eleanor began to go for long, solitary walks in the pine-treed hills behind the house, her face solemn and faintly uneasy, her eyes searching for something that no one else saw. It did no good to remonstrate with her, they soon found, since she became irritated and avoided their company even more. Perhaps it was the beginning of influenza? Perhaps she was concerned about the political situation at home?

Gradually Sophie and Henry became close as they worried about their friend and thought of ways to cheer her up. The communication barrier seemed easily enough surmounted by each one speaking their own language, the other understanding and replying in their own tongue. Sophie admired Henry as she had never admired anyone else before. Not just for his intelligence or his sensitivity, not even for his charm. It was his integrity that she found most appealing. And she respected and loved him more each day.

On Christmas Eve, Eleanor was particularly withdrawn, barely able to muster the energy to unwrap her presents or express her thanks. Soon after dinner, she took herself off to bed, sweating and shaking as though she had caught an ague or chill.

At dawn the house was startled awake by the sound of Eleanor's screams.

John saw the roof begin to sag inwards, the walls folding and with a sharp, tearing groan the last of the supporting beams gave way and the house collapsed in on itself. The fire still raged on but it was consuming itself, not attempting to spread across the parched clearing towards the other buildings. John saw the house fall with relief. There, it was done.

He wiped his brow and stared down at the few belongings he had kept. A bag of clothes, a handful of books, his rifle and ammunition, some food, tobacco, cooking utensils. A sad pile to show for what had once been his. No matter. He didn't need any of it anymore. He would move into one of the Indian huts nearer the others. Grow some vegetables, hunt for his meat, fish. Maybe take a few trips up and down the Paraná, organize a little local resistance, churn up some thought. If the Indians let him through.

The thought that had sprung into his mind as he had set light to the bungalow now returned, stronger and more insistent. What protection did he have now against any raiding parties? Monkey and his few people would be no defence. The house and its sturdy shutters, shelter against attack, was lying smouldering on the ground. That, and its powerful taboo. What would keep the war parties away now? Now they knew he was back.

He stood in the middle of the clearing listening to the clicking of the cicadas, the drum-booming of the tree frogs, the shrieking of the monkeys and he leant his head back and stared up at the perfectly round dome of sky that capped his domain. There were two tribes who lived in this area, but he knew the Parecis would never harm him. He was blood-brother to many of their warriors. No, it was the tribe to the east – the Morcegos, the Bat Tribe, whose figures filled his dreams. The ones who painted themselves purple and their hair yellow and who had stalked Eleanor and him that time when they were children. Why hadn't they killed him then? John breathed in deeply. He wondered whether they would come for him now.

It was midday by then and he decided he would need to arrange a place to sleep. He gathered up his belongings and began to walk, heavily laden, over to the far end of the clearing. Monkey met John near an abandoned hut, his arms crossed and a sullen expression on his face. They were also without protection now the house was gone.

'You go now?' Monkey asked.

John shook his head. 'No. I stay. Here.' He gestured to the hut, the least damaged of those remaining unoccupied. Monkey's face became more sullen still. 'You get the others to help me fix it up, Monkey. Okay? I'm staying here,' John repeated firmly, wondering what he would do if Monkey suddenly decided he did not like his master anymore. He wasn't sure he really cared, one way or the other. Monkey seemed to read the expression in John's eyes because he nodded suddenly and turned away, as though he were afraid of John. Afraid of what he had glimpsed there in those blue eyes. John sighed and dumped his belongings on the ground.

'And get Shiri over here. She can look after me from now on,' he shouted after Monkey, and then was sick at the tone he had used and the words of casual command that had sprung so easily to his lips. Like a fazendeiro, a plantation owner with his slaves. Do this, do that. I command it. He spat on to the ground. But he needed help and they would not give it to him willingly. For a while, at least, he would have to live with it.

As dusk fell, Shiri, the youngest of Monkey's daughters, came to wait on John. She had been dressed by the women as though she were about to attend the harvest dance, her creamy bronze skin adorned with chokers of feathers, a shell belt, arm bracelets of beads and shells and teeth, thick ropes of iridescent beetle wings crossing her chest, bandolier-fashion, and crushed flowers and perfume spices, such as vanilla, scenting the tiny gourds that clustered like grapes on leather thongs and hung between her breasts. She was tall and straight-backed with fringed, chin-length shiny black hair, and a curiously blank, flattened face. She was nearly thirteen.

John ignored her. He didn't want to take a child as his woman. He just wanted her to cook his meals and clean up the hut. While he hunted and tried to get the fazenda back in order. She didn't seem put out by his reaction, simply squatting down outside the door to the hut and watching him with that same, unnerving blank expression. John carried on cleaning his rifle.

He had noticed that Monkey had one of the old flintlock muskets that his father had bought for the house servants. They were made in England, by P Dunoulin & Co, from coiled wire soldered over and filed smooth and they could be used to kill just about anything, even a jaguar, until the barrels began unravelling. He wondered just how old Monkey's musket was. And whether Monkey would help defend him, if it came to that.

Shiri had been fishing earlier in the day and she had caught a palometa, a plate-sized, silvery fish with orange spots. She cleaned it and wrapped the fillets in palm leaves and left it cooking in the earth for some time to kill the worms that infested all the fish in the jungle waters. John could smell it, oily and slightly pungent, when she unburied it and laid it out for the evening meal. He wasn't hungry but he forced himself to eat it and to sip at the clotted milk drink she brought him. Not chicha, just a native milk and better than water for him. He sipped at its sour taste reluctantly.

He knew the dream would come again that night and he dreaded falling asleep. Dreaded seeing that room again, seeing the blood and the lamp swinging the shadows across the room. Seeing, not his mother's dead body slumped across the bed, but Eleanor's. Gradually, though, he closed his eyes and slipped into an anxious sleep. He sweated and shivered in the night breeze and Shiri watched him, from where she sat in the shadows, with her dark eyes and her blank face. There was a faint possessive smile on her lips as she watched him. But she didn't disobey her father when he motioned for her to follow him into the jungle.

The Morcegos came in the night but John never knew. He was locked into the horror of his dream, sweating, screaming, crying out obscenities in the night when they crowded in around him, spears held high, ready to drag

314

him from his hut. They prodded him with their feet, kicking him, and John opened his eyes, wide and staring blue, and utterly mad. He screamed. And the Morcegos ran.

The fever raged in him for nearly a week before dying out. Monkey and Shiri tended John, brought him water and milk, pulped the strange medicinal roots that the Indians knew of and pressed the creamy, clotted mixture into his mouth. They bathed him and wrapped elephant's ear leaves around him, and lit fires from which coiled dense, drugged plumes of smoke. And Shiri lay beside him at night, her body pressed against his to keep him warm. They knew the raiding party would not come back. As long as John stayed with them they were safe. He would be their taboo now, in place of the house. He would keep the Morcegos away. Shiri knew the drugs in her native milk would cloud his mind, keep him with them in a stupor of half-remembered dreams. She smiled in the night.

Eleanor woke to find Henry, Sophie and Philipe all gathered around her bed. She could still hear the scream ringing in the night and she shivered and clung to Henry.

'Someone screamed,' she said, the horror still clear and she felt Henry tighten his arms around her, soothing her.

'Shh, sweetheart. It's all right. It was just a nightmare. You screamed, that's all.' He was warm and firm beside her and she couldn't understand why it was she felt herself still shaking, terrified beyond belief. She saw Sophie's face peering over Henry, her eyes large and troubled.

'I'm sorry. I don't know what made me cry out like that. I thought − I thought it was someone else screaming and I was so frightened ...' She shook her head and sighed, gave a small, embarrassed laugh. 'I'm sorry.'

'Don't be silly, Eleanor. Everyone has bad dreams. Now come on, lie down again and try to get some sleep. I'm right next door if you need me.' Henry coaxed her back under the covers, kissed her cheek, and ushered the others from the room. He left the door ajar.

Dear Henry, Eleanor thought. Always there for me. So sensible. So factual. But this time, he was wrong. It wasn't just a dream; someone had really cried out. John. She had heard him.

For days after the dream, Eleanor fretted over what it could mean. She worried that John was ill, that he was in danger. She tried, without success to think of ways of contacting him. All the time she smiled and made polite conversation and reassured the others she was fine.

Henry returned to his travels, promising to look in on them in Paris before he returned to Brazil, and Eleanor and Sophie returned to their studies. The new year was under way before Eleanor heard any news.

Isobel wrote that they had heard rumours that John was now down on the military lists too and had little chance of ever returning to normal life in the cities. No one knew where he was; no one had seen him in a long time. Teresa had gone to North America to make another film and had made it known she was no longer with John, in case of trouble. The country was preparing itself for another coup, perhaps not immediately, but sometime before Goulart's end of office. There were suspicions he intended to try and stay on as president and even the women were out marching against him.

Papa was worried sick and trying to disassociate himself from the president but it was already too late. He was known to be one of Goulart's cronies. There would be trouble, Isobel wrote, when John was known to be connected to the family as well.

Eleanor grew pale and restless, resolving to return to Brazil immediately, in one moment, and then remembering John's request that she not return for his sake, in the next. She couldn't do anything and the sheer inability to help was worse than actually being there and fearing along with the rest of her family. Sophie grew round-eyed with astonishment when Eleanor explained what might happen to her family if there were a coup. And she asked anxious questions about Henry that made Eleanor smile, in spite of her worry. The world revolved around Henry, as far as Sophie was concerned. Eleanor hoped she would not break her heart over him.

In February 1964 Sophie's father died. He had been ill for some time, his cough never clearing, the pains becoming more intense until it became clear there was something seriously wrong. Sophie did not return after Christmas, staying on with Philipe to nurse him and comfort him through the final stages. Eleanor missed Sophie's comforting chatter, her bright, sunny temper that paid no heed to the winter raging outside or the worries preying on Eleanor's mind. They wrote to each other and Eleanor flew down for the funeral but Sophie did not return to her studies. There was no money and too many bills that her father had left to consider such a course. Sophie kissed Eleanor farewell and promised to come visit. In time. Paris became a grey place without Sophie.

In the northern summer of 1964, Eleanor flew back to Brazil. She still needed another term in which to finish her degree but, in March of that year, President Goulart had been overthrown by the military and had fled to safety beyond the borders of Brazil. The military had taken control of the country themselves; Eleanor decided it was time to return home.

Chapter Sixteen

Vila Serrista
July 1964

John sat outside his hut and read. A steady dripping rain
fell but he was protected by the awning of palm leaves that
Monkey and he had built. It was the only cool place to be,
to try and catch some hint of air. He swung in his hammock
and paged through the book idly. He had been through all
the volumes he had saved from the house many times
already. But he returned, particularly, to the collected
works of Joseph Conrad, as though that writer had known
something about him when he wrote his tales. It was an
eerie feeling, to be found out by someone who was dead
and long gone. He wondered sometimes if he were
supposed to be Kurtz or Jim – or both. Perhaps neither. It
was hard to be sure of anything much anymore.

He glanced over at the other huts, where the Indians
were busy tending pots, weaving, curing skins. No one paid
him any heed except Shiri who smiled timidly. He shook
his head and carried on reading from *Lord Jim*:

'It is when we try to grapple with another man's infinite
need that we perceive how incomprehensible, wavering,
and misty are the beings that share with us the sight of the
stars and warmth of the sun. It is as if loneliness were a hard
absolute condition of existence . . .'

That's very true, John thought. No one could possibly share his thoughts, his desires, his needs. Everyone was different. Just look at little Shiri there, so sure of what she needed that she could not imagine he did not need the same. A place to sleep, food, a mate. She wanted him as her mate. And could not conceive why he turned her away. Different needs that made for loneliness in each and every one of them. Was that what made him stand aloof from the rest? Because he saw that as a necessity of life, just like Conrad, and the others refused to believe it? Maybe he was a little mad. His thoughts were often so clouded he thought he might be. Perhaps they thought him so.

He sighed and put down the book, wiping a white film of mould from the cover with the palm of his hand. It was the Wet. He wondered if his collection would survive many more rainy seasons. Probably not. But then probably neither would he. Not with the fever that ate away at him every few weeks, and the blurred, endless days that disappeared one into the other.

A faded photograph, yellowed and splotched from rain, slipped out from the front cover of the book and John hesitated, picking it up and turning it over and over in his hands. An old photograph of a child who did not exist anymore. He looked at it finally, pressing his lips together as though to be sure no sound could escape. A twelve-year-old Eleanor laughed up at him. He stared hard into her face.

There was no point to any of that anymore. He had learned to be alone. He didn't need anyone now, not even her. She was a memory inside him and that was all he needed. He peered up at the sky, gauging the time from the angle of the sun. Nearly six. The animals would be coming down to drink at dusk. He gathered up his bow and small pouch of arrows and stood up, his body lean from hard work and little food. He wore a loin-cloth, like the Indians, his skin tinged an unhealthy yellow and marked with scars. A sacred tooth, from a jaguar, hung on a thong around his neck, a filthy, faded bracelet of plaited ribbons that Teresa

319

had once made for him encircled his left wrist. Other than that, he wore nothing at all.

Soon, he thought, he would go down river, to Fra Janio's mission. See what the news was, maybe think about getting away, leaving the jungle for a while. If he didn't get away soon, he thought, he never would. But somehow, whenever he seemed to think about it, he would come down with the fever again. And the Indians would tend him, would look after him through the weeks of illness and macabre dreams, would tell him he must not go away. But he would go this time. It was now or never. Goulart must be close to falling. John was sure of it. Then he could go home.

He didn't think of the jungle as home anymore. It was his prison, his hell and, like a devil, he danced and sweated and screamed with fever through the long months of enforced seclusion, wondering whether he was to be there forever. Whether it was his punishment, his purgatory on earth. Sometimes he wasn't sure what was real and what were the phantasms of his deliriums, hearing the insistent beat of the drums through the night, the fires that leaped and whirled around in his brain. Such a sweet seduction that sucked at his life force and left him sweating and weak for days, weeks sometimes, blurring with the drugs and the milk and the medicines they gave him. Sometimes he knew he was a little mad, and sometimes he knew the Indians were responsible; he smiled ruefully at the thought and Shiri smiled back at him, her dark eyes shadowed beneath her swinging hair. She pounded a root between two stones, smiled again.

'We all seem a little mad to each other; an excellent arrangement for the bulk of humanity which finds in it an easy motive for forgiveness.' Conrad had his finger on it, as always. But would John be forgiven his madness if he were to leave here? He didn't think so. Anymore than he would be forgiven his sanity if he were to stay. Besides, he knew deep down inside the Indians didn't mean him to leave, not ever. He was their safeguard; their protection from the Morcegos.

320

He hummed to himself in the fading light, running along the trail, gliding like a wraith between the trees. Charcoal stripes covered his body and face. Only his eyes gleamed brightly in the gloom. A deep, enveloping blue.

The room seemed different, Eleanor thought. Smaller and more provincial than she remembered. She looked around at the window-seat, wondering if that too had shrunk, but it looked just the same. They were gathered in the library, she and Isobel and Louis and Mama, sitting stiffly around, wondering what to say to each other now that they were finally all together again.

Henry had already dropped by to greet her, his soft eyes full of pleasure and expectation. He had talked of his plans and of his new job, he had made hesitant suggestions for what she might like to do, now that she was home, but then he had noticed her air of abstraction and had left after little more than an hour, tactful as always as he realized the family would want to be alone together.

But Papa wasn't home yet. He was late, Eleanor thought with surprise. That wasn't like Papa. Not when he knew she would be here, waiting for him. She forced down her anxiety and turned to smile at Isobel again.

'I just can't believe you're a mother.' She thought of the sunny tempered little boy who had tottered across the floor to greet her. 'It's quite odd. And I'm an aunt! You must be so pleased with little Charlie.' It was odd how polite and formal they were all being with each other. But two and a half years away took its toll.

'And I can't believe you came back without some gorgeous Frenchman in tow,' Isobel said smiling, wondering at Eleanor's shrugged shoulder, indifferent expression. Was it still John with her? Surely not.

Isobel was looking good, Eleanor thought. Very pretty and very contented – actually happy. It was a surprise to see that motherhood agreed with her so much. And marriage. Louis obviously hadn't strayed.

'Where can your father be?' Clarissa said suddenly, as

though her mind had been mostly on other things and she could not quite hold in the impatience.

Eleanor looked at her and saw worry in her mother's eyes. 'What is it, Mama? What's wrong?'

'Nothing. Why should anything be wrong? It's just he's late and he knew you were coming home. I can't think what's delaying him.' But Eleanor knew her mother was lying and she sat straining to hear the sound of her father's car.

When it came, it was followed almost immediately by another and the sound of loud voices raised in the hallway, her father blisteringly angry, more harsh, authoritative voices riding his down, making them all stand up in alarm. They hurried out to the hallway.

There were men there, strange men in uniform, a captain who stood firmly in the middle of the hall, his face uncomfortably certain. Charles Fawcett was sweating before the man, arguing, but there was fear in his eyes, a hesitation in the anger of his voice and Eleanor felt that fear catch at herself, leaving her breathless. The rest of the family gaped.

'You will come with us, Senhor Fawcett, I promise you. Either willingly or otherwise. The arrest warrant is in order, as you can see.' The little man, so smooth and sure, so very unpleasant, smiled. Charles, who had been examining a paper in his hand, looked beyond the captain toward his family. His eyes caught Eleanor's and she read humiliation there, at having her see this. And fear.

'Papa!' She ran forward and caught at his arms, almost hitting into them as he drew them across his chest, as though in rebuttal. 'What's happening, Papa?'

'Eleanor, darling.' He hugged her briefly. 'Go back to the library, sweetheart. I'll sort this out. Clarissa? Take the girls back into the library. Louis can help me straighten things out. It's all a mistake, don't worry. Go on, then.' He pushed Eleanor away, his face seemingly confident, his eyes pleading with her not to stay and watch his humiliation any further. Eleanor, her eyes brimming with tears, gave way before him.

She hadn't even known what cassated meant before that evening. Hadn't really known why Papa had looked so bleached of colour, his face sunken in like that of a death-head. It was all impossible, it had to be a dreadful mistake as Papa had said. One that would be cleared up soon – any minute now. She knew the police captain with his smooth good manners and his lingering, offensive gaze would be punished when they found out about the mistake. Papa couldn't be put in prison or lose his political rights, could he?

Would they, as the captain had later hinted to them – after Papa had been taken away, when he had come insultingly into the library – would they all lose their rights as citizens now, or was it just intended to punish Papa and John? Papa hadn't done anything wrong. How could they just take him and imprison him, without even charging him first? What were these commissions of enquiry about?

She had called Henry after the police had gone. Told him what had happened and tried to still the flutter of fear in her voice that shook and beat against her throat, trying to break into a cry that would tear her world apart. In her tight, hard, little voice she told Henry how the police had come for Papa. 'They said he'll be imprisoned until he faces some commission of enquiry. I don't understand, Henry! What do Papa's business dealings with Goulart have to do with what's going on now? They've threatened to take away all his rights, cassate him and put him in prison. That vicious little man, the police captain! God! Henry? They can't do that, can they? Papa hasn't done anything wrong. Neither has John really ... but they've already taken his rights away. They're going to hunt him down ...' Eleanor repeated, the quaver becoming more uncontrollable, the pauses between snatches of conversation squeezed out, becoming longer. Henry had told her to hold on. He would do his best. And so they waited.

Where was John? Was he even alive? Eleanor sat in her chair in the library, her head down, her fair hair falling comfortingly around her face as though to shield her from prying eyes. She confronted the possibility that he was dead. There had been no word from him in two years, no sign from any quarter that he still existed. What was that scream she had heard Christmas Eve night? Was it John's death scream? She closed her eyes tightly but there was no feeling inside her, no sense that he was still with her, just an aching void. Was he really dead?

The pain of continuing such a train of thought became unbearable and Eleanor stood up abruptly and went to look out of the windows. In the shadows of the forecourt, in front of the house, she saw a policeman move. They were under house arrest. That was what the captain had said. Until they found John.

They had all been interviewed, separately, one by one, about John. His whereabouts, his friends, his wife. Nobody had known anything. Eleanor had wrapped her arms tightly around herself and stared defiantly at the captain. Nobody had known anything. Not even Teresa, the famous film star who lived in California now and didn't need her husband anymore. Eleanor smiled bitterly to herself at that.

She wasn't sure how long they intended to imprison them all in their own house. Days? Weeks? Months? Surely not. But the new powers the military government had been granted were beyond anything anyone could remember. The new Institutional Acts made a mockery of Congress's power to veto the president, the trade unions were dissolved and their leaders arrested, the universities had been purged and the National Union of Students abolished. And the peasant leagues had been disbanded. What hope then did a single man have against them? What hope did Papa have? Or John?

Eleanor paced anxiously to and fro until Isobel snapped angrily, 'Oh, for God's sake, Eleanor! Sit down! You're wearing a hole in the floor and I can't take that tip-tap, tip-tap of your shoes on the wooden boards anymore. When's Henry coming anyway?'

'I – I don't know. As soon as he could, he said,' Eleanor replied and sat abruptly in the window-seat.

Isobel sniffed. 'The whole thing's ridiculous. How on earth is anyone supposed to do business, or just live normally if they keep having coups and accusing anyone who has known the last government of being corrupt, of being traitors? How can you be a traitor to a new government that's taken power by force?' she demanded, her pretty face marred by anxiety.

Eleanor sighed. 'By being on the wrong side at the wrong time, Isobel. Don't be naïve.' She looked at Louis but saw he was uninterested in their discussion. He was looking thoughtful, his eyes shadowed and turned in, as though he were taking a personal inventory that did not include anyone in the room. Eleanor hoped he was not regretting his decision to ally himself with Isobel's family. She hoped he was not thinking – but no, Louis would never do that. He loved Isobel.

She caught his gaze as he looked up and they stared at each hard for several moments. Then Louis smiled and Eleanor instantly felt ashamed of herself. No, Louis wasn't going anywhere.

'Mama, do they know about Papa's heart condition? Has he got his pills on him?' Eleanor broke away from Louis's gaze and went to stand beside her mother, laying her hand on Clarissa's shoulder.

'I told them about it. I made them wait until I got the pills. But the captain was so impatient, I don't know how much good it'll do. They didn't want to see your father as a person, someone's husband or father, someone with a heart problem, because then they might pity him. And they didn't want to do that,' Clarissa said in a harsh voice. She clutched Eleanor's hand in her own. 'I don't know what we're going to do, you and I, my dearest. We'll have to get jobs but we can't keep the house, and the business – how is that going to run all on its own? Louis and Isobel will be all right. The bank won't come to any harm, but the trading business, I just don't know ...' There was panic in her voice. For the first time since her parents died, Clarissa had no one to lean on, no one to make decisions for her, to provide for her. And she was frightened.

'Don't be silly, Mama. We'll be fine. We're not going to lose the house. Papa will be out before you know it, and even if he is cassated, that doesn't take away his right to make a living, to run his own business. Henry'll get him out, just you wait and see,' Eleanor said firmly and she saw her mother give a tentative smile, a grateful look in her eyes.

'Yes, I expect you're right, dear. We'll have to rely on Henry. He'll help us.'

So they waited until past midnight but no call came and no Henry came and eventually they went to bed.

In the morning, Henry was there, looking tired and rumpled and in need of a shave. He was drinking coffee at the breakfast table when Eleanor walked in, and he didn't even attempt to stand for her.

Eleanor kissed him on the cheek and looked at him with worried eyes. 'Henry, you look like you've been up all night. Have you been with Papa?'

Henry ran a hand over his face, kneading the pain in his temples, pushing his hair back from his eyes. He tried to smile.

'Yes. My father and I were trying to find a way of getting your father released but we couldn't do it. He'll have to go before the commission of enquiry. The only thing we could do was get the process speeded up. They'll review your father's case before the end of the week. That way they'll have less time to dig up any incriminating evidence, find witnesses to malign his integrity, the usual tactics. They'll have to provide hard evidence on the spot before the end of the week or your father will have to be released. Best we could do, I'm afraid.' He looked disappointed, as though his efforts had been ineffectual.

Eleanor reached out and took his hand. 'Oh Henry, thank you! You and your father. I don't know what we'd do without such good friends at a time like this. Mama will be so relieved. Did you see Papa? Is he in good spirits?'

'Fair. He's shocked, understandably enough. And

326

nervous. But he promises none of his business dealings have been illegal. There's been some leverage used, I'd say, to get contracts that might not otherwise have gone to his company, but nothing out of the normal for Brazil. We may just be able to get him off without any charges. At the worst, he'll be cassated and maybe imprisoned for a year or so. I don't know at this stage. It'll depend upon who's on the board of the commission. And how many scapegoats they're looking for. No one seems to know that yet.'

He tried to break the news gently, to sound cheerful about their chances, but Eleanor stiffened and held her breath, her face appalled. She had thought Henry would fix everything for them, that life would go back to normal and now he was talking about a year's imprisonment! What would Papa do? How would he survive it, survive the shame? And what would Mama and she do? She could get a job, of course, but it wouldn't pay enough to keep both of them, or the house. Mama would die if she had to lose the house. What were they going to do?

Henry saw the fear and doubt in Eleanor's eyes and he clasped her hand tightly in his, trying to find the energy to reassure her despite the fact that he had had no sleep at all and had been on his feet for most of the night. The police had not been the most gracious of hosts.

'You'll be fine. We'll get someone in to manage your father's business, or maybe promote someone within the company. It'll keep going and you won't lose the house, so you needn't start fretting about all that. Your father knows his chances and he's prepared for the worst, just in case. It won't come as a total surprise, so his heart should be able to cope. He'll get special treatment, we'll see to that. Fresh food, better living conditions. And that's only what would happen at the very worst. We may well be able to get him off altogether.'

He heard footsteps approaching, the measured pace of Clarissa coming across the hall towards them. 'Just keep your chin up and remember how much your mother's depending on you, Eleanor, all right? Can you do that for me?'

He looked intently into her eyes, gauging her strength, wondering if she could cope with the times ahead. What he saw reassured him. Her face was thin and gaunt from stress. But her eyes radiated warmth as always. He smiled and Eleanor felt as though she could lean against him and all her troubles would slowly melt away. He was her rock.

She nodded. 'Yes, I can do that. Thank you, Henry. For always being there.' She kissed his cheek, feeling the stubble rough and curiously pleasant against her skin.

'Where else would I be?' Henry smiled and then he kissed her gently, very gently on the lips.

Charles Fawcett was found guilty of corruption and was fined one half of his personal fortune and cassated for ten years. He was not, however, imprisoned. Henry fought hardest of all against that and, at the end of the commission of enquiry nearly two weeks later, Charles came home leaning heavily on Henry's arm.

The police report mentioned that the whereabouts of John Campos de Serra were still unknown, although his fazenda had been raided and the Indians living there interrogated. They insisted they had not seen him since he was a boy and that the house had burned down when hit by lightning in a storm. Their huts had been searched but nothing found. The report suggested that John Campos de Serra must, indeed, have fled the country since no sign of him could be found anywhere. The case was shelved until new information came to light and the house arrest was lifted.

Eleanor thought about that burned house and the scream she had heard in the night. And she wept, alone.

Charles had aged in the last few weeks, his hair greying, his face sinking in around the once strong face. There was a bewildered look in his eyes, and he clung to Henry or Clarissa as though frightened to let them out of his sight. Eleanor couldn't bear to see him look so lost and had to walk away hurriedly so that he wouldn't see the tears in her eyes.

Slowly, over the next few months, he regained some of his strength and vigour, returning to business and inviting close friends again to dinner at the palácio. Henry and his family were by far the most frequent visitors. Many others declined Charles's invitations, others came once but no more. Their circle of friends diminished and Charles spent more and more time trying to put his business affairs in order, setting up small trust funds to provide for his wife and daughters.

So few contracts were granted to his company now, so few people dared do business with someone who had been cassated, someone under the shadow of treason to the state, that finances began to occupy more and more of Charles's mind. Inflation was taking a savage bite out of what was left of his funds. The business limped along, losing more than it made, and Clarissa began to make cut-backs in their style of living. Not with the servants. They were family and had been with the Fawcetts for years. They would stay as long as there was food of any sort to put on the table. But other expenditures had to be curtailed: the couture houses, the new cars, the delicacies for their guests. There was no question but that business was going badly.

Charles smiled grimly through it all and Eleanor had never loved him so much than in this time of hardship when he showed his true strength. She sat with him in the evenings, walked with him at weekends in the hills surrounding the house, and drove him into Copacabana to drink fruit juices at the sidewalk cafés and watch the people pass by. Slowly they regained the closeness they had both once cherished.

Baby Charlie was also a delight in a household of long faces and heavy sighs. He toddled around the gardens, shrieking with glee when he made a dash for the fountain and howling angrily when Isobel or Adélia, now appointed nurse, intercepted him and brought him back to safety. He had been a blond baby but already his hair was darkening down, like Louis's, and his eyes were quite brown. Isobel spoiled him outrageously and Charles senior sat and nursed his grandson on his knee with all the delight of a proud grandfather who had desperately wanted sons himself. Eleanor smiled and watched them together with relief. They were good for each other.

As Henry was good for her. His gentle strength, his good humour, his unfailing love all helped to repair the damage done during those days of her father's arrest and imprisonment. They also helped to ease the misery that told her John was dead and gone from her forever and that she must somehow go on without him.

The hours spent alone grieving for John were more bleak than anything Eleanor had ever known, ever even imagined. She felt as though half of her, the best half, had been gouged out leaving an empty shell. For a while she even looked out at the sea, shimmering in the distance, and thought of the nothingness that that silent dark could bring. Thought of the easing of the pain. But no, that wasn't her way.

She wandered, aimlessly, up in the hills behind the palácio, revisiting old childhood haunts, remembering each delight with a smile that would slowly still as reality came back to her. Henry watched her return from those expeditions with a face of stone.

'It's no good, Elly,' Isobel remarked one evening, late in November. 'He's gone, and he'll never come back. Let him go.'

They were sitting out on the terrace in the half-gloom, a candle flickering across the table cloth producing warm red tones of flesh, sudden black oases of dark. Eleanor stretched out in the chair, crossed her legs as though she hadn't heard her sister. They were alone, the others either dining out or in bed.

Isobel sipped her coffee. 'I used to envy you so much, you know. You and John.' Her face became solemn, remembering. 'You had your own exclusive little world just

330

between the two of you. Sometimes you'd invite the rest of us in, for a while. But it was only ever you two really. And I was so jealous of that.' She laughed almost painfully, as though the indignities and longings of childhood were still with her. 'Did you know that?'

Eleanor turned her head to look at her sister, her eyes seeming dark in the shadows. She shook her head. 'No, I don't suppose I did. It never really occurred to me. There was nothing deliberate about it – we just, were closer than, than ...' She trailed off, unable to put it into words.

'Where is he, Elly? Can you tell that anymore?' Isobel knew what Eleanor had tried to say, knew it and accepted it finally.

'I don't know. I just don't know.'

'I wouldn't have that closeness anymore, not for anything. God, how I pined to be together with you both, pined to be a part of that special bond you had. Now I thank the Lord I never was,' Isobel said, not with satisfaction or any trace of her old abrasive ways. She said it with sorrow and regret for her sister. Even perhaps for John.

Eleanor looked at her and nodded. 'I know.' She half smiled. 'But you've got Louis and Charlie now. You don't need anything more than that.'

'And you? You could have Henry.'

'Ah yes ... Henry.' Eleanor looked at Isobel, her face quite still.

Fra Janio stooped over the chicken pen and pushed the stakes more firmly into the ground. The rain had washed the earth away in the night, bringing down one side of the pen and embedding it thickly in the mud. Luckily none of the chickens had strayed far. The earth ran slick red and oozed between his toes and sucked at his sandals, coated his cassock hem so that it slapped wet and unpleasantly against his legs. He shooed the last chicken back inside and firmly latched the gate. Stupid creatures, he thought and made his way back to the main building. Maybe Sister Eugénia had put some coffee on?

331

When he entered the lodge, he was aware that something was amiss with the nuns. They moved in agitated, purposeless circles, wringing their hands and glancing up at the ceiling as though the beams might shine light down on them and help them. Fra Janio grunted in irritation, mentally equating the chickens and the good sisters in less than favourable terms. He was in a bad mood already. He didn't need more trouble.

'Well?' he demanded from where he stood in the doorway, rain dripping from the eaves, his robe, his hair, his eyebrows, his nose. The sisters fluttered towards him, eyes rolling, fingers pointing. To the rear of the room, to where the curtain marked off the confessional.

Fra Janio sighed deeply. 'What is it?' he asked sharply. They nodded, long, mournful faces in their sad sacking towards the confessional. Their plainness gave him no pleasure anymore, their gentle manners gave him no consolation. He was tired of the jungle and tired of the Wet. Perhaps he was even tired of – but no, he could never bring himself to think that. Fra Janio gave a rueful mental apology to his maker. He pushed past the women towards the back of the room.

'Well, young man, you in there?' he bellowed and John twitched aside the curtain, remaining seated. Fra Janio frowned. 'Thought I heard you had gone north. Up Bahia way. We had the national guard looking for you, here and up at the Vila Serrista and a few other fazendas around a while back. You're a hot number where they're concerned.'

John smiled faintly and leaned back against the wall, feeling ill. 'A "hot number"? My, we're becoming "hip", father! And yes, I know about that but it was some time ago now. At least, I think it was. Time becomes difficult to gauge.' He paused and looked uncertain. 'That's why I'm here. I thought I'd get out for a while, maybe even work my way back down to São Paulo or Rio. They must have shelved my file down there by now, surely?' He glanced at the priest who remained stolidly silent. Then he became more positive, more determined.

'Anyway, it's good to see you, father. You're looking in fine form.' His voice mocked gently at the old priest, his eyes red and blurred with fatigue.

Fra Janio stared intently into those eyes. 'Hmm! Thank you for that, even if I'm not looking fine at all, as the good Lord can bear witness what with all this rain and blessed heat. Where have you been all this time, John? We thought at first you must have been up at the Vila Serrista but when they raided the place and there was no word of you these two years now ... Have you travelled far?' He saw the young man start, looked shocked. And the priest, seeing the almost naked body under the cassock that the nuns had loaned him, wondered at some of those scars, the lines of pain in such a youthful face.

'Two years! Has it been so long?' John was silent, aghast at the time that had been robbed from him. He shook his head. 'I was at the Vila Serrista – or hiding in the jungle. All that time! I knew something was wrong, that I couldn't have been having fevers that long, that everything shouldn't have been so blurred – I had to get out, get away, but I couldn't get a grip on it. The Indians wanted me to stay, you see. Finally, I decided I'd slip away – come and see you. I mean, who else could tell me how things stand? I know you get all the news.'

He sat back, glancing across at the priest with troubled eyes. 'Funny thing. I went home to feel safe and it got so that I was more nervous about staying there any longer than about braving the guarda. I was nervous about eating or drinking or falling asleep. And it seems I was right.' He smiled ironically. 'I slept for two years. My memory's practically blank.' He sighed, holding his head in his hands. The priest's expression softened, became more understanding. He nodded when John continued.

'Nothing like being an enforced drug addict for two years. I don't totally blame the Indians. I guess I was their protection. Their evil eye. They didn't dare lose me or the Morcegos would come back.' He was silent a moment and then said tentatively, 'Well, I thought I might stay here a

333

few days. Would that be all right with you and the sisters?'
He looked worried, almost desperate as though he thought
the old priest would deny him shelter.

The priest saw the fear and the illness that still plucked at
the young man's body. He put out a hand and touched
John's shoulder. 'Do you really think I would turn you
away? How could I? The Lord is our shepherd,' Fra Janio
replied simply and saw John's face relax, a smile form on
his lips.

He took a deep breath. 'Thank you, Fra Janio. You've
been my sanctuary twice now. But, don't worry, I'll go if
I'm inconveniencing you or putting you in danger. Just as
soon as I can.'

'No, John. I would always wish you to consider this place
a shelter for you in your troubles, as it was to you as a child.
Come, come and eat with us and tell us your news and I
will tell you about the government's doings and how the
country is being wrapped in chains, more tightly and more
impenetrably every day. It is a tale of woe and best heard on
a full stomach.' He sighed and stretched out an arm to
John.

Over breakfast the priest told John about the purges that
were taking place in all the major cities, how Mazzilli, the
temporary president, was nothing more than a puppet for
the military and how General Humberto Castelo Branco
was to take over the presidency the following year. There
was hope that he might be more democratic than the
powers who were in charge at the moment, particularly
General Costa e Silva who seemed to be running the whole
show from Rio. Fra Janio advised John to stay away from
Rio for at least another year.

In turn, John told the priest how he had escaped the
Indians one night, when everyone was asleep and made his
way across country to near Ricki's place where he had
managed to steal a canoe.

'Ricki lives there alone now. His mother went to live with
one of his sisters, who's married. The other one lives in Rio.
He's growing strange there, all alone. I didn't let him see

me.' John was matter of fact. No one wanted a fugitive on their hands. It was too dangerous. And he had never trusted Ricki. Never forgiven him. He had even thought about confronting him about Eleanor but there was no point anymore. Ricki was living his own personal hell – that was punishment enough.

The priest told him about the resentment further north that, despite having helped back the coup that had brought Goulart down, they were being given no say in the new régime. Other supporters, such as the governors, Ademar de Barros of São Paulo, José de Magalhães Pinto of Minas Gerais and Carlos Lacerda of Guananbara were also agitating for more reform, for more rights and becoming increasingly vocal in their disappointment. The word was out on the street, Fra Janio said, that the government meant to crack down further and that the governors would be some of the first to be taught obedience.

'Which will play right into our hands,' John remarked as he sipped his coffee and rolled a piece of bread around in his fingers. The priest shook his head, unconvinced. 'Yes, it will, father – the harsher the régime becomes, the more oppressive measures it uses and the more people it arrests, the more the people will cry out against it and resolve to bring freedom about for themselves. I have to believe the people are strong enough, somewhere deep down inside them, to finally lose their fear. The military just goes from one atrocity to another. In time, the people will stand up and shout, "No more!" And you, and I, and all the others who have fought for so long for that moment, will be there to show them the way. Freedom will come, I know it.' John shrugged, thinking how melodramatic his words sounded. But he couldn't help it; he believed in them.

For a moment, listening to the compelling voice, seeing the vision in those eyes, Fra Janio almost believed in them too. But then he remembered that this young man's life was forfeit if captured and he shook his head again.

'Brave sentiments, John. You are truly the sort this sad country needs. But I fear I won't see the change come in my lifetime nor, perhaps, in yours. Should you outlive me, that is.' He smiled and John nodded and smiled too, both aware of the risks. The priest patted John on the arm. 'But come, tell me how your lovely little cousin is. I haven't seen Eleanor since she was a child, but I remember her well. What does she look like now?'

John reached into his pocket and pulled out his wallet, taking a small photograph from inside. He passed it to Fra Janio.

'That was taken a couple of years ago, in Paris. Eleanor's studying there now,' he said. The priest bent over the photograph, peering with failing eyesight at the girl who sat on a balcony, sun streaming across her hair. She was smiling but there was a look of something in the eyes, sadness, desperation perhaps, that Fra Janio remembered. Looking at the person taking the picture with an intensity that seemed to look straight into his soul. The priest pretended not to notice.

'She's turned out a fine looking girl. In character too, I would say. Have you heard from her lately?'

John took the photograph back and put it away in his wallet. He hesitated, swallowed. 'Not since I took that shot. I went to see Eleanor, for a few days before I came back to the Vila Serrista.' He took a deep breath. 'Father, it's been many years for me now but I – I would like you to hear my confession.'

The old priest looked up and nodded, his old eyes dulled with compassion. 'Ah, yes, I rather thought it might come to that,' he said, and then he took John's hand in his. 'Just remember, John, God forgives everything, all sin. As long as the heart is true. Come, I will hear you now.' He stood up and led the way to the curtain at the back of the room.

Henry knew Eleanor did not love him. She had told him so, once, very sadly when he had tried to press her. But she would in time. He was sure of that. And she certainly felt everything but love for him. There was no one she cared for more. Except John. But John was gone, perhaps dead, and

Henry would take that risk. He had enough love for both of them.

His eyes followed her across the room, the way she paced between the windows and the drinks table, as though hoping someone else would come into the room. She knew he meant to say something to her. Why else would he have asked to see her alone?

'Elly? Elly, come and sit down. I can't talk to you if you're running up and down the room. Please.' He patted the arm of the chair beside his own and Eleanor, halted by his words, looked at the chair in dread. For a moment her mouth opened, as though she would say something, anything to deny the moment that she knew was upon her. But then she closed it silently and nodded, her mouth very stern. She sat in the chair.

'Elly, I think you know already what I'm going to ask you and I want you to consider a couple of things before that.' Henry was desperately uncomfortable, desperately determined and Eleanor dropped her head to avoid his eyes. She felt so sorry for him and almost worse for herself. This was all so wrong.

'Firstly, we're old friends, closer than most friends can ever be. We share all the same memories and background, we know the same people, we understand each other. That's very important.' He paused, wondering if his words were making any difference. He wished he could just swoop her up in his arms, make her laugh and flutter with excitement the way any other marriage proposal might be made and accepted. But he knew that would not do for them.

'Secondly, your father is old and ill now. You need someone to look after you – to look after all the family and its affairs. I'm willing to do that. I want to do that,' he repeated more firmly, not wanting it to sound as though it were a burden. He truly did want to look after them all.

'So, I know you said once before that you didn't actually love me – not in the way that I love you.' He paused painfully. 'But you also once said you hoped that if you ever

337

fell in love with anyone, it would be with me. I think that's very important, very – significant.' No, that was all wrong. He was sounding pompous. No wonder she was looking away now, her face very pale.

Eleanor was sad beyond belief that Henry felt it necessary to sound so humble, so logical about how much their marriage made sense. She would have been happier by far if he had just blurted out his love for her and thrown himself down on to one knee. She was sadder still that she knew she was going to accept. How unfair to him; how unfair for her.

'Please, Elly, I want you to marry me. Please.' There, he had said it at last, even slipping off the chair so that one knee briefly brushed the ground. Eleanor, feeling detached as though she were not really there, but was watching the farce from afar, could find time to think how silly Henry looked like that and how terribly sincere he was. Poor, poor Henry.

'Yes, I will. Thank you, Henry.' She saw the surprise, the wild expectation that flashed into those eyes and the pride that made him jump to his feet, pulling her up beside him, pulling her into his arms. His kiss was awkward and unwelcome but she forced herself to respond.

'Oh Elly! Oh, my darling,' He crooned and she closed her eyes briefly. But no, he was too dear not to realize how much it cost her and he released her gently. 'You will grow to love me, Elly. I'll be a good husband to you, I promise.'

She smiled at him and stroked his cheek. 'I know you will, Henry. I'll try to be a good wife.'

The wedding took place quietly three weeks later with none of the fanfare that had accompanied Isobel's wedding. Only close family attended.

Eleanor was not sure how to write and tell Sophie the news. For days before the wedding, she deliberated over whether it was not kinder to never tell Sophie, or to let her find out for herself. But that was just cowardice trying to take control of her mind, Eleanor decided, and eventually

338

she composed a loving letter telling Sophie everything. About Papa's troubles, about how Henry was taking care of them all now. And how she hoped Sophie would understand and would come visit them soon. Sophie did not write back.

Henry agreed, reluctantly, that Eleanor and he should also take a wing in the palácio in which to live. Papa needs me, Eleanor thought and so does Mama. Henry has always been like a son to them. It's natural they should want us to all stay together at the moment. Who else can we rely on, if not family? Later, perhaps, when Papa is better and the political situation more stable, then we can move out and get an apartment of our own. Later, when there's more money. But not yet.

Eleanor shrank from the thought and Henry would do anything to please her. They stayed.

Chapter Seventeen

October 1965

Eleanor lay on a blanket on the grass, in the shade of the rose arbour, and blew bubbles at the infant beside her. Barely five weeks old, Katherine Arreas de Botelho smiled and waved her tiny fists in the air. She gurgled and Eleanor laughed, making silly faces and holding out her finger for the fists to clench on to tightly.

'Who's a clever girl, then? Who's a clever girl?' Eleanor asked and lifted the baby into her arms, rocking her gently. Katherine gazed absorbedly into Eleanor's face, her eyes a deep, deep blue. In the heat of the afternoon, the cicadas shrilled and the sun blurred and blinked between the leaves. Eleanor felt drowsy. She had been tired ever since the birth, it seemed, drifting through the days in a cloud of fatigue. It would be so nice to have her strength back again. Perhaps she would, soon. She tucked Katherine in beside her and lay back against the pillows, drifting with the sounds of the garden, the insects, the birds calling joyously to each other, the gentle splashing of the fountain into the pool surrounding it. Drifting, smiling, she fell asleep.

It was the sound of the bells that woke her. The church bells calling in their flock and chiming discordantly in the still air for miles around. She yawned and leaned over, a smile forming as she went to touch her daughter. Already the shadows were longer on the ground, the heat of the afternoon evaporating into the blue of dusk. The baby might catch a chill, if she stayed out much longer, she thought. But Katherine wasn't there. With alarm, Eleanor looked up. Looked around, frantically.

Behind her, sitting on the stone bench that she had shared with Henry that time at Isobel's wedding, was a man, his legs outstretched, his blond head bowed over the blanketed figure in his arms. He was holding Katherine, staring down at her with a quizzical, amused expression as she chewed on his finger. He looked up and smiled painfully at Eleanor when he saw she was awake.

'Yours?' John asked.

Eleanor stood up, pushing back her hair in a dazed fashion, her mouth opening and shutting again, without a sound. Finally she managed a nod.

'And Henry? Your husband, I would assume?' John was looking down at the infant now, as though aware of his own eyes and needing to conceal their expression.

Eleanor nodded again. Finally she found her voice. 'I – I heard you cry out. And then they said the Vila Serrista was burned down. I thought, oh God! Oh God ...' Eleanor leaned against the arbour, her hand across her mouth to stifle the words that wanted to pour out in regret and pain and sorrow. Words that wanted to explain. But that would be unjust to Henry. He deserved better than that. She kept her hand, steady and eventually was able to control the quiver in her voice. 'Where have you been, John? We thought you were dead.'

John looked up at that. His face was serious and regretful. 'I've been all over the place. The Vila Serrista, Fra Janio's, up in Bahia, just lately in São Paulo. I'm sorry I couldn't contact you. I didn't think it would be safe – for either of us.' He smiled down at the baby. 'She's beautiful. Just like you. Makes me wish ...'

Eleanor came to sit down beside him. 'Makes you wish Teresa's baby had lived?'

'That, too,' he said and Eleanor understood what he had meant to say. They stared at each other greedily, shamelessly, neither one broaching the distance between them.

'She is beautiful, isn't she? Five weeks old. I can't quite believe she's mine yet. I keep thinking someone's going to come along and claim her and I'll realize I was just looking after her, that's all.' Eleanor smiled tentatively and John nodded.

'That's how I feel. I can't believe she's yours either. How's Henry? You two getting along all right?' He wanted to hear the opposite. Eleanor knew that as clearly as she knew she had been mistaken in thinking she could forget John for Henry, in time. Her mistake and she would have to live with it. She flushed and breathed in deeply.

'Yes, we're fine together. Henry's well, getting into local politics now. He's pretty busy. But he's a good husband.' Eleanor couldn't go on and changed the subject abruptly. 'You heard about Papa?'

'Yes. I'm sorry. How's he coping?' John chewed his lip, knowing in some sense that what had happened to Charles was his own fault. If his name had not been connected to Charles's, the punishment would not have been so severe. John looked at Eleanor, wondering if she blamed him.

'Better now. It was very hard at first. For everyone but particularly for Papa. You can imagine how much his pride suffered, how unbearable it was for him to have friends drop his acquaintance, refuse his phone calls. Some friends!' She gave a hard laugh and John saw the damage that the past year had done to Eleanor herself. She was thinner and more wary, more ready to add a cynical tone to her voice. He held out Katherine and Eleanor took her back, holding her tenderly. John saw her smile down at the infant and looked away abruptly.

'You mentioned hearing me cry out? What did you mean?' he said suddenly and Eleanor glanced at him uneasily. She explained what had happened that Christmas Eve in France, how sure she had been that she had heard his voice and she saw him pale in recollection.

'Did you cry out? Was it you?' she asked.

John nodded slowly. 'I had a fever. A raiding party of Indians, the Morcegos, came for me that night, just after I burned the main house down. But I was raving, a lunatic and they ran in terror after I screamed. I never really woke up out of that fever for two years. Monkey and his people made sure I didn't. They wanted me to stay. Odd, isn't it, that you should have dreamt of my cry. Gives me the shivers, doesn't it you?' They were silent in recognition of the force that bound them, one to each other. Exulting in it, scared of it.

Finally, Eleanor broke the silence, trying to sound normal. 'Can you stay, John? Or is it too dangerous? I must say I'm surprised you risked coming here at all. How do you know they haven't got the place under surveillance?'

'They? The police, or the military, you mean?' He waited until she nodded her head. Whichever. It didn't make any difference these days. 'I don't think they've got enough resources for all that. I'm dead or out of the country as far as they know. No one's spotted me in three years now. I think it's safe to come home for a few days. As long as everyone keeps their mouths shut. Maria and Adélia especially. You know what gossips they can be.' He laughed at some distant memory and Eleanor thought how good it was to see him laugh again. He seemed better than the last time she had seen him, less bitter, less angry, rested.

'How is Fra Janio, anyway? Still trying to save a few souls and convert some young men?' she said and shifted Katherine so that she lay more comfortably across her. John reached out and brushed his fingers through Katherine's wispy blonde locks.

'He's well enough. Getting tired of the jungle and the good sisters, I think, although he would never say as much to me. He heard my confession last time I saw him.' He looked at Eleanor steadily and she opened her mouth in surprise, colour flooding her face.

'You told him about us?'

343

'That's the point about confession. You tell everything. Confess all sins.'

'Am I now a sin to you?' There was a quiver of pain in her voice.

John shook his head, reached across and touched her face, cupped her cheek with the palm of his hand. 'No. Never. I told Fra Janio that and he said he could not absolve me, unless I repented. And I didn't repent. I never will.' He smiled and gradually Eleanor smiled too. She rubbed her cheek against his hand.

'I've missed you so much, John.'

'I know. I've missed you.' They looked at each other, saying things between themselves that no one else could hear. Around them the shadows deepened.

Henry watched them from the verandah, trying to still the ache inside him. He had been so happy in the last year, so sure that Eleanor was beginning to love him as he loved her. And the baby had made it all perfect. Recently he had seen Eleanor smile more and more, shedding that fear and hurt that had threatened to always come between them. Opening herself up to him in thought and emotion in a way that he had thought she would never be able to do with anyone except John. And now John had come home. Henry slapped the hard stone of the balcony with his hand, barely feeling the pain. He was enveloped in a greater pain still.

He heard footsteps behind him and he turned, awkwardly, to see Louis standing there.

'Drink?' Louis asked. He looked out across the gardens, obviously aware of what Henry had been watching. He held out a glass and Henry took it.

'Thanks. How did you know?'

'Saw them from my bedroom window. Charles know yet?'

'I don't really know. Hopefully not.' Henry smiled that charming, awkward smile of his that made so many people realize how very kind he was and how much they liked him.

Louis smiled back. 'Should be fun at dinner tonight. Give the old man something to rave about. He needs to have a good blazing row every now and then. Clears the spleen for him. And listen, don't worry about Eleanor. She's a good girl and she loves you. She just doesn't know that yet, that's all. John'll disappear again, off to whatever personal war he thinks he needs to fight, and Eleanor'll miss him for a while and then she'll remember you and her baby – and she'll be content,' Louis said with conviction.

Henry shook his head. 'Content? I don't want Eleanor to just be content. I want her to be happy. Totally and blissfully happy.' He put his head back and poured the whisky down his throat, not really liking it but needing the burn. 'Besides, you know the really odd thing? I admire John. I wish to God I had the guts to be doing what he's doing. He's fighting for all of us, for our country and we're sitting around drinking and having dinner and making polite conversation, trying not to get into trouble. It makes me sick. I make myself sick!' He focused on Louis for a moment, his face pale and serious. And then he smiled again. 'Think I'll go pay my wife a visit. Excuse me, Louis. I'll see you at dinner.'

Louis watched him leave as he went to join the couple in the garden. He sighed.

Eleanor lay in bed that night, listening to Henry's quiet breathing and a hundred wild schemes ran through her mind. She and John would run away together to England and bring Katherine up there without ever telling her the truth about her father. Or John would turn himself into the military and beg forgiveness, insist it was just during Goulart's term that he had agitated against the authorities – and then she could divorce Henry and go and live with John. But no, none of them would work. Most of all because she could never bring herself to hurt Henry like that. He was everything she could ever expect or want from a husband and yet, despite that, he wasn't enough. He wasn't John. She hated herself for thinking such a thing. If

345

anyone was to be unhappy, it would have to be her. Henry must never be hurt.

She thought about dinner that night and the strained, awkward atmosphere that longed to expel the one outsider amongst them, to return to the comfortable ease of previous nights. John was more a member of the family than Henry or Louis could ever be. He was a blood relative. And yet, he was the outsider. The stranger in their midst who upset the delicate balance. And while John was present, Papa refused to eat downstairs. Instead he had his dinner in his bedroom and kept the door firmly shut. He did not want to see John, and did not want anyone to mention John's presence in the house. As far as Papa was concerned, John did not exist, Eleanor thought unhappily.

As far as she was concerned, only John existed. Well, no, not quite. There was Katherine, of course. She was the most important one of all, and another reason why it was impossible to run off with John. John had never been stable. How could she risk her baby's life and future with the sort of insecurity John offered?

But how was she to manage how she felt? How was she to behave as a normal wife to Henry now, when the thought of making love with anyone else but John repulsed her? Oh God, what was she to do?

She wished, desperately, that Sophie were there to advise her. A Sophie who could understand this dilemma and not think only of Henry but of everyone involved. But Sophie wouldn't want to understand; she had never liked John. No, Sophie would not help.

Henry stirred beside her and moaned, a scarcely heard sound that wrenched at Eleanor's heart. She stroked the hair back from his brow, ran her hand over his shoulder, soothing him with her touch. Trying to still some of the pain she had glimpsed in his eyes that night, some of the uncertainty he felt. He turned and pulled her in against him, his hand claiming her body. She could feel the warmth of him against her. She lay perfectly still, hoping he would sink back into a deep sleep. But he was aroused now and his mouth sought hers in the dark, his hands slid along her body, pulling at her nightdress.

Eleanor thought of the many other nights they had made love and how she had come to welcome his gentle caresses, his caring. It was nothing like when she was with John. She had never felt a part of Henry. But he loved her and she was his wife. And he needed her desperately not to reject him now. She reached around and pulled him to her.

John lay awake in his own room, the narrow bed hard and monastic, the walls still painted the same colour, the furnishings never changed. It was his room, but a forgotten one in a house that flowed and ebbed with changes and growth. He was the forgotten one of the family. And he couldn't blame them for it. They wanted a happy, steady life, and he caused turmoil. They wanted everyone to conform to the strictures of their society and government. He wanted change. He understood only too well why they welcomed him so tepidly, and changed the subject when he began to discuss awkward subjects, why they hoped that he would be gone in the morning, or if not that morning, then the next. He didn't really want to stay either. Only Eleanor held them all chained together. And she was the unhappiest of them all.

He sweated at the thought of Eleanor in bed with Henry, perhaps making love with him even now. He wondered if she had felt that way about Teresa. But no, surely not. Teresa hadn't cared about him, hadn't wanted him as anything more than a stepping stone to respectability and to furthering her career. A nice enough girl, Teresa, but not a threat. Not like Henry. He ground his teeth together, staring up at the ceiling. Slowly the night ticked away.

When Henry woke, it was only five o'clock and he turned in the dim light of the room, looking for the noise that had woken him. There was nothing there. Not even his wife. He sat up, about to go and look for her, and then he stopped himself. He stared at the floor for a long time. And then, with a sigh, he lay back against the pillows and closed his eyes again. He trusted Eleanor. Even if she were with John, it would only be to talk. Eleanor was not the sort of woman who could climb straight from her husband's bed into another man's. He knew she wasn't. Eventually he drifted off to sleep again.

In the nursery, Eleanor sat holding Katherine in her arms, the blanket tucked in around the tiny body, the pink, puckered face of an infant in deep sleep resting against her breast. She rocked in the chair.

'I thought I heard someone moving around. Are you all right?' Isobel said from inside the doorway and Eleanor glanced around in surprise.

'Yes. Of course. I'm sorry if I woke you. Charlie's fine, fast asleep.'

'Charlie would sleep through a war,' Isobel said with maternal pride. She sat down opposite Eleanor. 'I wish we could have another one just like him but nothing seems to happen, and it isn't for lack of trying!' she said pointedly and Eleanor smiled. Isabel was a good mother and a good wife. She wished she could be more like her. The thought brought Eleanor up sharply. She had never wanted to be like her sister before. That made it seem as if all her values had turned upside down. But Isobel was a better person now than she had been as a child. Loving Louis had done that for her. And was she, herself, a worse person? Vaguely Eleanor heard Isobel saying something and she focused back in on the words.

'You just having trouble sleeping, or is it John?' Isobel heard Eleanor give a gusty sigh.

'Oh, Isobel – it's always John. Ever since we were all children, there's never been anyone else for me. I used to shock myself with dreams about him, about us, but I don't think I really care anymore about our being first cousins. It just doesn't seem an issue compared to all the others. The real barriers, like Henry and now, this little one.' She smiled tenderly down at her daughter. 'How could I ever leave either of them for John? I couldn't.'

348

'You and John have been lovers in the past, haven't you?' Isobel asked. She didn't seem surprised when Eleanor nodded. 'Umm, thought so. I think Mama suspected too. So now what? What're you going to do?' Isobel tucked her feet up under her dressing gown and settled herself more comfortably in the chair. She looked at Eleanor expectantly.

'I don't really know. Nothing, I suppose. It was so hard not knowing where John was before, or whether he was alive at all. But I could cope when he wasn't here. Now he's back, I just don't know. I wish – God, I wish, in some ways, he hadn't come back!'

Out in the darkened passage John leaned against the wall, his eyes shut. He had never thought he would hear Eleanor say those words but he had heard them plainly enough. His face became quite still, chiselled features bathed in moonlight as the words revolved around and around in his mind. She wished he had never come back. She was like all the rest of them now, feeling him an outsider, a stranger, and wanting him gone. And he couldn't blame her either. Without a sound he made his way down the passageway, back to his room.

Neither Eleanor nor Isobel heard John beyond the door. They continued talking, strangely pleased with the closeness that had sprung up between them of late, and aware how easily it could be shattered by a careless remark. They nurtured it until full light and then returned to their bedrooms and their husbands.

In the morning John was quiet and withdrawn. He rebuffed Eleanor's attempts at conversation and sat silently through breakfast, the newspaper held up in front of him. Louis and Henry exchanged glances across the table, Henry looking away abruptly when John cleared his throat and spoke to Louis quietly, from behind the paper.

'Can you find me a place in town, down near the docks? Just a room and bathroom. Pay for it yourself and give your name. No one'll check you out. I'll give you the money for it. I don't think it's safe for me to be here much longer, not for any of us,' he said softly.

Louis glanced at him awkwardly. 'Well, okay. If that's what you want. You don't think your face'll be recognized down there by someone? They've had posters of you up all round town in the last year. Most of them've faded or been pulled down now, but it's still a risk.' Louis also kept his voice low, not wanting the rest of the family to hear.

He wondered whether this was not simply a ruse, a chance for John to get Eleanor away somewhere, on her own. But looking at John's set face, the way he compressed his lips, Louis began to think otherwise. John and Eleanor must have had words sometime last night. And Eleanor had told John to leave. It was the only thing that made sense. Suddenly, Louis felt desperately sorry for John. He smiled and gripped John's arm.

'Don't worry, Johnny, I'll find you something. We'll go straight after breakfast. You can rely on me, as always,' he said and saw John look at him assessingly, returning the smile. John needed someone to turn to, for God's sake, Louis thought. And if Eleanor wouldn't help, then it was up to Louis himself. Someone round here had to remember John was family and take his side. He helped himself to more toast, anger in his eyes.

Henry watched the exchange. So, Louis was backing John again. That made things easier. John needed financial help but he wouldn't take funds from Henry himself. With Louis in the middle, maybe they could prevent John knowing the source of the funds? It was at least something Henry could do. A beginning.

He looked down at his breakfast, deep in thought. Then he glanced at his wife – and smiled.

Eleanor knew something was wrong with John. How could she miss the hardness in his eyes, the indifference with which he answered her questions. He was telling her something that she understood only too clearly, but could not see the reason behind. What had provoked this change in him? She couldn't think. And it made saying goodbye to

350

him all the harder, knowing she had offended him in some way, and unable to put it right. She kissed his cheek, as they all stood in the hall saying their goodbyes, and clung to him for just a moment. John remained stiff, her embrace barely acknowledged. She released him and stepped back, not looking at him.

'Will we see you again soon, or not for another three years?' she joked. Beside her she felt Henry put an arm around her waist and had to control a spurt of irritation that wanted to push him away, tell him to leave her alone.

John gave a gentle smile but his heart was not in it, the pain showing briefly in his eyes. 'Who knows, Eleanor? That's what makes life exciting – the not knowing.' He turned away and was gone, Louis by his side, before any of them could say anything further. Eleanor looked after him, feeling as though half of herself had walked out the door, perhaps never to return. She breathed in deeply and then slipped from Henry's hold.

'I'll be upstairs,' she said and she walked slowly and firmly across the hall and up the stairs, her back quite straight and her head held high. Henry and Isobel watched her with misgiving. And Clarissa went to tell Charles that John was gone, yet again.

'I want a job, Henry,' Eleanor said. Henry looked up from the papers he was reading. It was two weeks since John had so suddenly appeared and disappeared again in their lives and Henry had begun to hope that Eleanor had settled down. He frowned slightly.

'What sort of job, something like Mina's got, you mean? Start up a boutique?' He sounded amused.

Eleanor shook her head impatiently. 'No, no, nothing like that. I'm serious, Henry. I'm nearly twenty-two and what have I ever done with myself? Been a rich, pampered daughter, and then a rich, pampered wife and mother. That doesn't make me anything at all. I'm tired of – oh, I'm tired of being useless!' She paced up and down, her arms wrapped tightly around her, her face strangely disturbed.

351

Henry put down the papers, taking her seriously at last. 'You're not just someone's daughter or wife – you're you! And you always have been. Isobel or, if you'll excuse the liberty, your mother are the sort who are content to have their lives revolve around the men in the family. And that's fine for them. You've always been different. I'm so sorry, darling, if I've been giving you the impression you're nothing more to me than my wife. You're everything, my friend, my lover, my confidante, my sounding-board, my support. How on earth could you think you're useless?' He went to stand beside her, putting his arms around her. She stood still, looking down at the floor. He didn't hear all the possessives. Couldn't understand the difference between something that was his and something that she was in her own right.

'Then you don't mind if I get a job?' she asked and she heard him sigh again. No matter that Henry was half-English, the other half of him was Latin. And Latin men didn't like their wives working. Eleanor pushed on. 'I want to start a school. I taught in one before, remember? Before I went away to Paris? It was just a little one for some of the women of the favelas and it was badly run and almost without money of any kind. But I could do it better, if you could just lend me some money. Papa won't, I know, and he seems to be so worried about money all the time now that I just couldn't ask him.'

She saw the doubt in her husband's eyes and rushed on, 'But, Henry, you've said yourself that change is never going to come about until the population is literate and I know I can't do much but I can make a start. Get some of the girls I went to school with involved. They're all bright, talented girls wasting their time, wasting all those educational skills that took so long to learn, on sitting at home and having tea parties. I speak French and English and Portuguese fluently and I very nearly completed my degree in History and Literature. I don't mean to brag, Henry, but I'm bright. I was in an honours programme. Don't you think it's a criminal waste to just let all that sit around, doing nothing?

How would you feel if you were told that your law degree was very nice and now, what are we having for dinner?'

She hadn't meant to sound so fervent, her eyes glowing, her cheeks flushed but somehow the need to convince Henry had run away with her and she had said more than she intended. Revealed more of her own frustration than was good. Henry was looking hurt.

'I had no idea you'd been brooding about being taken for granted. I try very hard to never take you for granted. I do think you're being unfair, Eleanor,' he said. He dropped his arms and went back to his desk, shuffling the papers into order.

Eleanor closed her eyes briefly. 'I'm not saying you're taking me for granted, Henry. How could I? You're the most thoughtful, appreciative husband anyone could hope to have.' She saw him smile a little at that. 'I'm just asking for your approval to help others learn something about the world. I'm asking your approval to share some of my incredible fortune, my schooling, my spare time, my – oh, how can I make you understand? I feel selfish, Henry. I have so much and most of those people out there have so little. I can't given them money because I don't have any of my own. All I can give them is my time. And I want you to approve of that. Please.' She held out her hand and reluctantly he took it, smiling in spite of himself.

'You always were more eloquent than was good for you – or me. What about Katherine? Don't you want to spend time with her, and with whatever brother or sister comes to join her?' He pulled her in against him, holding her tightly.

Eleanor forced herself not to pull away. She patted his arm. 'I'll be there for Katherine too. Just not all the time, the way I am at the moment. Katherine's quite happy with Isobel and Charlie. She doesn't need me one hundred per cent. And,' she hesitated, 'I've been feeling so run down lately, Henry, that I was hoping we could wait another year or two before we have any more babies. It's an exhausting thing, you know, carrying a child around for nine months and then giving birth. I just don't feel like I can do all that

353

again for a while. I need a break. You understand, don't you?' Contraception was not available in Brazil and besides, Henry was Catholic; he knew what she was asking. He sighed, a forceful expulsion of breath that sounded more irritated than usual. Eleanor waited.

'All right, if that's what you want. You may start your school and I will back you. For one year. After that, the others – whoever you have recruited – will have to carry on without you because then I will expect you to return to being a full-time mother. I will want another child. Is that understood?' He sounded as though he were lecturing one of the clerks in his law office.

Eleanor bristled. 'Henry! I'm not a chattel! This is 1965, not the Middle Ages. If you won't help me without preconditions, I'll find someone who will. And I'm not sitting around here twiddling my thumbs any longer. Do you understand?' Her voice had regained the strength it once had had to demand her own rights.

Henry looked startled. 'Why ask me, if you intend to do whatever you want anyway?' he said coldly.

Eleanor snapped back, 'Because, as I have already said, I wanted your approval. It didn't occur to me that you would disapprove of something that you have spoken about so often as one of the main needs in this country. I feel like we need to do something to help the country out, help it crawl its way out of the mess it's in and towards democracy. Those were, I thought, your ideals too.'

'And I'm already doing what I can to help. I don't want you getting mixed up in things. I want you to stay clear of political problems. There's enough being done in this family already, without you getting mixed up,' Henry retorted but Eleanor wasn't about to give in.

'Oh, what? You mean John, I suppose? Yes, he's helping, and I'm proud he is. But I don't see anyone else doing anything. Louis? Papa? You? What are you doing, Henry? Tell me?' She could be wounding when she was angry and she wished she could stop the words that poured out of her, but they had been held in too long, the growing frustration that had built within her over the last year showing all too clearly. It had to come out.

'I'm doing more than you know, Eleanor,' Henry said harshly, goaded into saying what he had promised he never would. 'And from where I stand, what I'm doing is a hell of a lot more effective than what John's doing. He's the next best thing to a terrorist. But I expect you'd be proud of that, too, just as long as it's John doing it.' Henry picked up his papers and walked abruptly out of the room, slamming the heavy doors behind him.

Eleanor stood where she was and then picked up the vase on the table and went to throw it in the fireplace. But she couldn't. She had never done anything destructive in her life and she couldn't do it now. She didn't even like it, she thought staring down at the milky green celadon. But she couldn't break it. She replaced it very carefully on the desk and closed her eyes.

How could she have lost her temper with Henry like that? After everything else she had put him through? She was ashamed of herself and, perversely, still angry with Henry. Why hadn't he fought it out, forced her to see his point of view? Why did he have to go slamming off like that, never giving her a chance to finish the argument? Now it was going to hang between them, like some foul-smelling piece of game, until someone said they were sorry and climbed up and cut it down. Until someone gave in. She didn't want Henry to give in; she wanted him to understand. And she wasn't about to give in, herself.

What on earth had Henry meant about he 'was doing more than you know'? What was he doing? He was a good lawyer and occasionally he would take a charity case on, for free, if he thought the cause were just. He was also an aide to the mayor of Rio, dealing with a lot of political problems and advising the mayor as to the best course of action from a legal point of view. But that was it, as far as Eleanor knew. What else could Henry be doing? The thought worried her.

She left the study and wandered along the passageway, wondering where Henry might have gone. In the distance, she could hear the front door bell ringing and the sound of voices, raised in greeting. Her bedroom was empty, the large, canopied bed seeming curiously forlorn now that she had argued with Henry. She sat down on it, smoothing her hand over the starched white cotton cover. Oh Henry, I'm sorry, I didn't mean to argue with you like that. I didn't mean to suggest you weren't doing enough or that John was better than you. I'm sorry.

Her guilt increased as the moments passed and Henry did not return to kiss and make up, as he had always done in the past. She stood up and went back out into the passageway, listening for his footsteps. The east wing was silent. Reluctantly, she trailed downstairs into the main house.

There were voices coming from Mama's sitting-room and she wandered in that direction, thinking that perhaps Dr da Silva had turned up again for tea. He was recently widowed and said to be grieving as punctiliously as he displayed every other emotion. Mama seemed to like his company and Eleanor herself thought him a charming man. She hoped his was one of the voices she could hear.

But when she opened the door, she was surprised to see it was Henry and that he held someone in his arms, all that could be seen being two slim arms encircling his back in embrace. Eleanor stopped in astonishment and would have retreated if she hadn't seen her mother also standing in the room, smiling. For a moment, Eleanor couldn't think how it was that her mother could be smiling at Henry embracing some other woman until, with a gasp, she cried out, 'Sophie?'

Henry and the unknown female drew apart, Henry stepping aside, so that a tiny, delicate figure in a ridiculously short dress was revealed, her dark hair flashing and fizzing with energy as it was tossed in the air and her grey eyes laughing.

'Eleanor? You see, I did come to have my bottom pinched but alas I could not convince Henry to do so, so you will have to take me out and have some wildly sexy

356

Brazilian man do so at once. I am in danger of feeling neglected!' She stretched put her arms and Eleanor gave a cry and ran forward.

'Oh Sophie! You wretch! Why didn't you let me know you were coming? How could you just make your own way from the airport when you know I'd have been there to meet you? Oh, I don't believe you're here! It's so good to see you!' They hugged each other for a long time, while Henry and Clarissa looked on.

Then Sophie broke away and said, quickly and nervously, 'I hope I'm not going to be a nuisance because I didn't actually have enough money left after the flight to stay in a hotel so I, um, rather hoped you wouldn't mind putting me up here, just for a while. Would that be all right?' They hastened to assure her she could stay as long as she wanted, weeks, months, years even, Eleanor said with a laugh and Sophie smiled her impish grin and glanced beyond Eleanor to where Henry stood, eagerly seconding his wife's invitation. For a moment they looked into each other's eyes, seeing confusion on the part of Henry, a pained longing in Sophie's. She dipped her eyes away immediately when she saw Eleanor's mother intercept the look, her face stilling for a moment, the smile half slipping. Clarissa angled her head to one side to examine Sophie more carefully.

'Are you thinking of staying out here long then, Sophie? You've obviously been studying very hard with your English. It's immaculate! Have you also been studying Portuguese?' Eleanor asked, impressed that Sophie had been doing all that and working to pay off her father's debts at the same time. So much more than she had been doing herself. Apart from having Katherine, that was. Nothing could detract from the wonder of Katherine.

'Of course! My Portuguese is disgraceful but I expect it will get better. As for how long I will stay – I don't know. I have decided to be true to my bohemian father's blood and explore the world. And where else should I start than where my best friends are?' She laughed and Eleanor drew her

357

arm through Sophie's, eager to show her Katherine. For a moment Eleanor looked into Henry's face, but saw no forgiveness there. He could be as pleasant as possible to Sophie, but Eleanor was not yet forgiven. He looked at her coldly and she was dismayed.

'Sophie, dear, come upstairs. I have to show you Katherine before all my maternal pride makes me burst. Come on. Mama, Henry, you'll excuse us for a moment, won't you?' And taking their assent for granted, she led Sophie out of the room and upstairs without a look back.

'Sophie, thank heavens you're here,' Eleanor said quietly as they were going towards the nursery. 'I've had the most dreadful row with Henry today and he's barely speaking to me and all because I want to start a school to teach poor people to read and write. I don't think that's so terrible, do you? But he thinks I'm going to be neglecting him and Katherine if I do and I ended up shouting at him that I wasn't his chattel and oh hell, you know how it goes, everything thrown at each other and God knows I would never want to hurt Henry. He's so good to me! So you'll have to help convince him for me, be around a lot, take my place. You'll do that for me, won't you Sophie?' she said in a hurried voice. She glanced at the girl beside her. 'Sophie?'

'Oh, yes, of course I will, Eleanor! Goodness, you and Henry arguing! I can't quite imagine it.' Sophie was silent for a moment and Eleanor was puzzled.

'Well, husbands and wives do occasionally. It's just that normally Henry comes and makes up immediately or else I do, but this time we've both dug our heels in and I don't know what to do. It's all so silly, really. And I didn't help things by telling him I didn't want any more children for at least a couple of years.' She sighed. 'Anyway, enough of all that. How are you? Where've you been living? What's been happening?' Eleanor asked eagerly and Sophie laughed.

'I've been living with a very rich old man who took a fancy to me and paid off all my debts and made me appreciate the meaning of wealth and then, suddenly, a few days ago, I decided I just couldn't take it anymore and that

I was tired of his jowly, fat face and creeping fingers and I decided that what I really wanted was adventure and young, gorgeous men and lots and lots of fun so I pawned some of the jewellery he gave me and bought a plane ticket here. And so, here I am!' She grinned as she saw Eleanor's mouth part in astonishment.

'Sophie! You haven't! My God!' Eleanor was appalled and too surprised to be able to conceal it with any success.

'No, actually I haven't.' Sophie's grin grew wider still, painfully wide. 'But it seemed more exciting than what I've really been doing which is working in a chemist's shop and paying off all Papa's debts myself and studying English and Portuguese from books in the evenings and hoarding my savings so I could come and see you. No lovers. Boring as hell.' She shrugged and looked away.

Eleanor laughed, her voice almost cracking with relief. 'Oh you dreadful girl, you really had me believing that tale. I'm infinitely more proud of you having done all that by yourself. What a little heroine you are!' Eleanor hugged Sophie and then stopped at a door, holding her finger to her lips. 'She's having a nap and so is Charlie, so we'll have to be quiet. Come and have a look.' Eleanor entered and Sophie followed, a strange expression on her face as she saw the sleeping children and the delight Eleanor had in them. For a moment Sophie looked – almost angry.

'Have you and Eleanor had a quarrel, Henry?' Clarissa asked once the two women had left the room. Clarissa hated to probe but she had felt a moment of uncertainty in that look she had intercepted that rocked her steady world almost as much as her husband's imprisonment. She sat down and gestured to a chair beside her. It wasn't a request.

Henry sat. He looked irritable and uneasy, hesitating over his words so that he could choose exactly the right tone of blandness. 'Yes, sort of. Eleanor wants a job, and I want her to stay home. She doesn't want any more children for a while and I do. The usual sort of husband-wife argument, I should imagine. Why? Does it bother you, Clarissa?' Henry didn't think his mother-in-law would press things further if he became uncommunicative. She liked an easy life.

As though agreeing with his thoughts, Clarissa frowned. 'Henry, you know I don't like there to be trouble in my house. Of course it concerns me if you and Eleanor aren't getting along. What I want more than anything is for everyone to be happy. So please will you do your best to patch things up? I'm not trying to interfere, I'm not telling you who's right and who's wrong. Just please don't let there be an "atmosphere" in the house. I don't want that, at all costs. You know how much it upsets Charles.' And me, Clarissa thought. She wondered whether to bring up the matter of Sophie but decided, more from embarrassment than anything else, not to intrude. Henry was a good man; he would never do anything to hurt Eleanor.

'There won't be, Clarissa. My word on it.' Henry stood and leaned over her, kissing her briefly on the cheek. She smelled of a heady floral scent that would have been too strong on many women but which suited her perfectly. The gentle rose set to bloom gracefully in her garden, determined to never allow any weeds. Even if it just meant digging the weeds under, so they didn't show. Henry smiled ironically and said he was going to his office; he had work to do. He left her still protesting the fact that it was a Saturday.

Henry's political mentor, Rodolfo Pereira, Mayor of Rio de Janeiro, was coming up for re-election in the next year, as were the vice-mayor and the municipal assembly. Since last week when the second Institutional Act had been enacted, there were now only two parties allowed in the country and the thirteen parties that had previously existed had been dissolved into the government party, ARENA (the National Renovating Alliance) and a loyal opposition, MDB (the Brazilian Democratic Movement). A new wave of cassations had already begun with civilians subject, for the first time, to the military courts for offences against the armed forces. The Supreme Court had been strengthened from eleven members to fifteen, the additional four tilting the pro-military balance. Henry was desperately worried by the way the democratic reforms of previous governments were slowly being stripped away by the military. Worried? No, he was frightened.

Somehow, through this maze of dangerous new political measures, he had to steer Rodolfo Pereira to success in the elections or the situation would deteriorate further. It was not a task he was looking forward to. He especially didn't have the time to waste thinking about a difficult wife who didn't want to be a mother. He put her out of his mind with an unhappy shrug.

Rodolfo Pereira was a good man, fair, democratic, conservative. Just the sort of man Rio de Janeiro needed as mayor. He was now a member of the ARENA party, albeit reluctantly, so the military should have no problem with his re-election. But the opposition were better organized than last time, and were themselves a faction of the ARENA party, which could be difficult. It would have been so much easier if they still had the old populist leaders to campaign against. They were brilliant, born-politicians but the coarsest of administrators, Henry thought, and easily enough unseated.

But when two different chapters within the same political party were squaring up against each other, anything could happen. And he didn't trust the opposition. They were hard-line members of the new régime. Just what would happen, if they got into power?

Right now he was in a perfect position for seeing most of the important and relevant information that passed over the mayor's desk in time to whisper snippets of news along to Louis and sometimes a journalist friend of his, before the information could be acted upon. Many of the people slated for cassation, or military enquiries, had somehow managed to disappear before the police came for them, thanks to that prior information. But if the opposition came to power, Henry would have to return full time to law, and no information would be passed at all. The cause would have to find its information elsewhere and that could be dangerous for everyone.

He sat at his desk, massaging his temples, the glasses that he had taken to wearing lately pushed up on his forehead. Damn the military hard-liners and damn the second Institutional Act! What was a shoo-in had now become a grim battle for power and he had no way of knowing how much the people understood what was being asked of them. Maybe Eleanor was right? Educate the people and the rest would follow naturally? He sighed and bent over his papers, yet again.

Eleanor and Sophie had taken the afternoon to go sight-seeing around Rio, starting with the more well-known sights like the Sugar Loaf and Corcovado, where the statue of Christ, arms outstretched, rose one hundred feet into the air, and the cable car up to Sugar Loaf swayed gently with the wind, displaying the whole of Rio harbour flashing in the afternoon sun below. The waters of Guanabara Bay rippled and flowed from greens and blues into dark black, marking the shallows and depths and the sun shimmered across the bay and beat steadily through the glass of the car, building with heat as it slowly crawled towards the summit.

Far below, the fort, the shipping, the naval academy had been reduced to toy size, as had the Racecourse and the Jockey Club and the smart residential districts of Ipanema and Leblon. Eleanor looked down with relief, putting all that seemed so important when standing on the ground, into its true perspective. Dots, childish toys against the grandeur of the mountains and the land itself. What did it matter that Papa had been thrown out of the Jockey Club and banned from the racecourse? They were silly, man-made pastimes that mattered not a jot compared to all this. She looked around with pleasure.

'It's been years since I've been up here,' she said to Sophie. 'Not since I was a child, really, on a school outing. Makes you think how petty the whole human thing is compared to the magnificence of all these natural formations.' She laughed. 'Oh dear, don't I sound pompous?' She wished she had not spoken her thoughts aloud.

Sophie glanced at her, quizzically. 'Does it make you feel better, diminishing all that?' She waved her arm out at the city spread out below them. 'Sort of snap your fingers, click your heels, and it all disappears into a fantasy-land?'

'Dorothy-like? Yes, I suppose so.' Eleanor sighed. 'But it doesn't stay like that. Somehow you have to go back and then they all loom up again, life-size problems and all.'

'It seems pretty calm to me. No one would guess the military are in control or that there was coup just over a year ago. Brazilians obviously take it all in their stride,' Sophie said and Eleanor glanced at her, interested in seeing how a foreigner saw the situation. Did it really seem that calm?

'I guess it only matters when it hits your own family, or the business where you work, or perhaps a friend – a lover. Then you see what's really going on,' Eleanor said softly. She glanced around at the other sightseers but no one was paying attention to her.

'Like your father? And John?' Sophie said. 'What's really going on there now? Are you still seeing John? Are you both still – lovers?' She watched Eleanor's expression intently.

'No. That was over long ago. Three years ago, when he left Paris. I've only seen him once, for a day, since then. Besides, I'm married now, remember.' Eleanor shrugged, trying to seem indifferent. She wasn't sure why she felt the need to conceal her feelings from Sophie but something was different between them now. The old Sophie and, to be fair perhaps the old Eleanor, were now different people. Nearly two years of experience lay between them. She couldn't discuss John with Sophie anymore. That much, at least, she knew.

Sophie's eyes were clear and light in the glare of the sun, and Eleanor almost felt guilty concealing her feelings from the girl. But it was better that way. John was out of her life and Sophie need never know the full truth. No one need ever know.

Later they took the train from Cosme Velho station on a roller-coaster journey through the mountainside vegetation up to the statue of Christ on Corcovado. They wandered around the base of the huge statue, staring out at the view, at the protective arms of land that curled in around the bay, defending it from the sea. They craned their heads back to stare up at the statue, shielding their eyes against the harsh light on white stone. Then they climbed back into the train and returned down the mountainside. About halfway down, the train halted for twenty minutes at a little inn set amongst the pines and named, aptly enough, Pinheiro.

Sophie insisted on trying the soft drink, guarana, made from tree bark and they both ordered a bottle and wandered off from the inn into the shade of a wooded glade. A statue of Ceres beckoned, her lips rouged by some less than classical tourist, and Eleanor sipped on her drink and tried to relax. She had been tense ever since they arrived at the way-station, expecting something to jump out at her from the shadows. Ridiculous really.

'This isn't half-bad. Kind've fizzy apple tasting. Hey, I could get to like Brazil. Maybe I'll stick around a while,' Sophie said and Eleanor smiled. It was nice to have Sophie back, with all her energy and spirit.

She raised her bottle so that they clinked together, in toast. 'To your staying here then. And to our friendship.'

Sophie grinned and put her head back, draining off the last of the guarana. 'And to my finding a man suitable to my own inimitable spirit, great beauty, and total lack of funds.' They both laughed but Sophie didn't really seem all that amused.

Watching them from deeper in the shadows, beyond the statue, was a tall, fair-haired man wearing a blue, cambric work shirt and faded khaki trousers. He leaned comfortably against a tree, knowing they could not see him. Not now that they had stopped to finish their drinks and laugh like giddy schoolgirls. For a moment, he had wondered if

364

Eleanor didn't sense his presence. He had seen her looking around uneasily, staring into the shadows. But now she was diverted again, and she had forgotten that feeling.

She had on a white dress and was slim, her head small with a wary shine to her green eyes. The neatness of her figure and the way she stood, for an instant, looking around her, was cool, steady and infinitely appealing. Her hair was pulled back from her face, revealing small ears studded with pearls that gleamed milkily in the half-light. He relaxed and watched them with a funny feeling of almost pleasure. He hadn't felt much pleasure in anything lately, so it was strange that two such idle, indulgent women should be able to make him smile.

They sat down for a few minutes beside the statue and, although he could not hear their words, he could tell from the tone of their voices, from their laughter, that they were enjoying themselves. But then the bell rang, calling them back for the rest of the journey down the mountainside and they gathered their things together and stood, brushing themselves down. In sadness, he saw them returning to the inn where the train waited. He still missed Eleanor.

When they returned to the palácio that evening, Henry came to greet them at the door, smiling and ruefully commenting on how he had passed the day when they had been off enjoying themselves. He kissed Sophie on the cheek, and slipped his arm around his wife, leaning in to kiss her gently on the lips.

'Sorry, my love. You were quite right and I was acting like a medieval despot. You may have your school. Unconditionally,' he whispered and he saw her look at him with such a grateful and guilty expression that he could only wish to kick himself harder for having put her through such an afternoon.

'Oh Henry, I'm so sorry for everything I said. I never meant to hurt you. You really are such a good husband, such a good friend, that I could never manage without you. I've been so miserable thinking you were still angry with me.' She hugged him tightly. 'We'll have more family soon. Really.' And she smiled so that the whole room seemed to light up, to share the pleasure she felt. Sophie felt dark and drab in comparison as they walked into the drawing-room where the rest of the family was gathered. Clarissa watched carefully and was relieved to see the equilibrium restored.

For the rest of the evening, the palácio rang with the sound of laughter and good spirits, Sophie entertaining everyone with her dry brand of wit and Eleanor recounting endless tales of past exploits that kept everyone amused. Henry sat on the arm of Eleanor's chair for most of the night, his hand on her shoulder. And Eleanor reached up occasionally to pat it, or look up into his face. Clarissa sighed with relief. And Sophie's humour became drier still.

Isobel and Sophie had, surprisingly, been pleased to make each other's acquaintance. Normally Isobel suspected any and all women of trying to attract Louis's attention, and was correspondingly cool and wary towards them. And from what Sophie knew of Isobel from Eleanor in the past and even from Henry's letters, she had expected to find a girl not very much to her liking. But Isobel had blossomed of late and Sophie was patently not interested in Louis and, in each of them, they found an amusing and unthreatening presence. They sat and talked away most of the evening about clothes and children, parties and gossip, and enjoyed each other thoroughly. Eleanor was pleased.

Chapter Eighteen

August 1967

The school was a success. Even without Henry's support, Eleanor was sure she could have found the funding from amongst her more liberal friends and their families, but with Henry's help it was destined to run well and prosper almost from the moment the doors opened.

The idea was that each student would be sponsored personally, rather than the school itself which would run on a not-for-profit basis and take in fee-paying students. Each pupil was chosen from amongst the poor of the favelas because of demonstrated ability, a desire to learn, a willingness to make a success of themselves. The sponsors sometimes funded only one student, sometimes several, according to how generous and liberal-minded each of Eleanor's and Henry's friends were. Isobel was drafted in to beg funds from her friends, as was Louis, and each of those sponsors then asked friends of their own and so the ball rolled on and on, gathering a surprising amount of moss and generating a good deal of pleasure for all concerned.

Eleanor taught a class in reading and writing, another in history and geography and a third, to some of the more advanced students, in English. Various other women from Eleanor's old convent school taught mathematics, basic science subjects, nutrition and hygiene. And Henry taught political science quietly and discreetly, twice a week, in the evenings.

The students were eager and determined to learn, knowing already what kind of life they were condemned to if this one chance at gaining an education failed. They studied hard, asked increasingly bold and attentive questions, and competed fiercely for top marks in each class. Eleanor was surprised at how hungry their quest for knowledge was and she worked longer and longer hours to impart what she knew.

No permission had been requested to start the school. The Church provided a building, free of charge, for the classes and there was no question of trying to provide diplomas of certification. The students knew they would not be officially qualified. But they would be taught, for free, and what could be wrong with that? Henry waited, daily, for the police to arrive and close down the school but, with time, even he relaxed and began to enjoy the feeling of satisfaction in having helped, in a small way, to change life for the better.

By the time the elections took place, in June of 1966, re-electing Rodolfo Pereira to the post of mayor and quite a few of the more liberal local politicians to the municipal assembly, the hard-liners were beginning to question the wisdom of allowing the old politics to come in through open election doors and there was a move to annul the disliked candidates' mandates. One general even went so far as to try and force the issue with the threat of troops. Henry was pale and anxious for several days, his hands almost shaking as he sat at dinner or drank alone in the library. But the storm passed and the election results were allowed to stand.

By July of that year, various state assembly representatives had been cassated for criticizing the government too openly and the opposition MDB was threatening to resign en masse in protest. They were promised a ten-year cassation themselves and their resistance folded rapidly. Costa e Silva, the general who had originally taken control from Goulart, was selected as candidate of the ARENA party for the next elections, virtually guaranteeing him the presidency in the following year. People began to watch their words even more closely, to question their friends' best intentions, to survey the world with unfriendly, suspicious eyes.

John was equally busy. He divided his time between Rio and São Paulo, sometimes travelling on false papers further into the interior to attend meetings, rallies, to urge resistance, to hand out pamphlets outlining positive steps that could be taken to help oppose the power of the military as it grew stronger and more tentacled in its encroachment on civilian affairs.

Long talks took place with the various Church authorities for each of those regions, who, for the most part, had aligned themselves strongly with the Left and the masses. But there were always the odd few who towed the party line and promised the people paradise in heaven for the extra suffering they endured on earth. John wrote to Father Dominic, his old mentor at Wykham, for help in contacting sympathetic sources and was not disappointed by the letters that flowed back on a steady basis.

When the government began talking about 'reforming' higher education, John and the other student leaders arranged with the Church to hold a secret congress of the banned National Student Union. They decided on Belo Horizonte as the site for the congress and in July of that year, John travelled secretly to attend the meeting.

He was an eloquent figure, sure of his political knowledge, even surer of his own burning mission to help. Many who were wavering fell under the spell of the tall, blond fugitive who spoke with such fervour and conviction. Many more were already convinced.

A year later, a further congress was called, in São Paulo, and John, again, was asked to speak at it. His was a voice that held both reason and vision, and many of the radical Left or the militant Church were as eager to hear him as the students themselves. John agreed reluctantly, although he knew it was a risk, knew the guarda were closer on his trail than ever.

He travelled by night and waited, on the outskirts of the city, for the appointed hour to fall.

Lying in a ditch, at the side of the road, an old blanket pulled over him to shelter him from the rain, he was cold. The rain fell, not steadily but fitfully, and he shivered constantly as the wind lifted the sodden blanket and eddied in around him.

His companion, Pedro, was as cold and tired as he was and huddled miserably into his poncho, his thin, dark face looking old. Much older than the twenty-four years he had been blessed – or cursed – with so far. They would have liked to take shelter in one of the bars in the old part of the town, or perhaps in an abandoned building, but there was too much chance of their faces being seen and recognized. São Paulo was especially dangerous for them. They would wait until dark.

John tried to close his eyes and sleep but the shivers that rippled through him, shaking him like an old palm tree in the wind, rattling bones and teeth alike, kept him awake. He could feel the fever coming with it. It always came back at this time of year and he would drift, sweating and shivering through a twilight world for several days until it passed. Pedro glanced at him with concern, but knew better than to say anything. The congress went ahead tonight, or not at all, and John could not afford to be sick. The shivering continued, unchecked.

'Hey, Pedro, you ever hear of Carlos Marighela?' John asked, from between clenched teeth.

The dark young man stared across at him. 'Yeah, the terrorist. I've heard of him. Why?'

'You know anyone who knows him? I'd like to talk to him, maybe, sometime.' John wasn't sure what Pedro knew but there were strange depths to the young man that sometimes surprised everyone. His father was a powerful politician and newspaper magnate who was almost alone amongst the voices raised against the government now. Pedro was very like his father, both reckless and courageous and, at times, very wary. He was looking wary now.

'What do you want to talk to him about?' he asked. Rain streamed down his face, turning his sallow skin blue with cold. He had a thin, hawklike nose, much like his father's, that dominated his face, and dark eyes beneath heavy black eyebrows. John trusted him like a brother.

'About us. About maybe joining forces. Hit back against a few military targets, make the authorities sit up and take us seriously, make the public aware there are people fighting for their freedom. I don't like the thought of terrorism, but it might have its uses. We're not getting anywhere fast this way.'

'Then why are we here, John? What purpose does this congress hold if none of it is worth anything?' Pedro said furiously and John could see the light had not yet been extinguished in this man's crusade. He would never agree to terrorism, until he learned the realities of what their pathetic resistance produced. A pinprick in the side of the government, a minor irritation to the military, a small embarrassment to the police. Nothing else. He raised his hand.

'Calm down, Pedro. It was just a thought. Maybe a bad one. Forget it, okay?' He shivered again and felt ill. Desperately ill. It would be too ridiculous to succumb to the fever now though. Only another two hours and they could start making their way to the meeting-place. He would just have to hold on until then. He clenched his teeth together and pulled the blanket over his head again.

When it came time for them to go, John found he could barely move. His muscles ached and his head spun. He limped along behind Pedro, sweating and uncomfortable. But the meeting-house, approached from down a dark alley near the old railway yards, was already nearly full, the hushed and shadowed figures sitting patiently on the cold

371

floor awaiting them. John slipped past them towards the platform they had erected at one end of the warehouse.

'Can you speak?' Pedro whispered from behind him, when he halted and leaned against one of the internal pillars, welcoming the cool feel of the metal. He was burning now, and Pedro eyed him uncertainly.

'Yes. But let me speak first. I can't hold on much longer. Get them to start, will you?' John was referring to the priests who gathered together in the corner, their robes hanging limp and sodden with rain, their whispers harsh in the echoing vaults. While Pedro organized things, John tried to focus his mind on what he would say. He had written a speech some time ago and had meant to deliver that but now he knew it was too long and he could not remember it well enough. His mind was already wandering, inserting strange, dream-like sequences to the night, so that he was unsure what was reality and what his fevered imaginings.

'John? John, they're ready for you now.' Pedro had somehow materialized by his side and he hadn't noticed. In fact, the darkened warehouse was almost completely silent now, shadowed faces directed towards him. They were all waiting for him to speak.

He walked haltingly over to the small platform which had been lit up with two kerosene lamps. In the glare, he saw several familiar faces, priests he knew and he smiled.

They watched him expectantly, as though they knew he alone would be the one to turn the tide of failure and pessimism sweeping the reform movement. John felt deeply tired. Why did they all want so much from him? He was only one man and a sick one at that. A disillusioned one. Couldn't they see that?

He stood facing the crowd, estimating its size. Two hundred, perhaps a little more. Not so many really. But all of them had risked their lives to be there. That made each worth a great deal.

He cleared his throat, forcing his mind to function. 'I will not speak for long tonight. As you can see, there are many others here who have come a long way to speak to you. And there are many of you who would like a chance to stand up and say your own piece. So I will keep it brief.

'For some years now we have been struggling against an increasingly repressive military-backed government. One that has promised reform, promised land, education, economic and social development. And in return they have given us the three "Laws" of contemporary Brazilian politics. You all know them. The Law of the Miraculous solution, that is if this particular president can't sort it out, the next one will. The Law of the Vacancy – political musical chairs. And the Law of the Scapegoat: make someone else the butt of all that ails the country. Blame the foreigners, blame the Left, blame the Communists but never, never blame the government.

'That has all got to end. They are corrupt and inefficient and intent on strangling the country's economy just so that they can keep the masses ignorant and compliant. Well, we are here this night to condemn Costa e Silva, to condemn his government and its total lack of social justice, its neglect of the land reform it promised us years ago; we are here to condemn the way the Institutional Acts rob our citizens of their rights, to condemn a cabinet that is dominated by military men and business interests, to condemn the increasing rape of our land by foreign powers.' He paused and wiped his forehead, shook his head and peered out into the shadows.

'In the past certain people have tried to provoke the government into over-reacting by bombing the newspaper "O Estado de São Paulo", by trying to bomb Costa e Silva when he was only the presidential candidate, and by sporadic guerrilla activities in Rio Grande do Sul. These actions were, for the most part, unsuccessful. And why? Because they were isolated, performed by a handful of dissatisfied people. What we must do is overwhelm the government by our sheer numbers. We must have the people out on the streets, shouting, demanding reform. We must get the workers out, must make them understand that it is not just us students who are being repressed and imprisoned. It is them as well. They are being imprisoned in their own lives, with no hope and no money. Their wages have effectively fallen by thirty per cent in the last year alone and inflation has made their future increasingly uncertain. They are being made prisoners in their own country. And they must be made to see that they are the lifeblood of Brazil. We need direct election ...' He faltered, the room swinging around him, the lights blazing into spots of colour, the silence suddenly loud and ringing in his ears.

'We need direct election,' he repeated and broke off again. There was much more he wanted to say, much more that needed to be said and he could tell that they were listening.

But suddenly he felt as though he were in a tunnel, the walls closing in on him, and he couldn't tell which way was up. He started to move forward and the lights swung again, sharply, angling above him. And then he closed his eyes and felt the cold floor beneath his cheeks, and sighed with relief. He would tell them later.

Sophie sat with Katherine on her lap and pointed to the clowns. Beside her, Isobel and Charlie were clapping their hands in glee and the clown was blowing bubbles out of his mouth now, huge pink, translucent balloons of gossamer that floated up towards the roof of the tent and hung there, quivering. Katherine shrieked with delight, slapping her palms together.

'Look, Sosee, look!' she laughed and Sophie hugged her tighter and grinned at Isobel.

'I guess this is what being a mother is all about. I could get to like it,' she said and Isobel laughed, her own belly large again, finally, with her second child.

'This is the good side. You have to go through the bad bit first,' she warned and Sophie smiled, her eyes turning in on little Katherine. The child, at nearly two years old, was like a miniature adult, Sophie thought. Perfectly proportioned and full of confidence, speaking clearly and carefully in

374

fully formed sentences. Please can I have some milk? Thank you. Aren't you having any too? It staggered Sophie. She stroked the child's hair and wished, desperately, that Katherine belonged to her. That Henry belonged to her. She could make them both happy in a way Eleanor never could.

Eleanor who only thought about her school and perfect strangers and how much they needed her. Never mind her own family. They could manage, there were always other people to look after Katherine, someone to be nice to Henry. Eleanor didn't need to bother. Sophie's face became stony at the injustice that had given Eleanor so much and herself so little.

'Can you believe Eleanor wouldn't come today? I thought Katherine was going to cry the house down but Eleanor didn't budge. She can be very – determined – sometimes, can't she?' Sophie said and Isobel glanced over at her, not really giving the words much thought.

'Oh yes, Eleanor's always been determined. It's a shame she didn't come though. Katherine's first circus and Eleanor has to miss it. They grow up so fast at this age.' She ruffled the brown hair beside her, Charlie turning to grin good-naturedly up at his mother. 'Don't they?'

'Very. But I suppose I can always fill in for Eleanor, take her place. My job's not exactly demanding,' Sophie suggested, knowing Isobel was beginning to think of her as another member of the family. Another sister. None of them would hear of her moving out, once she had managed to get a job with the French consulate. On the pittance they paid her, Henry had said with horror, and instantly appealed to the Fawcetts. And Charles, thank the Lord, had said she must stay. There was so much room in the palácio and rent could be so expensive in Rio. Why would Sophie even think of leaving? Eleanor had also insisted, grateful for the time Sophie devoted to Katherine and Henry, when she was not there herself. And Sophie had gracefully given in, ignoring the slight frown on Clarissa's face that wondered just how long the French girl meant to make her home with them. Sophie could have told Clarissa. But not yet. She could wait.

Eleanor closed the door behind the last student and turned back into the room to straighten the chairs and wipe down the blackboard. It was late afternoon and she didn't have any further classes that day. She wished, somehow, she could have made it to the circus with Katherine, Isobel and Charlie. She felt guilty. But it wasn't her choice. If she missed a class, all these people had to come again, on another afternoon, to make it up. Many of them had to get special permission from their places of work to attend these classes and they had families and responsibilities that had to be taken care of. She couldn't just say, sorry, come tomorrow instead because I want to go to the circus with my daughter.

Still, it was a pity and she would try to make it up to Katherine. Take her somewhere special – just the two of them, on their own. Make her realize just how much her mama loved her. Eleanor stretched and arched her back, weary with standing for so long.

There was a rustle from the back of the room, from behind the connecting door that led to the Church offices and she called out, wondering if it was one of the sisters coming to see her. But no one replied. Puzzled, she walked over to the door and opened it, looking inside the passageway. It was empty. She returned to her room and collected up the pencils, putting them away in the cupboard and locking the door. The blackboard was dusted down, the wastepaper basket emptied. Eleanor liked to leave the room tidy for the next day.

Another noise, a sliding, scraping noise this time, made her stand quite still, her heart pounding. It was silly to be frightened. It wasn't even dark yet. But, still, she was. She called out again, and this time there was a sound. A voice. Indistinguishable through the walls, but clearly non-threatening. Laughing at herself and her fears, she walked towards the door and pulled it open. It must be one of the nuns.

But the figure that stood there, leaning against the door, was not a nun, nor even a priest. It was a tall, unkempt figure with a few days' growth of beard and clammy, sweaty skin the colour of parchment, wet clothes sticking to him under a dark blue peacoat. Eleanor opened her arms and John fell forward into them.

'John? My God, what's the matter with you? Are you wounded or just sick? Here, lean on me.' She staggered over to one of the desks, propping John on the chair and supporting him against her so that he did not loll sideways and fall over. He didn't answer her, his eyes glazed over, his mouth hanging slackly as though unconscious. Where had he come from? What was she to do with him? She smoothed the hair back from his forehead, feeling the fever raging in the heat of his skin. There was no wound. Just fever. She looked around her, uncertainly.

There was no one in sight. Not even through the windows of the classroom could she see anyone. They were all going home, wanting their dinner, and the dusk was falling rapidly now. John breathed heavily, coughing, and she held her cheek to his, trying to fight the tears that wanted to fill her eyes and trickle wetly down her face. She must help him. But how? He needed a doctor, and a place to recover, a bed and warm blankets, food. More than any of that, he needed time. This fever could take weeks to burn out, for all she knew. She gave a cry of frustration and urged herself to think!

The night watchman would be doing his first rounds shortly, checking that the doors and windows were all locked and the lights switched off. He would report John to the police immediately, Eleanor knew. He was an unpleasant enough character enjoying his little bit of power, swaggering around in his uniform and swinging his night stick. He would recognize John's face and John would be taken and imprisoned, maybe tortured. Eleanor could barely think for the fear in her chest, tightening with every second.

'John? John, listen to me! You've got to stand up. I can't

377

carry you and we can't stay here. You've got to stand up and walk with me out to the car. Can you do that? Please darling, can you do that?' She was almost pleading and he slowly seemed to straighten, the words penetrating the fog and mists that swirled in his brain. He nodded, placing his hands on the desk and forcing himself upwards. He staggered and Eleanor slid in under his arm, supporting his weight on her as he pushed away from the desk. Slowly, painfully, they made their way to the door.

Eleanor could smell the sweet stench of fever sweat and the gaunt bones of John's ribcage pressed into her side. She wondered how long he had been like this. His skin was yellow and slick with perspiration, both cold and burning, raging hot at the same time. She eased him against the wall and opened the door carefully.

Her car was a long way from the building and she told John to wait while she dashed across the forecourt and climbed into it, bringing it up as close to the building as she could. She hurried out and half supported, half carried him down the few steps and into the back seat of the car. He fell across the bench seat and Eleanor pushed his legs in hurriedly, throwing her raincoat across him. A cardigan was wadded up and placed beneath his head and then the door was shut on him and Eleanor climbed back into the driver's seat and headed out into the deepening evening shadows. Behind her, some distance in the rear, she saw the night watchman come out of his hut and begin to walk across the forecourt towards the schoolroom. Eleanor swung the car out into the rush-hour traffic.

Dr da Silva lived downtown, off the Rua do Ouvidor, less than twenty minutes' drive away. Eleanor was sure he would take John in, for a while, maybe a day or two until she could think of somewhere else to take him. She couldn't take him home. Papa had forbidden John to return to the house, since the last Institutional Act had been passed. He wouldn't risk everyone who lived there just for John's sake, he had said. And Eleanor knew he meant it. She drove carefully, heading for the Avenida Rio Branco.

378

In the back, she heard John murmuring something over and over, calling for someone called Pedro. She didn't know any Pedro. One of his student friends perhaps. She told him he was safe and not to worry and he was quiet again, for a while.

It was dark by the time she pulled into the maze of narrow back lanes off the Rua do Ouvidor and she edged slowly past parked cars, hoping she didn't scrape anything. The last thing she needed was for the police to arrive when she was miles from home, after dark, with a known political agitator in the back of her car.

There were no lights in the lanes and she wished her car lights were better. It was all taking so long and she was desperate to get John inside and cared for as soon as possible. He was delirious now, calling out about bats and chicha and flailing about wildly in the back of the car, the raincoat thrown on to the floor. Eleanor tried to soothe him but it had no effect.

Oh God, it was past eight o'clock, she saw as she glanced down at the dashboard. Everyone would be at home by now and they would be beginning to worry about her. The thought struck her and she felt sick – she hoped they didn't call the police. But no, nobody called the police anymore. When she got to Dr da Silva's, she would call home and let them know she was safe. Oh, please let Dr da Silva be there and let him be kind. Don't let him turn us away. She prayed under her breath as she parked the car tightly against an old stone wall with a brass plate set into it.

Dr da Silva lived in an apartment in part of what had been a huge walled town palácio, the wooden gates that opened on to the inner courtyard set flush into the thick outer walls with a smaller door set into them. It opened when Eleanor pushed against it and she stepped through into the courtyard, threading her way past bicycles and motor scooters towards the far left corner. Dr da Silva's surgery and apartment were on the ground and first floor levels. She pressed the bell and waited, impatiently.

When Dr da Silva finally opened the door, it was obvious

he had been dressing to go out. His dinner jacket swung immaculately back to reveal a snowy, starched evening shirt that glowed in the dark of the courtyard. He was surprised to see Eleanor standing there, her hair in disarray, her face strained and pale.

'Eleanor, my dear, what on earth is the matter? Nothing wrong with your papa, is there? Your mama?' His tone of anxiety sharpened when he mentioned Clarissa.

Eleanor smiled awkwardly. 'No, no. It's John, Dr da Silva. I've got him outside in the car. He's burning up with fever, delirious. I didn't know where else to bring him. Papa won't let him in the house and I can't just take him to a hospital. He's wanted. Can you help me, please, doctor? Please?' Her voice rose in agitation and Dr da Silva swallowed and looked unhappy, glancing out towards the front gates. He looked back at her, soulful, dark circled eyes seeking her understanding in a smooth face.

'But my dear, how can I look after a fugitive? I would lose my licence, go to prison, if anyone found out. I daren't!' He was a small man, fussy and particular in his movements, even in moments of stress like this. He was pulling his cuffs down now, so that the required amount showed whitely under his jacket sleeves, adjusting the cufflinks.

Eleanor wanted to scream. 'Please! I don't know where else to go. At least look at him. I'm scared. He's so sick, and he looks like he's been like this for days. Can't you at least look at him?' she pleaded and he hesitated, glanced around, and nodded abruptly.

'Wait here while I get my bag. I know where we can take him. I shall also have to cancel my evening engagement. I'll be with you in just a moment.'

'Could you – um, could you call Mama, Dr da Silva? They'll be worried about me. Tell them, oh tell them the truth but ask them to keep quiet, for my sake. Speak to Mama. She'll be the easiest. She loves John too. She'll want me to help him.' Eleanor thought that was the best way to enlist the doctor's support. Say Mama cared about John. Then Dr da Silva would be doing this for both of them. She saw his eyes soften at the mention of her mother.

'All right. I shall be five minutes. Perhaps you had better wait for me out in the car. Keep him quiet, for heaven's sake,' he said rapidly and disappeared into the apartment, walking both quickly and pedantically in his own particular manner.

Eleanor returned to John. He was sitting up, staring around him in fright, and Eleanor climbed into the back seat with him.

'It's all right, John, it's all right. Lie back down. I'm here. Come on, that's it, lie back down.' She coaxed him back against the seat cushions, out of sight, kneeling on the floor herself so that she would not attract attention from anyone passing by. The lane seemed deserted but people lived along here and there was a steady passage to and fro at this hour of the evening. She crouched over John, using her handkerchief to wipe the sweat from his face, his hair plastered wetly against his skull. He looked as though he had already died, she thought, and the faint rise and fall of his ribcage was a mistake, a trick of the light. She wrapped the raincoat over him again.

'They've arrested Pedro's father,' John said suddenly and quite distinctly.

Eleanor looked at him in surprise. 'Who's Pedro, John? Is he a friend of yours?' she asked but she saw immediately that he was not awake, the statement made somehow through the delirium that held him hovering beneath consciousness. She stroked his cheek and waited for Dr da Silva to arrive.

The doctor knew her car. He had seen it often enough in the forecourt at home. Now he climbed quickly into the passenger seat and gestured for Eleanor to return to the front seat and drive.

He led her out of the city, north along the coast road, the street lights fading behind them as they drove out between open fields and the dunes of the sea. In time, the fields faded into undergrowth, half-jungle, and the road sped on straight as an arrow and completely deserted. Half an hour later, Dr da Silva indicated a road up on the right and Eleanor took it, wondering where they were going. The road was little more than a track and it led in amongst the dunes and across flat marshes, winding its way narrower and narrower. The doctor was being uncommunicative, telling her to wait and see. He was nervous, glancing around and behind them constantly, to see if they were being followed. Eleanor wished he would sit still.

Finally the track petered out completely and a small shack of a house became visible nestled in amongst the dunes and grasses, gleaming palely in the moonlight. Between them, they half carried, half led John towards the shack, letting him slump on to the verandah while the doctor checked around one last time and unlocked the door. He pushed it wide and they carried John in and laid him on an old sofa, the springs protesting even at his emaciated weight.

Dr da Silva then disappeared into another room, emerging with two kerosene lamps that he lit quickly and efficiently. He placed one on a hook on the wall near the sofa and brought up a stool on which to sit.

'Whose place is this, Dr da Silva?' Eleanor asked, as she looked around.

The doctor looked up and smiled. 'I don't know. Nobody's, really. Or maybe mine, now. I come here sometimes to get away from – all that.' He waved his hand in the direction of the city. 'I found this shack, abandoned, and I fixed it up a bit, brought in some furniture. Nothing I care about if anyone ever turns up to claim the place. And I just take it easy here, go for walks, birdwatch, read. It's very peaceful,' he added, meaningfully, as he looked John over, probing his liver and spleen, poking hard fingers into sensitive areas, palpating in strict order of rotation. John groaned.

'Hmm. He'll need lots of bed-rest, lot of fluids, quinine. I'll give him a double dose now and you can give him the rest on a daily basis. He's had this fever before, I take it?' From the yellowness of John's skin, the fever was obviously well along.

382

'Yes, I think so. He mentioned having a pretty bad bout of it a couple of years ago, out in the Backlands. The Indians kept him alive, gave him their medicines, but I think it recurs from time to time. Especially in the rainy season. Is he going to be all right?' She was bending over John, soothing him with her touch, and Dr da Silva watched her uncomfortably. She stroked her cousin's face lovingly – like a lover. He snapped his black bag shut.

'In time, yes, I think so. Maybe not for a long time. You'll have to look after him well, make sure he takes the quinine and the fluids. No alcohol, of course. The rest is in God's hands.' He sighed. 'I'll have to take your car back to town. I'll return it to your house and tell your husband exactly where you are. If I can, I'll come out and see you on Friday night. Be very careful, Eleanor. If you see someone coming, whom you don't recognize, go and hide in the sand dunes. You understand?' He saw she was looking up at him in consternation now, her mouth open.

'But – I can't stay with John! I thought you would stay with him, Dr da Silva. Until we can find some of his – friends, to take over. I have a school to run and a family and – I can't stay!' She felt panicked at the thought.

'Well, my dear, neither can I. I have a practice to run. You can leave him here, without anyone, if you like. But I don't know if he will make it. He needs care and time. And a lot of both of them. You should have thought of all that when you brought him to me.' He sounded reproving, chiding her as though she were still a ten-year-old child who had made a thoughtless remark.

Eleanor flushed and looked down at John. 'Then I suppose I must stay. I can't leave him alone.' Her voice became thick, blurred with emotion that she would not show. 'Thank you for what you've done, Dr da Silva. I'm sorry if it's put you in a difficult situation but I couldn't think who else to turn to. Mama will be grateful too.' She held out her hand and the doctor shook it, smiling awkwardly.

'I'm sorry to leave you here. But I don't expect it will be

383

for long. Your husband will, no doubt, come after you quickly enough. And bring extra hands. Well, I must be going. Help yourself to whatever is there. I'll bring more supplies on Friday, if I can. Goodbye, Eleanor.' He had been edging towards the door for most of his last speech, and now he made it out on to the verandah and escaped.

Eleanor stood in the middle of the room for some time after the doctor had gone, listening to the night sounds, hearing the distant pounding of the sea on the shore, the rushing wind between the dunes and the soughing of the grasses. It was soothing in its blankness. Then she snapped herself out of her reverie and went to see to John.

His clothes must come off, she thought, and it would be better if he were in a proper bed. She explored the rest of the shack with the aid of the kerosene lamp, and found a bedroom near the rear with a mattress of striped ticking rolled up neatly at the foot of the wooden bed frame. There were sheets in the cupboard, and she quickly made the bed, thinking how damp the sheets felt in the salt air.

But the doctor, it seemed, had thought of that too because, in the back of the cupboard under another set of sheets, was a hot water bottle, smelling unpleasantly of rubber and metal. She carried it through into the kitchen and heated some water on the gas top, exploring impatiently while she waited for the water to boil. Butane bottles kept the cooker going but there was no water piped into the house. All the water was in large rainwater drums by the back door. There were basic supplies in the kitchen cupboards, enough to allow her to live out of the few tins there until fresh supplies came. The doctor had never bothered to furnish the shack with more than essentials for a day or two. Certainly his wife had never accompanied him out here, while she was alive. Eleanor wasn't sure what sort of bathroom there was, and imagined, rightly, the worst. But, for now, it was a sanctuary. And she gave thanks for that small mercy.

The hot water bottle filled and rubbed over the sheets to take the chill from them, Eleanor returned to the front room for John. She wished she could give him a bath but it would take too long to heat the water and, right now, what he needed was bed. He stumbled along beside her into the bedroom and submitted meekly enough to her stripping his damp clothes from him and wiping him down with a flannel of hot water. Then she lay him back against the pillows and piled an eiderdown on to him, that had also been rolled up in the cupboard. The doctor liked some creature comforts, clearly. John lay quietly against the pillows, his mouth partly open, his breathing shallow and ragged. Eleanor pulled the eiderdown up around his chin.

She was cold herself and she returned yet again to the kitchen to make them both some hot tea. The night air was falling dank and chill now, through the open door, and she shut it and bolted it, shivering in the mist. She had left her cardigan in the car and wore nothing more than a thin blouse and trousers, both damp and soiled where they had brushed up against John. But Henry would come soon. She knew he would. With a start, she heard the kettle begin to wail.

Chapter Nineteen

It was nearly midnight by the time the doctor arrived at the Palácio Lampedusca but the lights still blazed brightly in the house. He was admitted quickly and Henry met him in the hallway, forestalling his entry to the drawing-room where the others were gathered.

'Dr da Silva. Thank God. Where's Eleanor? Isn't she with you?' Henry was pale with anger and the doctor viewed him cautiously.

'I am afraid not, Henry. It was necessary that someone stay with John. He is very ill. I came back with Eleanor's car to tell you how you may reach your wife. You see here, I have made a little map for you.' He handed over a piece of paper. 'But, if I may make a suggestion, I would not consider travelling the roads tonight. There are many road-blocks, many police checks. Perhaps they are expecting trouble, I do not know, but it would be better if you did not travel until the morning. Safer. I, myself, will trouble you to call a taxi. A late evening, too much wine – a taxi is perfectly understandable.' He was precise and calm, not allowing Henry's ill mood to deflect him from his purpose. He was uncomfortable when Henry pressed him, further.

'Just how sick is John? What's wrong with him?' Henry

demanded and the thought was there, between both men, that Henry did not entirely trust his wife.

Dr da Silva shrugged. 'Too sick to stand. Too sick to be left alone. He may take weeks to recover his strength. Your wife is very brave and loyal, staying alone with him, which she did not want to do. I'm sure you must be proud of her.' He barely smiled, the irony tinging his words.

Henry stiffened and looked away. 'Dr da Silva! There you are! Henry, why didn't you bring the doctor through? Please, you must be in need of a drink after such a night. Do come in.' Clarissa came out of the drawing-room to discover the delay and took the doctor by the arm and led him through. Henry, coldly furious, walked behind.

The next half hour was difficult for the doctor and he hoped, sincerely, never to have to repeat it. The house had been split into factions, Charles Fawcett, Henry, Isobel and some young woman, whose role in the house the doctor could not quite fathom, called Sophie, aligned on one side and his own beloved, the Senhora Fawcett, and her son-in-law Louis Preston on the other.

Dr da Silva had not wanted to be in the middle but that was, unquestionably, where they placed him and the atmosphere had been unpleasant. The husband, Henry, was most unlike his normal self. There must be problems there, in that marriage, that no one knows about, the doctor thought to himself. This matter of Eleanor and John. There had always been rumours. Perhaps, just perhaps, they were true. Why otherwise would Henry behave in such a fashion when he was normally such a charming young man? But, the doctor thought hastily, he wanted nothing more to do with it. Let the family sort out their own problems. Dr da Silva cast languishing eyes at Clarissa and was relieved when his taxi arrived.

Clarissa, as usual, saw the doctor to the door while the rest of the household continued to argue in the drawing-room. Henry cut across what Louis was saying about family ties with an abruptness that Louis had never seen in his brother-in-law before.

'I don't care whether John is twice as much family as the rest of us, he's still putting my wife in danger. That's what we're talking about here. Eleanor. My wife! And that makes my opinion the one that matters.' He stabbed a finger at his own chest and Louis sat down, looking away.

'If it weren't for the fact that Eleanor's with him, I'd turn him into the police myself,' Charles said angrily from his corner of the room and was instantly rounded upon by everyone, their voices rising one over the other to be heard. Isobel stamped her feet, Louis threw down the book he had been pretending to look at and Charles waved the fire irons angrily above his head. Sophie was alarmed and, finally, Henry held up his hand for peace.

'Look, what we've got to do is find some way of getting to John's companions. Find a couple of them who'll look after him. Then I can persuade Eleanor to leave and, once she's home and safe, I'll make sure she stays that way. Dr da Silva was right, there's no safe way to get to Eleanor tonight without being conspicuous out there on the roads. I'll go out there tomorrow. Louis, do what you can, will you? You know his crowd better than any of us here.' He saw Louis nod.

'And what if you can't find any friends of John? Is Eleanor going to continue to stay out there? Who's supposed to look after Katherine or the precious school? Or does John always come first?' Sophie said from where she sat, near the door, and saw Henry's lips tighten angrily. Good. She sat up straighter, looking from one to the other. This is the real issue here, her eyes seemed to say. She saw they all knew it.

'Sophie, my dear, I hardly think this discussion involves you, does it?' Clarissa's voice cut through sharply and Sophie turned in surprise, not having heard Clarissa's return. She looked contrite.

'I'm sorry, Mrs Fawcett. I didn't mean ...' Her eyes flinched and she hunched over in her chair, holding her hands tightly together.

'Leave her alone, Clarissa, for God's sake! What she says

is perfectly true and we all know it,' Henry said abruptly. He stood in the middle of the room, one hand massaging his forehead. The others looked at him with embarrassment, not wanting him to say any more. But he could not be stopped. The anger and the hurt overrode normal restraints. Henry shook his head, as though admitting the truth at long last.

'John always comes first, even before Eleanor's own child, even before me!' he said quietly, and then he stared around the room, smiling sourly. 'Doesn't he?' When they didn't answer, Henry turned and walked out of the room. For a moment no one knew what to say.

Then Isobel remarked acidly, 'It's taken Henry this long to realize that? I thought he was supposed to be the bright one in the family.' She subsided when she saw both Clarissa and Louis give her a withering look.

Charles turned to confront his wife. 'Now, now do you see, Clarissa? He's doing it again, breaking this family apart, setting us one against the other. I've always said that boy was like the devil, bringing no one any good. I won't have him set foot on this property, ever again. Do you all understand me? Even if he's dying, he won't die here!' he cried furiously and then bent over, coughing and holding his chest. Clarissa hurried over to him, soothing and helping him to swallow his tablets. Everyone paused for a moment. Sophie looked down at her hands, contemplatively, waiting for the argument to start up again. When it did, she slipped from her place near the door, and went to look for Henry.

Eleanor took the tea back into the bedroom and put it on the nightstand, leaning over to see if John slept. His face was turned into the pillow, relaxed and, for the moment, undisturbed by dreams and deliriums. She drank the tea herself, sitting beside him. The heat of the liquid through the china warmed her hands as she cupped them around the mug. Let him sleep. It was the best thing for him.

It was curious the way no matter how much time passed

389

between them, no matter how often they were apart or what was said in anger when they were together, they both turned automatically to each other for help. And knew they would receive it. John had found her somehow, in his sickness, and now that he knew she was there, he had abandoned his fight to remain conscious and had slipped away in the fever, knowing she was there to care for him. Such absolute trust must have been built up between them as children, she thought, because it was inside them as deeply and irrevocably as the blood running through their veins. She caressed his cheek but he didn't stir.

Now that she knew she would miss her classes the next morning or even for several days, she felt a sense of release. Someone else could do the worrying, plan the classes, mark the homework. For a few days Henry would have to be without his perfect wife who was there for him every evening, dressed for dinner. Even little Katherine would have to miss her mother, just for a few days. That was the only regret Eleanor had. She saw little enough of her daughter as it was. If it weren't so dangerous, she would ask Henry to bring Katherine back with him the next time. What could be nicer than to spend a few days alone with her two favourite people? But Henry would never agree. She sighed and set down the mug.

There was nowhere for her to sleep, and no extra blankets either. She would have to share John's bed tonight. Like old times. But not really. She smiled ruefully to herself and then, turning the wick down on the lamp, slipped into bed beside John. It was warm under the quilt and she knew John would be unaware of her presence. She curled into his back and closed her eyes.

'Henry? Are you in there?' Sophie tapped softly against Henry's bedroom door. She had already checked the library and the nursery. He had to be in his bedroom. She tapped again. 'Henry, it's me, Sophie.'

The door opened without Sophie hearing anyone approach and Henry stood there in his shirt sleeves, looking tired and upset. He tried to smile at Sophie but it was a poor effort.

'What is it, Sophie? Is there more news?' he asked, the hope there in his eyes that perhaps Eleanor had come home.

Sophie shook her head. 'No, I'm sorry. I just – wanted to be sure you were all right? I'm only an outsider, I know – Clarissa certainly pointed that out – but Eleanor and I've known each other a long time now. I just wondered whether you wanted to talk? I'd do anything to make you feel better.' She was tiny and delicate, her face puckered winsomely, a solitary tear trickling down her cheek.

Henry sighed and opened his arms, hugging her to him. 'Don't cry, Sophie. Shh, it's all right. I'll find Eleanor tomorrow. There's nothing to cry about.' He was surprised how protective he felt towards her, her tiny figure making him feel strong and in control. He hadn't felt like that for a long time.

Sophie was crying harder now and Henry brought her into his room and closed the door, leading her over to the small sofa by the window.

'Come on now, Sophie, chin up. It'll be fine, I promise you. Now sit down and take a deep breath. Here, use my handkerchief.' He sat beside her on the sofa, gently wiping the tears away from those huge, clear eyes that always reminded him of water running over grey granite. They blinked wetly at him.

'I'm not crying about Eleanor, I'm crying about you,' she murmured and Henry stilled for a moment, staring at her.

'Me? Why me? I'm quite safe,' he said quizzically.

'But you're being so badly treated. You do everything for Eleanor – for everyone in this family, and all they can think about is themselves. Eleanor doesn't love you. She only loves John, just like she always has. Just like when he came to Paris and they pretty much threw me out of the apartment so they could be together. I could kill Eleanor sometimes, the way she treats you and Katherine. She got everything, the best of everything and she doesn't care, just

391

goes running after her lover as always, never stopping to think how much hurt she's putting you through.' Her voice broke and she cried some more, leaning in against Henry who cradled her against him almost absentmindedly, stunned by what Sophie had said.

John had been in Paris, had been Eleanor's lover? When? How could it have possibly happened? He stared down at the dark curls, soothing the girl who hiccupped and sobbed against him.

'Sophie, I don't understand. Are you telling me they're lovers? I find it hard enough to believe they ever once were, but that they are now? No, I can't believe it. Eleanor would never do that to me.' His voice quivered, the hurt so real and so near the surface that he couldn't think, his mind churning around and around in turmoil. He looked at Sophie who lifted her head. Her face was tragic, the small nose pink, the mouth trembling, the eyes staring at him from behind a ring of wet lashes. She didn't answer him. Just stared.

Henry groaned and closed his eyes, holding his head in his hands. 'No, no. It's not possible – she wouldn't! Oh God! God, what do I do now? Eleanor! God damn you!' He felt Sophie stroke his back, murmuring consolation and the first bitter, heavy tears filled his eyes.

Then it was Sophie's turn to hold him against her while he cried, in anguish and anger, and when, some time later, he felt her cheek against his, he found it natural to hold tightly to her, to press his cheek against her soft skin. He wasn't sure quite how it came about, but Sophie was there, loving and comforting, and her arms were so very tender, her lips so very gentle that he was kissing her and then more, and the pain and humiliation were lessened and for the moment there was no guilt. He picked Sophie up in his arms and carried her to his bed.

The dawn was cold and grey, washing over the room and picking out the bareness, the cracked woodwork, the fading paint on the walls. Eleanor lay beside John, feeling the shivers that racked his body, and the clamminess of the sheets. She touched his forehead. It was hot.

Her watch said it was just after seven and she pulled back the covers, sliding out on to the cold boards. The chill hit her and she shivered herself. Would Henry think to bring extra clothes for both of them? Or would he assume she would be returning with him immediately? That thought had worried her through most of the night. Someone had to look after John. Someone who cared. She wasn't leaving there, no matter what Henry said, until they found a good enough replacement. She slipped her feet into her shoes and wandered through into the kitchen with the clothes that John had been wearing piled up in her arms.

There was a copper pot outside the back that she could fill with water and boil the clothes in. The sooner they were washed and dry again, the better. At least then John could be mobile, if he had to be. She busied herself in the kitchen, putting on the kettle to boil, searching for something to eat, and rearranging the mess the doctor had left on previous occasions. For someone as fastidious as Dr da Silva, she was surprised at the disarray throughout the house. But then, this was his escape. Why should he be tidy here too?

The bathroom was nothing more than a washstand with a tin basin and jug and a shower in the corner, water poured into a receptacle suspended near the ceiling that worked on a stop-cock basis. Pull on a chain and the water ran straight down into the showerhead and then through a hole in the floor to the ground below, dissipating in the sand beneath the house. Ingenious, she thought, and wondered whether the doctor had thought of it himself. The lavatory was a tin bucket into which sand could be ladled after each use, or a small shed outside the house that smelt abominably and which Eleanor refused to look inside. She would cope with the bucket.

She filled the container above the shower with warm water and stepped out of her clothes, hanging them up to air. She couldn't wash her clothes and John's at the same time or there would be no one to greet any visitors who might call. But, as the morning wore on and she had showered and dressed again without any sign of company, Eleanor began to feel as though she and John were lost in their own particular sand-duned world, and that no one would ever come that way again. She grew weary of looking out of the windows towards the track, weary of seeing nothing but sand and grass and grey sky. She wrung John's clothes out and hung them up to dry, and then carried a bowl of hot water through to the bedroom. Time to bathe him down again.

He was awake when she entered the room, listlessly staring at the ceiling. He smiled weakly when he saw her approach.

'Hullo there. How're you feeling?' Eleanor said in pleased surprise. She lay the basin down on the bedside table and went to feel John's forehead. It was still hot.

'Aching, irritable, tired, the usual list. I'll live,' he said and she smiled quickly, in response. His voice was husky from lack of use and dehydration.

'Well, while you're still awake, how about some medicine?' She poured out a glass of water from the pitcher beside the bed and added the quinine drops. 'Here, get this down and I'll get you some soup and biscuits. They're a bit stale and the soup's from a tin. Makes me miss Maria,' she said and John smiled again, drinking the cordial down without anything more than a sour face. He lay back against the pillow, exhausted by that simple act.

When Eleanor returned a few moments later, his eyes were shut and she wondered whether he had fallen asleep again. His face was so thin, she thought uneasily, thin and yellow and totally defenceless. He opened his eyes, catching her staring at him.

'What?' he asked. Eleanor shrugged and sat down beside him, holding the bowl up to him so she could spoon the soup into his mouth. He didn't have the energy to feed himself.

'You look like you've been ill for a while,' she said after he had managed to swallow a few spoonfuls. 'Why didn't you come to me sooner?' She held up the spoon but he shook his head.

'I didn't want to involve you,' he said and sighed, deeply. He closed his eyes again and seemed to sink deeper into the pillow, relaxing his whole body.

'Can you manage any more? A biscuit maybe?' she coaxed but he shook his head, rolling it slowly and deliberately so that he would not have to speak. Eleanor put the tray aside and wrung out the flannel in the bowl of hot water. 'Here, this'll make you feel better.' She wiped his face, pushing the hair back from his forehead, running the flannel down to his chest. She saw him open his eyes again, the lids heavy over a narrowed slit of deep blue. He watched her, a faint smile on his lips, as she washed the rest of his body down and then towelled him briskly dry. When the eiderdown was once more tucked in around him, he swallowed and dredged a voice up from somewhere within him.

'You won't go away anywhere, will you, before I wake up again?' She saw the fear lurking in his eyes, in the tenseness of his neck. There was a bluish tinge around his mouth that told of exhaustion.

She shook her head. 'No, I'll be right here. I promise. She leaned over and kissed his cheek, smoothing hers against it. 'Go to sleep, John.' And he closed his eyes and drifted away.

She sat watching him for several minutes, wishing they could go back to childhood again. Lately that was an all too frequent if silly wish.

'Very touching,' a voice said from behind her shoulder and Eleanor turned around anxiously. She didn't recognize the man who leaned in the doorway, his skin swarthy, a beak-like nose dominating his face.

She drew in her breath sharply. 'Who're you? What d'you want here?' Instinctively she rose and blocked his view of the bed.

The man seemed amused. 'Don't worry, Eleanor – it is Eleanor, isn't it? But yes, you look so very much like John.

I'm Pedro.' His eyebrows rose as he saw recognition in her face. 'John has told you about me?'

'Not really. Just – he mentioned your name a few times and said something about your father being arrested. Is that right?' She was tentative, not sure if he could be trusted or not. Pedro's face became blank, only the eyes still darting their dark, liquid messages. Eleanor wasn't sure what they meant.

'Yes. But he will be released again. He is a difficult man to hold without good reason. I came as soon as I could be spared. Is John very ill?' He was approaching the bed now, walking around the other side so that Eleanor could not step in front of him. She watched him carefully, half expecting some signal of his would bring armed men bursting into the room, John's life given in exchange for this man's father. She narrowed her eyes, searching for a weapon. Only the water pitcher came to mind.

Pedro glanced at her impatiently. 'Relax, Eleanor, please. I am John's friend.' With gentle, sensitive fingers, he felt for John's pulse and pulled back his eyelids, peering at the pupils beneath, the colour of the whites. He checked John's temperature quickly and sighed.

'You have quinine? Good, that's a start. Has he been conscious at all?' Pedro seemed quietly efficient and Eleanor began to wonder, as she told him about John, whether he was a doctor himself. Perhaps he could take over and she could return, shortly, to her husband and baby? The thought was curiously unappealing.

'Well then, I'd say everything's been done that could be done. It's just a matter of bed-rest now. You can handle that, I assume?' Pedro said finally and Eleanor stared at him.

'I thought my husband sent you to look after John? Are you telling me you're not staying?' she demanded and she saw him flush slightly.

'I owe my family some time, right now. You can look after John perfectly well. And, to answer your question, no, your husband did not send me. I heard, via various people, that Louis Preston was looking for me and so I called him. He told me John was here and needed help. I wouldn't have bothered to risk coming all this way if I knew you were here,' he added, as though he felt he had been duped.

Eleanor shook her head. 'Hold on. I'm confused. How did you know who I was if Louis didn't tell you?'

'John has a picture of you. He showed me once. Besides, I told you, you look like him.' He watched her steadily and Eleanor flushed and looked away.

'How did John get this sick? Why didn't anyone else help him? One of your other friends?' she asked, her voice choked and awkward.

He sighed and walked over to the window, leaning on the wall as he looked out. 'We were all supposed to attend a meeting – a secret political meeting – in São Paulo. But just before John and I got there he became sick again, chills, fevers, even convulsions. Halfway through his speech he collapsed, so I took him to – to a safe place and went back to the meeting to speak instead. But, by the time I returned, someone had tipped the guarda off and the place was surrounded. I got away but most of our friends didn't. Some of them were killed, some taken by the guarda. Perhaps it would have been better for them to have been killed. They will disappear now, and we will never know. Those that got away like me, well, who can say? They're hidden all over the place, I expect, frightened to even breathe in case someone denounces them.' His voice was bitter.

'I got John back to Rio but then I heard about my father and I had to leave John to fend for himself. He seemed better by then and he told me he'd be fine. I had no idea he was still this sick.' He scratched his nose and looked back into the room.

'There isn't anyone else to look after him right now. You're his family – and his ...' he hesitated. 'Well, you know better than anyone what you mean to each other. You'll have to stay with him. I need to be with my family right now. They're not finished with my father yet, I

397

suspect. It is difficult for me to help, when I am on a list but I will do my best.'

'I see. I'm sorry, I had no idea about all this. Did, did Louis say whether anyone else in my family would be coming out here? I've been expecting my husband all night and all morning and it's after two o'clock now. He should've been here by now.' She looked worried when Pedro shook his head.

'Look, I've got some supplies in the car, quinine, some blankets and food and extra clothes. I wasn't sure what sort of place this was. It's a lot better than I could've hoped for. Maybe we can use it again in the future.' He grinned for the first time and Eleanor realized then just how young he was. About the same age as herself.

She smiled. 'Yes, nice and secluded. Just don't use the bathroom. I'll come and help you bring the things in. Tell me, are you a doctor, by any chance?' She saw him glance at her in surprise.

'I was studying medicine when all this happened.' He waved his arms out wide, encompassing all the atrocities of the last two years.

Eleanor nodded. 'Will you ever finish your studies?' She was walking beside him out to the car and, for a moment, he looked up at the sky, dull and leaden like unpolished pewter.

'One day, maybe. If we all live. But for now, I am a fugitive − like John. And life does not progress smoothly under those conditions. Take care you don't end up on a list too.' He carried the boxes from the car and stacked them quickly, almost angrily on the verandah, not allowing the conversation to continue. Eleanor felt guilty for the luxury of the normal life she lived. Guilty that she was not in fear every day of her life, like these men. She bit her lip and said nothing more.

When the last box was stacked by her feet, Pedro looked up at her curiously. 'I always wondered what you were like. Give John my regards when he wakes,' he said abruptly and then he walked back to the car, raised his arm in salute, and slammed the door after him. The car rocked and bounced off into the distance, lost to sight as it rounded a corner and disappeared behind a sand dune.

Eleanor stood staring after him. What had he meant by that? What had he wondered about her? She didn't like to think. Shaking her head, she turned and picked up the first box. At least now they could be warm and eat.

By dusk, Eleanor was seriously worried. Why hadn't Henry come? What could possibly have held him up? Could he have had an important case in court where not to appear might have made everyone suspicious? Or perhaps he thought she would be relieved by Pedro and would have found her own way back? But no, Henry would never leave her to manage like this – unless, he was so angry with her that he didn't want anything more to do with her? The thought, unconsidered until now, of how much trouble she would face when she returned home, left her breathless and trembling. Papa would be livid and Henry too. That must be why he hadn't come. He was too angry with her. She swallowed and finished unpacking the last box and stood up, brushing her hands down her trousers.

'Well, damn Henry and damn Papa too,' she said aloud and crossed her arms defiantly. But, even to herself, the quiver in her voice was apparent. She stared out at the gathering night, her lips tightly compressed.

'I've already told you, Captain Almeida, we haven't seen John in years. Not since my sister-in-law, Isobel's, wedding in, when was it? December 1962? The family doesn't get on well with him and Senhor Fawcett has forbidden John to ever return to this house. I don't understand the purpose of all this questioning, yet again.' Henry had been elected spokesman and the captain of the guarda civil was trying to be polite. It was obviously an effort.

'So you say, Senhor Arreas. So you say.' He looked around, glancing one by one at the others gathered in the drawing-room. Counting them. 'And your wife, senhor?

Where is she?' For a small man, the captain was imposing. It was there in the self-importance of his stance, the heavy-lidded stare, the fleshy, determined lips. Henry remained calm.

'My wife is visiting friends in São Paulo. She will be back in a few days. Why? Are we under arrest, captain? On what charge?'

'No, you are not under arrest, senhor. You are very quick to assume the worst.' The captain smiled without showing his teeth. 'But I would like to talk with your wife. She is – close to her cousin, isn't she? The one most close to him in the family, so I understand. It is natural I should want to speak to her. And yet, she isn't here. How very unfortunate.' His eyes glinted beneath a drape of skin, dark pouches beneath the eye sockets making him look ill.

Henry shrugged. 'If we had anything to hide, captain, we would have made sure my wife were here to speak with you. As we had no idea we would be called upon to answer yet more questions about John, I am afraid we did not take any precautions and my wife is visiting friends. It's that simple. As I said, she will be back in a few days and I will be happy to bring her along to your office to answer any questions you might think of in the meantime. Is there anything further, captain?'

For a moment it looked as though the captain would give way before Henry's determination. But then, looking round, he clicked his fingers at the two men standing in the hall.

'Search the place,' he snapped and turned back to confront the people standing before him. He detested this sort. Weak, pampered, fina gente with no backbone for the fight they financed and spread. He smiled. 'No objections, are there?' He wasn't surprised when there weren't. 'Good. And, these friends in São Paulo, you have their name and address, I would assume? Please be so good as to write it down for me here.' He held out his notepad and Henry breathed deeply, the tension reaching his shoulders. He almost snatched the pad from the captain. Thank God he knew the de Souzas were away up in Brasília this week. He

400

would give their name and hope for the best. Damn Eleanor and damn John! This had gone too far.

'Here. But I'm not sure whether they will be there or not. They mentioned taking a trip into the interior while Eleanor was with them, so they may be away. You will no doubt check that out yourself.' Henry turned away from the captain and went to sit down at the desk, trying to control the trembling in his limbs. He glanced up at Louis who half grimaced.

'Really? How convenient. Then you will understand perfectly that, should I not be able to contact your wife, senhor, then you and everyone else in this house,' the captain bowed to them all in a mixture of courtesy and mockery that marked his whole demeanor, 'will remain here under house arrest until such time as her return. Please,' he raised his hand, 'please don't think I do not appreciate how difficult this is for everyone but we know John Campos de Serra is here in Rio and we know he is ill. Who else would he turn to but his own family? It is natural. And I want the man in custody. So, that is how things must be. You will excuse me, I trust?' The captain bowed again and left the room.

No one said anything, Henry's quickly raised hands preventing the outburst that was threatened on all sides. He stood up and went to look outside the door. A guarda looked back at him impassively. Henry closed the door and returned to the others.

'There's nothing we can do. They're not going to believe John isn't or wasn't here and they're not going to believe Eleanor isn't with him, until she returns here. So we'll just have to be patient for a few days. Isobel, you perhaps should check on the children. The men might scare them. I don't know whether Sophie's thought to go to them or whether she's still in her room. And Clarissa, would you be so kind as to fetch Charles's pills? He's looking a little strained.' Henry crossed to stand by Charles, frowning with concern into his father-in-law's face. He pressed his fingers insistently in Charles's arm.

401

'Yes, of course. Darling? Are you all right?' Clarissa was worried and would have tried to flutter concernedly around her husband, but he waved her away in irritation.

'Fine, fine. Go and get the pills.' He sat heavily in the chair Henry led him over to and Clarissa gave another worried look and went off to fetch the pills. Isobel accompanied her.

As soon as they had left, Henry pulled out a piece of paper and wrote on it. 'Keep talking normally. Indignant. Deny all.' He flashed it under Charles's and Louis's noses and then threw it into the fire. Instantly he began writing another note as Louis broke into a monologue and began to earn his reputation as a first-rate debater. Charles was happy to fill in any gaps in the conversation. Occasionally they appealed to Henry who grunted morosely, or said, 'I'm thinking', or 'What the hell am I going to do about my court cases?' where appropriate. He finished writing and passed it to each in turn, before again throwing it into the fire and stirring the ashes with the poker.

The note read as follows: 'Charles is going to become sick. Heart trouble. Dr da Silva will have to be called and Charles can tell him to contact Eleanor and get her back here in a few days with her story ready. The de Souzas must be warned somehow – I will give Dr da Silva a note to send to them in Brasília, explaining all. For God's sake, keep calm and remember we are innocent. Tell Isobel and Clarissa when you can do so quietly. They may be listening at keyholes, for all we know.'

'Ah, here's Clarissa now. Louis, can you get some water? I don't know whether they're questioning the servants or not, but I expect Maria'll be a little anxious right now. Reassure them all, if you can. Come on, Charles, just sit quietly and take deep breaths.' Henry spoke clearly, for the benefit of the guarda outside the door. Charles leaned back against the chair and began to look convincingly ill. Henry wondered how often he had faked it before.

Isobel and Sophie had not returned yet. For a moment Henry felt a sickness rise in his throat at what he had done

402

last night. How was he to explain to Sophie that it had just been a moment of weakness, despair? How could he explain to Eleanor? But then, she was with her lover right now, so there was no need for any explanations there. After all, if it weren't for Eleanor and John, they wouldn't be under house arrest, and their lives would not be in danger. He owed Eleanor nothing.

The anger helped assuage the guilt and Henry continued to pace the room, glancing around it as though he were seeing it all for the first time. Now that they were so close to losing all, he realized how much he considered this room to be his home. This was the heart of the palácio, with its tall ceilings and dark woodwork, its tapestries and oriental rugs, its beautiful porcelains and mahogany furniture. A gracious, formal room that still managed to create a feeling of warmth and belonging. He wondered how much longer they would call this home. Long enough for his children to grow up there? Or only a few more days? It was an unsettling thought.

John woke again in the evening and his temperature seemed to be down, his fever chills less severe. Eleanor had found an old windchime on the verandah and had brought it through to the bedroom for him to ring when he needed her. With her help, he was able to make it into the bathroom, although he was still weak and had to lean on her. His body was gaunt, the belly stretched taut, the ribs showing clearly. Naked, he looked even more ill than dressed. But neither of them was embarrassed by Eleanor having to help him. It seemed natural to them both.

When John was back in bed, Eleanor gave him another hot wash-down with a flannel and fed him some more soup and medicine. He managed to eat more this time, even a little bread, and Eleanor was encouraged. She tucked him in tightly again and sat beside him.

'Pedro came to see you today. Did you know about the meeting? About the guarda being there?' She held his hand, rubbing her thumb over his knuckles absentmindedly.

John sighed. 'Yes. I know. Pedro got me away. How is he, how's his father?' His eyes were on her, trying to understand the tension he felt in her. She was more fearful now, than earlier in the day. Had Pedro said something to her?

'He seems to think they'll let his father go. I don't know much more than that. He didn't stay long. He said his family needed him right now.' She smiled and squeezed his hand tightly. 'So, it looks like it'll just be you and me again, for a while. Like old times.' There was a nervous note in her voice and John stilled her hand, pulling her in closer.

'What is it? What's wrong?' he asked. Eleanor knew she could not deceive John. She didn't try.

'Henry hasn't come. No one in the family's been out to see me – us – at all. I can't think why, unless they don't want anything more to do with – all this.' She looked at him.

He was staring at her, his eyes worried. 'They won't cut you off, Eleanor. They'll never do that. You go back tomorrow, all right? And I'll be fine here. I'm better already.' And he was. Much better. But still not strong enough to stand unaided, still not strong enough to feed himself. Even now he was beginning to fade, the colour bleaching out of his face, the yellow becoming more prominent.

Eleanor shook her head. 'No. Not until you're well. I don't really miss any of them, anyway, except for Katherine. Oh, I wish she were out here too! Wouldn't that be lovely, just the three of us?' She smiled and John smiled back, his eyelids beginning to droop.

'Go back soon then, before you don't want to,' he said and closed his eyes. It was odd, Eleanor thought, how he always read her thoughts. But it wasn't just her choice. Did he still want her? It was years since they had discussed anything of the sort. She didn't know how he felt anymore. Only how she did. She left him sleeping and went to fill the hot water bottle.

The day dragged on, much the same as the one before. But this time no one arrived to break the monotony. The weather began to clear from the east, a blazing red sunset promising a beautiful day to come and the waterfowl flocking back from further inland where they had been waiting out the storm. Seagulls keened over the dunes, swooping and shrieking over the scraps Eleanor threw out in the sand. The air was warmer and moist, rolling into mist as night fell and seeping through the cracks in the windows. Eleanor wrapped herself in a warm jumper and sat on the sofa, trying to think.

Not about why Henry hadn't come or whether they would all be angry with her when she finally returned. Eleanor had thought all that through before and come to no good answers there. No, she was thinking about the future. What did she really want out of life? Was it enough for her to continue to be Henry's wife and to live with her parents as if she were no more than a child herself? Was it enough to teach a few people what little she knew? Was that the sum of her life? And what about children? Henry wanted more and she knew she couldn't hold him off forever. But their lovemaking now was infrequent and carefully restrained, so that she almost flinched away when he leaned over to touch her in the night, knowing what he wanted. She loved Katherine but could she bear to have any more children by Henry?

She stopped, shocked by those last two words that circled in her mind. By Henry. Who else would she have children by? If at all? She stood up abruptly and walked over to the windows, staring out at the blackness that enveloped the land and sea and sky in one inky, impenetrable bag. She was trapped in that bag, fighting to find a way out. And terrified of looking towards the opening, where the light shone brightest for her. Angry with herself, she walked up and down, trying not to think what she had been thinking. But it was there, hinting, tantalizing, licking its way around the corners of her mind, ready to jump out at her and say, ha! Here I am! See!

The kitchen seemed a perfect retreat. She would put some tea on. John would need some more soup soon and

405

perhaps, perhaps ... But the thought of John had brought it all back, and she knew there was no stopping herself now, knew the idea was fully formed and ready to be looked at. Reluctantly she let it in. What if she were to have a baby by John?

In the morning, Eleanor began to clean the shack. She pushed all the furniture into one corner of the sitting-room and swept the floors and then scrubbed them, wiped down the woodwork, cleaned the windows and beat the rugs. She picked grasses and weeds and arranged them in large, unrestrained bunches in old jars she found in the kitchen and even carried some through into the sick room. John was better again and Eleanor filled a tin tub with hot water and let him soak in it, while she changed the bed linen and aired the quilt. Then she dressed him in pyjamas that Pedro had brought, his long, bony limbs protruding well beyond the pyjama sleeves and legs. She combed his newly washed hair back from his face and shaved the fuzz from his face and was surprised at how much better he looked. She kissed him quickly and left the room.

The night had been a long one for her, huddled in blankets on the sofa, thinking painful thoughts. But she was almost decided now. She would return to Henry and ask for a divorce. Such things happened, although perhaps not to many people that she knew. But it was better than trying to live out this lie anymore. She would take Katherine and they would go and live by themselves somewhere. Perhaps in England? Somewhere where they would not be under suspicion by the military if they so much as stopped to speak with a neighbour in the street. Somewhere where she could earn a decent living for her daughter and herself. She didn't add, somewhere where Henry could not try and take Katherine away from her, but the thought was there. Henry was Catholic; the chances were slim he would agree to a divorce, or to his daughter being taken from him. She tried not to think of it.

John would have to do whatever he felt best. She couldn't

become involved with him while she was still married to Henry. It would be deceitful and unkind — and really more than she could bear to live with. It would be hard enough to hurt Henry by leaving him. She couldn't commit adultery as well.

Sophie lay on her stomach, her legs crossed and waving in the air. She was reading a silly novel about a young nobleman who fell in love with the wrong sister and came to realize his mistake just in time. She was enjoying it thoroughly. She knew everything would come right in the end. It always did in these romances. If only it could be like that in real life, she thought with a sigh. Then Henry would realize he had married the wrong girl and would fall madly in love with her instead. And Eleanor — well, she would run off with that dreadful cousin of hers and leave Henry happily in Sophie's care.

For a moment Sophie wondered whether to have Katherine stay, or leave with her mother. But it didn't really matter that much. She didn't mind. As long as she got Henry. Then they would have children of their own. She smiled and stretched luxuriously, remembering the past two nights.

He had thought he could turn her away last night. Thought he could make it into nothing more than a mistake, a moment of passion and despair. Sophie snorted to herself. Well, he had found he was wrong, when she had slipped into his bed after everyone was asleep. And he had found that making love with her was quite different to making love with Eleanor. There would be no comparisons worth making, after these few days were over and Eleanor tried to return to her place as wife. In fact, Sophie said softly to herself, there would be no place to return to. She would make quite sure of that.

She rolled over on to her back and stared up at the ceiling of her bedroom, admiring the intricate carving in the plaster-work. Henry had been surprised by some of the things she had taught him, she thought. Surprised and —

yes, delighted. He must wonder why Eleanor didn't arouse him in quite such a way. And it was so easy to say nothing when Henry asked about Eleanor's infidelities with John. Henry was so ready to believe in them. And, for all she knew, such infidelities were actually happening. Eleanor didn't confide in her about John anymore. That in itself was significant. Almost certainly she was John's lover.

Sophie smoothed the satin nightgown over her hips, admiring the gentle curves and undulations of her body. All she wanted was Henry. Nothing else. She had loved him long before Eleanor had married him and Eleanor had known it too. So, really, it was Eleanor who had stolen Henry from her, rather than the reverse. Eleanor didn't deserve to have two men, when Sophie, herself, had nothing at all. No, Eleanor could have John and she would have Henry. There was nothing wrong with that, was there? Everyone could be happy that way. Just like in her book.

She looked at the clock beside the bed. Nearly two o'clock. Everyone would be asleep now. And the guarda weren't in the house itself. Only outside. She smiled and sat up. Time to go see Henry.

Isobel tucked Katherine back into her cot, and pulled the covers over her. She was sleeping soundly now. Across the room, little Charlie was sprawled across his bed, his bottom rucked up in the air, his thumb in his mouth. The blanket had fallen down so that he lay almost without covers. Isobel smiled and rearranged him, pulling his thumb gently out of his mouth and wrapping the blanket tightly around him before tucking it in. She kissed his cheek and breathed in the sweet, warm smell of baby skin. His brother or sister would be along in just a couple of months. She rubbed her hand over her stomach and prayed that everything would be all right.

The guarda weren't letting anyone in or out of the house except the doctor and they had even searched him. Thank heavens Henry had changed his mind about giving the doctor that note and had made Dr da Silva memorize the telephone number instead. Now it was all up to that fussy little man who had probably never done anything under-handed in his life. The thought made her want to hide herself under the blanket with her son and never open her eyes again. Oh, please, Dr da Silva, please get it right!

She stood up and switched off the light, gently opening the door to the hall. A noise, a creaking of a board, a rustle of fabric against skin, made her pause. The nursery was in the west wing, where Henry and Eleanor slept. No one should be there now except Henry, who had gone to bed some hours before. Isobel peered carefully through the crack in the door.

In the morning, Isobel was particularly silent over the breakfast table. She had said nothing to anyone so far, not even to Louis. She wanted to talk to Henry alone first. Perhaps there was an explanation, some reason why Sophie should have visited his room in the middle of the night? But she knew there wasn't. She knew what had been going on.

Looking up from her reverie, she caught Sophie's eye and had to look away abruptly before the anger could show. There was no point in confronting Sophie. The woman had no morals at all if she could move into her best friend's house and then steal her husband. There was no point in appealing to any higher conscience there. Sullenly, Isobel helped herself to more coffee. Sophie needn't think she was going to get away with it. Because she wasn't. With a hard chinking sound of metal on china, Isobel stirred her coffee.

Henry was looking unhappy, Isobel thought. A little seedy even, his eyes not as freshly alert as normal, his bearing slack as he sat heavily in his chair. There were guilt pangs at work there, all right. And so there ought to be. Maybe Eleanor had once been John's lover but that was years ago and long before she was married. Henry had no excuse. None at all! He looked up and caught her examining him, his half-smile fading into nothing. He looked embarrassed, aware and glanced away.

'How long do you think this is going to go on?' Sophie

said abruptly into the silence and everyone looked at her. For a moment, Isobel wondered whether Sophie were talking about her own nightly affairs, and then she realized that it was the house arrest that was being called into question. Henry didn't offer a reply, didn't even look at Sophie really. He seemed to stare past her at a portrait of Eleanor on the wall.

Charles cleared his throat. 'A few more days probably, Sophie. Until Eleanor comes back. I shouldn't worry. They'll understand at the consulate.' Charles was tired of looking pale and dragging himself about the house but it was better than being confined to his bedroom. He looked across at Clarissa and smiled. She was a good woman, never complaining, never pulling a long face like this little French girl. It had taken years but he was finally beginning to appreciate his wife. She had her own special qualities. He winked at her and Clarissa smiled in pleased surprise.

'But, won't they want to question Eleanor when she comes back?' Sophie pressed and saw Henry shift abruptly in his chair, as though she had hit him. She bit her lip. 'What happens then?'

Louis stood up and glanced quickly into the passageway. There was no one there. They had been left pretty much to themselves once the house had been searched and the guarda were all now stationed outside. A small courtesy but one they all appreciated.

'If you mean, what happens if they try and beat the truth out of Eleanor and she breaks, then the answer is we don't know, Sophie. I would've thought you'd be more concerned with Eleanor's position than with anything that comes after that,' Isobel snapped and she saw the girl turn her head slowly to look her full in the face. The anger and dislike was there for both to read. Sophie's eyes dropped.

'Oh, for God's sake, I won't let them question Eleanor without my being present. That's all there is to it,' Henry said irritably, the fear warping his voice and making him sound older and harsher. He dropped his pretence of trying to eat and drank his coffee instead. Nothing would happen

410

to Eleanor. He would make sure of that. Nothing must ever happen to her. Life would be – pointless – without her, he thought in vague surprise. No, she would be all right. She must be. He set his jaw grimly and stood up. 'Please excuse me, I have papers to look over,' he said and left the room.

No one said anything more, the table becoming silent and uncomfortable as each person tried not to let their spoon clatter noisily in its saucer, as they tried to eat quietly. The atmosphere became unpleasantly strained. Isobel laid down her napkin and made her excuses, smiling lovingly at her husband on the way out. Maybe he did cheat on her, she didn't know. But if so, he did it discreetly with women who never moved in the same circle of friends as she did. There was never any chance of her finding out. And he didn't cheat in their own bed. Isobel gave Sophie a venomous look and closed the door after her.

Henry was in his own suite, sitting at his desk, when Isobel knocked and entered. She caught him unaware, holding his head between his hands, a look of such despair on his face that her own anger was instantly abated. Henry was going through enough hell. He didn't need her to lecture him. She tried to smile.

'Isobel! What is it? Has something happened?' Henry asked. She thought, for a moment, she saw his eyes glinting but then he blinked and looked away, frowning over something and when he looked back, his eyes were the same as always.

She nodded uncomfortably. 'Last night, I was checking on the children. Quite late. I saw Sophie,' she said quietly and she saw the colour leave his face, his mouth twitching in humiliation.

He nodded. 'I see.' His voice was low, barely audible.

'I'm not going to say anything, Henry. I know you love Eleanor and this was just – a stupid, thoughtless fling, I suppose you could say. But I want it to stop.' Isobel forced herself to sound stern. She couldn't bear the pain she could see in Henry's eyes.

'Isobel, you know everything, don't you, about Eleanor?

She tells you everything?' he asked finally and Isobel looked puzzled.

'Yes, I suppose she does. Why?'

Henry was standing now, wandering over to the curtains, pulling them to one side and staring out. He didn't look at Isobel.

'Is Eleanor having an affair with John?' he said after a moment and turned quickly, to catch Isobel's expression. He saw only outrage.

'No, she is not! What on earth made you think something like that, Henry?'

'Don't lie to me, Isobel, please. I know he spent time with her in Paris. I know they were lovers then. Are you telling me there's been nothing since? Or didn't you know about Paris?' His voice had steadied and become harder, more businesslike. Probing out the truth in courtrooms was his business and Isobel felt exactly as though she had been put on trial. Her sympathy for him began to dissolve.

'Yes, I know about Paris. And I also know Eleanor made a decision, when John came back and she realized he hadn't been killed, to put him out of her mind and to stay loyal to you. She talked to me about it and she said you and Katherine would always be the most important parts of her life. She must have told John that because he left the next morning and she hasn't seen him since. You know that, Henry, you were there. You saw John's face. There's been nothing between them since Eleanor married you and there won't be. If Sophie told you otherwise, then she's the liar, not me. Eleanor wouldn't ever hurt you the way you've hurt her. She deserves better than that, Henry.'

Isobel turned angrily and would have left the room but Henry caught up with her and put a hand on her arm, restraining her. When she looked at him, she saw his face was lit up, filled with such joy that she stopped and stared.

'Thank you, Isobel. Thank you for putting me out of my hell. I can't begin to tell you what I've been going through ... May God forgive me for ever doubting her.' He leaned down and kissed Isobel's cheek. 'Please keep this to yourself. I'll deal with things and, I promise you, I'll never hurt Eleanor again. I give you my word.' He held her arm and she nodded, reluctantly smiling at him.

'Then you better keep it, Henry, or I'll see you back in hell!' she said gruffly, and then kissed him back. 'I better see to the children. Why don't you come and help me with Katherine? It's time you learned to change a nappy.' She smiled and he put an arm around her, opening the door.

Sophie stood there, a hand raised to knock. Both Isobel and Henry looked at her grimly. She stepped back a pace, her smile faltering.

'I – I just came to see you, Henry. For a talk. Is this an awkward time? Shall I come back later?' She saw the anger in Henry's eyes, the – yes, she had to admit it – hate, there. And her own eyes filled with tears.

'I don't think so, Sophie, do you?' Henry said quietly and then he led Isobel past the dark-haired girl and they walked down the passageway. Behind them Sophie stood perfectly still, staring after them.

Chapter Twenty

The windchimes tinkled tinnily, the sound threading through the air and almost lost in the pounding of the surf and crying birds. Outside the sun washed over the sky a clear stain of gold, tinging towards a pink dusk. Eleanor paused, near the open door where she had been airing the rug, and stood up. Was that the windchime? Perhaps John was ready to eat something again? She wandered through to the bedroom and leaned in the doorway, smiling.

'You rang?' she teased and John, lying against his pillows, thought how very beautiful she was, even wrapped up in an oversize jumper and wearing a pair of men's jeans. Her hair gleamed in its tight plait, her olive skin was smooth and unblemished, her eyes radiated warmth and love. He wondered how he could have ever thought he was over her. That he didn't need her. The thought made him laugh. She was what made everything else in life worthwhile to him; she made him see things as they really were, not as he pretended they were to the world. He needed her, he admitted finally. Needed her completely. And if that made him less than a great man, then he was happy to be so humbled.

But 'I need my brow soothed' was all he said and

Eleanor hooted with laughter, in a way she hadn't since they were children.

'My Lord and master! Shall I find some clusters of grapes to peel and feed to you, one by one? Or perhaps some dusky, dancing maidens?' She clapped her hands, as though to summon them.

John groaned. 'Too predictable, far too dull. Come and entertain me yourself. I've no mind for Beaudelaire's fantasies.' He sat up, awkwardly and, when Eleanor reached over to help him arrange the pillows, he leaned close, smelling her clean, fresh scent of soap and skin and salty sea air. His mouth hovered, less than an inch away from her, as though he would press forward and kiss her slowly and lingeringly on that long column of throat.

Eleanor jerked away. 'Unfair tactics, John. Stop it.' She tried to pass it off lightly but it was difficult. Particularly so, when all she wanted was to press against him as though they had never been apart, as though she had never been married, never had a child. But she couldn't. She looked away and tidied up the plates beside his bed.

'I never touched you. You're still a chaste married woman. Does that keep you warm at night, knowing how good you are?' John said mockingly and then sighed, holding up his hands. 'Sorry, sorry. I know that was uncalled for. Forgive me.' He took her hand in his, holding it tightly. 'I can't help the – jealousy, sometimes. It all seems so unfair. But I'll try and be good. You deserve that much, at least.'

'Do I?' She paused awkwardly. 'John, I think you should know. I'm – I'm going to leave Henry. Take Katherine and go away somewhere, maybe to England,' she said suddenly and she looked at John, at the expression of blankness in those eyes. He wasn't giving anything away. 'It's nothing to do with you, so don't start thinking you've ruined my life. I just can't – carry on the lie. Maybe if you hadn't come back, things might have gone on all right. I don't know. They've been bad for a long time now. And I think this is the only solution.' She wondered, for a moment, whether

John only ever wanted her when he knew she was un-available. Perhaps it was the frustration that piqued his interest? Would he care so much now? She really didn't know.

She stood up and moved away from him, going to close the window as the afternoon drew into evening, blues turning to indigo, shadows stretching out fingers across the sand.

'Just like that? You think Henry's going to let you go?' John lay against his pillows, paler now, staring at her. 'He won't, you know. He'll fight it every step of the way. And he won't let you have Katherine. And you won't leave without her, not for anyone, will you?' He sat up. 'Will you?'

Eleanor turned back into the light of the room, the curtains pulled snugly behind her. 'No, not without her. But I don't know how Henry feels anymore. The fact that he hasn't been out here makes me wonder whether he wants me back at all. Perhaps not. I don't know. I haven't been able to think that far yet. It was hard enough to make the decision in the first place. Maybe,' she paused, 'maybe I've never had the time to myself before to really think anything through. We'll have to wait and see. Don't make this more difficult, John, please. I don't want you playing devil's advocate this time, all right?'

'What do you want me to do then?' John said. He lay back again and held out his hand, tiring again as the fever pulled at him. He was watching her intently, trying to read something in her face but she didn't know what. She went to sit beside him, holding his hand up to her cheek. It was hot and dry.

'Just get well. And think about what you're going to do. The guarda must want you pretty badly now. They'll bribe people for information on you, they'll – torture people. You won't be able to go back anywhere you've been before, in case they're waiting for you. Do you really want to go on leading this sort of life? What sort of future is there for you? You'll be lucky to stay alive the rest of the year.' Her hand trembled slightly at the thought and he gripped it more

416

firmly. Pulled a face that reminded her of him as a boy, rueful, regretful, disillusioned.

'To be honest, Eleanor, I'm about as tired as can be with it all. But they're not going to let me just step off the merry-go-round and say enough! It doesn't work that way. I'm what, nearly twenty-seven now, and I suppose I'm beginning to lose my illusions. Maybe Brazil will become democratic one day, but I don't think anything I'm doing is making a damned bit of difference. It's the politicians, like Henry, who will win the day. My group's split up, mostly arrested, and I'm out of money, and I'm tired of being on the run. If I could think of a way out, a way of returning to normal life, I'd jump at it. But I can't. You know that old saying about youth being wasted on the young? I'm beginning to finally understand what it means. Maybe I'm finally growing up.' He glanced at her, his face gaunt and ill. She had to look away.

'Who knows?' He shrugged. 'Maybe I'll go join the terrorists for a while. You know, Carlos Marighela and his lot? At least they're organized and have proper funds. There's a lot of anger built up inside me, you know, that just wants to lash out and hurt the people who've been making my life hell. I'd say it's my turn to get a little back on them. Not particularly worthy, maybe, but at least I'm honest.' He sighed at her expression. 'Oh, what the hell, I don't really know, Eleanor. I've got a wife somewhere in the United States. Maybe I'll try and get to her. Get out of this pisspot of a country altogether.' He was tired and becoming irritable with the fever. Depressed because he had nothing better to offer.

Eleanor pressed her hand to his lips. 'Enough. You've used up quite enough energy for one day. I'll go and get you some dinner if you promise to have a nap for an hour or so. Then we'll talk again, all right?' She gathered up the glasses and plates from beside the bed and walked out of the room quickly before he could see how much he had upset her with his talk about terrorism and hating Brazil. Well, at least she knew where she stood now. John wasn't planning on ever being a part of her life. That was what she had thought. She took a deep breath. All right, she could cope with that. As long as she had Katherine, she could handle anything. She forced herself to hum a tune, so she wouldn't – couldn't let out the shake in the back of her throat, the pain that was clenching at her throat muscles, in a tearing, screaming, cry. No, she would manage. She hummed some more.

Dr da Silva turned up as she was ladling out spaghetti into a bowl and chopping it up so John could feed himself easily. She saw the car beams swing across the sand before the car even turned the final curve and rolled to a stop in front of the house. When the headlights were extinguished, she could see nothing at all. Nervously, she went to investigate.

'Eleanor? Eleanor, it is I, Dr da Silva. Is everything all right?' she heard him call from the darkness and she took a deep breath of relief.

'Yes, everything's fine, Dr da Silva. You're just in time for dinner.' She smiled broadly as she saw him appear in the outer fringes of light and walk towards her. She kissed him on the cheek and led him inside, out of the chill night air.

Dr da Silva looked around him in surprise at the transformation Eleanor had wrought in the sitting-room. It looked old and threadbare still but she had managed to instil her own casual elegance to the way the few pieces of furniture were arranged, to the flowers and grasses in clear glass jars positioned around the room. Everything shone with the fervour that a day of nervous energy could put into it.

He smiled with pleasure and patted her shoulder. 'How very welcoming you have made it all. I wish I had thought to make it more comfortable before. And I wish,' he sighed heavily, 'that you could stay here longer. But tomorrow or perhaps Sunday I must take you home. Things are not well.'

Eleanor glanced at him, her own sense of foreboding now confirmed. She crossed her arms nervously. 'What is it? What's happened?'

418

'Everyone at the palácio is under house arrest. The guarda suspect you are with John, even now, and they are holding your family until such time as you return.' He tried to quiet the panic and fear in her face, leading her over to the sofa. 'Now then, don't worry, Henry's thought of a way out.' The doctor explained quickly about the de Souzas and Eleanor nodded, closing her eyes at the image the doctor drew of the family anxiously waiting to see whether they would all be imprisoned or not. She cursed under her breath everything she could think of, the government, the military, the country, herself and even John. Oh God, what should she do now?

'They'll see through it at once, doctor. Why should the de Souzas or their friends in Brasília lie for me? They barely know me,' Eleanor said finally and the doctor sighed again, lifting his glasses back on to his nose with one finger. He saw the fear in the girl's eyes, not for herself, but for those she loved and he squeezed her hand gently.

'They say they will cover for you. But I don't know. We must just hope for the best. I'll come for you on, say, Sunday, that would probably be best and you can come back to my place and telephone the de Souzas, get your story straight. The guarda don't know where they are, just off travelling in the interior, so we've got a few days' grace. You talk to them and then take a taxi back to the palácio and we'll have to pray all goes well. And John must go,' he added, as though such a course of action were obvious. Perhaps it was, Eleanor thought, and her mind simply wasn't functioning.

'He's not well enough yet, doctor. He hasn't any transport or any friends left. The guarda got them all. So where can he go?' There was more than fear now, there was pain at the thought of losing John again, perhaps forever. The doctor wondered whether she knew how much her eyes revealed.

'Teresa's back,' Dr da Silva said, pleased with the effect his news had on her. Good, now perhaps she would stop thinking of her cousin as her own particular problem. John

419

had a wife, let her take care of him. 'I called her and she agreed to send someone to get John. I didn't ask anything more. I didn't want to know. She doesn't dare come herself. She thinks she's being watched and they've questioned her too, several times. But she'll send a friend for John, tomorrow, she said. Get him away somewhere. And then you can go home.' He smiled brightly, as though that took care of all her problems.

Eleanor shook her head. 'Why is Teresa back? I don't understand. She's a big star now, even in the United States. Why would she want to risk all that for a husband she's barely seen in four, five years and whom she never loved anyway? Are you sure she isn't working with the guarda?' She flushed, even as she said it, knowing it wasn't true.

'Eleanor! Really! Who says Teresa never loved John? I always thought she did.' He snorted crossly. 'Anyway, she's back here to do a film, for a few months, and she's offered her help. It's the best we can do right now. It isn't safe for any of us, especially John, to stay here much longer. They may even have followed me, for all I know.' He laid a hand on hers, when she started and looked out at the black windows, the black night. 'No, no, I don't think they did – I checked as best I could. But I'm an old man and a doctor. I'm not cut out for all of this cloak-and-dagger stuff. This has to be the last time, Eleanor, and you must do as I say. It's the only way.'

'Yes, the doctor's right, Eleanor, it's the only way.' They both turned in surprise to see John standing in the doorway, his face calm and decided. He leaned against the doorframe for support and Eleanor got heavily to her feet and walked over to him. She regarded him for a moment before shaking her head.

'John, what're you doing? Come on back to bed, please. If you have to go somewhere tomorrow, then you'll need all your energy.' She would have tried to lead him back into the bedroom, but he refused to go, his face as stubborn, as tired as hers.

'Wait a minute, Elly. Let's sort everything out, while

420

we're at it.' He looked across at the doctor, seeing the thought in the old man's eyes of what a dreadful waste his life had been and he glanced away again, glanced down, gathered his breath.

Dr da Silva was still communing with himself about John and didn't notice the younger man's averted head. What had happened, the doctor wondered, to have made John so? What compulsion had so wrecked his life when he had so much potential, so much given to him, and now so little to show for it all? All that presence and intelligence, such courage, and where was it leading him? Straight to a painful death. It was enough to make an old man weep. He listened, sadly, to what John was saying.

'If, for some reason, your alibi doesn't work, Eleanor, if the de Souzas don't cover well enough for you, or the guarda find you out in a lie, then you'll have to tell them something else that they will believe. Something so embarrassing and shameful that you would have tried to cover it up with a false story first.' He hesitated, aware that he had their attention.

'Tell them you and Henry haven't been getting along. That he's been playing around and you found out and couldn't take it. You had to get away, you were hysterical and you turned to the doctor for help. He let you stay out here for a few days, so you could think and decide what you wanted to do. Henry didn't know where you were, so he invented this tale for the rest of the family and then had to stick by it when the guarda came. Okay? Think you can do it?'

He looked seriously into Eleanor's face, reading the shock and denial there. No, she wouldn't! How could she humiliate Henry like that, after everything he had ever tried to do for her, after he was risking his own life to cover for her? She shook her head abruptly.

'It's the only way, Eleanor. Can you think of anything else that they might possibly believe? And anyway, it's only an insurance measure. Hopefully you won't have to use it.' He appealed to the doctor, who was looking thoughtful.

'What d'you think, Dr da Silva? Is it believable, or not?'

The doctor ran a finger down the side of his nose, easing his glasses away from his face so that he could massage his eyes. He cleared his throat, his particular sign of indecision.

'Possibly. As you say, it's a good idea to have a back-up story in case everything goes wrong. But does it have to be so very unpleasant? Are you sure you can't think of something else, John?' For a long moment the two men looked at each other, the older one gauging the younger one's intentions, both cynically aware how much distrust there was between them.

'Feel free to try. But I told you, the whole point is that it is unpleasant, that you would've fabricated any story rather than have this come out. The guarda only believe the worst of people. I think they'll believe this. But nothing less.' John's voice became hoarse, his body sagged slightly where he leant against the door. He coughed and the doctor saw the way his whole body shook with the effort.

'Go back to bed, John. We'll sort this out,' the doctor said firmly and Eleanor took John's arm and led him into the bedroom. He fell backwards on the mattress, as though his energy was totally spent. He closed his eyes and shuddered.

'You're not well enough to go anywhere,' Eleanor said stubbornly above him and his lips moved in a brief smile. But he didn't open his eyes or speak. When she felt his forehead, it burned beneath her skin. She pulled the covers over him and went back out to the doctor.

They argued late into the night but eventually Eleanor had to give in. There was nothing more she could do for John, that wouldn't put the rest of the family in more danger. And she couldn't do that. She agreed John should leave the next day and that she would return with Dr da Silva on Sunday. What alternative was there?

Eleanor had no appetite herself but she served the doctor with spaghetti and took a bowl through to John. But he was asleep, his eyes sunken deeply into the sockets, a fine mist covering his skin as he shivered and mumbled, tossing his head from side to side. She sat beside him, holding his limp hand in hers, and she prayed as she had never prayed before. And Dr da Silva, watching her from the doorway, wished he could spare her the pain. But he couldn't.

He called his farewell, 'Until Sunday', and left. Eleanor did not even look up. Her face was slick with tears.

When Dr da Silva called in at the palácio on Saturday morning, to see how Charles Fawcett was progressing, he was met with suspicious stares from the guarda captain. It was four days now since the house arrest had been imposed and nothing new had come to light. Captain Almeida was becoming impatient.

He accompanied Dr da Silva into the sick room and remained standing there while the doctor examined Charles and took his blood pressure.

'Is this entirely necessary, captain? It must be obvious the good doctor isn't going to produce John out of his black bag, and I can't imagine what other reason you might have for standing there like that. Or do you actually enjoy watching me take my shirt off?' Charles was particularly withering and the captain pursed his lips angrily before leaving the room. He closed the door with frightening composure.

'You will be sorry for baiting him like that, Charles. He's not the sort to stir. And he looks particularly unpleasant when he pushes his lips together like that and squints at you from under those heavy lids. I would as soon poke a scorpion,' Dr da Silva commented mildly and Charles laughed.

'Yes, dare say you're right, but how the hell else could I get rid of him. What's the news?' Charles listened intently while Dr da Silva filled him in, especially to John's particular suggestion. He snorted angrily at that.

'Yes, and I'll just bet he was laughing his head off at the thought. Well, things'll have to come to a pretty pass before we let anything like that get spread around. Henry, of all people! No one would believe it anyway.' He saw Dr da Silva shrug delicately.

'Who knows? But, right now, I must tell you, as your doctor, that you are not in good shape. Take it very easy, Charles. Your blood pressure is too high, and your colour is bad. I want you to take these pills twice a day, and remain calm. The others are for emergencies. Stay out of the way, if there's likely to be a problem. I don't want you getting excited or upset. This imaginary illness of yours is not so imaginary as you would like to believe. Please, my old friend, take care.' They shook hands and patted each other on the back and Dr da Silva took his leave.

It was late afternoon before Sophie came to a decision. Henry hadn't spoken a word to her since the day before, when Isobel had been to see him, and Sophie knew now he was not going to forgive her. Somehow Eleanor had emerged untarnished in his eyes from all this, and he would welcome her back into his arms without a thought for the nights he had spent with Sophie – or the danger Eleanor's thoughtless actions had put them all in. Sophie kicked the wooden desk in her room in frustration and anguish. But it was no good. She would have to leave, and soon, before she saw Henry again. She couldn't bear to see that look of hate in his face. Not when she loved him so very much. She pulled down her suitcase and began to pack.

When Dr da Silva left the beach shack, Eleanor slipped off her shoes and climbed carefully into bed beside John, pressing herself tightly against his side. The water bottle was warming his feet, but the rest of him was chilled despite the quilt over him. Eleanor tried to stop the shivering. These few hours would have to last her a lifetime, she told herself, and the thought was a hard, aching misery that lodged in her throat and chest, and made her wish passionately they had both died that night in the jungle. Then none of this would have happened and she would have always been with John. She closed her eyes and pressed her

424

face against his shoulder.

John found her like that when he woke in the early hours of the morning. Her face pressed into him, her cheeks stained with tears. He eased himself over to face her, pulling her in against him. He touched his lips to her cheek, the skin warm and slightly salty. She was soundly asleep.

'My poor Elly. I'm so very sorry,' he whispered. So very sorry for ruining both their lives, he thought, both their futures. But he couldn't have done otherwise. And she knew that. At least she always understood, always forgave, even if no one else did. 'I love you, Elly,' he breathed softly into her ear but she didn't stir. Gently, he stroked her hair back from her face, wiped the tear stains from her skin with his thumb. He stared at her for a long time.

When John heard the car, he slid from the bed and went to peer out of the window. An old, beaten panelwagon was parked some distance from the house, the driver looking about him, as though unsure. John recognized Moreira with surprise. It had been a long time since that storm on the way to Santiago. He smiled to himself and stood up and waved. Then, he returned to the bed and leaned over Eleanor again. She smiled in her sleep, as though she were somewhere happy and he smiled back at her, stroking his finger across her mouth.

He gathered his clothes up and made his way, slowly, into the other room. Eleanor slept on, undisturbed.

When Eleanor awoke, the sun was high in the sky and the light was streaming in through the thin cotton curtains, bathing the room in an orange wash. She sat up, wondering for a moment where she was, and then as the memories slid into focus, she looked around for John. He was gone.

She threw back the covers and hurried across the bare boards to the bathroom, calling his name. There was no answer. He wasn't in the bathroom, nor the sitting-room, nor the kitchen. He wasn't anywhere. Frightened, she called his name louder and wandered outside, on to the verandah.

It was a golden day, filled with gentle heat, the air soft and moist against her skin, gusting occasionally to fill her mouth with its salty taste. She breathed in deeply to still the panic and wandered down on to the sand, surprised by how cool it felt against her bare soles, where the shadow of the house still lay over the ground. John wasn't anywhere in sight. She returned to the sitting-room, looking around, and there it was. The note.

She picked it up with trembling fingers.

My dearest Eleanor,
I will be long gone by the time you wake and read this and perhaps that is for the best, since I could not bear to have to say goodbye. Thank you, as always. I owe you everything. Please take care to remember my story. I think it will be the only way out. I wish I could stay with you but you are safer with me gone. Don't forget to hide everything I might have used. Bury it in the sand dunes, if necessary.
I love you,

John

She folded the note carefully, smoothing the creases between her fingers, her mind quite blank. Gone. This time, almost certainly, was the last. They were too close to him, too determined to hunt him down. She had seen him for the last time.

'Oh ... John ...' It came out as a long exhalation. She leaned against the verandah post and stared out at the sand for some time.

Finally, she took a deep breath and looked down at the note again, the way it was folded in her hand. So very stupid of her. This wasn't just her life, it was everyone's. Henry's and Katherine's and all the family's. She went into the kitchen, lit a match and burned the paper completely. Then she set about erasing any evidence of John's existence.

426

*

It was evening, Sunday evening, when the guarda arrived. Eleanor did not hear the cars, nor see any lights until it was too late. She was sitting on the sofa reading, her legs outstretched along it, when the door burst open and the guarda entered.

She looked startled, Captain Almeida thought, but not particularly frightened. As though she knew they would find nothing. Her beauty surprised him. Here was a girl who almost unnerved him with her cool, well-bred looks, her long, graceful body. So very fina gente. It annoyed him that she should be able to make him feel that way, and still retain her calm. His shoulders straightened in irritation and his voice took on an unpleasant edge.

'I am afraid the good doctor has been careless, Senhora; he didn't check his rear view mirror enough. Right now he is waiting for us out in my car, under arrest.' He noted her expression, the pallor of her skin. 'So, now you see, you will come with me, instead. But firstly, there is the matter of your cousin, John Campos de Serra. Where is he? What have you done with him?' he asked softly and the woman looked up at him with large green eyes, the colour of peeled grapes. There was fear in those eyes as she assessed him, he saw, finally. He smiled.

'John?' she asked, as he had known she would, and he slapped her. Hard enough to throw her back against the sofa cushions, her hand coming up to ward off another blow. An ugly red blotch appeared on that smooth skin. The captain smiled again.

'Yes, senhora. Your cousin, Campos de Serra. Where is he? I'll ask you nicely just one more time.' The captain's voice had become hushed, as though he only raised it when he lost control. The soft, silken voice was infinitely more frightening.

Eleanor shook her head. 'I don't know. He hasn't been here —' She broke off as he hit her again, rolling on to the floorboards in an attempt to escape the blows that rained

427

down on her. She gasped in pain and fear. 'I don't know!' she screamed and then her mind seemed to explode with pain as he kicked her, again and again.

When Henry was brought in to see her, she was barely conscious. She knew she had been taken, at some point, from the shack and driven a long way. But where, she wasn't sure. Perhaps the guarda civil headquarters in Rio? It seemed likely. The beating had been severe but she knew she hadn't said anything incriminating. In fact, she would almost have smiled to herself if the discomfort of moving her mouth were not so severe; they had beaten her so hard she had lost consciousness for most of the time and they had had little time to question her. That was the little captain's fault. He seemed so terribly angry with her. Now she really didn't care what they did to her. She had reached the point where the pain was outside of her, somewhere, and she felt as though her body belonged to someone else. She felt curiously strong in that bodiless form. Let them try. She didn't know anything.

She saw Henry, vaguely, hovering over her and Papa behind him, his face stricken, and she tried to tell them it was all right. She had told them nothing. But then they slipped away again and she heard voices shouting but they weren't shouting at her this time so she closed her eyes again and drifted off. It was too late for them now. John was safely away.

'You've no right, you son of a bitch! John wasn't with her. He was never with her! She left me, God damn you, because – because ...' But Henry's voice broke at this point and he couldn't continue, kneeling beside Eleanor's inert form, wiping the blood from her face. Behind him, he heard Charles shouting at the captain, threatening him with every empty, useless threat he could think of.

The small room was grey in the early morning light. Grey like the captain's uniform, like Henry's face.

Captain Almeida seemed unimpressed. 'You were saying, senhor? Your wife left you because ...?' He leaned over the desk and Henry looked up at him, hate in his face.

'Because she found out I was having an affair with someone.' He bit off the words.

The captain smiled. 'Ah yes, the exquisite Senhorita Gastambide, was it not? She explained as much when she requested permission to leave, to return to Paris. I escorted her on to the plane personally. Ah, I see you do not deny it. But that is beside the point. We know your wife was hiding Campos de Serra. Unfortunately,' he examined a button on his uniform with interest, 'he made his escape before we arrived, leaving your wife and the good doctor to take all the blame. But neither one of them has proven helpful. I should think you would want to help us find your wife's cousin, senhor, when he has put her in such danger. And perhaps for other reasons? There have always been rumours about them, I understand.' He smiled when Henry looked painfully away.

Charles, his face mottled and his voice shaking with emotion, leaned in over Captain Almeida, dwarfing the man with his height.

'My daughter has never had an affair with anyone in her life. But you wouldn't understand that, would you? You don't come from the sort of family where your women are loyal and faithful. Beating up women, that's about your size, isn't it? And for what? Some ridiculous tale of infidelity? Since when has that been a crime? Besides, what you're suggesting is laughable, they're first cousins –'

'And that has been known before, too. Besides, why else would your son-in-law be having an affair with Senhorita Gastambide. Because he knew that his wife and her cousin were lovers, no? It is so very obvious. Two adulterers in one marriage. That, I suppose, is how the fina gente carry on?' The captain laughed tightly, mocking Charles.

'You're wrong. I'm the only adulterer here, not Eleanor. She never did anything wrong.' Henry's voice was anguished as he kneeled beside Eleanor. He could see she was breathing slowly, as though it hurt to draw breath.

Captain Almeida was puzzled. Either Arreas was a good

actor, or this really was the truth. But then, his wife need not have been having an affair with her cousin. She might simply have been helping him. He was supposed to be ill, after all. The captain watched Henry with interest.

'Henry! Stop it. What are you saying? Adulterer? You and Sophie! Don't be ridiculous. I won't have such slurs being put on the family.' But Charles paused when he saw Henry's face. Paused and became silent, stunned. 'My God!' he said, finally seeming to realize that Henry was telling the truth, not some tale that had been thought up beforehand.

He wiped his face with his sleeve, the sweat seeping down into his eyes and stinging. 'You can't have! It's not possible. You and Sophie! In my house?' He looked bewildered, hurt. He looked down at his daughter. 'You? You're responsible for this, for what they've done to my Elly? You and your filthy little –' but he broke off as his voice dropped to a rattle, his fingers clutching at his throat. He groaned.

That pain that he remembered so well sliced across his chest, worse than before, worse that he could ever have imagined. He groped blindly for his pills, feeling the empty pocket, knowing too late he had left them at home. He groaned again, harsh and high-pitched and staggered forward.

The captain saw the old man begin to totter, holding his arms tightly to his chest, and he shouted for the guards to get help, get a doctor. Perhaps it was a bluff; perhaps it was just histrionics? Captain Almeida watched scornfully, his mind half in doubt.

When the old man fell, it was the son-in-law who caught him, who held him in his arms, while Captain Almeida watched them in fury and indecision. He shouted again and then pushed the son-in-law away, slapping the old man's cheeks and shaking him, but it was too late already. Fawcett's eyes were open and staring, his nose pinched in as though he were desperately sucking for air. There was a blue tinge to the lips.

Henry thrust the captain away and leaned over Charles,

trying to breathe life back into him until he had to sit back in exhaustion, gasping for air himself. It was too late. Charles was gone. Just like that. A matter of seconds. The captain swung his hand against his trousers in fury.

Henry sat back against the desk, Charles's body cradled in his arms, looking sick and the officer who entered the room didn't catch his attention. He continued to stare blankly over at Eleanor, the tears filling his eyes now so that the room winked and wavered around him, insubstantially. There were voices, some raised in anger, some in explanation, but Henry didn't listen to them. All he could think was that Charles was dead and his wife was near death and that he didn't care what happened anymore. He hoped they got on with it soon. It wouldn't make any difference to him to live, if Eleanor didn't. Just let them get on with it!

When they took Charles from his arms, he tried to resist at first. But they held his arms down and then Charles was gone, carried from the room, and when he looked around Eleanor wasn't there anymore either. He started to struggle, screaming at them to bring her back, but they weren't listening and then he felt a sharp pricking pain in his arm and the room began to dissolve like wet plastic, spinning out and around, sucking him into it.

It was only a small boat but it held the seas well, climbing sturdily over the slight swell as though it knew it could tackle much stronger waves with ease. John sat huddled below in case there were watchful eyes from the shore. Moreira had said it would take thirteen hours if the weather stayed steady, and he was willing to let them take charge. He felt worse than when he first went to Eleanor for help. Not just from the fever, but from the fear of what he had involved Eleanor in. The whole family. He cursed under his breath and shivered.

The bilge water slopped beneath his feet, under the wooden slats, and he had to close his eyes and lean against the bulkhead. Once they reached the landing place, there would be a truck to take him inland, Moreira said. To a safe

431

place. He sighed and wondered how many more safe places he would have to hide in. They were running out. His luck was running out. Time to change jobs, maybe, he thought with what might have passed for amusement a few days before. Now he began to consider it seriously.

Teresa wasn't coming to see him. Too dangerous, Moreira had said and John had been relieved. He didn't want to deal with Teresa right now, and he didn't want to be responsible for hurting anyone else. Moreira owed him and was glad to pay back the debt – a life for a life. It was good of the man and he had never expected it. That had all happened so long ago, in another lifetime. God, he hoped Eleanor would be all right. The thought wouldn't leave his mind. He stared at the water sloshing up and down.

Henry woke in a small room, screened off from prying eyes. His head hurt and his mouth tasted thick and unpleasant and, for a moment, he wondered whether he had been in an accident. Perhaps been hit by a car? But then the memories came flooding back and he opened his mouth and cried out, 'Eleanor! Eleanor!' He could hear someone running towards the screens and he picked up the metal tray on the table beside him and hurled it out into the larger room, where it clattered off in the distance.

A man appeared, dressed in a white orderly's uniform, and then another and they held him down on the bed while Henry shouted at them, hurling abuse, calling for Eleanor until the fight suddenly went out of him and he went limp. They stared down at him, blocking the ceiling and the light with their huge heads and Henry shut his eyes tightly.

When he opened them, there was a third man present. A colonel, it would seem, from the pips on his uniform epaulettes.

Henry looked at him, feeling old, feeling tired. 'Where's my wife?' he asked quietly. 'What have you done with her?'

'Relax, senhor. Your wife is being taken care of. I must apologize for the way you have all been treated. It was most unfortunate.' The colonel seemed upset and Henry wondered whether Captain Almeida had exceeded his authority, whether Eleanor was not supposed to have been hurt. He swallowed with difficulty.

'I want to see her.' He saw the colonel begin to shake his head and said quickly, 'Charles Fawcett is dead because of what you did to my wife. Now I want to see her.' He felt light-headed, as though he had been ill for a long time, and he fumbled when he tried to sit up, falling sideways unexpectedly.

'Please, Senhor Arreas, you really are not in a fit condition to travel. Your wife is not here. We had her taken to hospital. You are in our clinic, our sick-bay if you like. You should rest a little longer. The sedative you have been given has not worn off yet. We will take you to see your wife in time.' The colonel hesitated when another guarda leaned in the screens and whispered into his ear. 'Ah, I understand your father is here to see you, senhor. You will permit me to show him through?' Henry closed his eyes for a moment, wondering how he could tell his father the truth. But it had to be faced. He opened his eyes again and nodded.

'Yes, show him in.'

There was a greyness to his father's face that Henry had never seen before. He had never thought of his father as old, but now he saw he was. Henry tried to smile.

'How are you?' Senhor Arreas stepped forward and then glanced coldly at the orderlies, waiting for them to leave. The colonel raised his hand and they filed past and out beyond the screens.

'I'll be better when I see Eleanor. They've – they've hurt her, Father. Beaten her.' His voice was unsteady and Senhor Arreas gripped his son's hand tightly, nodding his head.

'Yes, I know. About Charles too. I'll go and see Clarissa when I leave here. I don't know what I can say to her, how I can explain.'

The colonel shifted uncomfortably behind them, cleared his throat. 'There will be an enquiry, Senhor Arreas. I will see to it personally. Nothing like this should have been

433

permitted. You have my sincerest apologies. We – I am not a barbarian, despite what people think of the military. I would never have permitted such a thing, had I been here. Some people ... well – we will see there is – restitution.' The colonel looked sincere and Henry wished he could tell the man that it was all right, that he understood. But he couldn't. It would never be all right again.

'John was never with my wife. She has done nothing – nothing at all. I want her released,' he said grimly and the colonel bowed his head briefly, embarrassed.

'As soon as possible, senhor. She and Dr da Silva. I will see to it personally. Captain Almeida found no evidence of Campos de Serra's presence out at the beach place. We have no reason to believe your wife would continue to lie through a beating like that. Dr da Silva has also confirmed her story. There can be no question as to its truth. The captain was too – zealous. I must, once more, apologize.' He pressed his lips together, nodding again, and then left, his footsteps loud and deliberate on the linoleum floor until they were cut off by a door shutting behind him.

Henry looked at his father and then closed his eyes again, briefly, trying to summon the courage. He swallowed. 'Father – oh God.' He stopped, almost breaking down while his father gripped his hand tightly. 'There's ... um.' Henry cleared his throat. 'There's something – I have to tell you,' he paused, not knowing how to say it. He saw his father shift uncomfortably, his eyes full of sadness. Henry continued with difficulty, 'It's all so long and involved, I'm not really sure ... Sophie told me Eleanor was having an affair with John. Since before we were married and then – during our marriage. I, I don't know why but I believed her. Maybe I was so jealous, I don't know.' He sighed heavily, not able to meet his father's eyes. 'I, um, slept with Sophie – several times.'

He groaned at the thought and swiftly told his father the rest, leading up to Charles's death. His father remained quite still throughout the recital, only finally shaking his head when Henry fell silent.

'Does anyone else know this, apart from this Captain Almeida? Isobel knows about your liaison with Sophie, yes, but I mean does anyone know that was what made Charles collapse?' Senhor Arreas asked and Henry shook his head.

'I don't think so. I don't know what I'm going to tell Clarissa. What am I going to tell Eleanor? Charles might have made it otherwise.' Henry felt as though he would never be able to live with the guilt of what he had done. He wondered if any of them would be able to.

'And just what purpose would telling any of them serve?' his father asked harshly and Henry looked at him in surprise. 'Who d'you think is going to tell them, if we don't? Hmm? No one. They'll just think it was the beating the guarda had given Eleanor that shocked him so much he had another heart attack. They'll put it all down to bad luck. No one's going to feel any better if you tell them the truth. Except maybe you, purging your guilt. But I don't think you deserve to feel better. So you can live with it. They can't.' Henry's father clenched his chin tightly, looking up at the ceiling, and then back at his son.

'I'll tell them Charles had a heart attack in Captain Almeida's office. That's it. Nothing else. And this Sophie. She's already gone, I gather? Good, that makes life simpler. I don't want Clarissa put through anything more. Nor Eleanor. You remember that, Henry, if you ever feel like unburdening yourself. They deserve better than that.' Senhor Arreas looked pained and Henry wondered whether his father would be able to forgive him. But when he looked in those old eyes, he saw only understanding. It was like a cup of water to a parched man.

Then Henry remembered Isobel had said the same. Eleanor deserved better than that. He nodded, grateful to his father.

Chapter Twenty-One

August 1969

President Costa e Silva was dead. The news had stunned Brazil, the flags flying at half-mast, a day of national mourning declared. Shops and businesses were closed. No radios could be played loudly, no unseemly behaviour could be indulged. Parties were cancelled, people stayed off the streets. Rio looked like a ghost town.

Eleanor, sitting on the floor beside Katherine and colouring in the picture book, wondered what would happen now. She stroked her daughter's blonde curls and took the crayon out of Katherine's mouth before the child could choke on it. She would be four next month. God, Eleanor thought, that made her feel old. She was nearly twenty-six herself, practically into middle age. The thought made her laugh. She had planned a birthday party for Katherine at Isobel's place. Their own flat was too small and there was no garden, but Isobel and Louis had been bought a house by Louis's parents and the party would be much more fun there.

Eleanor stared wistfully at the picture in her daughter's colouring book of a garden and fountain splashing out water. It would have been so lovely to have still been at the palácio. But that had gone almost immediately after Papa's death. Mortgaged to the hilt, the bank had said, and fore-closed before they could muster their finances. Not that they could have afforded to do anything about it anyway. Not once Papa's business affairs had been unravelled and the true state of financial distress had become apparent. She wondered how he had managed to keep juggling all those debts for so long without anyone knowing. Poor Papa.

Henry's parents had helped them to buy the flat but it had been difficult for them. No one had much money anymore and inflation ate up what little they did have. Her trust fund was going almost nowhere. Just enough to feed and clothe herself and Katherine. But Henry earned a good living. They were saving as much as they could with the hope of moving somewhere better in a year or two. And they were content. What more could she ask for?

She reached over and smoothed out the newspaper, ignoring the huge headlines about Costa e Silva and concentrating instead on a smaller article she had glimpsed while Henry had been reading the paper earlier. It was low down on the second page.

'... Urban guerrillas are forming a spearhead of opposition made up reportedly from students, clerics, and labour leaders and the incidents of atrocities have escalated sharply in the last year. Despite the Communist party's disassociation with such violence, a variety of radical leftist groups have undertaken both urban and guerrilla war in order, many officials feel, to provoke a reaction against the party. By forcing such a confrontation, the leftists hope to arouse popular anger, thus making possible a revolution and seizure of power ...' The article went on to enumerate the shootings, hijackings, bank robberies and even kidnappings that had occurred in the past twelve months, denouncing them only as an afterthought. The media censorship was clearly not as effective as it thought itself. Eleanor smiled grimly to herself. Perhaps finally John was getting rid of some of that anger of his.

'Look, Mama! I made the water purple,' Katherine giggled, waving a purple crayon under her mother's nose

437

and Eleanor, distracted from her thoughts, looked down and smiled.

'So you did, poppet! And what colour is it normally?'

'Blue! But I like it better purple. Don't you, Mama? Papa? Papa? Don't you like my water purple?' Katherine caught sight of her father walking through the room and was off the floor instantly and in pursuit, her happy cries filling the room. She adored her father, Eleanor thought. It would never be possible to take her away. Besides, how could she leave Henry after what he had done for her? After he had never murmured a word of blame against her, when it was her actions that had caused Papa's death. Hers and John's. Papa had been right. John was his nemesis.

She saw her husband pick Katherine up, swinging her over his head and back down to his arms, where he examined the drawing with approval. They were laughing together and Eleanor tried to see some resemblance between them, some hint that they were father and daughter, but it wasn't there. Katherine looked like a miniature of herself. With blue eyes. She smiled when Henry looked over at her.

'How about a respectful walk in the park? Would that be in keeping with the national gloom and doom, do you think?' Henry suggested and Eleanor nodded, stood up and shook herself down. She had dust from the carpet and bits of fluff from her jumper all over her woollen trousers. Henry came up behind her and brushed his hands over them, his eyes teasing her as he did so.

'I thought you wanted a walk?' she reminded him with a smile and he held his hands high, taking two steps back.

'Any sort of exercise would suit me,' he said mildly and then gave a deprecating smile as he saw her expression. 'Ah well, can't blame a fellow for trying, can you?' he asked and kissed her quickly on the lips, stroking the small scar on her cheekbone that was a legacy of her beating. His eyes clouded for a moment and Eleanor held his hand, smiling. She shook her head at him. Katherine, down by her father's knees, tugged on his trousers impatiently.

'Papa, is Mama coming too?' She danced around, showing off her latest ballet pirouettes and Henry laughed and scooped her up.

'Yes, my sweeting, Mama's coming too.' He carried Katherine over to put on her coat and Eleanor smiled painfully at the endearment Henry had used. 'My sweeting.' That was what her father had used to call her. She shook her head at that memory too.

'Katherine, darling, let Papa buckle your shoes up. You have to wear shoes to the park and then, if you're very good, we might go see Grandmama for tea. Wouldn't that be nice?' She saw the child's eyes light up and she winked at Henry. 'Mama called earlier,' she whispered. 'It's Carlos's birthday. Sixty. I said we'd come.'

Dr Carlos da Silva had married Clarissa nearly six months ago now and Eleanor gave thanks every day for the gentle, punctilious little man who had done so much for her family. All for love of her mother. It seemed fitting that they were together at last. And Eleanor knew her father would have wanted someone to take care of his widow. Who better than the doctor?

Henry nodded and finished wrapping Katherine up against the cold. He reached for his own jacket. 'What about presents?' he said and Eleanor shrugged.

'I wrapped up a bottle of port. Mama didn't give us much warning and all the shops are shut. It was the best I could think of. You don't mind, do you?' It was Henry's last bottle. They couldn't really afford to buy any more, for a while.

He shook his head. 'No, that's fine. Carlos deserves it, if anyone does.' He took Katherine by the hand and slipped his wife's arm through his free arm, leading them both downstairs to the park. It was a cool winter's day, suitably grey and forbidding for a funeral.

'How is your mother? Enjoying life?' he asked casually and Eleanor smiled.

'You know Mama. She likes things to be happy around her. Carlos makes sure they are. How could she not be enjoying herself? Once the shock of Papa's death was over, and the prospect of a life of petty economies had sunk in, Mama knew where her heart lay. She's a survivor.' There was no hint of reproach in her voice. She knew her mother had made the right decision.

'Like all of us. We're all learning to be survivors. What do you think of this new guy, Medici? He's talking about reconvening Congress,' Henry said and Eleanor leaned against him.

'So they can sanction his presidency. And then he'll put the boot in. Leopards don't change their spots,' Eleanor replied sharply. Henry grunted.

In the last year, students and workers had been shot down in wildcat strikes, the press severely penalized, priests tortured and killed, hundreds of civilians arrested, Congress closed, and the fifth Institutional Act passed making the president a virtual dictator. Senators, deputies and Supreme Court Judges had been purged, and repression and anti-subversive campaigns had spread a climate of fear and oppression throughout the whole of Brazil.

Eleanor had had no word whether John was alive or not but Henry knew she lived in hope. About him, about everything. They all lived in hope; there was no other way.

'No,' he said slowly, 'I don't think they do either. ARENA will win most of the municipal elections and those to the state assemblies and Congress. No one's willing to stick their neck out anymore. It's far too likely to get chopped. Oh, well, let's not talk about it. You know I'm representing Teresa against a company who's been illegally using pictures of her to sell their products? Her manager called yesterday and I said I'd look into it. I meant to tell you last night, but it slipped my mind with all this hoopla about Costa e Silva. How about that then? Nothing like keeping it all in the family!' He laughed, his tone lightening and Eleanor looked at him quickly.

'Good Lord, are you really? I'm astonished. I would've thought you were the last lawyer in Brazil Teresa would turn to. She never did like the family too much, now did

440

she?' She was startled and amused. And she wondered immediately if Teresa was fishing for news about John. She would be out of luck if she were.

'Um, I know, but I'm not about to turn down a lucrative case at this stage. Maybe, if it turns out to be a real money spinner, we might just be able to think about some more children? I think Katherine needs company her own age, don't you?' He looked at her, almost pleading in his eyes, and Eleanor forced herself to nod. She squeezed his arm.

'If you think we can manage, Henry. But not until you're sure. I'm terrified we're not going to be able to put Katherine through school as it is, let alone another brother or sister.'

'We'll manage, darling. That I promise you.' Katherine had run off to the monkey bars and, for a moment, Henry forgot about her, turning his wife into his arms and kissing her, his gentle face showing all too clearly how he felt. Eleanor held him tightly, fighting the squeamishness that wanted to turn away, to say no, leave me alone. How could she be so hurtful? What would she have ever done without Henry? He was the bulwark in her life. She smiled at her silly thoughts of leaving him, of running off to England. How could she ever do that?

'I love you, Eleanor. I just want you to know that,' he said, holding her face between his hands and staring into her eyes.

Eleanor smiled. 'I know you do, Henry. And I could never manage without that love. Or without you.' She caressed his cheek with her hand. Tried to say the words that he hoped to hear in return. But they stuck in her throat. She cared for him deeply. But she loved him still as a friend, not as a husband. She would have done anything to change that, or to be able to lie convincingly. But Henry would not be fooled.

And then Katherine's wail, where she had fallen off the bars, distracted him and Eleanor was able to pass it off, one more time.

I'm sorry, Henry, she thought, as she held her daughter in her arms and tried to comfort her. I'm so sorry.

Teresa sat stiffly upright in the chair and examined her nails. They were the latest shade of red, highly glossed and pointed. She could see her reflection wavering above them.

'Henry, we were once friends. What reason is there for not telling me about my own husband? I have a right to know, surely,' she said and Henry, hair falling down over his eyes as always, smiled uncomfortably.

'Of course you do, Teresa. And if I knew anything about John, I would tell you. But I don't. We've had no word for over a year. You probably know more than we do.'

'Not more than Eleanor. She always knows where John is, doesn't she?' The retort was quick and venomous.

Henry sighed. 'No, she doesn't. If people didn't go around saying things like that, maybe my whole family would be better off. Eleanor's still got the scars to show for her last brush with John and the police. I don't want anymore.' He looked at Teresa, thinking how different she was to the young girl who had first come to the palácio that Christmas Eve. This Teresa was as smooth and polished as onyx, and as darkly impenetrable. He had no idea what thoughts went on behind those black eyes.

'Look, Teresa, why don't you come to dinner tonight? Talk to Eleanor yourself. Then, maybe, we can get back on with the business of your law suit and put this whole business of John out of everyone's minds.' He smiled, charming her more consciously than he had known how to do when last they met. Still an attractive man, Teresa thought, but perhaps not quite as innocent. Some of the naïvety had worn off. A pity; she had liked him better before.

'All right. Thank you. I accept.' She waited while Henry rang home and checked with Eleanor, and then while Henry described how to reach their flat. Not the area she would have thought. But then, perhaps Henry's fall from grace had been financial as well as spiritual. She smiled tightly. 'I'll see you then.'

*

Eleanor was dismayed by the thought of Teresa coming to dinner. What could she say to the woman? The last time they had seen each other was nearly eight years ago when Teresa had hurled her accusations at Eleanor in front of the crowd at the couture house. Accusations that had subsequently proved correct. Since then Teresa had married and lost a baby, lost John and gained a career through who knew what means. There was nothing there to endear Eleanor to her.

Nervously she prepared a meal of fillet of beef in a heavy wine sauce that had cost her the equivalent of three days' food. But she would not have Teresa smirking at their loss of fortune. There were still a few good pieces of furniture that they had salvaged from the foreclosure, the Small Room's dining table and chairs, a secretaire from Mama's sitting-room, the desk from her own bedroom. The flat looked nice enough with bowls of flowers arranged around it, if a little spare.

Then, angry with herself for caring what Teresa thought, she hurried into the bathroom to wash and change.

Teresa was early. An hour early. Eleanor opened the door in surprise, wondering who it could be to come calling at seven in the evening, and there Teresa stood with her sinewy slim body draped in peach satin and her hair flying out in a cloud of dark curls. Eleanor stood quite still, trying to think of something to say.

Teresa had hoped Eleanor would have aged badly, perhaps put weight on that long, lean frame of hers but she was disappointed. The girl who stood before her, looking so surprised, was not much changed from the girl she had first met. The face was more aware, perhaps even more beautiful for that awareness, Teresa thought uncomfortably, and the long silken hair had not been chopped as was the fashion. It hung in a curtain of pale gold down Eleanor's back, peaking at the forehead in that way that John's hair

443

fell. They were so similar, it still came as a shock to Teresa.

Eleanor wore an ivory silk sheath, deceptively simple in the way it swung around her body and her skin was lightly gilded with sun. Teresa had thought to reduce Eleanor to plain housewife status with her own particular style but Eleanor could not be reduced. Angrily, she stared back at the girl.

'Am I early? I couldn't remember whether Henry said seven or eight. Either seemed so very early, that I couldn't make up my mind.' She raised her eyebrows gracefully and Eleanor stepped back.

'It doesn't matter in the slightest, Teresa. Come on in. I was just putting Katherine to bed, but you're in time to say goodnight to her.' A child, fair and golden like her mother, stepped out from behind the door, and clung to her mother's leg. Teresa bent down and looked the little girl in the face. It was John's face that looked back at her, his eyes. Teresa darted a hard look at Eleanor, wondering.

'Hullo, Katherine. I'm your Aunty Teresa. And how old are you?' Perhaps this was what her own child would have looked like, Teresa thought. She glanced up at the mother, seeing Eleanor smile.

'I'm four. Are you my real aunty or just pretend aunty?' Katherine asked and Teresa looked back at her, startled.

'I'm – well, let's see. I married your mama's cousin, so that doesn't really make me your aunty, but it makes me family.' She was intrigued by the child but couldn't quite understand why. Was it because she looked so much like John? Or was it because she was so very self-possessed? But then, the fina gente were born self-possessed.

'Why have I never seen you before?' Katherine prompted and Eleanor leaned down and picked her daughter up.

'Aunty Teresa's been away in the United States where she's a big movie star. And now she's back for a short time to see everyone. So say goodnight now, Katherine.' Katherine held out her arms and pressed her mouth wetly to Teresa's cheek.

'Night, night, Aunty Te-sa,' she called over her mother's

444

shoulder as Eleanor whisked her off to bed.

'Goodnight, Katherine,' Teresa called back and, when the two disappeared into the bedroom, she looked around the flat angrily, trying to distract her thoughts from the child. From the envy she felt.

The flat was small for a family, particularly after the life they had led before, Teresa thought. Rather spartan even with only a few rugs on the wooden boards. But it was elegant. You knew that whoever lived there was – someone. She examined the pictures in silver frames on the tables, laughing, happy faces, smiling into the camera. She breathed in sharply and walked over to the window, peering out at the view for some time.

'I'm sorry to leave you on your own like that, Teresa,' Eleanor said in a rush as she returned from the bedroom. Her face was flushed and amused still from something Katherine had said. 'Now then, what can I get you to drink? Wine, caipirinha, something soft perhaps? Then you must tell me all about your latest film.'

Teresa turned to look at Eleanor as she came back into the room, forcing a smile.

'Wine, please.'

Henry looked down at the report in his hands, trying to still the shake. It was already late, nearly an hour after he should have gone home, and he still didn't know what to do. He took off his glasses, scrubbing tiredly at his face. Oh God, why couldn't he have just missed this? What perverse fortune had put it down on his desk, what fate had made him look at it? If he hadn't seen it until tomorrow, it would have been too late. There would have been nothing he could do. But he had seen it. Oh God!

The police report was sealed and earmarked for the mayor personally. No one else was to look at it. That alone had aroused Henry's curiosity, his uneasiness. So, after everyone else had gone home, he had carefully opened the report and read it. And now he knew. A member of the terrorist group led by Carlos Marighela had been captured

445

and tortured. The information extracted had enabled the police to set an ambush, for the early hours of the following morning. And the list of names extracted was there too. John's was among them. Henry groaned and hit the desk, dizzy almost with the way his thoughts rushed this way and that, pulling him in two different directions.

Someone had to warn them, someone had to get to John. But who? His normal contact was away, and he didn't know anyone else. He didn't dare involve Louis in case it all went wrong. But should he risk himself? Why? For John's sake? And then the guilt bit at him, telling him this was his chance to redeem himself and he swung wildly the other way, thinking maybe he could bring it off, maybe he could get to them in time and Eleanor would be so grateful. He knew she would be.

No, that wasn't reason enough. He ought to do it because he believed in resisting this government, because this was his small chance to show he cared as much as John did for his country. He was sick of himself, keeping so carefully out of trouble, compromising his values all the time. This was his chance to do something more. He breathed in deeply.

'I can't think where Henry's got to, Teresa. I'm sorry if you wanted to discuss your case with him, but I expect he'll be here shortly. He tends to get caught up with things at night, after everyone else leaves, and sometimes he forgets the time. How about another drink?' Eleanor was nervous and trying not to show it. She stood up and poured Teresa out another glass of wine.

Teresa shrugged. 'It doesn't matter. I didn't want to talk to him but to you. It's probably better if we have our – discussion – privately. Then we can say what we really mean.' Teresa saw Eleanor stiffen, her face becoming cool and remote.

'Really? And what was it you wanted to discuss?' As if she didn't already know, Eleanor thought uncomfortably. Well, as long as they didn't let it degenerate into a shouting

446

match like last time. Perhaps it was best to clear the air.

'Oh come on, Eleanor. John, of course. When has it been anything else between us?' Teresa had become used to people deferring to her in the last few years. She was surprised by the resistance Eleanor showed.

'Oh, nonsense! We've met twice before, Teresa, and the first time I showed you nothing but kindness and the second time I said nothing to you whatsoever. I barely know you. I hardly think that makes John the pivotal point of our lives together, do you? As far as I'm concerned, we are distantly connected and nothing more.' She saw Teresa's eyes flash angrily.

'Then you won't mind answering me, if I ask whether you and John are lovers?' Teresa pressed. She took a small sip of wine, watching the girl over the rim of her glass. Eleanor shook her head, the small scar on her cheekbone catching the lamp light and glistening palely.

'You know, I'm really tired of that question. No, I am not John's lover. I'm married, happily and entirely faithfully, to Henry. I have always been faithful to Henry. Is that clear enough for you, Teresa?' She was angry and still nervous, wondering whether Teresa knew about Paris. Perhaps, perhaps not. How could Henry put her in a situation like this and then not turn up? It was unforgiveable!

Teresa was surprised. She thought she could read people well enough to know if they were lying or not, and all her instincts said this woman was telling the truth. Then why did John keep going back to her? It didn't make sense.

'And you don't know where he is now? You haven't any idea?'

'How many times can I say that? No, I don't. You're the one who took him away last time – or arranged it. I haven't laid eyes on him since, nor have I heard anything. What are you so afraid of, Teresa? John and you split up years ago anyway, so it's not as though you could think I was trying to take him away from you. John is John. No one can hold him against his will.' Eleanor tried to make Teresa understand, but she saw it was useless. The woman's face was closed and unapproachable.

'You can,' Teresa said stubbornly. 'You've always held John, ever since you were children together. He used to talk to me about you sometimes. About how he felt only half-alive when you weren't there beside him. You'll always hold him and there'll never be anyone else for him.' Her face was anguished at the thought and she bit her lip and looked away.

Eleanor was stunned. 'You do love him,' she said.

'Of course. Did you think I didn't?' Teresa gave a harsh laugh. 'Did you think only the fina gente have such feelings? But I realize now I'm just wasting my time. You and he are – inseparable, even when you're not together. I can't compete with that. So, tell him – when you see him – I want a divorce. I want my life to go on, instead of waiting, stagnant, for him to be killed. He won't ever return. I guess I always knew that.' She drank back the last of her wine and looked at Eleanor.

'Your daughter, she looks just like John – even more than she does you, really. She's got his eyes.' Teresa didn't ask but Eleanor shook her head anyway.

'Katherine is Henry's child. I hadn't seen John for three years before Katherine was born. In fact, I thought he was dead. You mustn't think that. It isn't fair to Henry.'

Teresa half smiled. 'Ah yes, Henry. He's a nice man. Perhaps you got the better of the two? Just neither of us realized that then and it wouldn't have done any good anyway. We both still love John.' She stood and held out her hand. 'I won't stay, I think. We might as well part on a good note. It was nice to talk with you again, Eleanor. I'm – I'm sorry about the last time we met. I hope you and Henry have a long and happy life together.'

'Thank you. I'm sorry too, Teresa. I've never wanted us to be anything but friends.' They shook hands awkwardly and Teresa was almost to the door when the telephone rang and Eleanor hesitated, and then went to answer it.

'Eleanor, it's me; let me talk with Teresa, will you?' Henry said and Eleanor knew from the tone of his voice

448

that he was agitated. She held out the receiver to Teresa.

'Henry wants to talk to you,' she said and Teresa took a deep breath, looked irritated, and then reluctantly returned and took the phone.

'Yes, Henry? What is it?'

It was a dark, almost moonless night, just a sliver of light waning yellow in the sky. Teresa drove. Her car was fast and she changed the gears well, snicking them in with strong, sure movements of her hand. Eleanor sat beside her silently. The miles sped by in a blur of darkened landscape. Teresa chain-smoked, her cigarette end glowing red in the night.

She had agreed to meet Henry some three miles away from the farm, at a crossroads, and to wait there for him to bring John to her. Henry didn't know Eleanor would be there too. He had rung off before Teresa knew herself. But, when she put the phone down, she had seen the determination in Eleanor's eyes and she didn't protest.

It was past midnight already and they were still fifty kilometers from their destination, the roads becoming potholed with the last of the rains and the distance from a major city. The speed dropped and Teresa threw out her cigarette, a whisked meteor of light showering in the slip-stream. She concentrated on the curves of the road. The ambush was set for two in the morning, Henry had said. And he had to get to John and have him away before that. They would barely make it.

Eleanor had been praying for most of the journey, silently mouthing her needs to her God, knowing in the pit of her stomach that something was going to go wrong. Desperately, irrevocably wrong. One of them would be killed. She knew it, felt it in every sinew of her tense body. Dear God, help them, don't let them die. She didn't know which man she ought to pray for more and so she blindly prayed for them all.

Her neighbour had taken Katherine, not asking questions when she saw the strain on Eleanor's face, the fear in her eyes. No one asked questions anymore. No one wanted to know.

Teresa glanced over at the girl beside her, seeing the set profile, the taut way she held her head, lips tightly compressed. There was a lot of control in that girl. Good, she was going to need it. Teresa looked back at the road, her own mind focused on just one thing. Making it to the meeting point in time. She changed gears going into a corner and accelerated away, the rear of the car fishtailing out for a moment before steadying again. Teresa put her foot down hard.

Henry had wasted valuable time searching for a garage that was still open, and he was nearly half an hour behind schedule by the time he drew up near the farmhouse. For all he knew, the police might already be there, lying in wait in the dark. He breathed quickly, trying to steady the shake in his hands. Was this worth it? Would it not be better to just let events take their course, and hope John made it away? What good would it do to end up being arrested too? Teresa would understand if he told her he had been too late. It was almost too late now. Henry sat behind the wheel of his car, listening to the silence of the night.

Just get on with it, he told himself sharply and was half out of the car before he was even aware he had moved. He hesitated and then realized that hesitation at this stage would prove fatal. Fearfully he walked forward, through the remains of an orchard, and climbed awkwardly over a half-demolished wall. The farmhouse sat, hunkered down in the dark and turned in on itself as though it contained nothing more than a peasant family in sleep. Henry stared at it from the shadows.

It was a long way across that field. And nothing to hide him along the way. He looked up at the sky, cursing even that sliver of light. How did he know there weren't other men all around him, sitting quietly in the dark, staring across at that building? And what was he supposed to do, when – if – he got to the farmhouse? Would the terrorists

450

just shoot him down, before he had time to say who he was? He shivered in fear and felt an unpleasant prickle of sweat break out across his face. He wished he hadn't come.

The night smelt of dry earth and almond trees, and Henry breathed it in deeply, steadying his nerves. He glanced at his watch and saw it was just one o'clock. An hour to go before the police moved in. It was now or never. He swallowed and stood up, walking forward across the field.

His suit was dark and the collar of his jacket was pulled up over his shirt and held across the chest so that there was little to see in the gloom. He walked quickly, almost running in places, and swerving from side to side when he remembered. His back ached with the tension and he held his breath as though waiting for something to smash into his flesh. There was no sound and no movement from the shadows. He reached the side of the farmhouse safely and leaned against the wall, gasping for air.

They would have a guard, almost certainly. Probably two or three. He couldn't see anyone but he was sure they were there. He closed his eyes for a moment and then, slowly, made his way towards the archway in the third wall.

They came up from behind, pinning him face-first to the wall, as soon as he passed through the arch. He felt a gun being pressed to his neck and he gasped, holding on tightly to his panic.

'I'm John Campos de Serra's cousin. Please, I must talk to him. It's urgent,' he said quickly and he felt a boot roughly kick his feet apart, pushing his face against stone.

They searched him thoroughly, murmuring in whispers to each other and Henry felt the seconds ticking away.

'For God's sake, get John out here to identify me. I must talk to him,' he repeated, and the desperation in his voice must have reached the others because one of them broke away and Henry heard him walking into the house, the door slamming behind him.

'What do you want with John? How did you find us?' a gruff, almost gutteral voice behind Henry's ear asked. He

451

had been prepared for this question, knowing it would be stupid to lie to them. He swallowed.

'I work for Pereira, the mayor of Rio. There's going to be an ambush here tonight, in one hour. You must all get out, right away. I came for John,' he said and there were exclamations from behind him, and he was suddenly pulled around so that he fell with his back to the wall and stared at two figures. They were dressed in black and their faces were darkened with mud. He didn't recognize them.

'Who are you? What's your name?' the one nearest him asked and Henry breathed in shakily.

'Henry Arreas de Botelho. I'm married to John's cousin. For God's sake, listen to me! The police are probably on their way here right now. You've got to get out!'

The door to the farmhouse opened again and Henry saw John come out, his fair hair gleaming in the dark. He saw Henry and started to run.

'What is it, Henry? Is Eleanor all right? Has something –'

Henry cut across his words. 'Shut up and listen. The police are coming. They know you're here. I don't care how you all get away, but start moving now. John, I've got a car and Teresa's on her way to meet us. For God's sake, come on!' He had thought there would be a protest from John, or disbelief the way the others were reacting. But John simply nodded and turned to the other two.

'Henry's telling the truth. I'd stake my life on it. Get out of here. Leave everything, just get out.' He turned back and grasped Henry by the arm, hustling him out of the courtyard towards the field. 'You too, get out of here, Henry. I'll make my own way. Just go. And tell Teresa to get out of Brazil. I'll be all right.' He paused for one moment, patting Henry on the back. 'Thank you. I owe you my life several times over, you and Eleanor. I won't risk yours again. Give her my love.' He pushed Henry towards the dark and turned back into the courtyard, hustling the other two into action.

Henry hesitated and then, knowing suddenly that he had only a few minutes left, he set off across the field at a run.

452

He had reached the orchard and was nearly to his car when he heard the first gunfire.

It came from the south, across the marshland on the far side of the farm, and Henry hesitated, almost turning back. Then he saw the dark figures running across the field, in his direction, and his mouth filled with fear. He ran, faster than he had run in years, his heart pumping, his mind shrieking terror. But his shoes were slippery on the rough ground and he fell from time to time, rolling and pulling himself up to run on again, his breath coming in ragged spurts. The car was just beyond the grove of trees at the end of the orchard, and he turned and looked back briefly.

Behind him, close behind, he saw John and then, further back, another figure. He didn't know who the second figure was, whether friend or foe and Henry didn't wait to find out. He ran on, making quickly for the car and throwing himself into it. He started the engine, praying John would hurry, his stomach pulsing in dread.

The police were so early! He could have been there, himself, if they had come moments before. The thought shocked him and he peered out through the windscreen, searching for John. There, there he was, breaking through the trees now. Henry gunned the engine, throwing open the passenger seat door and rolling the car forward. John made a diving leap for it, holding on to the door and roof of the car as he ran along beside it. With a last, convulsive effort, he threw himself forward into the car.

Henry accelerated out towards the road and John leaned over and pulled the door shut, shouting 'Go! Go!' at the top of his voice. And then the side window exploded and John slumped back against the seat, out of range.

Henry put his foot to the floor and the car rocketed across the last few feet of clearing, leaping into the air as it hit the side of the road and then swinging wildly across the road. He fought to control it and then he was heading out of there, towards Teresa, and the sound of the ambush was dying behind them. He quivered with fear, disoriented beyond anything he had ever expected, by the night and

453

the danger, the fear that made his tongue curl and stick bitterly to his mouth, his forehead slick with sweat. He drove furiously, looking straight ahead.

When the terror subsided slightly, Henry was able to breathe again, even give a shaky laugh. He glanced over at John, wondering at his silence.

The bullet had caught John in the neck, just above the collar bone. For a moment, Henry thought he was dead. But the wound was still bleeding, pouring out great clots of dark red blood that flowed down his shirt and across his chest. John's eyes were shut, his face slack. Henry stared at him and then tore his eyes away back to the road, swerving violently into a corner he had not seen in time. The car almost went over, sliding sideways off the road and into the reeds. But Henry coaxed it forward again and back on to the road. He cursed as he drove.

Eleanor could not sit inside the car. She opened the door impatiently and stood up, searching the crossroads for any sign of a car approaching. Henry was late. Very late. What on earth could be happening?

It was a still night and they both heard the gunfire clearly, carrying across the fields in the cool air. Eleanor stopped pacing and stared in the direction from which the gunfire came, her sense of foreboding coming back again twice as strongly. She stared back at Teresa. Teresa started the engine.

'Get in, Eleanor. We may have to take off fast. Get in and be quiet. I'm trying to hear.' Teresa didn't seem to feel fear, Eleanor thought. She was calm and loose, her body showing none of the tension Eleanor's displayed. Maybe she couldn't imagine anything happening to John? Maybe she thought he was invincible, Eleanor wondered. And what about Henry? Did Teresa care what happened to him? She glanced angrily at the woman beside her but Teresa wasn't watching her, just staring out through the windscreen. They waited in silence.

Teresa heard it first and she peered out along the road

that lead from the south, her foot hovering over the accelerator. Their lights were extinguished. The other car wouldn't see them lying in the shadows, the car as black as the landscape around it. They waited, seeing the lights wavering along the road, the scream of the car's engine apparent as it roared towards them. At the last second it braked, slewing sideways as though it had only just seen them. Eleanor was out of the car and running towards Henry's before Teresa could tell her to stop. Angrily, Teresa edged her car out on to the road, as close to Henry's as possible.

The blood was everywhere. Eleanor couldn't think what to do with all that blood. She pressed her finger tightly against the entry point, hearing John gasping, gurgling for breath, and she gave a terrified look at Henry. He was sitting, staring straight ahead, his hand clenched onto the wheel.

'Get out of the way, Eleanor. Henry, Henry! We've got to get him into my car now. You lift on one side, I'll take the other, Eleanor, you get his legs.' Teresa's voice was sharp and it penetrated Henry's fog, making him blink and stare over at them and then come shakily around the car to do as Teresa said. Together they carried John over to Teresa's car, putting him in the passenger seat. Teresa strapped him in tightly, pushing a pad of material on to his wound and holding it in place with the seat belt. She slammed the door on him and looked at the other two.

'I'll take him. You get going. Get out of here. I'll call you, if I can.' She didn't waste time with farewells, but climbed into the car and drove off swiftly in the direction they had come. Eleanor looked at Henry, at the terror on his face, and with a cry put her arms around him, holding him tightly against her.

'Come on, Henry, we've got to go now. Get in the car.' But he continued to shake with the horror and the fear of the last half-hour and would not move. Eleanor kissed his cheek, murmuring to him. The shudders stopped after a while and finally she was able to push him towards the passenger seat, throwing her raincoat over it to cover the blood.

'Get in, Henry. I'll drive. You're not up to it. Come on, darling. Quickly. We must go. They'll be coming for us.' She coaxed him into the car and shut the door, running around the other side to climb into the driver's seat. Her hands trembled and she wanted to cry, wanted to scream, but the shock of seeing John bleeding his life force out of him, held her in such a tight vice of horror, she could barely begin to think. She turned the key in the ignition and glanced in the rear view mirror.

There were lights. Just one set but they were coming fast. She gave a gasp of terror and pressed her foot down on the accelerator, spurting forward across the gravel of the cross-roads and taking the road to the left. She had no idea where it went but perhaps they wouldn't see her if she could just get around the next bend, just out of sight. She drove furiously and Henry sat beside her, glancing back from time to time, as though he were living all his childhood terrors in one night. Something was chasing him through the dark, something that would kill him – and kill Eleanor! It was close behind now, gaining. He stared at his wife.

'I love you,' he said but his voice was cracked and shaking, and Eleanor barely heard him. She swung the car hard left and then the rear window exploded, shattering in on them and Eleanor gave a cry of terror and drove faster still, her foot already hard against the floor. They wouldn't make it; she knew they wouldn't.

Watching in the rear view mirror, Eleanor suddenly saw the police car swerve too fast as it took the corner, a patch of slippery road catching the car unaware so that it continued to go forward instead of turning with the road. It hit the ditch front on, the tail coming up in the air, falling over, rolling.

Eleanor dragged her eyes back to the road and exulted. 'They crashed, Henry! They crashed! We'll get away now. Just see if we don't!' She took her hand from the wheel to grab Henry's hand and squeeze it and then she saw the way his eyes were staring sightlessly ahead, the way his head had slumped to one side against the window. A small smear of blood was caking the window and Eleanor braked sharply, bringing the car to a halt. She turned and stared at her husband. The night was hushed and still.

'Oh Henry, no. No.' There was so little blood. Not like John. This was just a trickle, a smear. But it was from his forehead. His face seemed tired as it lay propped up, the hair falling forward over his eyes as usual, the laughter lines around his mouth smoothing out. Gently she eased his head around so she could see the back and then she turned away, sickened.

'Oh no, no. Oh God, not Henry, please!' she cried and she held him tightly against her, feeling the terror and fear becoming numb, the ache in her throat overwhelming her in her grief. She held him in her arms and sobbed, dredging the pain up from deep inside her. The truth struck her, when she knew it was too late. She stroked his cheek tenderly.

'I love you, Henry,' she whispered. 'I love you.'

Chapter Twenty-two

The funeral was private, only immediate family present. Henry, lying so peacefully in his casket, looked much the same as he always had but without the charm of his smile. That was what had made Henry so special, Eleanor thought numbly. Not his good looks, his regular features but the personality beneath that came through in that smile. She sat stiffly in the front pew, aching at the loss.

It was only two days since he had held her in his arms, warm and strong and happy. Two days. The desert that had swept through her life in that time had changed it forever. If only she had told him she loved him, if only she had made more effort. The regret hurt more than anything. Henry had deserved better than her, and he had died telling her he loved her. The guilt that thought gave her, late at night in bed when the others had all left and she was finally alone, was almost more than she could bear. Such terrible, aching regret. Oh Henry, my poor love, I'm so sorry. Do you know that? Do you see how much I love you? Loved you?

Eleanor sat forward, thinking for a moment she had seen his cheeks move, his lips curve upward. But no, it was nothing. She sat back again as her mother took her arm, stroking it. Henry slept on peacefully.

Carlos da Silva sat discretely in the pew behind Eleanor, feeling the waves of pain almost buffet him as he watched the family grieve. A double grieving, for Henry and for John, his condition unknown, his death presumed. There would never be any peace for that poor girl again, he thought sadly. Her father and then a year later, her husband and her cousin. It was unthinkable that so much pain be visited on one person. He glared angrily up at the figure of Christ on the cross, unable to explain it even there, in God's house.

Further back in the church a slight shuffling of feet, a cough, reminded Dr da Silva of the presence of other higher authorities. The police. They hoped John would attend the funeral. They didn't know. Not about any of it. They thought Henry had died of a sudden stroke, an embolism in the brain taking his young life with it. Why should they think otherwise? He had signed the death certificate and Henry had been carefully prepared by the undertakers. There was no reason to think it was anything more than a tragedy.

He shivered at that. A tragedy. So very many seemed attached to this family. He let his eyes roam around the chapel, coming to rest on his wife's back. He smiled tenderly.

And then the family was rising, filing out of the church into the blazing sunshine that mocked their misery with its blue skies and shining light. Henry should have been buried on a grey day, full of rain and wind. Some howling elements appropriate to the silent howling pain of this family's loss. But no, the sun shone and the wind was light and playfully gentle as Dr da Silva watched Henry being lowered into the ground with bewilderment. He saw the same disbelief on the faces around him. Incredulousness. The sneaking suspicion that Henry would be waiting for them back at the apartment, laughing as though it were all some sort of odd joke. Only Eleanor seemed to know. But then, she had held him in her arms.

Dr da Silva watched her scatter some soil, standing close,

459

dreadfully close to the edge of the grave as though she were half of a mind to simply join Henry, there and then. Why wait for death? Why not embrace it now? He saw the signs on her face, even through the gauze of her veil. He saw the sagging shoulders, the sudden buckling knees and he was darting across to her side before anyone could move.

They laid her out on the grass, Katherine wailing her displeasure and uncertainty from her aunt Isobel's arms, and everyone pressed forward with cries of concern. Eleanor's face was sharply defined against the black of her dress and veil, so very pale that it seemed set in stone, a deathmask. But Dr da Silva found a pulse at last, a thready wisp of pressure that reassured him. They carried her to the car and then the mourners hurried to their own. Henry was left alone at last.

Weeks passed and Eleanor gradually grew to accept that Henry was gone. She didn't know about John. Everyone else was so sure he was dead, but she didn't know. All good sense said he must be but still, she clung to the hope that it might not be so. Teresa was gone again, back to the United States and Eleanor dared not write in case her letter were somehow intercepted. Perhaps, in time, she would try and call from a phone box. When things were more settled.

But for now she had Katherine and she had her family who insisted on including her in everything. They made sure she had little time to think except late at night, alone in bed. Those thoughts were so painful that she refused to retire until she was exhausted and she rose the moment she woke, hurrying around the apartment cleaning and sorting, denying her mind any chance to dwell on past events.

She took a job in one of Mina's boutiques to supplement her trust fund income and Isobel was happy to welcome Katherine into her nursery. Charlie, at six, was already at school but there was little Sarah now who, at two, was close to Katherine's age and a happy playmate. Katherine, confused by her father's disappearance at first, rapidly forgot in the pleasure of her new company.

460

So it went on, life gradually assuming a semblance of normality but deep within, the tremors and cracks were there for anyone with astute eyes to see. Dr da Silva saw them and, perhaps, Henry's father. But he was old and broken with his son's loss and he hadn't the strength to sustain both his wife and Eleanor. Once the initial grief was over, they gradually drifted away from Eleanor, choosing to see Katherine alone. The little girl, with her happy prattling and joyous laughs, could be enjoyed; Eleanor, with her huge eyes and pale face, could not.

Eleanor wrote to Sophie, something she had not done since Sophie had left so abruptly during the period of house arrest. Not even to ask if Eleanor was all right. But Henry had said Sophie had grown uneasy about the political situation, the house arrest and the danger they were all in and she had insisted on leaving Brazil. He had been bitterly dismissive of Sophie's lack of loyalty and had insisted Eleanor break contact with the French girl. Eleanor, puzzled, was still uneasy enough not to push the issue. Whatever had happened, she didn't need to know. She had left it alone.

But now, nearly a year after Henry's death, Eleanor thought Sophie should be told. It was a painful letter to write. But the news was sent. She never received a reply. Perhaps Sophie had left that address, perhaps she no longer cared about her old friends, not even Henry. Eleanor, sensing that to probe more deeply would only cause pain to them all, let the matter rest.

In time, Eleanor complained to Isobel about the cost of clothing in the boutique Mina owned and how there was almost nothing ready-to-wear that was either current fashion or good quality. Isobel commented, in turn, about the lack in Brazil of the cheap and cheerful furniture, china or glassware that she had noticed in Europe on one of her latest trips. It didn't take them long to realize that they could easily supply what was lacking and, from there, it was but a short step to forming their own trading company.

461

By the end of 1971, the second year after Henry's death, Eleanor and Isobel were partners in a startlingly successful venture. Perhaps, Eleanor thought, it would be the beginning of a new decade for all of them.

After the official year of mourning was up, Eleanor was surprised by how many invitations she received to go out to dinner from the various men of her acquaintance. Many had been friends of Henry's, some friends of her own or Isobel's. They all called with one thought on their mind, she realized ruefully. Consoling a widow.

She accepted a few but always stopped them firmly at the door of her apartment. The calls began to diminish. Only the nicer, kinder or perhaps more persistent continued to call. And Eleanor felt the months, the years, slipping away while she lay alone at night and she hoped, against hope, that there still might be some word from John.

Isobel lost patience with her. 'You can't go through life thinking Henry was some sort of saint and you have to remain faithful to his memory, Eleanor. He was just a nice, ordinary man with as many faults as the rest of us. Don't cut yourself off from life. Somewhere out there, there might be another man, equally nice. Katherine needs a father – and you need a husband,' Isobel nagged and Eleanor would try for a few weeks to see other men. But she couldn't tell Isobel it wasn't another Henry she was looking for. It was John. The guilt that provoked was unbearable.

She had tried to call Teresa but found her number unlisted. A letter, carefully impersonal, requesting Teresa's telephone number and sent to her manager, was never answered. Eleanor had no way of knowing about John and Teresa obviously had no intention of telling her.

In March 1974, four years after Henry's death, President Geisel came to power and there was a definite turn towards relaxation and democratization. Eleanor read the papers sadly, thinking what a waste Henry's death had been. It had all come about as he had said it would anyway. In time. Except that now she was a thirty-year-old widow with a child who needed a father. And a good man's life

462

had been senselessly cut short. She shook her head and then called to Katherine, smiling as the child came through the door.

'There you are, darling. Let me see how your dress looks. Oh! Aren't you beautiful! Turn around?' She caught her breath in pleasure at the sight of her daughter, at eight, wearing her first 'grown-up' dress. It was for the opera. She was going with Henry's parents. Katherine swirled the deep green velvet out around her.

'Do you like it, Mama? Aunt Isobel said that it was really for someone a little older but I'm so tall already that none of the clothes for my age would fit. It doesn't look silly, does it, Mama?' Her face became pensive, and she looked at her mother with lips folded in, chin jutted out. Just like John. It gave Eleanor a jolt.

'It looks wonderful, Katherine. Truly. I can't think of anything that's ever looked better on you.' She had to stop herself before she said something silly, like 'your papa would have been proud of you'. Katherine barely remembered her father. There was no point in bringing up painful memories.

Katherine's face cleared and she smiled broadly, running back out of the room to change out of the dress. When she returned, she held several letters in her hand.

'These came in the post today. I forgot to give them to you,' she said with an apologetic shrug and Eleanor smiled and gave her a hug.

'Well, it's not every day you get a dress like that. I couldn't expect you to remember everything, now could I? Did you hang your dress up again?' When Katherine nodded, Eleanor pointed to the pile of books on the dining-room table. 'Good girl. Now it's time for a little homework, I think, isn't it? I'll start getting dinner ready as soon as I've been through these.' When Katherine nodded, Eleanor smiled, 'How do omelettes sound to you?'

She saw the girl pull a face. 'Oh Mama, must we? Can't we have chicken or something? I hate eggs.'

'Since when? Or is that because Charlie hates eggs?'

Eleanor saw the quick look of defiance on her daughter's mouth, not quite a pout. And she remembered how she had felt at the same age when she had only liked what John liked. Could the pattern be forming again? For a moment, she was disturbed, understanding perhaps for the first time how her father had felt. But then she shook her head at herself and her fears. Katherine and Charlie were just children. There was nothing to worry about.

'Omelettes. There's nothing else. But you can have a chocolate mousse for pudding, if you're a good girl and finish your homework first. All right?' She leaned over and kissed her daughter's head and pushed her gently towards her books.

Eleanor carried the letters into the kitchen and shut the door behind her. Several were bills, for electricity, water, telephone. She sighed at those and put them to one side. One was from Isobel, detailing the list of contents on the next shipment. She laid that aside also. Two were invitations to parties that Eleanor knew she would have to attend and also knew would involve fending off some man who had been invited especially to entertain her.

The last was from England. Eleanor picked it up in surprise and turned it over. No return address. Perhaps it was something to do with the business? She slit it open, wondering.

It was from a Maximillian Fawcett Esq. Cousin Max. Eleanor read it through hurriedly, trying to still the lurch her heart gave.

My dearest Eleanor,

Forgive me the liberty of writing to you in such a familiar manner, but I feel as though I already know you so well. I have heard so much about you, both when you were younger and now again, more recently. In fact, in the last year I have heard about you so unceasingly that I ventured to write to you to invite you to visit us here in Winchester. We should all so enjoy seeing you, and the family ties should be kept up, don't you think?

Possibly your family would be kind enough to spare you to us for a few short weeks? I know it would be greatly appreciated and we have so much, after all, to talk about. So much to catch up on.

I have enclosed a return ticket, as you will see, with his letter which perhaps will seem a great piece of impertinence as, I am afraid, it is, but I must hope that your sense of family and what is owed to the blood will allow you to overlook this one transgression.

Waiting in hope of a favourable reply,

I remain, yours,

Maximillian Fawcett.

Eleanor stood perfectly still, looking down at the page in her hand. Outside the kitchen door, she could hear Katherine singing to herself as she sat down to her homework. The street lights glinted in the night through the window and Eleanor stared blankly at her reflection in the window. What is owed to the blood. Yes, that was true. John was her other half. It was time they finally made a whole.

Slowly, as though her heart had been held in a tight vice for four long years, Eleanor began to laugh.

In August 1979, some 7,000 political exiles were allowed to return home, to Brazil. John was one of them.

how to cure himself with their strange plant medicines, how to find the secret war trails that criss-crossed this seemingly impenetrable jungle and how to avoid the snares that were put along those trails for the unwary – and most of all, how to kill. They had taught him like one of their own sons and he had learned it well. She shook herself, trying to clear the foreboding from her mind. He would be all right. They both would.

Eleanor came running back, her hands carefully cupped around something, her face bright with success. 'I've got one, Aunt Elizabeth. I've got one!' Slowly she opened her hands and a single, pink butterfly rose into the air. It fluttered above their heads before disappearing towards the garden. Eleanor looked after it wistfully. 'I just wanted to show you it – I couldn't keep it. It would've died if I'd put it in a box to keep it safe. But I wish I could've,' she said.

Elizabeth stroked the girl's hair; she knew how Eleanor felt. But she was thinking, not of a butterfly, but of her son. 'I was wondering whether you'd like to take a look at the waterfall today. I haven't had an excuse for going up there in ages and if the men are going to be hunting, it'll be pretty dull for you around here,' Elizabeth said.

Eleanor blinked with pleased surprise. She had assumed the picnic would be off now that the hunt had become more important. 'Oh, could we? I mean, it won't be dangerous for us to go out there when they haven't caught the jaguar yet?'

'No, not up there. The jaguar stays down in the basin mostly, trying to get easy pickings from the fazenda. Besides, Michael's men tracked it early this morning and they say it's over to the south, beyond the clearing. It took one of the dogs last night so it won't be looking to hunt again until this evening, probably.' She smiled to dispel any nervousness the girl might feel. 'The jungle's pretty wild, Eleanor, and if you worry about everything, you end up not going out the door. And I like my freedom,' she added firmly.

Eleanor nodded but didn't voice her thoughts.

53